T0014446

PRAISE FOR
WHERE THEY WAIT

"*Where They Wait* is so readable, you'll be a couple of hundred pages in before you realize you're terrified . . . and then you can't put it down. Mesmerizing."

—Stephen King

"Tense and twisty."

—Charlaine Harris, #1 *New York Times* bestselling author of the Southern Vampire Mysteries

"A taut, creepy techno-chiller that will leave you hearing ghosts."

—Paul Tremblay, author of *A Head Full of Ghosts* and *Survivor Song*

"*Where They Wait* hums with creeping dread and mounting horror. It's smart and scary, and the final act is like that last downhill plunge on a rollercoaster—terrifying, exhilarating, and unforgettable. I loved every page."

—Richard Chizmar, *New York Times* bestselling author of *Gwendy's Button Box*

"Compulsively readable . . . Easy to get hooked and hard to forget . . . Pure horror."

—*New York Times Book Review*

"Uber-creepy horror thriller . . . Superior prose enhances a craftily twisted plot, which sticks its landing. Peter Straub fans will hope for more from Carson."

—*Publishers Weekly* (starred review)

"Horror knows no bounds in this supernatural thriller about a new mindfulness app, behind which lurks something much more sinister."

—*Newsweek*

"Readers will be terrified."

—*Booklist* (starred review)

"You should read this book."

—*Goodreads*

"A creepy horror novel that goes places I didn't expect, *Where They Wait* is eerie and unsettling and made me side eye my mindfulness apps."

—*The Library Ladies*

"If you've ever suspected that your relaxation app was secretly trying to kill you, this is the book for you."

—*New York Post*

PRAISE FOR
THE CHILL

"Wow! This is one terrific horror/suspense/disaster novel. Characters you root for and a story that grips from the first page."

—Stephen King

"*The Chill* features a clever and chilling premise, and Scott Carson delivers on the promise of it with swift clear prose, well-defined characters, and terrific suspense. This is a must-read for fans of eerie, gripping storytelling."

—Dean Koontz, #1 *New York Times* bestselling author of *The Night Window*

"Horror has a new name, and it's Scott Carson. *The Chill* is an eerie dive into the murky depths of the supernatural. A story that has you looking back over your shoulder on every page."

—Michael Connelly, #1 *New York Times* bestselling author of *The Night Fire*

"The year's best spine-tingler is already here. *The Chill* is a good old-fashioned ghost story, meticulously researched and brilliantly executed. If you've ever wished for a cross between *Chinatown* and *The Fog*, Scott Carson has answered your dark prayers . . ."

—*John Connolly, New York Times* bestselling
author of *The Nameless Ones*

"Scott Carson's *The Chill* may be the perfect thriller. Great characters. Creeping dread and explosive reveals. Pacing that never lets up. Maybe some of the best conversation with the dead since Stephen King's *The Shining*."

—Alma Katsu, author of
The Deep and *The Hunger*

"Scott Carson's *The Chill* is a hold-your-breath horror thriller, full of mounting dread. Carson weaves classic chills and nuanced characters into a story both compelling and creepy as hell. Don't miss it!"

—Christopher Golden, *New York Times* bestselling
author of *Ararat* and *Snowblind*

"Part old-fashioned horror story, part supernatural thriller, *The Chill* is a breathtaking story of justice— and revenge. Once I started this book, I couldn't put it down. Prepare to be chilled."

—Rene Denfeld, bestselling author of
The Butterfly Girl and *The Child Finder*

"With *The Chill*, Scott Carson has written a spooky, thrilling, and genuinely moving tale of righteous obsession from beyond the grave, with a setting and characters that leap off the page. If you like Stephen King or Joe Hill, you must read Scott Carson."

—Nick Petrie, nationally bestselling author of *The Wild One* and *Tear It Down*

"Reading Scott Carson's *The Chill* gave me shivers like the ones I got when I first read Stephen King's *The Shining*. Set in a remote town in upstate New York, the novel starts ordinarily enough, with a fractured relationship between father and son, but swiftly cascades into a story about vengeful ghosts and a cataclysm generations in the making . . . The result is a fast-paced, frenzied tale of survival against both natural and supernatural forces that will leave you gasping for air."

—*Bookpage* (starred review)

"The tension of the novel is masterful . . . as the past hauntingly plays with the present."

—*Booklist*

"Based on the true history of a drowned town . . . this novel provides an alluring mix of truth and ghost story which will draw interest and keep readers hooked."

—*Library Journal*

"Fans of Stephen King won't want to miss this one."

—*The Real Book Spy*

ALSO BY SCOTT CARSON

The Chill

SCOTT CARSON

WHERE THEY WAIT

A NOVEL

POCKET BOOKS

NEW YORK   LONDON   TORONTO   SYDNEY   NEW DELHI

The sale of this book without its cover is unauthorized. If you purchased this book without a cover, you should be aware that it was reported to the publisher as "unsold and destroyed." Neither the author nor the publisher has received payment for the sale of this "stripped book."

Pocket Books
An Imprint of Simon & Schuster, Inc.
1230 Avenue of the Americas
New York, NY 10020

This book is a work of fiction. Any references to historical events, real people, or real places are used fictitiously. Other names, characters, places, and events are products of the author's imagination, and any resemblance to actual events or places or persons living or dead is entirely coincidental.

Copyright © 2021 by Scott Carson

All rights reserved, including the right to reproduce this book or portions thereof in any form whatsoever. For information, address Atria Books Subsidiary Rights Department, 1230 Avenue of the Americas, New York, NY 10020.

This Pocket Books paperback edition January 2024

POCKET and colophon are registered trademarks of Simon & Schuster, Inc.

Simon & Schuster: Celebrating 100 Years of Publishing in 2024

For information about special discounts for bulk purchases, please contact Simon & Schuster Special Sales at 1-866-506-1949 or business@simonandschuster.com.

The Simon & Schuster Speakers Bureau can bring authors to your live event. For more information, or to book an event, contact the Simon & Schuster Speakers Bureau at 1-866-248-3049 or visit our website at www.simonspeakers.com.

Interior design by Lana J. Roff

Manufactured in the United States of America

10 9 8 7 6 5 4 3 2 1

ISBN 978-1-6680-3349-4
ISBN 978-1-9821-0464-1 (ebook)

*For Kaleb Ryan,
with thanks for friendship
and support across the years*

PART ONE

1

I was never a dreamer.

I mean that in the most literal sense. Figuratively speaking, I absolutely consider myself a dreamer. Aspirational, at least. Optimistic? To a point, although my profession—journalism—mandates a certain cynicism. When I say I was never a dreamer, I mean at night, in the depths of sleep.

No dreams. Just didn't have 'em. Not good, bad, happy, or sad.

Slept well, though. I slept well. That's hard to believe these days, but I know that it was true once.

People talk about their dreams all the time. I dated a woman for a few years who would wake up and recite the bizarre and vivid stories that had accompanied her through the night. Sometimes, I'd be tempted to pretend that I could share the experience. Dreaming seems normal, right? Seems like something that *should* happen to all of us. And yet we don't know much about the mechanisms of dreams, for all of our scientific research and psychological theorizing. We believe dreaming is tied to memory, that REM sleep is an archival process.

We believe dreams are indicative of repressed emotions, or perhaps harbingers of maladies that haven't yet offered physical symptoms. Warnings. Messages from the dead. From God. We believe all of these things and more, but what we *know* is this: dreams are still not fully understood after all these years. They come and they go.

For most people, at least.

Until I returned to Hammel, Maine, in the autumn after I was laid off from my newspaper, I enjoyed deep and untroubled sleep. Not for long, maybe, but enough. Five or six hours were plenty.

Whitney, my ex, was a nightly dreamer who always seemed bothered by my blank-slate sleeping. When I returned from a stretch as an embedded correspondent covering troop drawdowns in Afghanistan, I think she was waiting on nightmares, PTSD terrors, cold sweats. That didn't happen. The visions that came for me from the war zone were— and remain—real memories.

Once, she asked me to explain what dreamless sleep felt like. We were in bed in our apartment in Tampa with the windows up and a humid spring breeze fanning through the screens, coffee cups cooling on the nightstands, a lazy Saturday morning. She'd just recounted her latest theater of the mind that passed for sleep and returned to the question of whether I'd dreamed that night, too.

"Maybe," I said. "I don't remember them, that's all. I'm not like you."

"Everybody remembers *something* from a dream," she said, dark blond hair falling over her face before she pushed it back.

"You'll have to ask me before I wake up next time," I said, a dumb joke I offered just to move on to another topic. She'd minored in psychology and loved to guess at the meaning of a dream, loved to hear opinions on what the subconscious or unconscious mind was trying to tell her. I think that's one of the reasons the empty archives of my nights bothered her—there was nothing to dissect.

"What does that feel like, then?" she asked.

"What does *not* dreaming feel like?"

She nodded: The hair fell across her face again, and she swept it back again. Whitney and her hair had a war each morning and she always surrendered first but on a Saturday morning the battle could go on for quite a while.

"It doesn't feel like anything," I said.

"Come on, writer. You've got to do better than *that*. You fall asleep, you wake up, and that sensation feels like . . ."

She hung on that dangling unfinished sentence, waiting for me to turn a phrase that explained the experience. I could see that she was serious and so I tried to come up with an honest answer.

"Blackness," I said. "It's that simple. The world is black, and then I crawl out of it—float out of it, if there's no alarm going off—and the world is light again." I shrugged, sensing her disappointment. "It's the best I can do. Sorry."

"That sounds sad," she said, and her expression was so forlorn I couldn't help but laugh.

"At least I do wake up," I said, leaning over to kiss her. "Beats the alternative."

She cocked an eyebrow, giving me mock scrutiny. "*Something* goes on in that brain at night. It *has* to."

"You say the same thing during the day, and you're wrong then, too."

"False. I've never accused your brain of working during the day." She propped herself up on her elbow, studied me. "Promise me you're not hiding them?"

"Hiding my *dreams*?"

She nodded. "I want to know what they are. Even if they're always about that bitch from Chicago you dated back in—"

"Now, that's not nice."

"I want to hear. Actually, don't tell me if they're about her. Turn her into someone more interesting, would you?"

I laughed, and she did, too, but then her smile faded and she said, "You *will* tell me when you remember them, Nick? Even if they're bad?"

"I'll tell you," I said, and I meant it then.

I really did.

I also knew better than to believe it was my literal lack of dreams that put up the wall between us.

Yet, when the breakup finally happened, I couldn't help the thought. I remembered the combination of scrutiny and concern in her eyes when she asked those questions, remembered her emphatic insistence that *everyone* dreams something sometime, and I wondered what she saw in my own eyes when I insisted that I did not. Whether there was something in them that scared her.

Nonsense, right? It had been a silly conversation in a loving relationship that had simply run its course. There was a gap between us, and eventually in a long-term relationship you ride up against that chasm, judge its risk and reward, and make the hard choice: try to make the jump on faith, or retreat?

She retreated and tried a new path. Last I heard, she was dating a man who owned a sailboat and they were talking about taking a year off and cruising the world, untethered.

I have a feeling that guy's dreams made for the right kind of conversation.

Better than blackness, anyhow.

I don't know if the happy couple ever actually weighed anchor. Whitney and I fell out of touch, the way you do. Except I'm not sure you ever *really* do. Everyone insists they've lost track, of course. "Where's the ex? No idea. Haven't heard from her in years." But there are days when I'll think of people I lost touch with long ago and have a near-physical certainty that they're thinking of me, too, right then, as if there's some electric current riding through the atmosphere and we happened to connect on the same circuit one more time. It's always a good feeling, like a kind touch.

For a guy who can't dream, that's not bad, right?

I returned home for the reason most people do it: a lack of options.

It wasn't a formal move. Just a visit. The kind of visit without dates that you can make only when you've got no demands on your time. I was unemployed and doing what you do—calling in favors, hunting for leads. *Networking* is the polite term. Begging is the feeling.

I started with editors, working my way through contacts in an industry that was hanging on the ropes. Even the more optimistic colleagues I spoke with couldn't promise a job. On down the line I moved, from the overseas bureau folks and the managing editors at big metro dailies to Patrick Ryan, the oldest friend I had who was connected to anything remotely related to journalism. Pat ran the PR department for Hammel College, one of those tony New England liberal arts schools that have been around long enough to justify the tuition rate with a straight face.

I'd graduated from Hammel at a discount because my mother was a faculty member. The student loans were still equivalent to a mortgage payment, but in exchange I emerged with a degree in journalism—a dinosaur of a profession and a historically low-paying one at that. (I have a theory that some basic finance class should be taught in high school. It's the kind of theory you arrive at in your late twenties, but rarely before that.)

I loved writing, though, loved newspapers, loved the daily grind of reporting. First draft of history, and all that. Pat had started in the J-school with me, but he read the industry's writing on the wall and bailed for a degree in folklore—which he claimed was the same thing as journalism—and a heavy focus on schmoozing with anyone who could hire him for . . . well, for anything. In the end, he didn't have to leave at all, remaining at Hammel to work in the bold world of college PR. Yawn. But, hey, nice benefits package.

Pat had come east from Montana for school, and although I was technically a townie, I'd lived in Hammel for less than two years, a move we made following my father's death, and I still felt like an outsider when college began. I was used to that, though; as my mother's academic star ascended, we'd moved frequently. There was always another school that could entice her by promising fewer lectures and more research time. I attended four different schools in four different towns between the ages of eight and eighteen, so moving into the dorms with out-of-state and international students didn't feel all that unusual to me. Fresh starts were standard operating procedure in the Bishop family.

Pat Ryan and I bonded the fall of our freshman year over two things: beer and bullshit. Much of the latter was based on endless arguments over who was tougher, Mainers or Montanans. He was a big, rangy Irish kid who sunburned easily—no small feat in Maine—and loved fly-fishing and hiking and sailing. He bought three sailboats while we were in college, each one cheaper than the last, and the first one set him back only fifteen hundred bucks, so you can imagine how seaworthy these tubs were. I answered the phone one Friday night when the harbor master, a cranky old Yankee named Bobby Beauchamp—who was also the caretaker of my mother's cabin in the off-season—called to report the sinking of the boat Pat had christened the SS *Money Pit*.

Pat was far too drunk to drive down and do anything about it by then, and he reasoned the boat wasn't going to be hard to find, because it was still tied to the mooring buoy, the buoy was still above water, and he'd paid for the space, so what did it matter whether his boat was on the water or beneath it, shouldn't his renter's rights remain intact?

Hell, let's have another beer and deal with the boat in the morning, he said, and so we did.

Needless to say, he had a strained relationship with the harbor master after that.

On the day Pat offered me the job that brought me back to Maine, he was long removed from his carousing days, a respectable staff member of an esteemed college, one with enough clout to offer me a freelance job.

"Five grand for a puff piece," he said. "Nick, you *gotta* do it."

"I *gotta* find an actual job, man. Not a Band-Aid."

"I love a man who's bleeding out on the battlefield and still waving off Band-Aids."

Fair point.

"We'll even reimburse your mileage," he said, and that was the first time I realized he expected me to show up in Maine. I'd been viewing it as a phoner, Hammel College covered from a Tampa condo, because that was the way it usually went. Nobody had travel budgets.

"I'm in Tampa. If I'm coming to Maine, I'm flying."

"Yeah, we can't reimburse that, brother. I can probably spring for one-way mileage, though. I'll siphon it from the intern fund. Those little shits don't need the help. Drive north! Live a little! Seriously, it's summer. You *want* to stay in Florida? What happened to my Main-ah buddy?"

In point of fact, I didn't want to stay in Florida. I was sick of the trapped heat, of the stagnancy I'd begun to associate with the summer air in Tampa—hell, with *everything* in Tampa. I also hadn't been home in years, and there was an instant, just thinking about it, when I swore I could smell pines and clean water.

"Be good to get up here for a visit," Pat pressed, as if sensing my nostalgia. "See your mom while you're at it."

That made me feel guilty, but only a little. I spoke with my mother twice a week, and yet I hadn't had a conversation with her in more than a year. That was when the stroke had claimed her mind. She verbalized plenty now but didn't *communicate*, her mind stuck in a slow spin cycle, churning on the same details but never able to add anything fresh to the load. A lot of us are headed to that place, be it through a stroke, Alzheimer's, or dementia, and I think it is one of the great fears of my generation—we are, after all, obsessed with remaining connected, and narcissistic enough to believe that the rest of the world wants us to be.

For my mother, though, it was a tragedy that transcended family. Alice Jane Bishop had been one of the nation's preeminent scholars in the field of memory research. She published in leading medical journals and spoke at conferences around the globe. She knew the intricacies and mysteries of the human memory as well as anyone—until she lost her own.

Cruel joke, right? Cruel world, kids.

She had been hiking alone in the Camden Hills on a favorite trail along Mount Megunticook. When the stroke came a fall followed, and she tumbled down into the rocks. It was early December and light snow was blowing in—hardly a foul-weather day by Maine standards but still cold enough to kill you if you were exposed to the elements all night. Mom always hiked with a headlamp, though, even on a day hike—a habit I'd teased her about mercilessly—and it was the headlamp that saved her life. She fumbled it out and succeeded in not just turning it on but in setting it to the blinking red distress strobe. The last hiker in the park that night found her. He crawled down through the rocks to look for the light source.

I'd been optimistic when the first doctor called. My mother was alive but disoriented, he said. Just disoriented. Then days turned to weeks and months and it became clear that the Alice Bishop who had departed the trailhead that morning wasn't going to return to us.

"Hell, just come to see *me*," Pat Ryan said now, maybe realizing that a face-to-face with my mom wasn't as appealing. "I'm offering you a paid vacation."

"That makes it sound worse, Pat. Let's at least pretend it's a job."

"Fine, fine. It's a job. Crucial work."

"Doing what?"

"I've got a profile for the alumni magazine that won't write itself."

A profile for the alumni magazine. Two years ago, I'd been reporting from Kabul for international syndication. How quickly things come apart.

"Who's the pride of the alma mater these days?"

I asked, trying to keep my tone light, trying not to let Pat hear any humiliation. He was, after all, doing me a favor.

"You'll dig it," he said. "Some young tech guy who—"

"Oh, no."

"Got a bit of VC money and—"

"Heaven help me."

"—built an exciting little company right here in Hammel that—"

"Has a billion-dollar IPO?"

"Not yet. Give it a month. Your profile will be ahead of the curve! Bloomberg and *Wired* and even our austere friend the *Wall Street Journal* will be madly envious."

"Terrific." I opened a bottle of Blanton's bourbon. "What did the precocious young lad do, pray tell? Invent a blender that sources private consumer data to retailers in real time?"

"That's next year. This year, he's working for the good of the people!"

"I bet."

"Seriously. He's developed an app—"

I held the phone close to the glass while I poured the bourbon into it, and I could hear Pat laugh.

I put the phone back to my ear. "Go on."

"In *total seriousness*, the app is for the human good."

"Uh-huh."

"It's a mindfulness app."

"Aren't there already about a hundred of those? I see ads everywhere. 'Still your mind, calm your soul, and do it on the go!'"

"Yeah, I know. But there's only one of them that is headquartered in the old Hefron Mill. They've injected some serious capital into the place."

The Hefron complex had been a sprawling brick dinosaur looming over the Beaumont River when we were in school, a long-defunct pulp mill, its impotent smokestacks cutting a bleak silhouette just past the pristine campus.

"Donors like revitalization projects," I said, and sipped my bourbon.

"Exactly! And you'll be paid a princely sum to capture the young titan in your eloquent yet concise prose. Everyone wins."

"Five grand."

"Five grand more than you're making this week, right?"

It was indeed.

"It's a no-brainer," Pat said, and I had to laugh.

"What?" he protested.

"I'm thinking of how many times you said that about something that nearly left me dead or in jail."

"And you regret *none* of those adventures."

That was the truth. I could see Maine then, the dark pines and blue water and the gunmetal November skies and the fogbanks that floated in thick as bed linens. I could see it, and I missed it. Badly.

Plus, I needed the money, and it was a chance to see my mom.

"All right," I said. "And thanks. Sincerely."

"My pleasure. Be great to see you again."

"Likewise."

He turned serious then. "This guy *is* interesting. He's got a team that's very talented, and the app has some big-league neuroscientists as consultants."

"What does a neuroscientist bring to the table beyond credibility?"

"That special thing that separates it from all the rest. Gotta be different, right?"

"What's their special thing?"

"Shaping your dreams."

I laughed.

"No, really," Pat said. "That's the gimmick. That's how they intend to separate from the pack."

I lowered my bourbon.

"Shaping your dreams?"

"Yep. Consider your quality of life if you could remove every nightmare and replace it with a sweet dream. Think that might have an impact on anxiety, stress, blood pressure, et cetera? Can you even imagine that?"

"No," I said.

As a non-dreamer, I truly could not. And something strange happened then, while I stood in my kitchen sipping bourbon and talking to an old friend: the pleasant memories of the Maine coast were gone and I had a flash of Whitney's face, of the concern in her eyes when she asked me to explain what my sleep was like.

Blackness.

Had she recoiled, then? No. Surely not. It had been an inconsequential conversation.

She'd have liked the idea, though. Shaping your dreams. She'd subscribe to that app, no free trial needed.

I thanked Pat once more, promised to see him soon, and then went out onto the balcony and let the Florida heat envelop me. I thought of Maine, of my mother and of my friends, and I waited for a cooling breeze that never came while I imagined a blond woman on a sailboat beneath a starlit sky, pushed ahead by a freshening wind.

Then I went inside and went to bed. Sleep came and sleep went. Blackness rose and blackness receded.

Reliable as the tide, back then.

I miss those nights.

2

I returned to Maine on the last week of October.
By the time I drove north, it had been nearly four months since I'd lost my job and I was past the bitterness and feeling okay, as if I understood the plan ahead. Because there *was* a plan. I would head to Maine, stay a few weeks, and work it all out up there. Reimagine my future and fortify my resilience. Shit, what else can you do? Get knocked down, you best get back up.

I was back up. By the time I crossed the Piscataqua River Bridge from Portsmouth into Kittery—saluting when I passed beneath the *Welcome to Maine* sign—I was actually feeling pretty damned good. I'd run out of podcasts and playlists somewhere along the eastern seaboard and had the radio on, the real radio, which I never listened to, and WCLZ was playing Tom Petty, "Runnin' Down a Dream," and how could you not laugh at that? A little on the nose, right? But there was Tom, on cue, when I needed him.

I felt so good, like anything was possible . . .

Not so hard to buy into it. I was broke, yes, but

I was young and had a plan and was a tough SOB. Those were the things I knew in my bones.

There's something good waitin' down this road...

Damn straight there was.

Rest in peace, Tom Petty.

The song ended before I reached the York toll booth, but the good mood lingered on up the turnpike. I wasn't missing anything crucial in the rearview mirror. My job was gone, I was single, I was tired of Florida, and I'd come to think that the layoff was the nudge I needed, if not something even grander: an actual sign—or, as my mother would've said, "Your guardian angel giving you a swift kick in the ass."

My mother had an interesting sermonizing style. I was ready to see her, or whatever was left of her. Even if she didn't recognize me it would be good to see her face. My father was long dead, gone when I was sixteen, courtesy of black ice on I-295 just north of the Portland Jetport. He'd been hurrying to catch a flight that, unbeknownst to him, was already canceled. I think he'd have laughed at that. I did the crying, but I think my dad would have laughed, and knowing that just made me cry harder. The friend who can laugh on the bad days is the one you need the most, after all.

Until he died, we'd lived in Camden, Maine, a short drive up the coast from Hammel, and my mother commuted to the campus. She'd loved the drive, particularly in the winter—no traffic, Penobscot Bay hugging you on one side, low snowcapped mountains on the other. After the wreck, though, she didn't care much for those winding roads in winter. We sold the family house and moved to Hammel, staying first at our old seasonal camp on Rosewater Pond and then moving into a house near campus. I finished high school there, a year and a half that went by in a blur, and then moved into the dorm. Our house in Hammel never felt much like home to me, and I sold that without hesitation when my mother's medical bills started to flow, but I still had a free place to crash in Maine, due mostly to nostalgia and more than a little guilt. Our camp—or *cabin* for you non-Mainers—on Rosewater was still in my possession, although I never visited it now, and obviously neither did my mother.

The mind, though, is a mysterious beast, and while my mother seemed not to retain an iota of memory about the house, she held *vivid* recall of the camp. In our phone conversations, she would mention it again and again, getting into the weeds of detail, asking me if I'd remembered to put Rid-X in the septic, or if the light above the kitchen sink was still out. Her house and husband and son were all gone from her mind, but the camp remained. That was a bad reason to keep the place, particularly considering I wasn't investing in its upkeep, and yet I never got around to listing it.

When I made my triumphant return to Hammel, then, I arrived with a residence on the water. That sounds impressive until you look at a map of Maine and realize how much water there is. In most places, Rosewater would be called a lake, but in Maine it's got to be a hell of a big body of water to classify as anything more than pond. Rosewater lived up to its name in the right sunset, when the granite gorge at the western end funneled the dying light across the water and gave it a ruby shine. Most of the day, though, it was hard gray, like unpolished pewter.

The camp had been in my mother's family for two generations, and we'd spent happy weekends there when I was a kid and a less happy spring and summer there after Dad died. Maybe that period tainted it for me, because I'd stopped spending time there after college. I'd seen that the property taxes were paid and basic maintenance was done by Bob Beauchamp, the old-timer who'd been the harbor master for Pat Ryan's boat scuttling. Despite Beauchamp's efforts, it was an old cabin in a place of long winters, and it looked rough when I arrived in the slanting light of late evening. The clouds killed the sun, and there was no signature rose-colored glow to the water.

The camp was tucked in a cove and screened by pines and birches. The paint had been a deep, rich red but it had faded into a rust color and seemed to blend with the fallen pine needles that carpeted the massive rock on which the building rested. I parked my Ford Ranger in the rutted drive and then unpacked, swatting at mosquitoes. The spare key was still taped to the bottom of the propane tank that fed the stove and the space heater. The key was rusted but it worked.

Inside, everything smelled like an attic, the scent of trapped memories. I opened every window that still had a screen, lit a couple of old candles, and went outside to sit on the decaying dock in the darkness. It was a strange feeling, being back, but there was a loon calling on the other side of the pond, that beautiful mournful cry, and I had so many good memories wrapped up in that sound that it felt welcoming.

Rosewater.

I was back.

I sat on the dock for a long time, refreshing myself on the uselessness of citronella against Maine mosquitoes. The privacy and silence were striking after the constant backdrop of human sound in Tampa. To the right, across the cove, was a camp that had once belonged to the Holland family. I'd had a terrible crush on their daughter. The yellow-sided house was dark and quiet now. Beyond that was my least favorite house on the pond, a sprawling postmodern monstrosity. The lawn looked like a putting green sweeping down to a stone wall. A long dock extended from the shore in front of the house, and two oversized, bright green reflectors marked the dock for a boat that never arrived. Why green, no one knew, but the combination of the green light and extravagant home led my father to nickname the place the Gatsby House.

Across from the Gatsby House was a log cabin with a forest-green metal roof that blended into the pines. There were log flower beds, log walls, even a log flagpole. This land o' logs was owned by none other than Bobby Beauchamp. Beauchamp was the de facto caretaker for half the houses on the pond. He was cranky but reliable and affordable—qualities that are often mutually exclusive.

While I sat on the dock, Bobby's ancient Dodge Ram came rattling down the drive (which was lined with log barriers and ended in front of log parking blocks; you see the pattern with Bobby and the logs) and the door opened and there was the retired harbor master with a paper bag in one hand and a six-pack of Pabst in the other, staring at me. I lifted my hand and waved.

He faced stiffly ahead. "You lookin' after Bishop's place, or is the kid rentin' it out?"

"It *is* the kid, Mr. Beauchamp," I called back. "It's Nick."

"Ayuh, I should've recognized you," he bellowed, never mind that he hadn't seen me in years, we were separated by a good two hundred feet, and the light was fading. Harbor master vision is a superpower, apparently.

"Good to be back," I said. "You doing well?"

"Course I am," he said, as if offended that there could be any question over his well-being.

"I'm glad to hear it." I rose to my feet, thinking we might catch up on whatever news there was around Rosewater. He cut me off.

"Gotta get the groceries in the fridge," he said, lifting the six-pack without any apparent irony. "I'll come over and talk tomorrow. You got some dyin' trees need cut. I can do it, but not for free."

Ah, Mainers.

"Thanks," I said. "We can talk it over."

"Camp needs staining, too," he said. "I could do it, but—"

"Not for free," I finished. "Sure. I appreciate it, Mr. Beauchamp."

Why I couldn't call him Bob even to this day, I had no idea. He grunted and rattled the six-pack in what was possibly supposed to be a wave and then he was gone into his cabin. I smiled and shook my head. The list of suggested repairs wouldn't stop with cutting and painting, I knew. I'd have to make reference to my status as an unemployed man early in the conversation, before the numbers began adding up.

When I'd donated enough blood to the mosquitoes for one night, I went inside and found some linens for the ancient twin bed with the creaking box spring. I'd just made up the bed when my phone chimed with a text message. It was an unfamiliar number but a 207 area code—somewhere in the state of Maine. I opened it.

Hello, Mr. Bishop! This is Renee with Clarity
Inc. Pat Ryan at Hammel gave me your number.
We are looking forward to hosting you for a
tour of our new headquarters at the Mill tomorrow. Please confirm that you made it in, and I'll
pass along parking details.

Clarity Inc.? And parking details? Last I knew,
the mill had enough empty asphalt surrounding it
that you could pick your parking angle and leave
the vehicle for days. I'd also wanted a day or two
to get settled, see my Mom, and catch up with Pat
before I did any interviews. But, what the hell—I
was here to do the job, and the quicker I started,
the quicker I'd have the check in hand.

Thanks, Renee, I pecked out. I'm looking forward to it as
well. How does 10 a.m. work for you?

Within seconds, a response:

Perfect! Please park in the garage off Ames
Street and we will validate. No recorders and
no cell phone, please. Pat promises me that
you can work with a pen and paper.;-)

I sat with the phone in my hand, smelling the
cool, dusty cabin around me, and tried not to be
pissed off about some techie wunderkind's security
concerns. Tried not to be tempted to write back that
I'd dealt with Department of Defense clearances, so
I could probably manage the Clarity Inc. process.

I wasn't working with the DOD clearance anymore, though, and there was no need to be a dick, so I wrote back Sure thing and left it at that. It occurred to me that I hadn't told Pat I was back in Maine yet. I'd planned on calling him in the morning. Oh, well. The app developers were eager for their publicity. That was fine. Eager sources make a reporter's life easy.

I turned off the lights and lay with my head on a flat, musty pillow and waited for sleep. It was a long wait. The loons were out, and the loons were loud. Two of them, maybe three, all engaged in busy squawking chatter that didn't resemble their standard mournful cry. The rapid-fire exchange suggested that they were reacting to a disturbance or a threat, most likely some unwelcome creature near the nest. The signature sound of the loon is a solitary sound. It's a haunting cry of undeniable beauty with an undercurrent of sorrow. An announcement of peaceful northern isolation, the Thoreau of birds.

The sound is a lie, though. Loons are not solitary, nor are they peaceful. The loon's life is a violent one. The birds will stab each other with their beaks, beat each other with their wings, and pull each other under the water. The midnight cry that makes people think of Thoreau at Walden Pond is anything but serene.

I wasn't sure what triggered the battle between the birds on the pond, or what ended it, but eventually they reached a cease-fire and silence returned to Rosewater.

Then I slept.

3

The old Hefron Mill had changed so dramatically that I might have driven by it the next morning if not for the structure's sheer size.

The last time I'd seen it, the mill had been a blend of red brick and concrete, weathered and dulled, the windows cracked or covered with boards, the building tagged with the half-hearted graffiti of bored high school kids. A few attempts at converting the space had been made over the years, but nothing stuck, because what company in Maine needed 300,000 square feet of industrial space? The town was always trying to "gift" it to the college, and nothing sent the Hammel board of trustees scurrying away faster than such an offer.

Now, though, it stood in splendor, painted a clean cream color that contrasted with the tiered flower beds of pink beach roses below. A new entryway was highlighted by two stories of glass. A deck and footbridge lined with flower boxes led across the Beaumont River and the thundering falls that had once powered the mill. On the other side was a freshly paved parking lot, gated and fenced. There were five cars inside the lot, and there were twenty empty spaces on the street in front of it. Money well spent.

I parked on the street.

For the first time since Pat had referenced the story, I had authentic curiosity in it. Not because of the app, but because of the money. Surely they hadn't been able to generate *this* much venture capital backing for an unreleased product in an already crowded market?

A reporter with a question is a happy human. It was a small question for a minor-league story, but it was still a hell of a good feeling.

I walked across the new footbridge, the falls pounding down to my left, the flower beds fragrant to my right, and made my way to the main entrance. Pulled on one of the giant glass doors.

Locked.

Ah, yes, the security procedures. I'd forgotten my instructions. I dutifully pressed the buzzer on the outdoor intercom box, and a bright-voiced woman answered.

"Delivery?"

I gave my name and the purpose of my visit.

"Oh, sure. I see Renee in the hallway now. I'll send her down."

I stood and waited and enjoyed the morning. The harbor—where once a young Patrick Ryan had lost a sailboat to the high seas while it sat at anchor— was straight down the steep hill that followed the river on its way to the bay. There, on a clear day, you'd be able to make out the islands and see all the way across to where the coastal towns of Rockland, Camden, and Belfast were scattered along Route 1 on the northbound route to Bar Harbor and Mount Desert Island and Acadia.

Behind me, the glass door of the revitalized mill opened and a smiling young woman with dark red hair and green eyes extended her hand.

"Mr. Bishop, I'm Renee."

"Good to meet . . . ," I began, and then, "Hang on! *Renee!*"

Her smile widened, and for a moment I thought the handshake was going to turn into a hug, but it didn't. Instead we just stood there grinning at each other. Renee Holland had been my first real friend in Hammel, and a Rosewater neighbor for as long as summer lasted. After Labor Day, everyone scattered. She was two years older than me and ran cross-country and read philosophy books with absolute earnestness and knew more about gangsta rap than anyone I'd ever met. The ideal eighteen-year-old enigma.

Being two years older would've usually made her too cool to hang out with me, but summers are different. We'd bonded over music and then started running trails together in the humid afternoons. In her basement we listened to countless spins of Nas and Tupac and Dr. Dre and fiercely debated the merits of Eminem. Renee dismissed almost every current rapper as trivial pop music; only the past held an allure for her. I had a ridiculous crush on her, but like most summer crushes, it was never realized. She went back to college and then transferred to a school out of state, Indiana or Iowa.

"Didn't recognize me!" she said now, teasing. "I can't believe it."

"You're disguised. What's with the red hair?"

She laughed. "I know, I know. It's a bit much."

"No, it looks great."

"You have to say that."

"I'd never lie to you."

"He lied lyingly."

I smiled. "Why didn't you tell me it was you last night? You were so formal: 'Renee from Clarity here to tell you about parking validation.'"

She grinned. "That wouldn't have been any fun. A surprise is always better in person."

"It is," I agreed, and it *was* better. Seeing her, I felt at home in a way I hadn't on my return to Rosewater. Home is always more about the people than the place.

"Come on in," she said. "I'll show you the empire."

We entered a rotunda of polished floors and gleaming white walls. Everything was white, almost too vivid, that line where brightness becomes harshness.

"You guys have poured a lot of money into this place," I said.

"Well, it's not all about Clarity. We're just the

flagship tenant. They're hoping for many more, of course. They want it to be an incubator of sorts, the destination for newer businesses, tech jobs, anything and everything that stops the brain drain, you know?"

She waved a key card in front of a sensor beside the elevator. The doors opened. We stepped in.

"I'll let Bryce explain the rest," she said. "It's his baby."

Bryce. I tried not to wince. Of course, he was a Bryce. I could see him already: trust-fund baby, college dropout, boyish CEO of overvalued tech company.

We rose one floor, two, three, and then stopped and the doors chimed again. There were no buttons in the elevator except for an emergency intercom switch. The key card automatically directed the elevator to the proper floor. Sophisticated. And expensive.

The elevator doors opened, we stepped out, and there was a soft chime. Renee turned to me immediately.

"Uh-oh," she said, mock chastising. "I thought we agreed no phones?"

"I won't use one."

"I believe you, but we really can't have it in the building from a security standpoint. Hang on." She crossed the room, which was an open industrial plan a few years behind on the curve of cool, with exposed brick and ductwork and black fixtures offsetting refinished wooden floors. Wood-and-glass partitions broke the space up into separate workstations. There were sleek black lounge chairs in one corner of the room, a whiteboard, rolled-up yoga mats. It looked like the space someone might design for a tech company if their only sense of Silicon Valley came from the old HBO show. They were missing the Ping-Pong tables and smoothie bar, but not much else. Maybe those were on the roof.

Renee Holland returned carrying a small black box. When she lifted the lid, I saw that it was felt-lined. It looked like a miniature casket.

"If you can put your phone in this, kind sir, we'll see that you get it back when you leave."

I looked back at the elevator and realized belatedly what had happened.

"There's a sensor?"

"Pardon?"

"That chime when we walked off the elevator told you I had a phone?"

"You really are an investigative reporter. I'd assumed Pat was lying about that. Yes, there's a sensor." She smiled brightly, as if this was a wonderful innovation, but I felt vaguely disturbed by it.

"Lot of security," I said, dropping my phone into the casket-box, which she promptly snapped shut and returned to the table.

"Do you know what Calm's valuation was?" a voice from my right said.

I turned back to see a man who was maybe a few

years older than me, somewhere in his early thirties, with an unevenly trimmed beard obscuring a chubby face.

"This is Bryce Lermond," Renee said.

He wore faded jeans and a fleece vest over a long-sleeved T-shirt, as if he'd been torn between hiking the Appalachian Trail and creating a tech start-up. The only problem with that rumpled look was a pair of boots so new I was surprised I couldn't smell the leather from where I stood.

"One billion dollars," he said. "So do I worry about security?" He laughed. "It's a nice ego stroke, at least, imagining people would want to steal our genius."

His smile was warm and genuine, at least, and his handshake was relaxed, not trying too hard.

"I've come to chronicle your genius," I assured him, "not steal it."

"I know, I know." He looked at Renee, smiled. "I understand you go way back with our COO."

Renee Holland was the chief operating officer of Clarity. It seemed like a surprising fit for the girl I'd known, the would-be philosopher and part-time rapper. I'd have expected to see her in academia or maybe publishing. Or running a marijuana farm.

"Way back," I said. "'Memory Lane.'"

That had been her favorite Nas song. She smiled at the reference, but only slightly. She was probably not inclined to throw a verse in front of her boss. A damn shame.

"Shall we sit?" Bryce Lermond inclined his head in the direction of one of the portioned-off cubicles. It was larger than the others but still part of the open plan, with no door or other indication that this was the CEO's space. He didn't need to worry much about privacy, though; it seemed to be just the two of them.

I took one of the leather chairs across from his desk, which was an unpretentious piece of butcher block. Renee took the chair beside me.

"We really appreciate this," Bryce Lermond said. "The college has been a crucial collaborator, so the chance to say a few words about that is important."

"Terrific." I was far more interested in Renee's journey than Bryce's, but I had to play my part. "Mind if I just wade in with some questions, get the ball rolling?"

"By all means."

And so we began. I learned that Bryce Lermond was originally from Boston and had attended Hammel briefly before dropping out and finishing his degree at UMass Lowell; that he'd flirted with a PhD in psychology before taking a job as a coder for a cloud computing company; that he'd become interested in the idea of mindfulness applications while studying meditation; that his company currently consisted of a grand total of five employees, only three of whom lived in Maine—the others were coders in New York and Seattle—but that they had high hopes to employ as many as fifty from the company headquarters in the grand old Hefron Mill, which was an inspiring facility because of its history, and blah, blah, and blah.

I'd just gotten to the questions about slowing the "brain drain" of young talent that flooded out of Maine each year, which was catnip for the donors who might read the piece, when Bryce Lermond interrupted me.

"You don't buy it, do you?" he said, smiling.

"What's that?"

"Us. The idea. The potential." His smile seemed authentic. Not unfriendly, and not surprised.

"Sure I do."

He chuckled. "Come on."

I glanced at Renee. She was watching me, and she was not smiling. She looked vaguely disappointed.

"I don't think it's relevant," I said, turning back to Lermond. "Neither should you. My job is to get the word out there about the company, what you're doing, and what your ties to Hammel College are. I'd love to pretend it's more than that, but it isn't."

"To *me* it is, though," he said, leaning forward, blue eyes earnest above the beard that showed the first few gray hairs of his life. "I mean, I get your gig, but anytime I talk about what we're doing, I'm curious to see the responses. And you . . ." He wagged a finger at me. "You are not a believer."

My job wasn't to do PR for the company, and it certainly wasn't to accept all of Bryce Lermond's claims without scrutiny, but I still felt guilty. He seemed like a decent guy, Renee was definitely a decent woman, and they had big dreams. No reason to breathe cynicism in their faces.

"Sorry," I said. "Reporters are skeptical creatures."

"And?"

I raised my eyebrows. "And . . . what?"

"Seriously, Nick—may I call you Nick?" After I nodded, he pushed ahead. "I'm appreciative of any ink we can get at this stage, but I'm more interested in what *you* think."

"Why?"

"Because I'm going to have to figure out how to sell it," he said bluntly, and his smile faded and he looked vulnerable. His eyes flicked to Renee and then back, as if he wished he hadn't made the admission in front of her. Entrepreneurs needed to exude confidence. Bryce Lermond wasn't putting off much of it.

"I'm sure you won't have any trouble," I said.

"Bullshit," he answered, and then, quickly, "Sorry. But where you see this as an interview, I see it as a test run. Do you follow?"

"I guess. But you've already raised plenty of money. Seems like you've passed the sales-pitch test with more important people than me."

The smile returned, rueful now. "My mother," he said, and Renee shifted in her chair, crossing her legs and smoothing her black slacks. I didn't need to look at her face this time to read her displeasure; she seemed a few seconds away from shouting at him to shut up.

"Your mother is one of your investors?" I asked.

"She was the *only* investor."

I tried not to show my surprise, but he studied my face and then nodded, satisfied that he'd seen whatever he wanted to see there.

"Yeah. Not ideal, right? We've got a board of directors and everything, we've got input from first-class people, but as far as money, one source."

"She must have a lot of it," I said.

He laughed. "To chance wasting it on such a dumbass bet?"

"Not what I meant."

"That's exactly what *I'm* afraid people will think. But, yes, she did have a lot of money. I won't deny that. Which means, since her death, *I* now have a lot of money. And people view that with . . ."

"Skepticism," I said, because he seemed to want me to provide the word.

"Contempt," he said. "It's beyond skepticism, trust me. I'm fine with that. But when I talk to you about the tech, about the real *idea* here, the *magic* here, the *potential* here, I feel like you're being polite by not yawning." He paused. "Actually, you did yawn once."

Truth.

"Look, Mr. Lermond, I'm not an ideal target market. Not really a tech guy."

"But that's the point!" he said, voice rising. "I don't want to sell this thing to tech guys. I want to sell it to the whole damn world. So tell me—*please*—why doesn't it intrigue you?"

His face was so earnest, the question so plaintive, that I decided to give him an honest response. I didn't look at Renee.

"I feel like it's already out there," I said. "Calm, Headspace, Ten Percent Happier, etc. I guess it doesn't seem *new* to me."

He looked crestfallen. When I glanced back at Renee, she was staring at me like I'd stomped on her puppy while telling her kid that Santa wasn't real.

"But again," I said, more to her than him, lifting my hands in surrender, "I'm not the ideal market."

Bryce Lermond pushed back from his desk and swiveled back and forth, the hangdog expression lingering.

"It's a challenge," he muttered. "I won't disagree with you. It is a crowded space."

They both looked so damn disappointed that I felt as if I had to offer some reassurance. Hell, I wasn't there to *report* on their business, not in any real way; I was there to shine them up and make the old alma mater proud of its alumni. It wouldn't be a great way to thank Pat Ryan if said alumni called him in tears, which suddenly looked plausible from Bryce Lermond.

"The stuff about dreams interested me," I said. "You haven't even mentioned that."

It was like watching the sun rise and set—he brightened and dimmed and then went dark, scowling, face turned to the ceiling.

"Pat Ryan told you about that?"

"Yes. I thought it was . . . very intriguing. The whole bit about shaping dreams."

His eyes snapped back to me. "You don't believe that either, though?"

"I'm intrigued by it," I repeated.

Holy shit, what had I gotten into here? I just needed a few quotes about the way Bryce Lermond had found inspiration in the hallowed halls of Hammel, and now I was being asked to hold the guy's hand.

He nodded distantly, tugged on his beard, and stared into space. I was just about to break the silence when he said, "Would you try it?"

"Pardon?"

"The app. As a beta user."

Renee said, "Bryce—" but he put up a hand.

"No, no, we'd make him sign all the waivers and NDAs and stuff."

"Not if it's going in my story, you won't," I said, the reporter's instinct rising. Puff piece or not, I wasn't signing any nondisclosure agreements. The *disclosure* part of things was my business.

Then I remembered that I was writing this for an alumni magazine that needed to win Bryce's favor. It wasn't journalism, it was public relations.

"Forget it," I said. "I'll sign whatever is required."

He turned his attention to Renee. "We *do* need beta testers."

"We have a process for finding them, too," she said, her voice one degree warmer than scolding.

"Is there any reason he *can't* be one?"

She clearly wanted to argue but chose not to. Examined a fingernail instead, as if it were suddenly of great interest.

"Try it?" he asked me. "Two weeks. Every day. My only request would be that you follow the prompts and the process. Don't just binge through it. That's a poor idea. The product is designed for microdosing."

"Microdosing? I thought that was what you did with LSD."

Bryce Lermond didn't laugh. Neither did Renee.

"Similar concept," he said. "That's why we have a process with clear prompts. The graphic interfaces aren't finished yet but the content is there. The guided meditations, the breathing exercises, the sleep songs."

"Sleep songs?"

He nodded, a trace of enthusiasm returning. "So cool," he said. "So, so cool. Our brains are wired for song, you know. Story and song. Combine the two, and—" He brought his fists together with a smack, as if the collision was a good thing, but it looked like a head-on crash that bruised his knuckles.

"Powerful," I said.

"Damn straight, it's powerful! Try it?"

"Sure," I said. Why not? At this point, all I wanted was to get out of the office without making him cry.

"Awesome!" he said, and smacked his desk with delight. Beside me, Renee's interest in her fingernail deepened. It appeared to be the first fingernail she'd ever encountered.

"Renee, he brought a phone," Bryce said. "Can you get it for me, please?"

"How does everyone know I brought a phone?" I said.

He looked like I'd caught him at something. "It's quiet here. The chime . . ."

"Right. That's one hell of a sensor. Is it triggered by the phone's signal?"

"Yeah. It's pretty cool. I mean, do we need it? No. But I thought it was pretty cool."

Pretty cool. I felt like I'd climbed a rope ladder into a kid's clubhouse.

"Who makes it?"

"Hell, I don't remember." He waved a dismissive hand. "We can download the beta version of the app to your phone and you can tell us what you think. Just don't share it with anyone else, okay?"

"I won't share your app," I said. "I can promise you that."

"There you go," Bryce said enthusiastically. "We've got a beta tester, Renee. Your old friend, too. Keeping it in the family, almost. Let's do this!"

He drummed on the desk, grinning.

Renee took a deep breath—in through the nose,

out through the mouth—and then got to her feet and went to retrieve my phone and whatever paperwork would threaten to sue me right out of existence if I violated the trust of Clarity Inc. All the warmth of our reunion outside was long gone. My guess was that she knew her company was a long way from the next big thing, and to have an old friend see that embarrassed her.

"She'll be fine," Bryce said, as if reading my thoughts. "She's just . . . you know, so *private* about everything."

When she was seventeen, she'd been the queen of oversharing, impossible to shame.

"Sure," I said. "That's Renee."

It felt awkward sitting alone with Bryce Lermond, staring at each other from across the empty desk in the office space that looked like a stage-set rendering of the Big Tech Start-up.

"The science," he said, tapping on the side of his skull with his index finger, "is a cut above. *That* is the thing. When it comes to understanding the mind and the"—he hunted for the right word—"*guidance* of the mind, we are so, so far beyond the rest. It won't even be competitive."

He grinned then. His bearded face split and his white teeth showed. "I'll make a believer out of you yet, Nick."

"I'm sure you will," I lied.

4

Renee Holland showed me out. The good humor and warmth of our reunion was gone from her now, and I felt that she was disappointed in me.

"How's the family?" I asked, though I didn't remember much about her family. Two parents and a kid sister.

We were in the elevator then, and she didn't say anything at all until we hit the ground floor and the doors opened into the lobby.

"Terrific," she said. "They're terrific."

When I looked at her, she was gazing at the ceiling. I followed her eyes to the dark globe of the security camera mounted there.

I said, "Fun place to work?"

Her eyes flicked down to meet my gaze and she smiled thinly.

"It was good to see you again, Nick."

"Likewise," I said. I lifted my cell phone and waved it. "I'll do well by the brand name, I promise. I've always prized clarity, you know. Much preferred to confusion."

"I'm glad."

I stared at her, waiting for some reaction, some crack in the strange façade, but all I got was that thin smile.

"Okay," I said. "See you."

"See you."

The elevator doors sealed across her like gravedigger's dirt.

I stood alone in the lobby for a moment, then shook my head and walked away. My shoes were loud on the polished tile and in the room with all the glass. No receptionist, no art, no plants, just all those cold surfaces and an elevator loaded with sensors and cameras. Expensively unwelcoming.

I stepped out of the building and onto the sidewalk. The smell of the beach roses greeted me, and the sun was warm on my face. The freshly poured concrete of the sidewalk was white and gleaming and harsh. I reached for my sunglasses but fumbled with them because the phone was still in my hand. As I looked at the phone, I had a strange desire to double-check that the promised Clarity app was actually on the device. I had not wanted the app until Renee acted as if I shouldn't have it. Now, like any journalist—or child—I was convinced it was important to possess.

The icon was there—a simple but elegant *C* in red with black bordering against a white backdrop. Nothing to draw the eye, and yet I stared at it, transfixed. It took me a moment to realize that the uninspired logo was animated. It had a shimmer, the black-and-red *C* undulating. The motion was strangely soothing, the *C* rising and falling like it was riding a deepwater wave. Easy to overlook, perhaps, but also the first animated logo I'd seen on an app. I wondered how Bryce Lermond had snuck that coding past the guardians of all things Apple.

I wondered if I liked that he had been able to.

I was still staring at the screen when a fat drop of blood hit the back of my hand. It was the size of a dime, red as a ruby. When I turned my head, another drop fell, this one dotting my shirtsleeve, and I realized it was dripping from my nose.

"Son of a bitch." I put the phone in my pocket and grabbed the bridge of my nose and squeezed. It was really bleeding now; even with the pressure, blood found an escape and ran between my fingers and across my palm, feeling too hot in that way a nosebleed always seems to. The closer to the brain, the warmer the blood is perceived, I think. Blood from a cut toe feels cooler than a nosebleed, as if the brain shouts, *Too close, too close!* as the injury nears central command.

I walked over to a bench where the spray from the waterfall of the defunct mill cast bright rainbows against the air, then tilted my head back and held my nose and waited for the bleeding to cease. It took a while. The blood on my hand was almost dry by the time I finally got it stopped. I couldn't remember the last time I'd had a real nosebleed, the kind that comes out of nowhere and is hard to stop. Irrationally, I found myself wanting to blame the building, all of that harsh light and loud sound in the empty lobby. The place was too damn bright.

There was something about that imagery—red blood against white light—that made my head throb. I closed my eyes, released my nose, and waited to see if the bleeding would resume.

It didn't. I stood up. Took a few breaths, sniffed. All was well.

Sprinklers hissed in a flower garden on the other side of the falls. I walked over and dipped my hands into the spray and rinsed the blood off as well as I could. The sprinklers threw more rainbows, but over here they didn't look as pretty; the shadows from the old, dormant smokestacks seemed determined to dull the colors.

I stood up, shook the water and blood from my hands, and looked back at the building as if it had dared me not to. They'd done a great job with the place. Even if nobody else ever showed up to work there, the revitalized structure was a gift to the town. Nobody minds an empty building if the exterior looks good.

Hell, nobody even notices it.

By the time I reached my car, the fog was rolling in and the crystalline sky was hidden behind it. I started the engine but didn't pull into the street right away. I called my mother's care facility first and asked to schedule a visit. They were agreeable—enthusiastic, even.

"It's been so long since she saw family," the man

who answered the phone said, and I felt like a bad son, just as he probably wanted. I knew it had been a long time since she saw family. I also knew she wouldn't recognize me.

You should make the visits, though. Even when they don't register, you should still make the visits.

They told me one o'clock would be ideal, and I said that would be fine, then drove down the hill to the harbor and found a waterfront restaurant with a deck and a good beer list. It wasn't quite noon, but what the hell, right?

I ate a haddock sandwich and drank a pint of Sebago Frye's Leap IPA and watched the fog roll in and erase the harbor from sight. The islands went first, and then the boats at anchor, and then even the high wooded hills on the opposite shore were gone and it was just me and the mist, no indication of what existed out there except for what I remembered of it.

Sailing in fog had always filled me with a cold, throat-tightening, stomach-clenching fear. I never told Pat Ryan this, both because I didn't want to look like a coward and because once you're in the fog, you've got no choice but to fight through it. To me, it was always a unique terror. The world was wiped away right before your eyes, and then you could be on a collision course with another boat, a rock outcropping, floating debris, who the hell knew? The best navigator in the world couldn't guarantee you open water. It was one thing to chart a course and another to know it was clear.

No, I never cared for the fog.

Watching it shroud the bay and pull off its vanishing-act tricks right before my eyes, I wondered if that was how it had felt for my mother. Was memory loss a tangible thing? Did you turn and reach for something with the certainty that you knew where it was, only to find fog in its place? Then whirl back to reorient, only to discover that the most recent landmarks were also gone?

I hoped it was nothing like that.

My father had died on black ice, pinwheeling across I-295, the contract between pavement and tires voided, the turns of the steering wheel meaningless to the car's actual direction, rules turned to broken promises. My mother had been on foot on a familiar trail when the stroke hit her. I didn't know the details of how it had gone up there on the trail to Maiden Cliff, just that the woman who'd once delivered a TED talk could no longer come up with answers when the paramedics asked for her name, her address, her birthday. Black ice. Rules gone, chaos conquering.

I paid the bill and walked back to my truck. It was where I remembered it being. This was how life moved along. Forward, then backward. Our brains don't allow us to press ahead without paying the toll of memory and making at least a short trip into the past. You can't drive to your next meeting if you don't remember where you parked your car. Can't remember where you parked it if you don't remember what kind of car it is. It's all simple until it's impossible.

5

My mother's care facility was called Harbor House, which seemed more suited for a bed-and-breakfast than an inpatient care home. It was well regarded and clean and spacious and expensive. All the elements that you tell yourself matter when you're signing off on the care of a loved one. A smiling young woman in blue scrubs shook my hand as if meeting a distinguished guest.

"Your mom is a favorite here," she said.

"She usually was," I said, and then I felt bad that I'd used the past tense.

The woman in the scrubs led me to Room 27, which, according to the literature, was a "garden-view suite." I suppose that was close enough. It was a hybrid hospital room and apartment overlooking lush flower gardens that were lined with bird feeders. My mother was seated, facing the windows.

"Mrs. Bishop?" the woman in scrubs said brightly. "You've got a visitor! Nick is here."

My mother remained facing the gardens. She seemed unaware of our presence until the woman in scrubs touched her hand gently. At the touch, she finally looked up. Smiled at the woman in scrubs. Smiled at me.

"Hey, Mom," I said, and my voice was thick. I cleared my throat, knelt beside her, and smiled. "It's good to see you."

She looked as if she were still there. Clear-eyed and focused. Looked as if she were one breath away from launching into an impromptu dialogue about a book she'd read or a piece she'd heard on NPR or a personal theory. She was a big one for theories. "I have a theory," she'd begin, and while sometimes a serious, scientific idea would follow, the same preface would be used for anything and everything. "I have a theory that we should have key lime pie. I have a theory that the dog is eating grass. I have a theory that you've got a crush on the neighbor girl, Nick."

Today she looked at me and said, "Grackles."

I looked out the window. There were three bright yellow goldfinches at one feeder, and a squawking blue jay guarding a birdbath. No grackles in sight.

"Yeah?" I said. "Have they been around?"

"You know that," she said, and her tone was so familiar—the kind, warm *You can do better* tone that I'd known my whole life—that it nearly brought tears to my eyes.

The woman in the scrubs said, "I'll let you two catch up now, and if you need anything, Mr. Bishop, there's a button right here."

Then she was gone, the door closing behind her with a soft click, and it was just me and mom.

She smiled at me. I smiled at her. I leaned down and kissed her cheek. Her skin was cool and felt thin as parchment. I eased into the chair across from her, and her attention immediately returned to the garden, as if I'd left the room completely.

"I've missed you," I told her.

"Well, sure," she said, and I laughed. This was the sort of thing she did on phone calls; she couldn't track a conversation, but she'd throw in an aside that made sense and, often, was amusing.

On the phone, though, I couldn't see her smiling. I wasn't sure if it was better or worse that way. It was good to see and yet it put a lump in my throat and an ache behind my eyes.

"I'm back for a while," I said. "Not long, but a little bit. It's good to be home."

"Grackles," she said.

"Right."

We sat for a few minutes and watched the garden. Finches came and went. The blue jay hopped sideways on the birdbath, cawing out loudly, asserting his dominance.

"I'm staying at the camp," I said. "Out on Rosewater."

Her expression didn't change in the slightest—that polite but distant smile remained, as if she were listening to a boring guest speaker but wanted to be encouraging.

She said, "We will need to do something about the chipmunks."

She was not wrong; the camp was plagued by

chipmunks, and the little bastards had often found ways to invade.

"I'm working on it," I said. "They haven't gotten in recently. The mosquitoes are bad this year."

"Sure they are," she said. Her blue eyes still had a special sparkle to them. I thought that the staff probably told every visitor that their family member was a favorite, and yet I suspected it was actually true of my mother. She had a great smile and great eyes. She'd had an amazing mind once, too, and a quick wit. It felt unfair that any of those things could be taken, but particularly unfair that it had been the mind.

"I forgot how big the mosquitoes get out there," I said. "They should require FAA clearance."

"Grackles," my mother said.

"Right. They're almost that big."

It was quiet for a minute. At length, I tried again.

"The camp could use some paint. Maybe I'll be able to get that done before I head back south. I probably can."

"Stain," she said, and she was right again—the camp was stained, not painted.

"Exactly. I'll pick some up at E.L. Spear or Hammond Lumber, sand everything down, and do it right. Shine the place up."

"With stain."

"Yes. With stain." It was surreal, how she locked onto details about the camp. I decided to try another tack, having made some progress here. "I'm going to swing by campus, too. Pat Ryan works at Hammel now. You remember Pat, Mom?"

"They lost the game last night," she said.

"Who did?"

"The Red Sox."

The Red Sox had been on a travel day, but the last time they'd played, they'd lost, so I was happy to agree.

"Think they'll win the next one?" I asked.

She shook her head. "Not with Wakefield."

Tim Wakefield. How many years had it been since he'd thrown a pitch in the majors? And yet there he was, bouncing around in the corridors of her memory.

"Knuckleballers giveth and they taketh away," I said.

"Isn't that the truth," she answered, and I laughed again. She smiled but she didn't join in the laughter. Out in the garden, the blue jay gave up on the birdbath and took flight.

"Grackles," she said.

"Blue jay, actually," I told her. She didn't react.

I sat there and tried to think of something else. Should I talk about my dad? I could never decide on that one. The doctors told me not to be afraid of it, but I was anyhow. Dad represented a lot of sadness to her. Unsure of what—if any—memory might surface and stick, I didn't want to play around in territory that might make her unhappy.

"I'll go by your office later," I said. "Good old Grossman Hall."

No reaction.

"Anyone you want me to say hello to at Hammel?" I asked.

"Wakefield," she said.

I smiled. "If I see him there, I'll tell him you're worried about that knuckleball and the chipmunks."

"There are traps," she said.

"For the chipmunks. Yes."

"Under the porch. Traps right there for you."

"I think you're right. I'll find them."

"You've got to trap them. Can't get in, can't get out. Just stay where they are."

It was a morbid thought but an accurate one.

"I know it. I won't let them get in."

"Under the porch."

"Sounds good. I'll look first thing when I get back."

She nodded and gazed out at the garden. She'd lost some weight but was still healthy in appearance, trim and with the angular jaw and chin that we shared and I hated but she carried so well, jauntily, like the prow of a ship captained by a confident sailor. I looked at her and remembered that she'd once addressed an auditorium full of international scholars in Berlin, that she'd met with Bill Gates and been pleased at how well he followed her ideas. Think about that: she was pleased to bump into someone like Bill Gates so she didn't have to dumb down for the audience.

I watched her smile as the flowers below us swayed in the wind. If she knew who I was, she couldn't indicate it. But she knew the camp and she knew where the chipmunk traps were. I hated the human condition then with a sudden, fierce passion. It was a terrible thing, what had happened to her, and I was enraged by it.

I didn't want her to feel that from me, though. I wasn't sure what penetrated the fog that surrounded her, but I thought that emotions sent stronger signals than words, and so I tried to seal in my sorrow and project only warmth and love and gratitude.

As I sought for something that might slip through the barrier between us, I said, "Oh—guess who I saw today, Mom: Renee Holland. Do you remember her? From the camp across the cove?"

She squeezed my hand but didn't answer.

"She has red hair," I said. "You wouldn't recognize her. It took me a minute. You remember Pat, though, don't you? He hired me to write a story, and Renee is—"

"Not at Rosewater," she said.

"What's that?"

She turned from the garden, looked directly at me, and said, "Should not be at Rosewater."

"Renee shouldn't be at Rosewater? Or Pat?"

"Nick," she said.

I felt an eerie prickle. It was like being in the deep fog and seeing something take shape, clear and undeniable and dead ahead.

"I shouldn't be at the camp?"

For a long moment she stared directly at me, and then she turned away, and the smile crept back onto her face when she saw the bird.

"The Red Sox lost last night," she said.

"I'll tell Pat you said hello. He always loved you. You remember Pat, don't you?"

"When they lose, they lose," she said. "You can't help that."

"No, you can't." I shifted, leaned closer. "What about Renee? Do you remember Renee?"

"Traps are right under the porch. Lewis knows. Ask him."

"I will," I assured her, promising to ask her long-dead brother about the rodent traps. "I'll make sure they don't get in."

She smiled and bobbed her head. A cardinal joined the finches. There was a flurry of wings as the birds redistributed to various feeders. A light breeze teased the flower beds and rustled the trees. Up here, the fog hadn't squeezed out the sun, and light fell in thick stripes across the garden. It was a nice spot.

"I am looking for a new job," I told my mother. "It's a little scary, but I know it'll work out. Just a matter of finding the right spot, you know?"

"Grackles," she said.

I nodded and took her hand and squeezed it. She squeezed back. Smiled at me. We sat and watched the birds. I managed not to cry.

6

How long do you sit with someone who doesn't know who you are? For me, the answer that day was: until she falls asleep.

When I left Harbor House it was midafternoon and I felt restless and adrift and hungry for a real conversation.

Grackles.

I called Pat Ryan while I wound my way back up the coast. Voicemail.

"It's Nick. Hard at work for you. Got back in town yesterday and already have an interview in the bank and—hope you're sitting down for this— the first beta release of the app! This is what an ace reporter brings to the table, my man. Worth every penny. Give me a call. I'd love to grab a beer if you're around. I'm . . ."

I was going to say *I'm just leaving my mother's place* but for some reason I didn't want to get into that yet. Didn't want to have to explain the visit, how it had gone, how it had felt.

"I'm staying at the camp on Rosewater. So any human companionship will be welcome or it's just going to be me and Bobby Beauchamp discussing maintenance budgets. Let me know."

I passed the Hefron Mill, its repainted walls blending into the shroud of white mist, and drove on to Rosewater. The camp was only three miles outside of town, but the elevation climbed by a few hundred feet on the way, and bright sun shone on the pond, no trace of the harbor fog evident here. In the winter, those few miles inland can mean the difference between four inches of snow and a foot of it.

I stood on the dock for a few minutes and watched circles form where fish hit at mayflies alongside a large boulder that rose from the water just offshore. Above the surface, it was an egg-shaped rock that seemed to sit on the water rather than protrude from within it. At the right time of day, the rock threw strange shadows that resembled an old-fashioned lock, the kind you'd open with a skeleton key. My mother had nicknamed it Balance Rock, because of the way it seemed to sit so perfectly on the water's surface, but to my father it had always been Big Bass Rock, a favorite spot to cast with poppers or an elk caddis. He'd sing to the rock in an off-key blues verse while casting, *Let me hear that Big Bass Rock,* and my mother and I would groan and tell him to keep it down. He'd ignore us and sing until he had a fish on the line. Then he was all business.

I'd brought my fly rod, and the temptation to

try a few casts was strong, but I decided to write instead. It had been weeks since I'd put anything down on the page, and the simple act of interviewing Bryce Lermond that morning had instilled an appreciated sense of normalcy. Of identity. Anyone who says he isn't defined in some way by his job is kidding himself. If you think I'm wrong, test the waters of unemployment for a little while and tell me if you feel whole.

I was too young, at twenty-eight, not to think about a serious change in careers, considering the grim outlook for journalism, but a change was the last thing I wanted. I loved being a reporter, loved how new each day was, how the only sure thing was that you didn't know what tomorrow's big story would be. Bryce Lermond didn't feel like anyone's big story, but he was the story I had, and I intended to do it justice. I dragged an ancient Adirondack chair onto the dock, tested its creaking stability to make sure I wasn't going to end up on my ass amid a pile of kindling, and then eased into it cautiously, notebook in hand. The chair held, but it swayed under my weight just enough to taunt me, like pinching fingers on love handles.

My plan was to review the notes I'd taken, make a rough outline of what was worthwhile and what was cuttable filler, and then go inside to begin working on the computer. I remembered the app, though—that sacred beta-user app—and took my phone out.

The simple, block-lettered *C* icon awaited. I watched it and waited for the animation to take over again, that undulating shimmer of motion. It was dormant. I tapped the screen, swiped left and right, waited. Nothing. Bryce had warned me that their graphics weren't finished, but the here-and-gone animation still bothered me. I finally gave up, took my AirPods out, fitted them into my ears, and tapped the icon.

SMILE AND BREATHE! the screen told me.

"You gotta be kidding me," I muttered. Smile and breathe. Oy. Whatever target audience the *Smile and breathe!* mission sought, a deadline journalist probably didn't fit. We're more of a *Shut up and type* breed.

The slogan vanished and an image of a lighthouse replaced it. Stock art, but I thought it was off the Maine coast. Maybe Nubble Head? Pemaquid Point? One of the famous, touristy ones. As I watched the screen, a white, pixelated cloud crept from bottom to top, obscuring the lighthouse.

DO YOU WANT TO LEAVE FOG TOWN BEHIND? the screen asked. TAP TWICE TO FIND CLARITY!

Ugh.

I was grateful that Bryce and Renee hadn't made me endure this little demo in their presence. Fog Town. Yikes.

"Smile and breathe," I said, then tapped the screen twice.

A menu appeared. There were guided meditations, breathing exercises, focus enhancers, sleep songs, and motivation melodies.

I thought that I probably should have mixed a drink before embarking on this life-changing journey. As I shifted, though, the Adirondack gave a warning—or was it a delighted?—creak, and I decided to stay in place. Drinking on the job was no way to get back into a professional routine. I clicked on the focus icon.

For the next five minutes, I followed along to a male voice that was almost certainly Bryce Lermond's as we counted backward from one hundred by sevens, then envisioned a bear, then counted forward to one hundred by sevens, apparently unbothered that you couldn't get from zero to one hundred by sevens.

Having finished our destruction of numerical logic, we moved on to envision sinking a putt to win a golf match, which might've been interesting if I gave a damn about golf. Then we imagined a tunnel. The walls were narrowing on me, Bryce said, but the light ahead was clear and bright. We were leaving Fog Town behind.

On the screen, a placeholder said: GRAPHICS PENDING.

Now that I was properly focused and Fog Town was in the rearview mirror, I jotted down a few notes and returned to the app. I suspected I had a good sense of the breathing exercises and could guess at the guided meditations. (I would probably be asked to envision a river or a sunrise or, if they were really on top of things, a river *at* sunrise.) The sleep songs, however, were a touch more interesting. I remembered how Bryce's enthusiasm had risen when he described those, talking about the ballads, the intersection of story and song, yada yada.

I clicked on that menu and found a "play" button with the caption *Sleep Song #1*.

I pressed "play," wondering with dread if Bryce Lermond had handled the singing, too.

The only sound was the soft churn and smash of waves breaking over rocks. Then a woman's voice came on, tinged with a musical lilt. "Please close your eyes while we enjoy this sleep song."

I obliged.

The sound of the waves carried on, soothing and hypnotic. I was reminded of one October when Pat Ryan and I had bailed on two days of classes and driven up to the Cutler Coast, one of the northeasternmost reaches of the United States, to camp on the cliffs. At night the waves pulled you down to sleep, and in the morning they tugged you back up. I could almost picture the scene—the jumble of jagged rocks, seaweed clinging to them around the tide line, the water blue but the sky pewter, white foam accenting it all. I could hear the deep-bass booms of the water thumping through a hollowed-out portion of cliff; I could smell the salt of the sea.

On my headphones, a new sound joined the waves. Low strings led the way, a bass or a cello, with the plucking of a higher instrument that I couldn't recognize carrying the melody over the top. Gradually, the melody rose and the wave sounds faded. The tune was catchy but not calming. If anything, it was energizing. Maybe Bryce should swap his sleep song with his focus enhancer.

Then the woman's voice returned, in full-throated song this time.

If they come for me
If they take us away
Do not fear, oh, do not fear
For others have gone there before

It was beautiful, though hardly soothing. *If they come for me, if they take us away*? There was menace beneath the beauty.

The strings returned for a brief interlude, and beneath them was a rhythmic creaking that reminded me of oars in oarlocks in the hands of a straining rower. Then the woman's gorgeous voice returned.

As we drift away
As they circle around
The night wind calls us forward
And dark seas welcome us down
No course is clear to us now
No guide but the voices we hear

I opened one eye as the strings returned. Scrawled *Ask Bryce who the singer is* on my notepad. Then closed my eyes again, almost guiltily, as if it was cheating to have them open.

Down, down in the dark
No stars, no guide, but no fear
We hear them thrashing around
And know our hour draws near
If you feel you must stay, now, now is the time
But if you follow me, dear,
I'll ask you to rise without fear

I scribbled another question—*Is the song an original or a cover?*—and then closed my eyes quickly.

The low strings returned, the buoyant, nearly giddy plucking notes soaring above them, and I reminded myself to inquire about the instrument just as the vocals came back.

Far, far down we go
Fearless though we are prey
Nothing ahead that we know
But all behind we must flee
So run, run on with me
Dive, dive in with me
Swim, swim deep with me
Rise, rise now with—

I woke when the Adirondack chair shattered beneath me.

7

I did what you do when you fall on your ass—looked around to see if I'd embarrassed myself in front of an audience, and then, having confirmed that I was alone, burst out laughing.

The chair had split where the back met the seat, depositing me onto the dock with my feet in the air and my hands gripping the armrests like a kid on a roller coaster. There being no graceful way to extract from that position, I rolled onto my side with the elegance of a beached whale and pushed the two broken halves of the chair far enough apart to allow me to rise to my knees. My sunglasses fell off my face and bounced on the dock, landing near the notebook, which had miraculously not gone into the pond. The pen had. My phone was wedged between two of the weathered planks, saved from sinking by an eighth of an inch.

Somehow, the sight of the phone leaning like a tilted tombstone amid the carnage of the splintered Adirondack only made me laugh harder.

I was in that position, on my hands and knees in a pile of broken furniture, laughing like a fool, when a woman's voice said, "Is this a bad time?"

I snapped my head up and saw Renee Holland standing at the top of the steep, rutted drive, shielding her eyes with a hand and peering down at me.

"Not at all," I said, and swept the right-hand armrest of the chair aside so I could stand. It promptly slid off the dock, splashed into the pond, and drifted away.

I was still sniffing back laughter as I put my sunglasses on and closed the notebook and then— carefully—retrieved the phone. The Clarity app was no longer running, and only when I noticed that did I think of my AirPods. One was miraculously still in my left ear, but I couldn't find the other. This was less amusing: they were expensive, and I was unemployed.

I put the one I had in my pocket along with the phone and walked down the dock to meet Renee, feeling a twinge in my tailbone that would remind me of the successful sleep song for a few days.

"How'd you know where to find me?" I asked.

"You mentioned the camp when you came by this morning," she said.

"Ah. Right."

She surveyed the dock and the pond beyond and said, "I see I caught you . . . relaxing?"

"Stress-testing the furniture," I said. "An old Bishop family tradition."

"How lovely." She'd come on down the hill and was now standing at the end of the dock. She smiled at me. It was the old Renee smile—more smirk, always with that undercurrent of private amusement and anticipation, as if she saw the full joke before anyone else did. It fit the woman who'd escorted me into the mill earlier that day but not the one who'd shown me out.

"We had fun down here, didn't we?" she said.

"Yes. Although I don't think Mrs. Peabody has ever recovered from the summer of indoctrination to Eminem that you gave her."

"That *I* gave her!"

"Absolutely. You had the speakers."

Now I was laughing, her smile had widened, and it felt like old times. I could remember the warm summer sun on us while we floated in the pond and Mrs. Peabody, who owned a camp down the shore, bitched at us to turn down that *horrid* music. Renee had a swimming float shaped like a lobster. She would lounge between its inflated claws, lithe and blond and tan, her hand pointed toward her mouth with an extended thumb, as if she were holding a microphone. *Hi—my name is! Hi—my name is!*

"You guys still own your camp?" I asked.

"Sold it when my parents moved to New Mexico on their great snowbird migration. It was worth too much and they needed the money."

"Makes sense," I said, well aware of how the pressing need to sell my own family's camp would squeeze me in the months ahead. Economics dictated a sale, but emotional attachments don't have numbers.

"So . . . ," Renee said, breaking the silence.

"So, yeah, what's up?"

"I feel as if our audition for you this morning didn't go so well," she said, and the warmth of those fun memories faded, taking her smile with it.

"Pardon?" I said.

"Bryce got rattled." A stray pine needle drifted into her dark red hair and stuck. I wanted to reach out and brush it away but stilled my hand. Her bearing was tense, as if any gesture I made was subject to scrutiny.

"He's too eager for approval," she said. "This morning, he lost confidence."

"It was fine."

She shook her head, a quick, birdlike gesture, dismissing my comment.

"No, it wasn't. You don't care, because you're looking at Clarity with the limited interest of someone who's been asked to write a small piece for a small magazine."

"No disrespect," I said.

"I didn't mean it like that."

"The profile in the Hammel alumni mag isn't going to make or break your company's reputation. I get it."

"Right. That's all I meant." She seemed flustered now. "I know you're a big deal in journalism, Nick."

"No, I'm not, and I also wasn't offended. I understand your point."

"Okay. Good."

I studied her. "Why do you care so much what I think of it?"

"*I* don't," she said, and then, with a faint smile, added, "No disrespect."

"Yet you drove out to see me in person."

She looked past me and out to the pond. The smile was gone. Her eyes were on the water and the pine needle was still in her hair when she said, "Please don't use the app."

"Excuse me?"

"He shouldn't have given it to you. It's not ready yet."

"I've got an Adirondack chair out there that would argue with you."

Her attention snapped back to me. There was a spark of something new in her green eyes, something beyond scrutiny, something that looked almost like fear.

"What do you mean?"

I gestured at the dock. "I was sitting out there, taking notes and trying out the app. It's a nice, relaxing spot, and I'm only a day removed from a very long drive, but I also don't tend to fall asleep in the middle of the afternoon. I was maybe thirty seconds into the first sleep song when I dozed off. So you can tell Bryce that it's effective. I'm not sure I can vouch for the breathing exercises or the meditations in the same way, but the sleep song was actually quite—"

"Which one was it?" she said, voice low and taut.

"Number one."

"Number one? There's only one song, period."

I spread my hands. "It said sleep song number one. That's all."

Her face suggested that this news was both un-expected and disturbing. A light breeze came down off the mountain and across the water and reached me. On the dock and in the sun it might have been refreshing, but where I now stood in the shade of the tall pines, it carried a chill.

"He told you he was breaking it up," Renee said, more to herself than to me. "Microdosing."

"Right."

"That explains the number, then. But what was it about?"

I opened my mouth to answer and suddenly felt very strange—disoriented, almost dizzy. I had no idea what it was about. I remembered loading the song, remembered the number, remembered the woman's beautiful, haunting voice, and yet . . .

"I'm not sure," I said. "It was a woman, I remem-ber that."

"It will always be a woman. But what were the lyrics? You don't remember any of them?"

The lyrics came back to me easily. I meant to say them—speak them—but found myself actually attempting to sing. I have a terrible singing voice and would never attempt to sing for an audience, and yet it was as if I couldn't remember the words without putting them into the melody.

"Down, down in the dark
No stars, no guide, but no fear
We hear them thrashing around
And know our hour draws near
If you feel you must stay, now, now is the time
But if you follow me, dear,
I'll ask you to rise without fear."

"Whoa, whoa, I don't need to hear it all," Renee said, lifting her palm as if to ward me off. She took a step back and turned her head.

I stopped, embarrassed.

"I know I'm not a singer, but I didn't think it was *that* bad."

"No, it's just . . . I don't need to hear it." She looked out across the water. After a long pause, she said, "You heard that song and fell asleep."

"Yeah." I snapped my fingers. "Like that."

"But you still remembered the song. After hearing it one time and falling asleep during the process, you remembered it well enough to *sing* it."

I nodded, feeling as uneasy about that as she seemed to. Nobody retains the lyrics to a song on first listen. The experience with the app itself was vague to me now but the song remained crystal clear.

I turned and walked back down the dock and retrieved my notebook. The armrest of the Adirondack chair thumped off the dock, riding the light chop that the wind had brought to the surface of the pond. I opened the notebook and read my last scrawled writing.

"I guess I didn't write down any of the lyrics," I said. "Just questions—whether it was a cover or an original, and who does the singing."

Renee ventured out on the dock, stood close. Her face had a fine-boned, porcelain quality, a fragility that was completely at odds with her hunter's eyes.

"I can assure you that it is not a cover. They're all original."

"Well," I said, "I guess it worked. That's good news for you, right? The prototype was successful."

"Yay," she said hollowly. "All the same, please don't play around with it again? Off the record, between you and me . . . it really isn't ready and shouldn't have been shared. Not at this stage. It would mean a lot to me if you just deleted it."

A request to delete something is a reporter's catnip. It's even more enticing than a request to go off the record. I'd just been teased with both.

"Of course," I told my old friend, and then I took my phone out and held my thumb down until the icons began to shake, giving me the opportunity to remove their applications. I made sure she saw this and then I said, "Poof!" just loudly enough to bring her eyes up from the phone and to my face.

Then I smiled at her while I deleted Twitter instead of the Clarity app and put the phone back into my pocket.

"All gone, and no harm done to the brand," I said.

"Thank you," she said, and she looked so grateful that I almost felt guilty for the lie.

Almost.

"No problem," I said. "In exchange, though, I have a request."

"What's that?" Gratitude shifted to wariness.

"I'd like to interview you without him around."

"That's not my role. Bryce is the—"

"Come on, Renee. Just a chance to catch up. I'm curious how you ended up in this kind of business, what your life has looked like these past ten years."

"Not a formal interview, then?"

I lifted my hands. "I'll leave the recorder and notebook behind." I wondered why it mattered so much, though—why she was so damn uneasy about speaking on the record.

She hesitated, then nodded. "Not today, though. I've got to be going. And Bryce is the public face of things for a reason."

The underconfident, overanxious Bryce? He might be ideal for a lot of roles, but as far as I could see, the public face of the company wasn't among them.

"Sure," I said. "But he's never rapped while floating around this pond on a giant inflatable lobster, so he's less interesting to me."

She smiled. "No, he hasn't done that. I remember your mom laughing at that lobster . . . She was the best. She really was."

"Agreed," I said, and then, to fill the air and avoid showing the sadness I felt: "So, you went off to Indiana to get a degree in philosophy. How does a would-be philosopher find her way to a job with a sleep app developer?"

"Not today," she repeated, still with the smile. "I promise, we'll get into it later."

"I'll hold you to that. I've got little else on my plate at the moment, so I won't be all that easy to brush off."

"I don't intend to try," she said, and there was the good-humored, teasing warmth again. Her fear was gone now that she thought I'd deleted the app. "I appreciate your time, Mr. Bishop, sir," she said with false formality, "and I apologize for intruding on your fine day at the grand Rosewater estate. Perhaps on my next visit an inflatable lobster will be provided?"

"Certainly. We have the highest of standards at Rosewater."

She smiled. "Take care, Nick. It was good seeing you."

"You, too."

She turned and started up the drive.

"Renee?" I said.

She half turned. "Yes?"

"You have a pine needle in your hair."

She blinked at me, then bent at the waist slightly while she reached up with her right hand and tousled her hair until she shook the pine needle out successfully. It took a little while and it was a fine sight to watch.

"Thanks," she said. "I don't want to come back to

WHERE THEY WAIT 75

the office with evidence of my escape to Rosewater."

She smiled, but I didn't think she was joking, at least not entirely.

Renee went on up the hill to where she'd parked, and then she waved, and so did I, and only when she was out of sight did I take the phone out of my pocket. I pulled up the Clarity app that I'd pretended to delete, intending to play the song again.

Sleep Song #1 was gone, though. We'd moved on to Sleep Song #2, which told me it was "pending." It didn't appear there was any way to retreat to the first option. That would have been annoying for my note-taking process, but the lyrics and melody had stuck with me, somehow. I wouldn't have any trouble transcribing them.

A lucky break.

8

That evening, I met Pat Ryan at Riptides, a dive bar a block off the Hammel campus. The bar had changed owners several times across the decades, but the house policy of "forgetting" to card college kids ensured that it sold plenty of pints of beer and shots of Fireball. It had a massive, scarred oaken bar and rough-hewn plank walls decorated with a schizophrenic collection of memorabilia: Hammel pennants, photos of Franklin D. Roosevelt in Rockland, basketball nets, lobster traps. It stank of stale popcorn and spilled beer, and crossing the room was like walking across a strip of tape. It was the first place you went when you arrived as a freshman and the last place you went after graduation. On your last visit, you would agree with your friends that the bar was symbolic of everything you were ready to move on from, everything you wouldn't miss once you were out in the real world. Then you made it out in the real world and, naturally, missed the hell out of those nights at Riptides. There's a bar like it in any college town in the country, and yet I'm sure ours was the best.

Pat Ryan hadn't added or lost a pound since college, and he looked so baby-faced that you'd think maybe he should be carded even at Riptides. I couldn't help but wonder what his old-friend assessment of me was, what tickets he punched in the mental checklist, like a mechanic reviewing a car.

Hairline receding, waistline about the same, new scar on forehead, no wedding ring . . .

"It has been too long," he boomed as he swung his lanky frame onto the bench seat of the booth. "Two years?"

"About that, yeah."

"Inexcusable, Father."

This was a nickname that went back to freshman year, a combination of the religious association of my last name and Pat's tendency to confess his various sins to me. *I drank too much last night, Father. I bombed that midterm, Father. My boat sank, Father.*

"I'll absolve myself," I said, shaking his hand. "Give me credit: I still pick up the phone. How many others still make that mistake with you?"

"Few indeed." He'd somehow already signaled for and received a beer, a good trick in a place with three overburdened servers.

"Come here often?" I laughed.

He grinned. "It's all business for me now, though. Rich alumni passing through on their way up to Bar Harbor might stop off to revisit the beloved alma mater, and somebody's gotta be here to buy them a beer, listen to the stories about their glory days, then remind them that the endowment needs their support."

I thought that he'd be good at that. Knew it, in fact. And somehow it still made me sad, because I remembered the nights we'd camped on the Cutler Coast or in Baxter and the plans he'd shared over the fire—the travel, the adventures, the screenplays or novels that would follow at their own pace. Now he was still living in Hammel, married, with a young kid and a job with good benefits. All that mattered was that he was happy, yes, but there's always something sad about seeing a guy who would've been voted "Most Likely to Be Arrested in Acapulco" settled into ordinary adult life. Good decisions often mark the death of wild dreams.

"Cheers," Pat said, and we clinked frosted glasses and drank and he looked at me appraisingly, like a doctor before the physical begins.

"What?" I said.

"How's it feel? Being back."

"Nice," I said. "It's always nice."

"Bullshit."

I was surprised. "You know I love this town. Hell, it's *my* town. You just passed through." I realized that was no longer true. "And stayed. Passed through and stayed. Is that a thing?"

"No," he said cheerfully. "For a writer, you are complete shit with words."

"That should be *completely shitty*, actually. And I'd omit *completely*. It's needless."

He waved a hand. "Editors. What I mean is, yes, I know you loved the town, past tense, but I don't know what you think of it now." He leaned back in the booth, propping up one foot and resting his forearm on his knee. He was too tall for the tiny booths at Riptides, always ending up sitting sideways and trying to find space for his long legs.

"I like the town," I said. "For a visit."

"But you couldn't stay here?"

I felt like that was treacherous ground, considering he had stayed, so I simply shrugged. "It wasn't an option for me."

"Seriously, though," he said, "what do you think?"

I was confused. "Of what? The town is the town. Maine is Maine. I like it."

"But could you *live* here?"

"Moot point. No job."

He smiled then. I remembered this particular grin; it came after a few leading questions and right before he delivered the idea he'd been teeing up the whole time.

"What job?" I asked, expecting that he'd say something at the college, in marketing or fundraising, and it would be very easy to say no.

"Harbor master," he said. "Bobby Beauchamp recommended you."

I burst out laughing. "I saw the old SOB last

night. He'd been down to the store, picked up six pints of dinner. Then he hollered over that I needed to cut some trees and stain the place, and he'd be happy to do it, but not for free."

Pat screwed up his face into a theatrical scowl and dipped into a heavy Maine accent. "Now, listen he-ah, it's none of my business, but—"

"Some people say," I finished with him, and we both laughed. That was a Beauchamp classic— spreading gossip with his preface of innocence and lack of interest. *It's none of my business, but some people say . . .*

"Okay, wiseass," I said, pointing at Pat. "You're deflecting. There *is* a job, isn't there? And it's not being the damned harbor master."

"Write a book with me," Pat said.

I managed to stop my rising laugh in the nick of time. I hadn't believed he could be serious, but beneath his affable expression I saw a light in his eyes that was almost hunger.

"A book."

"That's right."

"About?"

"Shipwrecks. My specialty." Now *he* laughed. "I'm mostly kidding."

"Mostly?"

"Sure. Writing a book together would be fun. You know I've always wanted to do that. It's what I was supposed to do after school, right? You were supposed to go off to save the world like the second coming of Edward R. Murrow and I was supposed to write a book about legends and ghost stories, sunken ships and pirates. One of us did his thing. The other never even got started." He grinned, but it was self-conscious this time. "Do I sound like the sad sack who should've left town and couldn't bring himself to do it?"

"I'm jobless, Pat. I'm not going to bust on you for staying in town and being smart."

He leaned back in the booth, trying to find room for his legs. "You don't come back much."

"Well, after my mom—"

"Relax. It's an observation, not an indictment."

Our waiter returned and set two fresh beers down. I hadn't even seen Pat signal him. Before I could thank the waiter, he was gone again, and Pat was leaning across the booth.

"I'm curious, that's all. Time slips away, memories fade, and coming back to a place then? It's different. When I go back to Montana, I always have that question—could I stay?"

"Well, could you?"

"Absolutely not. I say that every single time. Absolutely not. And then I ride a horse into the mountains and suddenly I want to live in the west so badly it damn near brings me to tears." He gave a crooked smile over the top of the beer. "Hometowns, Nick, are complicated places."

"That's the truth," I said, though I'd never really thought about it before.

"I'm ten percent serious about the book, too."

"Only thing I know about shipwrecks is from having sailed with you."

"An expert, then. It's not all shipwrecks, either. The stories in Maine go as deep as the cold sea around its shores, deep as its darkest forests, deep as—"

"Oh, boy."

He slapped the table and pointed at me. "See! I can't turn a phrase! But *you* know how to write. You know how to research. And, most crucially, you know how to deliver on a deadline."

"You find us a publisher and I'll consider," I said, a harmless line when talking about book ideas, because nobody finds a publisher easily.

Pat's smile widened, and he tried to hide it by drinking his beer, inconspicuous as the cat with a mouthful of canary feathers.

"You're kidding me," I said. "You've sold a book pitch?"

"Emphasis on *pitch*. I can't get the friggin' writing done!"

"You brought me up here to sell me on this? The puff piece was bait?"

"No! One's got nothing to do with the other."

"Yeah?"

"Sure! Except . . ."

"Except?"

"There's a small chance . . ."

"Here we go."

"I'm talking minuscule . . ." He held his thumb and index finger a fraction of an inch apart.

"That?"

"That Bryce Lermond is on the board of the Hammel College Press."

"How'd he land on the board?"

"Filled his mother's seat when she died."

"Mommy's been good to him. She supported Clarity, too."

"Marilyn Lermond left plenty behind."

"New name to me. Not local."

"Very local, actually. Family goes back a few centuries up and down the coast from York to Prouts Neck to Lubec. She was full of stories, man. You wanted to hear the old legends, from shipwrecks to windigos, you just needed to buy Marilyn a chardonnay. She could go toe to toe with Bob Beauchamp any day—and did."

"That folklore degree really did pay off for you."

He winked. "Told you from the beginning— today's news is forgotten tomorrow, but folklore is forever. This is why you need to join me on the book, brother. We'll find the future by looking in the past."

"Gag," I said. "We'll need a new slogan before I sign on. Where's the Lermond money come from?"

"Family owned shares of some mills back in the day and then seem to have invested better than Buffet himself."

"Based on the app, that seems unlikely."

He chuckled, sipped some beer. "That bad, eh?"

"Not bad, necessarily, just late to the game. But I'll admit this: the sleep song actually put me down. I was in the middle of taking notes and then . . ." I snapped my fingers. "Out."

"Really?"

"Yeah. Only to be disrupted by one Renee Holland, who came down to the camp in person and asked me to delete the app—said it wasn't for prime time yet."

A group of college kids were jostling just beside our booth now, laughing loudly over a dart game, and I had to raise my voice just to be heard.

"She was one of the few people I actually liked in this town before going to college. It was a weird year, when my dad died and Mom relocated us."

"Renee worked at Hammel for a bit." Pat gave a wistful smile. "I do miss seeing her around campus."

"I bet. Is she involved with Bryce?"

"Romantically?" He turned his hands palms up. "If she is, I haven't heard. Nobody gives me the good gossip anymore. They tell me which toddler gymnastics class I should register my kid in. If there's sex, drugs, or rock 'n' roll involved, old Pat doesn't hear of such things."

"You're a living, breathing tragedy."

"Don't I know it," he said, but I could see how happy he was. *Content*—that was the word. Pat was content with his life. I tried to remember the last time I'd felt the same, and the first memory that rose was of a converted cargo plane that flew me into Bagram. It didn't seem like the right memory, and yet there it was. Contentment had always been intertwined with reporting, for me. For Pat, contentment had been right offshore from Hammel, a sailboat on Penobscot Bay.

"Do you guys have a sailboat now?" I asked. "I can't picture you without one."

His smile missed a beat, but then he said, "Jess is less enthused about it, but, yes, I've still got a boat."

Jess was his wife. They'd met senior year, and while I knew her, we'd never become close.

"What's this one called? The bar was set high with the SS *Money Pit* and the *Andrea Fitzgerald*."

The *Andrea Fitzgerald*, a hybrid name of two famously ill-fated vessels, was the last boat Pat had purchased, a fifty-foot sloop that had once been a beautiful craft and might have been again if someone had a few hundred grand to invest in the restoration. Pat had a few hundred, period. The mast broke off on the day he'd tried to sail the boat to South Thomaston for engine repairs.

"The new one is the *Evangeline*," he said.

"Formal for you."

"Isn't it? Named after a poem, no less. How damn urbane am I?"

"Let me see this tub before I answer that."

"That's Nick Bishop, always verifying. Skepticism, doubt, and double-checking. Your coat of arms."

"That's not me."

"No?" His voice rose to drown out the argument that was happening in the dart game. "Why do you think we've stayed in touch?"

"Friends stay in touch."

"And I've appreciated that. Shit, man, you called me from Kabul once. Checking on me and Jess, day after our daughter was born. Remember that? *I* sure as hell do. But—how many of the old gang do you call?"

"Not many," I said, but the truth was: not any.

"That's my point. It's just me. You stay in touch only with me."

He seemed so serious, and almost concerned, that I was at a loss for how to respond.

"Fine," I said, trying to joke it off, "you caught me: I'm in love with you. From the first time I saw you peel one of those spectacular Irish sunburns and leave the dead skin on your desk in the dorm, I was head over heels."

He leaned forward, pushing the beer aside. "No, seriously. All those years, it was pretty much just the two of us."

"What are you talking about? There was Seth, Todd, Little John, Matt, Cisco. We were always in a pack."

"Really?"

I thought about it then, as the guys in the dart game roared over a bull's-eye that won someone a pitcher of cheap beer. There'd *been* a pack when we were at Hammel. House parties and basketball games and pub crawls. But for the most part . . . Pat wasn't wrong. We'd been an isolated cell within it. The bigger group was a social necessity, not our default setting. We'd been loners more than I'd realized, maybe.

"You still talk to Cisco?" he asked.

"No. What's your point, though? What're you getting at?"

"You don't trust people."

I set my beer down. "Hell of an accusation."

"No, it's not. It's a friend's observation. You'll glide with a crew, but not . . . *invest* in it the same way as others. You're introverted, maybe, an observer, definitely, but it's more than that. You don't like to hand out trust."

"I don't *avoid* offering it, either," I protested, a little too adamantly. I think we always push back hardest when we're called out on the truth.

"Don't be defensive. It's a natural reflex with you is all I'm saying. You're a skeptic's skeptic. By which I mean a reporter's reporter, too. Being embedded within some group but operating outside of it is *perfect* for you. 'Trust but verify' doesn't even go quite far enough. You're more like 'Doubt and verify.'" He paused, smiled. "'And then verify with a second source.'"

I tried to match his smile, but a "skeptic's skeptic" wasn't exactly how I wanted my oldest friend to think of me.

"What'd I say?" he asked. "You look somber all of the sudden, Father."

The old nickname helped lighten the moment, or at least distract from it.

"Father Bishop," I said. "It still doesn't make any sense."

"Made sense to me," he said. "You still do the tithing thing?"

I shook my head. I'd almost forgotten about it, in fact. When we'd been in school, I had a habit of walking into any church that was open—the denomination didn't mean a thing to me—and tossing some pocket change or spare bills into the offering box. I told everyone else I was just covering my bases—*want to check every religious box before I die, just in case*—but eventually I told Pat the truth.

And, I realized now, I told *only* Pat. Nobody else.

The arbitrary giving to random churches was actually my father's ritual. He'd been raised Methodist, but my mother didn't want anything to do with organized religion, would roll her eyes whenever he'd give money to a church. She didn't try to stop him, just seemed resigned. As a kid, I was curious about his behavior and her response, and when I asked about it, she would always offer the same response: *It's how he was raised. Some circuits stay lit, Nick.*

A dismissive, science-minded answer. I never knew my father's mother, but I knew she'd been devout, and I had a feeling she was on his mind when he put cash in those offering envelopes. We never talked about that, but sometimes you don't have to.

"I always liked that," Pat chuckled now. "Catholic church, synagogue, Methodist church, Buddhist temple—you'd throw a few bucks at all of them."

"Some circuits stay lit," I said, parroting my mother's old slogan just as the darts-playing guys broke into shouts and applause as another game closed out.

"What's that?" Pat cupped a hand to his ear.

"My mom would say some circuits you just couldn't put out, even if you tried," I explained. "My dad always kept that one lit."

"But you didn't?"

"I guess not."

"See," he told me, "a skeptic's skeptic."

"So," I said, ready to change the subject, "are you seriously going to ask me to pitch a book to Lermond with you, or can I get his genius on the record and get out of Dodge?"

"What do you actually think of him?"

"I wouldn't have given him much credibility until I tried the product," I said, and right then I could *hear* the song again, that haunting voice calling me down, down into the dark. I could hear the melody and the crash of waves in the background and, faintly, the creak of oarlocks and the sound of wind in the rigging. One listen, and yet it was all there, branded into my brain as if I'd lived the experience rather than dozed through it. Maybe, I thought, this was what it was like to be a dreamer, to wake and remember the bizarre imaginings of the sleeping mind.

"It really works?" Pat asked.

"It put me to sleep faster than an Ambien," I said. "And people pay a few billion dollars for Ambien each year even while it chews away at their brains, so is there some value to his creation? Maybe. Sure."

"And the dreams? Did it shape them for you, Nick? Did you awake a changed man?"

"I woke with full faith in humanity and not an ounce of skepticism in my blood. I woke to experience the world as Pat Ryan does. It's an amazing thing. Now tell me—what do *you* think of Bryce?"

"I think he's got old money and is willing to spend it on strange endeavors and thus he's a friend of mine. Until the money runs out, naturally. Then I'll have to reassess him."

As he grinned at me, I was certain that he wasn't telling me everything. He'd been an honest man for as long as I'd known him, and yet as I watched him smile over the top of his beer, I knew he was withholding. Reporter's instinct, we'll call it, mixed with very clear memories of Pat's mannerisms. It would've been easy to forget those, but I hadn't forgotten.

Some circuits stay lit.

9

The loons were loud that night, but I didn't stay outside to enjoy them. I'd had a couple more beers than planned with Pat—that was always how it seemed to go with him—and the clouds had covered the moon and left the dock and the rocks in darkness. Also, I didn't have a chair to sit on, with the Adirondack having become a casualty of the day.

I went inside and drank a glass of water and then stretched out on the old couch, my head propped against one armrest, feet on the other. The couch was so small that someone of my six feet, one inch was doomed to a stiff neck no matter the position. The camp was still and peaceful and the night air coming in through the open windows was as cool as water dipped out of a deep well. I thought that I would sleep easily and deeply. That was good, because suddenly I was exhausted, bone-tired without knowing why.

When my phone chimed and the screen illuminated, I assumed it would be a text from Pat, "home safe, headache tomorrow, great seeing you" and so on.

It wasn't a text. It was a notification from the Clarity app.

Sleep Song #2 is now available!

I sat up, switched on the lamp, and found my notebook and lone earbud. I didn't want to fall asleep this time. I'd lost the first sleep song completely, and when they played, they vanished. A good reporter could fix that, I decided, and I went into the little bedroom and rooted around in my battered flight bag until I found my voice recorder. I started the recorder, then cranked up the volume on the phone and pressed "play" on the sleep song.

An error message appeared.

Headphones required.

Well, damn it, that wasn't ideal for recording. It didn't seem ideal, period; wouldn't I want to be able to hear the soothing meditations without needing to jam earbuds in before bed?

I nestled my single AirPod into my left ear and heard the low chime that told me it was connected to the phone's Bluetooth signal, then pressed "play" again. For a few seconds, there was nothing but silence. I was just about to pick up the phone when a low, booming wave played in my left ear. Ah, the crashing coast of Clarity. Good to be back.

The water rose and fell, rose and fell, and I envisioned the Maine coast. This time, the memory was of a night sky alive with stars, glittering constellations above black water laced with white foam. It was fascinating, the way the images came so vividly with the simple sound as cue. I remembered jumbles of uneven granite, slick underfoot with tide-soaked rockweed. Above the tide line, I could see the dry rock gleaming bone-white beneath a full moon.

A strange, distorted chord broke the water noise, harsh with reverb. I winced and reached for my earpiece, then stilled my hand when the chord faded. A moment later, floating over the top, came a higher sound, one that was human but not singing. It was somewhere between a whisper and a moan, but on pitch, and quite beautiful in its own eerie way.

I clicked my pen impatiently, holding the notebook at the ready, and waited for the lyrics to begin.

The low strings played on. The moan-whisper rose to a subdued wail, a distant sound that made me want to lean forward, as if that might help me hear it. I saw an image then quite clearly: dark, forested hills, somewhere across a shimmering field— or a stretch of beach, maybe?—and on the other side were men with torches, and out in the woods beyond, baying dogs.

I wrote, *Hunters? Makes me think of a night hunt.*

An odd observation, considering I'd never been on any type of night hunt, let alone with men holding torches and chasing dogs, but that was the image that rose to mind.

I sat back and waited for lyrics. I knew they'd be coming. This time I would write them down.

But the voice did not come. Just that eerie, whispering wail, a sound caught between a warning and an invitation, a sound that could conjure thoughts of a night hunt with hounds and now one of a tall, ancient church with stained glass windows and high ceilings and flickering candles.

I wrote, *Church? Hymn? Hunters? Makes me think of a night hunt.*

The song played on. Rising and falling, chasing new paths of melody over the same low, tumbling river of distorted string music. I sketched the sound. Or, rather, sketched what made sense to me, as I had no musical training—a simple peaks-and-valleys line to represent the pitch.

And then I slept.

I slept as if it were an act against my own will, slept as if paralyzed, slept as if held down by strong hands. At some point, I realized dimly that the lamp was off and that I didn't remember turning it off. My eyes would flutter open and the shadowed room would present itself and then my eyes would close again. None of it felt like a product of my own intention or effort.

I'd been through this routine several times before the woman appeared.

She stood at the foot of the couch, close enough to reach out and grasp my ankle if she wished, and still I couldn't move, couldn't so much as struggle upright or roll off the couch and onto the floor. I lay there, trapped and staring, as she tilted her head to the right and then the left, studying me.

She was dressed in pale gray hiking pants that were stained dark with water and a black fleece top that glistened like oil on hot asphalt. Her hair was blond but looked dark because it was wet, dripping. Her complexion was as pale as sand under moonlight.

She watched me and waited as if I might take the lead in the situation, and I tried to move and tried to scream, but there were no options—I could only watch. Finally, she spoke.

"You don't want to follow them," she told me. Her voice scarcely above a whisper, and yet clear and almost musical.

I tried to say that I would not. Tried to ask her who she was. Tried to ask her to leave.

No words came.

Instead, my eyelids flicked like the tongues of snakes, then closed again. Darkness descended. I had the sensation of sinking—not falling; this was very different, a slow descent through soft resistance, *sinking*, deeper, deeper, deeper, and then—

My eyelids flickered and opened again.

She was still there. Watching me with a mournful expression. The room seemed to have darkened around her, but her face had brightened, that moonlit-sand glow deepening to a blue tint. I had the sense that I knew her, that she was familiar to me, though I couldn't say why.

"It's better when the days are long," she told me. "Easier to fight the night then."

Stop talking, I cried. *Please go,* I cried. But she didn't react because I couldn't make a sound.

My eyelids shut once more, an activity over which I had no control, and once more she was gone, and then I was sinking again, passing through the couch and through the floor and on through soft, yielding soil that stank of decay. Then came the now-familiar tug at my eyelids, the snakes flicking their tongues, and my eyes were open again, and the woman was gone from the foot of the couch.

There was an instant of relief, like a fever breaking.

Then she leaned in above me, her face directly above mine, that wet blond hair swinging toward me in the darkness, her face blue-white above bloodred lips.

The scream I would have uttered then would have been unlike any sound I'd ever made before, if only I could have made it.

Her lips were at my ear, and I could feel her breath, cold as winter rain, when she whispered.

"You need to go deeper," she said, the instruction at once erotic and terrifying. "Deeper now. Past them. You've got to go down past the place where they wait. Remember that, Nick. They can't follow you all the way down."

My eyes closed again. Involuntary but welcome this time. The sight of her was worse than the sound of her voice, so much worse, because once she'd leaned in above me, I'd confirmed what I'd already suspected when she stood in shadow at the far end of the couch:

She was dead.

There was no denying it. She was a dead woman come to whisper in my ear, come to pull me down into that damp earth.

And now she was gone and only her voice lingered, *all the way down, all the way down, all the way down,* each whisper a cold breeze against my ear that spread out in a head-to-toe tingle of electric nerves as the sinking sensation came on and then shifted to falling, falling fast, falling down through the darkness to—

Where I woke on the floor with the smell of copper heavy in my nostrils and my palm bathed in warm red blood.

10

The blood held my attention first, as blood tends to.

My palm was hot and sticky with it, and there was an instant when, looking at the literal blood-on-my-hand scenario, I had a visceral, near-certain thought:

I killed her.

Madness, of course. There had been no her. No woman had entered the house and whispered in my ear. That had been a . . .

Dream? A dream.

Yes, a dream. I'd finally had one.

If this was a taste of what I'd been missing all these years, I wasn't in a hurry to have another.

I sat up, realizing three things in a staggered sequence: my hand was hot not just from blood but from pain; my shirt was absolutely soaked with sweat; and I had broken the lamp when I rolled off the couch. I discovered the latter when I tried to move from the floor and stumbled over the lamp and heard the tinkle of broken glass. Even then, I wasn't sure exactly what it was. The only source of light in the room was a pinprick of red light from the coffee table. I couldn't identify its source—everything was confusing in the darkness and the pain—and thought irrationally but absolutely that it was the dot from a sniper's scope. I staggered across the room and hit the switch for the overhead light and flooded the camp with brightness and laid bare the reality that had emerged from my nightmare.

The red light was from the digital recorder I'd left running on the coffee table. The glass was from the lamp beside the couch that now lay on the floor, the bulb shattered. In my terror, I must have swiped out for the lamp and knocked it over, and that was no doubt responsible for the deep cut that curled across my palm like a crescent moon, moving from the base of my thumb to the base of my pinkie finger in an almost graceful arc that pulsed with fresh blood and deepening pain.

There was blood on the floor, too—a tidy handprint from where I'd pushed off the old boards. In between the distinct crimson outlines of my thumb and index finger lay my single AirPod.

It was only at the sight of the earbud that I even remembered the Clarity app and the sleep song. All that lingered was the nightmare, the dead woman who'd seemed so impossibly real, something beyond a vision, because when she'd breathed, I'd felt that cold breeze along my neck and known . . .

I looked at the front window. The old, dusty

curtain billowed out in a soft but steady breeze, pushed out of the northwest and right across the surface of the deep, cool pond.

"Nightmare," I said aloud, because I felt the need to hear a human voice in the empty cabin where I stood bleeding and soaked and shivering.

Yes, *soaked.* My shirt clung to my skin, cold and saturated. I peeled it off and tossed it onto the floor beside the bloodstain. The sweat on my torso was so chilled that it seemed as if I'd waded right out of the pond itself.

I'd heard of night terrors, interviewed soldiers who told me of the physical power of PTSD dreams, how fingers curled around imaginary triggers. One Army Ranger told me he'd wake with his hand to his face, convinced he was pulling down a microphone to scream for air support. All of this I understood as possible. I'd just never experienced it.

You should call Whitney, I thought. *Break the big news: not only can you dream, you can dream big!* I was trying for a smile that I couldn't quite muster as I walked to the kitchen sink and put my throbbing hand beneath a stream of ice-cold water, watched the blood run red and then pink into the drain as it diluted and the flesh on either side of the cut turned white, already dying, as if crying out for its companion across the way.

I wrapped a dishtowel around my palm and then went into the small bathroom to see if any ancient medical supplies remained. In the tiny vanity cabinet behind the mirror I found a bottle of hydrogen peroxide, Mercurochrome, and some small Band-Aids that wouldn't have a chance. The blood had already soaked through the dishtowel.

I sat on the edge of the tub, unwrapped the dishtowel, and poured a liberal amount of peroxide over the cut, gritting my teeth in anticipation of pain that didn't come. The cold water had numbed the wound, or maybe the existing pain was already strong enough. The peroxide had an expiration date from three years earlier, but its foaming assault on the wound suggested it was still virile enough. I added a second splash, then painted the cut with the Mercurochrome—which was also expired, naturally—wrapped the hand in a fresh towel, and went outside to get my first-aid kit from the truck.

Outside the camp, the breeze didn't feel as cold as it had inside. It was a pleasant, silent night. The stars were out and the air was fragrant with pine needles and dampness. I thought of the woman with the blue-tinted flesh and the deep-red lips and I shivered hard, almost recoiling.

A dream. A nightmare, yes, but everyone has those, so congrats, Nick, you've joined the club, lost your nightmare virginity.

I thought back on the music as I stood with the truck door open and the cab light on and lined the cut with wound-seal powder and then layered it with gauze and taped it tight. Had there been lyrics to the song this time? I didn't remember. The woman from my dream was clear, and I recalled her words just fine. Too well, in fact.

Deeper now. Past them. You've got to go deeper, go down, go past the place where they wait. Remember that, Nick. They can't follow you all the way down.

Those were dream words, though. Not lyrics, nothing from the app.

Right?

Right. Because she'd said my name, and there was no way my name had been uttered on whatever recording I'd listened to.

Right?

Hard to vet, since the recording was no longer accessible.

If the damn thing didn't require headphones, you might have it all, I thought.

It was almost as if the Clarity system had been designed to frustrate a reporter; I couldn't stay awake to take good notes, and I couldn't make a recording of what happened.

I grabbed two small packets of Advil from the first-aid kit and then went back inside. I pulled a dry sweatshirt on, downed the Advil with a glass of water, and went to clean up the mess. The recorder was still running, its tiny red LED glowing. I shut it off and saved the recording file even though there wouldn't be anything on it, and then I swept up the broken glass, dumped it into the wastebasket, and put the busted lamp back on the end table. It would take some work with needle-nose pliers to extract the remains of the socket from the fixture. I washed the bloody handprint from the floorboards as well as I could, but a faint, rust-colored outline remained. A task for the next day. I was exhausted again, wanted nothing more than to get in bed and sleep the way I always had—deeply and dreamlessly.

First, though, I picked up my notebook. Searched its pages. I'd been sketching the music, the pitch itself, and the clumsy peaks and valleys represented high notes and lows. The only words I'd written remained less clear. *Church? Hymn? Hunters? Makes me think of a night hunt.*

I knew those weren't the lyrics themselves, although I wasn't exactly sure *how* I knew that with such certainty. I closed the notebook and got into bed. Shut the door but left the light on, like a child comforted by the thin band of light that framed the doorway in the darkness. Then I propped my aching hand up on a pillow and lay back and waited for sleep, the kind of sleep I'd always known, the comforting blackness that would take me fast and return me refreshed to the new day.

It didn't come.

Not at all. The night was silent and I was awake and alone. The hours passed as slowly as any I'd ever known, an interminable, purgatorial wait. Several times I thought about getting out of bed to read a book or watch a movie on my iPad or do any

11

The pain woke me around noon. I emerged from a dreamless sleep, flexed my hand, and immediately regretted that as fresh blood seeped through flesh that had begun to knit back together—or, at least, had stopped bleeding. How long it took for healing to begin, I wasn't sure, but if pain was a part of it, then the healing had started.

I'd slept for almost five hours but had the groggy, semi-sick feeling that comes with a sudden inversion of sleep cycle. It was one I knew well from jet-lagged trips but it was a new experience on the home front.

I drank some orange juice to feed my blood sugar but all it did was stir cold acid in my stomach and add to the sick feeling. The daylight helped, though. The sun was out and I could smell the pines and the pond and it was certainly a damn sight better than last night. I sat on the massive rock above the water while I changed the dressing on my hand and realized that it was time for a doctor's attention, not Nick Bishop's DIY approach.

"Nick, that you?"

Bobby Beauchamp was standing behind me. I hadn't seen him up close when I arrived, and now that I could, it appeared he hadn't aged a day—although that wasn't to say he looked young, just the same. Short and heavily muscled, a square face with a prominent jaw. He wore rumpled work clothes and had a surprisingly well-groomed beard, the only part of his appearance he seemed to put any time into. His white hair was wild and straggly, usually concealed by a baseball cap, but the white beard was so perfectly trimmed you'd have thought he used a T-square on it. Hell, maybe he did.

"Figured you'd had time to think on the dead trees by now. Those boys"—he pointed at a copse of pines directly over his head—"are likely to come down on my property. Now those giants"—his stubby index finger moved to point out the enormous white pines at the base of the rock just below me—"they seem likely to live another hunnert years. You got lucky there. But these others are weakly, and if they fall on the south side, it's over my—"

"I'll get them cut," I said. I had no desire to debate the property line with Bobby Beauchamp. I just wanted to get my hand stitched.

"Ayuh, good, good," he said, coming closer, arms folded over his barrel chest, clearly ready for exactly what I didn't want—a nice long chat. "So, it's none of my business, but some people say your mother took ill. Heart attack, was it? Or stroke?"

Ordinarily, I'd have had to hide a grin at the *It's none of my business, but some people say* line, but not this morning, and not with that question.

"Stroke," I said shortly. "She's doing okay, though."

"Oh?" His face told me he knew exactly what condition my mother was in. "That's nice to hear. She'll be by, then?" he asked, knowing damn well that she wouldn't be.

I got to my feet, dusted pine needles from my jeans.

"Yeah, she may be," I said, just to screw with the nosy old bastard. "I'll tell her you said hello."

"Ayuh, do that, sure. She was always a nice woman. Quiet. Polite." His emphasis was on *quiet*. His eyes roved over the camp and down to the water. "Say, couldn't help but notice you busted up that chair on the dock. Old, sure, but good wood. I could fix the other one up for you—"

"But it won't be for free," I said.

"Nope," he agreed, unbothered by my anticipation of his phrase, if he even noticed it.

"Tell you what," I said, "fix it and paint it and bill me."

Mostly, I just wanted him to get the hell away. He seemed pleasantly surprised with the offer and went down to gather the surviving Adirondack chair as I went into the camp and got my truck keys. When I came back outside, he was walking toward me. I made a show of locking the door and even started the truck's engine remotely just to make it clear that I had places to go and no time for further conversation.

"Hey, Nick . . ."

"I've got to head out. I'm sorry, but—"

"Figure you'd want this, or am I wrong, and I should just pitch it?"

I looked back at him. His hand was outstretched. In his wrinkled palm was a white curl of plastic. The AirPod I hadn't been able to find yesterday.

The sight of it rattled me for some reason, but I thanked him and accepted it. I couldn't afford to waste money on replacements. Still, I thought it would be a while before I put it back into my ear.

"Thanks."

"Sure." He looked up at the camp, squinting. I was sure he was about to suggest another project, when he said, "Been a long time since you were here."

"It has. Too long. I missed it."

"What brought you back?"

"Just visiting."

"Oh?" He pulled a grimy rag from his back pocket and wiped his hands carefully. "Not seen your mother in all this time?"

I didn't have patience for questions like that. "I've got places to be. We'll catch up another time, I'm sure."

"Sure we will," he said, but his eyes were locked on mine in an unpleasant way, and I knew that I'd offended him but couldn't bring myself to care. He was a nosy man, a gossip. I turned from him and headed for my truck.

"Hope you take to sleepin' through the night better if you're staying long."

I turned back. He gazed at me placidly.

"What's that?" I said.

"Your lights shine right into my bedroom window. Hard to miss. So I hope you're not gonna be the night owl that you were last night. Or, if you are, I hope you hang some curtains."

I pictured him watching from across the water and wondered how much he had seen. If he knew what I didn't—the way I must have looked, flailing around, breaking lights, staggering in the dark with blood on my hand. I felt exposed and angry, suddenly very angry, and I closed my hand into a fist around the AirPod.

"If you hang some curtains in your own bedroom," I said, "my lights shouldn't bother you much. Take care, Bobby."

Finally, I'd been able to drop the *Mr. Beauchamp* routine.

I walked for the truck then, and if he said anything else, I didn't hear it.

12

I drove to Bayview Healthcare. It was the only walk-in clinic I knew that wasn't the ER, and that seemed ideal for a man without health insurance. First time in my life I'd had to consider that, and it unsettled me more than I'd expected. I filled out the paperwork, trying to ignore the flush of shame that came on with answering "No" to the insurance question, thinking about how many millions of people went through this every day, and was waiting in one of the uncomfortable vinyl-upholstered chairs, when my phone rang.

Renee Holland.

"Hey, there. Just the woman I was hoping to hear from."

"Oh?" She sounded wary.

"Yeah! I'm sitting here in a doctor's waiting room with a hand that's all cut to hell, you see, and—"

"What happened?"

"That is precisely what I'd like to ask you about. Because my experience with the, ahem, prototype last night was a little wild."

A beat. Then: "Your what?"

Her voice had dropped an octave and she seemed almost frightened. It wasn't far from her response the previous day when I'd said I had tried the app.

"I had one hell of a nightmare," I said. "Broke a lamp and ended up bleeding on the floor. And before you tell me that's the price one pays for a night of drinking with Pat Ryan, let me clarify that *I don't have nightmares*. Or dreams. So whatever you guys have cooked up is more interesting than I'd given it credit for."

"What was the nightmare?" she asked, voice even softer now, and I had the impression that she didn't want to be overheard.

"I'll get into that in person. Why don't I come by the mill after they've stitched me up here and we can—"

"No, no. Not here."

"Fine. Where?"

"I'll come to your place. Just name the time."

"I'll call when . . ." My voice wandered off as the memory of my mother's replaced it in my mind. *Should not be at Rosewater.* It was a crazy thing to take seriously, and yet . . .

"Let's pick neutral ground," I said.

"What?"

"If you don't want me to come by the mill, then pick a place that isn't the camp."

"Let's just meet in town, then," she said. "The harbor park is quiet, and it's a short walk for me."

I thought about pressing her on why it was so

damned important that I not come by the mill, but let it go. For now.

"Fine by me."

"Let's say four?"

"Four it is," I said. "See you then."

I hung up. An overweight sunburned man with a cough that sounded like a clogged garbage disposal raised his hand to get my attention.

"That true?" he asked. "About the dreams?"

"Pardon?" As a rule, engaging with strangers in doctors' waiting rooms isn't high on my priority list; engaging with eavesdropping strangers with whooping cough falls even farther down.

"Heard you say you never dream. I can't believe that." He smiled, coughed, then waved a hand in front of his face as if that were a courtesy, fanning the germs in my direction.

"I don't remember them, at least," I said, and took my phone back out, pretended to be checking a message. It didn't slow him down, though.

"Only way I know that I've had good sleep," he said, shifting his bulk, the chair squeaking beneath him, "is because I have dreams. And with this fever?" He pointed at his sweaty brow. "Man, the dreams have been *wicked weird* lately."

I was saved from having to respond to that by a nurse calling my name from the hallway, clipboard in hand.

"Good luck," I told the fever dreamer, and then escaped down the hall.

While I was stepping onto the scale, the nurse said, "You've been here before."

"Huh?"

"To the clinic."

"No."

"Yes."

I was quite sure that I hadn't, but she was nodding, looking at the clipboard.

"Been a number of years, but you were in here with an ankle injury."

I remembered the injury. I'd stepped on a defender's foot while driving to the basket in a pickup game, rolled my ankle so badly I was sure it was broken. It would've been better if I *had* broken it, the doctor later informed me; as it was, the ligaments took all of the damage. I did a couple months of physical therapy for that one.

"I was younger then," I said.

She adjusted the sliding bars on the scale, stopped them at 176, looked down at the paperwork, and said, "Weighed exactly the same, though. Good for you!"

"The weight has stayed the same. The quality of it has not."

She laughed harder at that than I would've liked. As I followed her down the hall, I tried hard to recall the details of my first visit and couldn't. Strange. I remembered rehabbing the ankle. All of that had been done on campus. Why hadn't I gone to the student health center to begin with? Meaningless, of course, but it bothered me that I couldn't recall.

I remembered the play. Cisco Taylor was guarding me, and I'd gotten him to backpedal and then rocked him just enough with a shoulder fake to get him off balance as I brought the ball from left hand to right and cut straight for the bucket, my eyes already on the rim as a defender on the baseline charged over to help. He was a step too late; I was absolutely sure of that as I began my leap—and planted my foot directly on his instead of the asphalt. My ankle snapped, a white-hot pain.

All of that was vivid. But why in the hell hadn't I gone to the student health center? Why had I ended up here? It didn't matter in the least, but it bothered me because struggling for memory made me think of my mother, of insignificant memories recycling like water in a fountain.

An unimpressed physician listened to my explanation of the cut across my palm—I described it as inflicted by a broken lightbulb, with no further color commentary on night terrors and sleep songs—and looked it over briefly before announcing that he would glue it.

"It'll scar, but hopefully less than if we stitched it up," he said. "You've got to be careful with lightbulbs, Mr. Bishop. Was the lamp plugged in?"

I acknowledged that it had been, and he shook his head.

"You're lucky the cut was all that happened, then."

Fifteen minutes later, I walked out of the office with a prescription for painkillers and a thick band of purple glue over the cut. It looked like a night-crawler was stuck to my palm, but the wound was clean and the bleeding had stopped and I'd been assured that the glue would also serve as protection from infection. I was batting a thousand at the walk-in clinic, apparently, although I still couldn't remember my first visit.

You've been here before, the nurse had said.

I saw Cisco in his defensive crouch, saw his body weight shift to his right foot as he bit on my fake, saw the opening ahead, could almost *feel* the ball switching from my left hand to right as I cut for the basket . . .

Then what?

I didn't remember the doctor's visit. A small, silly thing, and yet it troubled me.

13

Renee had asked me to meet her at the harbor park because it was quiet, but when I arrived the parking lot was full and there was a crowd spread across the lawn, with people crammed on blankets or sitting in folding camp chairs.

I found a space five blocks away, facing the old railroad trestle over the Willow River. A few years earlier the trestle had been featured in national news when a woman tried to race a train across it in her car to escape a man who'd kidnapped her. It was the biggest news to hit Hammel in years. My mother had sent me clippings of that one.

I walked across the pedestrian bridge and down to the harbor. Music was blaring from large speakers in the amphitheater—"Sweet Home Alabama," a song that made little sense in Maine, but there you go—and a man with a microphone sat on the roof of the harbormaster's shack, Bobby Beauchamp's old quarters.

"What's all this?" I asked to no one in particular. A woman in a camp chair smiled at me in a pitying way.

"The lobster crate races!" she said. "Last of the season, too damn cold for anyone but kids and fools to try. Makes it fun!"

And, sure enough, I could see the course now—a long line of lobster traps bobbing in the water between the seawall and the nearest dock, which was maybe fifty yards away.

"Want me to sign you up?" a voice whispered in my ear.

I jumped. Not a little twitch but a full-on jump, up and to the side. Renee Holland stared at me, lifting her hands, palms out.

"Whoa," she said. "Easy there. Didn't mean to scare you."

The crowd around us was staring at me, too, because I'd just reacted to a friendly voice in my ear the way you should react to stepping on a live rattlesnake. I tried to laugh it off, feeling heat rise in my cheeks.

"Maybe I should limit myself to three pots of coffee per day," I said. Renee gave it more of a smile than it deserved while the rest of the onlookers turned their attention back to the water.

"Sorry about this," she said. "I completely forgot."

"The big race? How could you?"

She smiled. She was wearing loose white linen pants and a matching button-down shirt that hung open over a blue tank top, and against all that white her dark red hair was even more striking. Titian, my mother would have called that hair.

"I'm sure you were planning on participating," she said, moving away toward a quieter corner of the park. "This is the reason you really drove back from Florida, right?"

"Precisely," I said, falling into step beside her. "I start small, picking up victories on my old home turf, and the next thing you know, I'm running across lobster pots for the world championships."

On the roof of the harbor master's office, the man with the microphone who was emceeing the big event refreshed us on the process: each participant had two minutes to run across as many traps as they could, and if you fell in the water, you were done. Once we were all clear on those complex rules, the harbor master bellowed for contestant number one. Or *numbah one*, as he said.

The crowd broke into applause when a blond boy of maybe eight or nine jogged down to the seawall. He was wearing swim trunks and a T-shirt that said *The Talent Has Arrived*. He hammed it up for the audience, waving his hands, demanding louder applause.

The harbor master loved it.

"Victah Havey was a joon-yah league champion last ye-ah, but you'll notice he's done some growin'! Before you place your bets, you might remembah that the key to this event is keeping a low centah of gravity. He's *too tall*, folks, that's what I'm tellin' ya!"

Victor Havey, the defending champ, cupped

his hands to his mouth and booed the harbor master.

"This kid is something," I said, laughing. "How many traps do you think he gets?"

"A thousand," Renee said. We were standing side by side under one of the old oaks that shaded the sloped lawn, watching the race almost despite ourselves.

The harbor master counted down from five and fired an airhorn blast loud enough to make half the crowd cover their ears. Victor Havey was off, hopping from floating crate to floating crate, moving nimbly, high-stepping his way across the water. When he reached the far end and had to turn around, there was a precarious moment when he was frozen in midair with his right foot searching for a trap that was still bobbing from his last footstep. The crowed drew in a collective breath, waiting for his splashdown, but he compensated by leaning left and waving his left hand, clawing air, holding balance long enough to let the trap steady before he leaped onto it and continued his run.

The crowd roared as if they'd just seen an interception on the goal line in the Super Bowl.

I was laughing until I turned to Renee and saw that her attention wasn't on the race but on my hand, where the line of purple glue covered the cut. She looked more concerned about it than she should have.

"It's fine," I said. "Believe it or not, the doc told

me that this stuff will actually leave it looking better than it would have with stitches."

"How'd you cut it?"

"Thrashed out during a nightmare, I guess. Knocked a lamp over and the bulb broke."

"Do you remember the nightmare?"

"Part of it. But I don't remember the song. That's what I'd like to talk to you about."

She'd been looking at the harbor but now snapped her attention back to me. "What do you mean, just like the other time? When you blamed the app for your nightmare, I thought you meant from the first listen. How did you play another?"

"I didn't delete the app." I saw the anger in her green eyes, and I nodded. "Yes, I lied. And I'm sorry. But . . ." I shrugged. "Old instincts, I guess."

"To lie?"

"No. To hold on to evidence."

"Evidence!" She barked out a laugh.

"Particularly when someone seems to want it destroyed," I said. "And it *is* evidence. Whatever you guys are working on, that app was the only tangible taste you offered me. The rest was just Bryce blowing smoke."

"You lied," she repeated, and all I could do was nod. I might've been more ashamed if not for the night that the app had produced. Now my curiosity overrode the shame. It clearly didn't do much to diminish Renee's anger at being betrayed, though. She glared at me. Then the harbor master shouted that Victor Havey was down to ten seconds left, and we both turned, reflexively, to watch him close out.

As the harbor master counted down, Victor picked up speed, his knees pumping as he cleared one trap to the next to the next and then momentum finally caught up to him. He was only three traps from the safety of the dock when his foot landed on a trap that was tilting to the left, and his recovery effort didn't work this time. He hung suspended for a moment and then splashed into the bay as the crowd burst out into laughter and applause. He surfaced immediately, clasped his hands together like a heavyweight champ, and then swam to the dock ladder.

"Imagine what happens if you give that kid caffeine," I said, but Renee had lost interest in the spectacle—or in any diversion from my lying, evidently. She stepped close and faced me.

"I didn't ask you to delete it because of some business concern. It's much more important than that."

"Why?" I shot back. "Why is it so damned important?"

She took a deep breath. Considered. Finally, she said, "You understand that much of the research that is at the core of Clarity has its origin in your mother's lab, right?"

I did not know that, yet I wasn't overly surprised. A lot of neuroscience research—particularly studies in memory—had their origins in my mother's work. For research based in Hammel, Maine, the overlap felt almost inevitable.

"Okay," I said. "So you're afraid that I'll, what, sue for shares of the company or something? Come on. Unless you're flat-out stealing something she had patented or—"

"We absolutely aren't."

"—then I don't see how I have much room for a claim."

"That's not the concern."

"Then what *is* the concern? My mother's not going to be giving any interviews critiquing your company, I assure you of that. She can't tell a blue jay from a cardinal anymore, so you'll be able to sneak plenty past her."

"It's not about the company," she said, "and it's not about your mother's work. It's about you."

I cocked my head and studied her. Behind us, one of the big speakers boomed with the announcement of the next race contestant and the crowd roared again, but this time neither of us so much as glanced toward the harbor.

"What do you mean?"

"Bryce pushed things along yesterday before I could really . . . articulate my concerns. I'm not sure the beta version should have been shared with anyone, but it certainly shouldn't have been shared with you."

"Why not?"

"Because of the amount of work your mother did with you."

"What are you talking about, Renee?"

"It probably doesn't even matter, but the idea of taking the same kind of stimulus that she used with you all those years ago and then playing around with the same approach now, in an uncontrolled environment, just seems like an invitation for—"

I lifted my hand to silence her. The ghastly purple wound drew her eye again, but she stopped talking.

"You're confused," I said. "I have only minimal understanding of anything my mother did, frankly. Her work wasn't all that exciting to a kid."

She looked from my hand to my face. Her eyes darkened.

"I'm talking about the lab work," she said.

"And I'm still not following."

She stared at me, disbelief clear on her face. I felt a prickle and chill along my spine and suddenly wished we were standing out in the sun with the rest of the crowd and not up here in the shadows of the big oaks.

"You were involved in some pretty extensive experiments, Nick," she said, speaking slowly and carefully, as if my confusion was a hearing problem and she wanted to be sure I could read her lips.

"Experiments," I echoed. I wanted to laugh, because it all seemed so absurd, but Renee's face was so grim that I couldn't.

She nodded. "As a test subject. In your mother's

lab at Hammel. Weeks and weeks of testing. Surely you remember that?"

I hadn't the faintest recollection of it. I was about to object, about to tell her that she simply had to be wrong, but the look on her face negated that approach. She seemed absolutely certain.

"I must've been too young," I said. "It didn't stick."

But if it had been at Hammel, I couldn't have been *too* young.

The harbor master bellowed as another race contestant splashed into the bay, the crowd cheered and laughed, and Renee Holland stared at me and took a careful step back, as if I'd threatened her.

"You were sixteen years old," she said. "She had you in there three times a week. It went on for months."

I felt like I'd come detached from myself and was floating above, watching but no longer part of the scene. I heard myself as if from afar when I said, "*What* went on for months, Renee?"

"The memory work," she said. "To help with . . . with your trauma."

"With my trauma," I echoed woodenly.

"Yes."

"And what, exactly, was my trauma?"

The breeze pulled her white linen shirt back from her tank top and she caught it and pulled it tight, wrapping her arms tight to her body, as if for protection.

"The accident," she said. "With your dad."

I felt some measure of relief. Here, finally, was something that I knew and remembered.

"I was sixteen when he died," I acknowledged. "It was rough. I mean, it was awful. But I don't remember . . ."

I was about to say *any work with my mother* but Renee spoke first.

"The scene?"

"Huh?"

"You really don't have any memory of the scene?" she asked, stepping closer, as if her curiosity was drawing her toward me despite her better instincts.

"Of course not," I said. "I never saw it."

I swear she blanched then. I thought I should reach out and steady her.

"Nick," she said. "You were there."

"No. I was at home. He was on his way to the airport. He had to—"

"Catch a flight," she interjected.

"Exactly. There was black ice on the highway . . ."

She was nodding along with my words, but her green eyes were glistening, as if she was close to tears.

"And he spun out of control," I finished.

For a moment, she didn't respond. The harbor master's heavily accented voice droned around us and the breeze fanned over us and Renee Holland stared at me in silence before she finally spoke again.

"Nick?" she said. "You were driving the car."

14

You were driving the car.

I laughed at her. The kind of harsh laugh that comes from the intersection of pity and scorn. And, maybe, a little fear. Yes, there was fear. Even that afternoon in the sunlit park where children played games as the crowd cheered, I was beginning to feel afraid.

"What's your deal?" I said, shaking my head. "I mean, the little app with its nightmare-inducing songs is fun stuff, but this? What are you trying to achieve here?"

She looked sad. "There would be police reports, wouldn't there?" she said.

I stopped. Looked at her as she pushed her dark red hair back from her face, saw those bright green eyes locked on mine, and suddenly they seemed less friendly and more feral, a black cat's eyes in a graveyard after sunset.

"Sure," I said. "But I don't intend to go about humoring you and reading them."

"Why not?"

"Because you're crazy."

"Then you should prove that," she said gently. "Right? If I'm crazy, and I'm involved in making Clarity a functional program, you should put that in your article. It would be good journalism."

"I don't intend to waste much time on Clarity," I said. "Writing the article was a favor from a friend, a chance to make a little cash, and that's how I'm going to treat it."

"Pat Ryan is the friend."

"Yes."

"Am I another one?"

I wasn't sure how to answer that.

"Do you still think of me as a friend, Nick?" she prodded. She had a very steady voice now, and a bearing that made me uncomfortable, as if I were being grilled by a prosecutor. Or a psychiatrist.

"I did. But what you're saying now is so crazy that I'm not sure."

"I would appreciate you humoring me enough to read the police reports about the accident. That's not asking too much."

"I don't need to, though," I said, and hated the petulant tone in my voice. I knew what had happened, so there was no risk in reading the police reports.

"One of us is wrong," she said. "It is that simple, right?"

"Yes."

"Okay. If I'm wrong, I need to know that. So . . . prove me wrong."

"You can prove yourself wrong. I don't need to do—"

"As a favor," she said firmly, "for a friend. Please."

I sighed and turned away. Renee shifted to stay in my line of sight.

She pointed toward the harbor. "Why did you want to meet here?"

"*I* didn't want to meet here. This was *your* suggestion."

"The place was. But why did you want to meet with me today? What were the big questions you had?"

"Whose voice is it, and what is the song? Those were my questions before you started with this bullshit."

She didn't react to the last jibe but leaned closer to me and said, "Okay, the song and the voice—why do those things matter to you?"

"They don't. Not anymore. Because I don't have the time to indulge you in whatever—"

"You're too smart *not* to check the police reports. You also know me, you remember those afternoon runs and those days in the silly floats on the pond. Give me an ounce of credibility."

"I can show you the police reports if you insist on it."

"I insist," she said. The strange sheen was back in her eyes, the liquid gleam that almost looked like tears.

I didn't say anything. I looked away from her,

out to the harbor, watching as another kid splashed into the bay to the delighted laughter of the onlookers. I felt for him—running across a shifting surface with an audience waiting to watch you slip, fall, and sink into that frigid, end-of-season water. Suddenly, the lobster trap race didn't seem like a good-humored event.

"Some things simply shouldn't be fair game," I told Renee. "Not even in the name of research or the greater good or whatever bullshit credo Bryce Lermond has. Trying to get me to question my memory of something like my dad's death? That's not fair game, Renee. Not even close."

"I agree," she said, her voice tender in a way that troubled me, as if she felt I needed to be handled carefully. "More than you possibly know, Nick, I agree, and I'll be happy to address the topic with you. But first? You need to verify your own memory. You and I aren't going to achieve anything until that happens."

She put her hand on my arm, a light touch, and said, "If you decide to do that, give me a call. I can share more with you then. *If* you want to hear it."

I didn't respond. She squeezed my arm and stepped away. I didn't want to look in her direction. When I finally did, she was already back on the sidewalk, headed up the street.

You were driving the car.

What a thing to say! And to what end? What was the point of such a bizarre claim?

I ran through the facts of my father's death: *Black ice. He was running late to catch a flight. The car spun. I know that because that's what they told us.*

But who were *they*? I tried to remember the call. That should have been vivid, right? Someone had called us. The police or the ER doctor or . . . someone. Who had it been?

Mom. She sat down with you and broke the news.

Sat me down where? In the house? The room should be easy to remember. I thought it had been in the kitchen. We'd sat there at the old farmhouse-style table with those uncomfortable straight-backed chairs and she'd held my hand and told me . . .

Wrong house.

That kitchen had been in Hammel. We'd lived in Camden when my dad died.

Black ice. Running late to catch a flight. The car spun. He was dead on arrival. He felt no pain. It happened very fast and so he felt no pain because when it is so fast there is no pain, when you are spinning fast on the black ice, there is no time and no pain, black ice, the car spun on black ice, he was driving fast, driving fast because he was late and so when he hit the black ice the car spun and then—

The sound of waves breaking on the rocks drew me out of my frantic, insistent memories. It was rare to hear waves in the protected interior harbor.

They were pounding in the way they did out on the breakwater, thundering.

I turned to face the water.

The bay was flat and the children ran across the bobbing traps and I could find no source of the sound of the angry water at all.

The sounds grew louder. Smashing waves underscored by a high, whistling wind and the snapping of a flag. Something creaked and then tore, an awful rasping of sheared wood, and I looked down at the dock expecting to see a pylon collapsing, the whole dock and wharf tumbling into the bay.

Instead there was just sunlight and blue sky and solid wood. Green grass unruffled by wind. But the wind *sound* was ferocious, terrifying, a rising gale, and I was facing into it, I was sure of that; I was facing directly into the storm and there seemed no possible way that the reality of the soundscape wouldn't be joined soon by the elements.

I lifted my hand as if to ward off the oncoming wind.

The last thing I saw clearly was the ghastly purple wound that laced across my palm.

15

"Buddy! Hey, pal, you okay? *Somebody call an ambulance!*"

I blinked. Saw bright blue sky, cloudless and endless. A shadow crossed the sky then. A face took shape, fleshy and sunburned and staring down at me with concern.

The sound of the storm was gone.

I was on my back in the grass of the harbor park and a small group had gathered around me, all of them staring down with troubled eyes. One woman had a phone to her ear.

"I'm calling," she said.

"No, no," I said, sitting up fast. "I'm good. I'm fine. Just . . ."

"Pal, you need to lie down," the sunburned man told me. "You dropped *hard*. Let's just hang out and wait for an ambulance, okay?"

"No," I insisted, struggling upright and managing to stay on my feet as a wave of dizziness smacked me. "I'm fine, really. It's my blood sugar."

Someone murmured the word *diabetic* and everyone seemed relieved. The woman who had the phone to her ear lowered it and fished around in her purse and found a chocolate in foil wrapping and pressed it into my palm—and right against the cut from the lightbulb.

The electric pain actually helped clear my head, though. I thanked her and tore the foil open and ate the candy while the onlookers watched. It was a York peppermint patty. The chocolate had melted and left a dark smear across my fingertips that seemed to match the purple glue over my cut.

"That'll do the trick," I said. "Thank you."

"You sure you don't need someone to look you over?" my sunburned rescuer said. "Man, you dropped like a sniper had taken you down."

"I'm fine," I assured him, and I thanked them all for their concern again and then pushed my way through the crowd and up the hill. My legs weren't steady yet, but I wanted to be somewhere cool and dark and isolated.

You need to verify your own memory, Renee had said.

No. I did not.

By the time I made it back to my truck, I was sweating and exhausted and felt nauseated, the taste of the peppermint and chocolate a sickly-sweet mixture on my tongue. I sat in the driver's seat with the air-conditioning on and the vents angled at my face and closed my eyes and waited for the nausea to pass and my heartbeat to steady. Instead, it seemed to both race and waver, a terrifying sensation. My breath caught and I gasped and then seemed to draw in too much air, like trying to take a breath underwater.

Call 911. You need an ambulance.

I fumbled my phone out, had it in my hand when it vibrated with a notification. The Clarity app: *Your Breath Is Your Body; Thirty Seconds to Calm.*

There was a "play" button waiting below it. Absolutely nothing about the Clarity app should have appealed to me right then, but as my heart surged and skittered and my breath came in paltry wheezes or overwhelming gusts, I was suddenly ready to try.

Thirty seconds. If it didn't work, an ambulance. I had thirty seconds. And the app was right—my breath was my body. If I could calm the one, I'd calm the other.

I fitted my AirPods in my ears with clammy, trembling fingers and pressed "play."

No voice this time. No song. Just the sound of running water. Creek noise, a gentle stream over tumbled rocks.

"*Close your eyes,*" a male voice intoned.

I did.

"*Breathe,*" he told me.

I did.

In three seconds, hold two, out four. Focusing on the exhalation. Imagining the exhalation as a powerful wind blowing filthy dust clear of my lungs, my body, my mind. The voice told me to focus on that visual; to see the cleansing, *feel* the cleansing.

Damned if it didn't work, too. By the time the vocal prompts ceased and it was just the sound of water streaming over stones, my heartbeat was steady and my breath came smoothly, filling my lungs.

I sat there for a long time listening to the water sounds and breathing deeply and waiting for another attack.

Nothing happened. I felt more than steadied; I felt restored. Strong of body and clear of mind. I took the AirPods out with a vague regret, almost curious to see how much further they could take me. That simple breathing exercise had hit me like an EpiPen, a shock of salvation.

I put the truck into gear, pulled away from the curb, and headed out of town, toward Rosewater. I was physically calm and no longer felt rattled mentally, either. Renee's stunning claim about my father's death wasn't disturbing; it was a problem to be solved, nothing more. I didn't *need* to verify anything about my father's death. I knew that. But that didn't mean that I wouldn't. Renee Holland had wanted to unsettle me—no, *scare* me—and while I didn't understand that in the least and couldn't begin to grasp the motivation behind it, I was determined to show her that it wouldn't be that easy.

Paul Nicholas Bishop had died alone on I-295 just north of Portland on a grim February day in the winter of my sixteenth year, and I knew that as well as I knew anything about my life.

Just as Renee had said, there would be police reports.

I would find them, and I would read them, and then I'd show up at her strange office in the old mill and ask what the point of that little game had been.

The truth was nothing to fear.

PART TWO

BURN THE NIGHT

16

PORTLAND PRESS HERALD

FEBRUARY 16, 2009

FALMOUTH—A Camden man was killed late Sunday afternoon in a single-car accident on I-295 that police blamed on black ice.

Paul Bishop, 49, was the only fatality. He was a passenger. The driver, a minor who was not identified, was treated and released from the Maine Medical Center.

The crash happened on the southbound lanes of the interstate just after 4 p.m. After the driver of the 2000 Subaru Forester lost control on the ice, the vehicle struck a guardrail and overturned several times, according to Maine State Police.

Police said they do not believe there were any influencing factors in the crash beyond weather.

Bishop is the 21st person to die on Maine roads this year.

FALMOUTH—Paul N. Bishop, 49, of Camden, was killed in an accident on I-295 just north of Portland. Bishop was the passenger in a 2000 Subaru Forester that spun on black ice just after sunset on Sunday evening. Witnesses said the vehicle made a full 360-degree spin before striking a guardrail, going airborne, and overturning on a snow-covered embankment on the western side of the interstate. Maine State Police and paramedics responded to the wreck scene within minutes, but Bishop was pronounced dead at the scene.

Lt. Rick Barra of the Maine State Police said that Bishop, who was not wearing a seatbelt, had been ejected from the vehicle. The driver, a minor who Barra said was a relative of the victim and possessed a valid driver's license, was wearing a seatbelt and was reportedly uninjured. Barra said a chemical test was administered as a matter of protocol but that the driver was not considered at-fault in the accident.

"It's just a tragic thing," Barra said. "This time of year, and that time of day, conditions that had appeared to be safe took a quick, bad turn. That's the risk with black ice. A few minutes earlier, the sun was out, and we had melting, but it was damp pavement, not ice. You get that moment when the sun goes down and the temperature drops and traction can change in a hurry. We just ask all Mainers to be alert to those changing conditions. It can happen fast."

17

I read each story four times, as if the words might change. They didn't.

I closed the laptop and took a beer out of the refrigerator and walked down to the dock. There was no chair left to sit on, so I sat on the dock with my feet hanging off the edge and I drank the beer and stared across the water. The autumn trees were taking color and in a few weeks the place would be lit up brilliantly and then the color would be gone, the skeletal limbs of winter exposed. I watched the trees brighten and then darken while the sun sank behind the western mountains and blackness enveloped the water and finally took me with it.

When I tried to set the beer down on the dock, I dropped the can into the pond because my hand was shaking. I fished it out, the cold water pleasantly numbing on my wounded palm, and tossed the can up onto the dock boards and stared into the darkness and waited for a memory to rise. I *worked* at it, like a problem that could be solved through sheer effort.

I envisioned the highway and the setting sun

and a guardrail protecting a snow-covered embankment. I thought of our car, that red Forester with its trusty all-wheel drive, a vehicle my parents had selected specifically because of its foul-weather handling and their soon-to-be-sixteen-year-old son. They'd balanced the statistical danger of the latter with the statistical safety of the former.

I remembered that car.

I did *not* remember that stretch of highway in Falmouth or the colored lights of emergency vehicles or a police lieutenant named Barra. I did not remember ever seeing my father without a seat belt on.

I also did not remember my mother breaking the news of the accident to me.

My throat was dry and I wanted another beer but I didn't trust my legs to carry me back down the dock and up to the camp, so I just sat there, breathing in the night and wondering about the past. Finally, I took out my phone and called Renee Holland. She answered swiftly, but when she said hello her voice was soft and tentative, an unspoken question in the word.

For a long moment, I thought that I would not be able to find my own voice.

"You always knew?" I said at last.

She paused for nearly as long as I had. "Yes," she said.

I felt like the emperor wearing his new clothes then, exposed and ridiculous, the only man in town who doesn't understand that he's the joke.

"If lots of people knew, they would've confronted me about that," I said. "Why didn't they? Was I known around town as the crazy kid, or . . ."

"I wouldn't say *lots* of people knew. Also, she made you move so quickly that it didn't really have a chance to develop into a conversation. You were gone fast. Out of Camden and in Hammel."

"She was scared of the long drives," I said. "If that was true. Now I don't know."

"It was probably part of the reason, at least," Renee said, but I felt as if she was giving my mother more credit than was deserved.

"And I was the rest of the reason."

"Yes."

"Changing my memory. *Erasing* my memory."

She was quiet.

"Is that why we drifted apart?" I said. "You and me, I mean. Was it because you saw what was happening to me and were freaked out by it, or scared by it?"

"No," she said. "I was freaked out by it, yes, but mostly because I helped."

"What?"

She inhaled sharply. "It's a lot, Nick. I'd like it to be in person."

"Will you tell me how she did it?"

"I can tell you what I *understand* of it, at least. That's all I can promise."

I told her that was just fine. It was already more than I had.

"I'll come down tomorrow," she said. "It should be face-to-face, and it shouldn't be anywhere Bryce can see us."

"Okay."

"Are you all right, Nick?" she asked gently. "I can only imagine, but it has to be overwhelming."

"I'm fine," I said, but then I laughed. Or tried to laugh; what came out was closer to a sob. I took a breath. "I'm a little rattled, Renee. But I'll be okay. I appreciate what you told me already. What I don't understand is how nobody else in my life ever let me know."

"We'll talk tomorrow," she said. "And, Nick? Please delete that app."

"Okay," I said, and I couldn't have had less interest in the app. My imploding personal history was plenty distracting.

Renee promised to come down in the morning, and then we hung up and the phone screen darkened and then it was just me and the silent pond again. I waited there for a few minutes, until a loon cried, a single, solitary call. It seemed like a signal to go back inside. I left the dock and walked back to the camp. I walked slowly. It was dark and hard to see what was underfoot and ahead.

The phone buzzed. A notification from Clarity.

A new Sleep Song is available! was announced in cheerful font, with graphics of exploding fireworks that turned into twinkling stars against a night sky.

I put the phone in the nightstand drawer so I wouldn't have to see it.

I slept with the kitchen light on that night. Laugh if you want. When I woke to the sound of the loon's call, though, it was good to be able to see the outline of the cabin around me, to know immediately where I was.

Better than blackness, anyhow.

18

The wind rose overnight and by dawn it was gusting hard out of the northwest and had scoured the clouds away, leaving a crystalline blue sky and whitecapped water.

I spent the early hours sitting on the dock, idle and uneasy, waiting for Renee to call or arrive, and trying unsuccessfully to avoid paranoid-reporter thoughts, planning my investigation into my father's death step by step. It was a death that I'd never pondered investigating before, because what was there to learn? I'd spent my whole life looking deeply into other people's stories, but I had no need to question my own. I knew how my dad had died. You don't verify something you know.

It's a scary idea to think that you might need to.

I would need to speak with the officers who'd responded, would need to do everything possible to replace fiction with fact, building a narrative of truth, piece by piece, reporting. A familiar exercise. The only difference was that it was now my own story.

My own identity.

As I drank coffee and stared across the pond, I saw the telltale ripples of fish striking in the protected shallows of the cove that ran alongside the rock just offshore. Balance Rock to my mother, but Big Bass Rock to my father. By the time the coffee was gone and I'd checked my phone for the fifteenth time, I gave up and returned to my truck and found my fly rod. I was in search of distraction more than fish.

I tied on a dry fly that I hadn't used in years, one that my father had fished constantly on our weekends at Rosewater. I no longer even remembered the real name of the fly, in fact; to me it was simply Bishop's Lunch Money. My dad's nickname for it.

A young maple crowded what had once been my favorite casting spot in the cove, so I took off my shoes and rolled up my pants and waded out a few steps. The water was warmer than the air temperature and so clear that I could see the darting shadows of fish. I could not see the submerged stump alongside Balance Rock, but I knew it was there.

I got a hit on my first cast but missed the fish. Another chance on my fourth, this one not wasted. I caught a second. A third. No trophies but bass with some shoulders to them, breaking the water with furious flips. I was catching and releasing, moving quickly, heartbeat speeding with the sacred sensation of a live fish on a light rod.

My father and I had always had good days out here. I'd light a fire on the bank and we'd panfry the fish or, when my dad was particularly motivated, season them and wrap them with vegetables in aluminum foil and bake them in the coals. There'd been no point to the shore meals, of course; there was a fully equipped kitchen just a few paces away.

Or maybe that had been the point. We didn't go on weeklong fishing trips together, never did the big drive north or flight west or anything, so those shore lunches had been an attempt to make it feel like more of a wilderness experience than it was. Down here below the rock and facing across the cove, you saw nothing but pines and sky. If you put your back to the camp, you could imagine it was just the two of you.

My father's profession was computer engineering. He provided tech support for large mainframe computers. I hadn't understood much of it as a kid and still didn't as a grown man, but any school my mother went to had a job for my father. Every college was caught up in the computer arms race back then—and I suppose is now and will be. He seemed to enjoy the work. He was from Boston, a city kid, and the pond in Maine was as wild as any country he'd ever see. He always seemed to be dreaming of trips he wouldn't take. He'd had a fascination with maps—globes, atlases, topos, you name it—and sometimes I'd find little notations made on maps of distant lands he had never visited and never would. There was a wanderlust beneath his surface contentment, and I'd thought about that when I flew into a forward air base in a mountain range that I'd only recently learned existed. My dad would have been interested in those trips, I think. He'd have enjoyed hearing about those places.

Another bass, much larger, hammered the Bishop's Lunch Money, the reel screamed, the water threw glistening spray as the fish broke water and shook. I had a smile on my face for the first time in many hours as I reeled it in, ignoring the throb that the butt of the rod put through my wounded hand. I'd just released the fish and was watching it vanish into the thin reeds when Renee spoke from behind me.

"Try into the shadows," she said.

I hadn't heard her car, hadn't heard any sound of her arrival until she spoke, and it startled me enough that I jumped a little, the way I had when she arrived at the harbor and whispered in my ear. That annoyed me, so I spoke without turning.

"They're striking in the sun over that stump, actually."

"Try farther into the shadows," she insisted.

It felt like a taunt. I decided to put a fly out there on the dark water where she thought the big fish waited and prove her wrong. I kept my back to her, executed a false cast to shed water from the fly, then double hauled and cast, driving the power from hip and shoulder, like throwing a punch.

The line buzzed across the cove, and I was pleased by the nice, flat path it carved through the air, no arcing excess, everything about the cast a model of efficiency. The fly settled onto the surface softly. Bishop's Lunch Money floated in the shadowed water, waiting for a strike.

The water was flat. I twitched the line, making the fly jitter across the surface. Nothing.

"You're not much of a fishing guide," I said, and finally turned to Renee.

She wasn't there. The rock was empty.

I twisted, scanning the pines, the camp, the traces of the gravel drive that showed through the trees. Nothing. I pivoted back, looked at the dock protruding out into Rosewater Pond. Empty.

"Renee?"

Silence except for the shivering limbs above me.

"Renee."

Silence.

The warm water around my feet and calves was contrasted against the chill of that pushing breeze now—an odd sensation, as if I was divided between worlds. I reeled the fly all the way back in, linked the hook to the metal ring at the base of the rod, and then set the rod down on the bank beside my shoes. I waded out of the water and unrolled my pants but left my shoes where they were, pine needles clinging to my damp bare feet as I walked up the bank and onto the rock and the full camp came into view.

There was no one in sight. The driveway was empty except for my Ranger, and the road up the hill was quiet. Out on the far side of the pond, a kayaker and a man on a paddleboard were visible.

Nobody was close enough to have been heard.

Try into the shadows, the voice had said. Renee's voice. Hadn't it been? I'd been so sure . . .

I sat down on the rock, then slid on my ass, scooting like a child who hasn't learned to walk, until I was in a patch of sunlight. I felt better out there in the sun. Not great, not hardly, but better.

Try into the shadows. Try farther into the shadows.

The voice . . . the *voice* had been real.

I sat on the rock in the sun and told myself that I was not losing my mind. I told myself that everyone has odd episodes following a period of real trauma, and what I'd learned last night certainly qualified as trauma. I'd seen my mother again. I'd suffered an injury. I'd learned about my father's death and my mother's work erasing my memory. And, oh, yeah, I'd also lost my job and had no idea of what came next. Imagining a voice guiding my fishing efforts was the least disconcerting of my troubles. I just wished the voice had a better knack for finding fish.

I made myself smile at that. It was a half-assed attempt, but it helped. Whistling past the grave-yard, maybe, but doesn't the whistling actually help? I think it does.

The sun on the rock helped, too, the blue of the sky and the glitter and glimmer of the bright water.

Bob Beauchamp was splitting wood—he always seemed to be splitting wood—and the steady *thunk, thwack* was a rhythmic soundtrack. I scanned the pond, looking for my nighttime companions, the loons. I didn't see any. The nest was probably across the pond, and once dusk settled they grew bolder, venturing farther. So many creatures gain courage in the dark.

"Didn't expect to find you fishing."

The woman's voice came from behind me again. I almost didn't turn. I thought that if I turned around and saw no one standing there, I would begin to scream and maybe not be able to stop.

I looked back eventually, though. At some point, we always do, even when we should know better.

17

Renee was standing on the rock.

"Hey," I said. "Good to see you."

There was such relief in my voice that she looked puzzled, and I laughed. The laugh was a sound that felt close to galloping away under its own power, like a horse that has thrown its rider.

"I'm glad," she said. "I wasn't sure, after everything I threw at you yesterday."

I started to get to my feet, then settled back down and waved her over. "Sit," I said. "It's the best place on the pond. And the warmest, today."

She walked down to where I sat in the square of sunlight. She moved gracefully over the steep, rough rock, with the surefooted stride of someone who'd hiked a lot of uneven ground.

"I'd offer you a chair," I said, "but I destroyed it."

"I arrived in the aftermath, yes. After seeing that, I'll trust the rock over your furniture."

I listened to her speak and I thought that the voice I'd heard in my head had been similar but a pitch lower, and with a quality that came out like a breath, like someone sharing a secret. It hadn't been Renee.

It hadn't been anyone, of course.

Just as she sat beside me, though, I had a flash of unease.

"How'd you know I'd been fishing?" I said.

"Huh?"

"I'm sitting here, looking at the pond. I'm not fishing. But you said that you didn't expect to find me fishing."

She stared at me for a beat and then pointed over my shoulder.

"Fly rod and shoes," she said. "You're barefoot. Perhaps I jumped to conclusions, but . . ."

I was embarrassed. "Good detective work. You passed the test."

"Great," she said, watching me with wariness. "You okay?"

"Yes. Yeah. The fishing . . . I, uh, had to kill time." I looked at her. "They're biting in close today. Not out farther. Not in the shadows."

Renee stared at me as if I'd spoken Greek. If the reference to casting into the shadows meant anything to her, she hid it completely.

"Okay. I'll keep that in mind if I come down to fish," she said. "But I didn't."

"Right. So . . ."

"So." She sighed and looked across the water at the camp that had once been her family's. She had sunglasses on and I couldn't read her eyes. "The accident story was all new to you. Really and truly new."

"Yes."

She shook her head slightly. "I was never convinced it would stick. I mean, I saw it work, but there's short-term memory and there's long-term and I just could *not* believe it would last over the long haul. Then, yesterday, I looked into your eyes when we were down there at the harbor, and you were so deeply . . . *convicted*—I think that's the word. Deeper than convinced, more personal."

"We're talking about my dad's death, and my sanity. Yes, it struck a deep chord."

"We weren't talking about your sanity. Don't let yourself go there. There's nothing wrong with your mind, Nick. There never was."

"Then how did this happen?"

She gave a sad laugh. "I wish I could tell you to just ask your mother."

Renee and my mother had gotten along well. Renee had a sense of humor that skewed smart and witty and over the heads of most of her peers. My mother got her. I didn't know—or remember, at least—if they'd had any communication outside of my presence.

"She's my professional north star," Renee said, as if reading my thoughts. "Or she's the shadow over my life. I really am not sure."

"Explain that."

She let out a breath. Gathered herself. "I had

an entire vision for my life when I was eighteen. Everyone does at that age, right?"

"I don't think so, actually. You were a bit ahead of the rest of us."

She shrugged. "Fine. I thought I knew how things would go. At the top of that list was leaving Maine. And yet here I am. I think, after that summer, I always knew I'd come back."

"What summer?"

She turned to face me. The wind fanned the dark red hair out over her fleece, and some of it floated above her shoulder, trapped in a cloud of static electricity.

"The summer we remade your memories," she said.

"'We.' As in, you and—"

"Alice," she said. "Your mother. Yes."

"You helped."

She nodded. "Signed a waiver, even. She was very pleased that I was already eighteen."

"Wonderful. I'm glad you didn't have any liability for playing with my mind."

She didn't react.

"It worked," she said. "And I saw it work, and then fall came and I went off to school. but it was all meaningless after that. Directionless. I wanted to come back and work with her again. I'd seen something that mattered. The impossible made possible."

She leaned toward me. "We fixed you," she

whispered. "Together. We just"—she snapped her fingers—"fixed you."

"*How?* The nuts and bolts of this approach are fairly important to me, as you might have guessed."

"Do you know who Elizabeth Loftus is?"

The name was familiar, but it took me a moment.

"Memory research," I said. "She was an early critic of the whole idea of recovered memories. Defense attorneys loved her, but a lot of people did not. *Do* not. Mom appreciated her research but not her approach to the media. Or hunger for media, whatever you want to call it."

Renee nodded. "One of the most famous experiments Elizabeth Loftus conducted was the implanted memory of being lost in a mall as a child. Do you remember hearing about that one?"

I shook my head.

"Okay. The gist is that she was able to demonstrate an astonishing success rate of convincing her subjects to believe that they'd had this traumatic experience of being lost in a shopping mall when they were very young. They would recall details of it—precisely, emphatically, passionately. But the experience had never occurred. It was offered first as a suggestion, using leading questions, and then it was reinforced with detail, and then she saw something extraordinary happen, something that changed memory research forever: the subjects took over the narrative. Creation of the false memory ceased to belong to Loftus and her team, and it became the creation of the subjects." She paused, studied me. "And they believed it. Deeply."

"I don't have a false memory of the accident," I said. "I *thought* that I did, but I really just remember the summary: late for a flight, black ice, all that. But I can't say anything has *replaced* the rest. I do not have any memory of hearing the news, for example. The funeral is the first thing I can recall with clarity."

"Your mother didn't want to create a false memory. She had ethical concerns with that."

I had to laugh. It was such an absurd qualification. "She was more comfortable with the idea of simply wiping the slate clean?"

"Yes."

"She found a way to erase my memory of the wreck. You really want me to believe that."

"I think you already do."

I wanted to object, but how could I? Suspension of disbelief occurs pretty damn fast when the impossible has happened to you.

I sat and felt the wind on my face and pictured my father casting a Bishop's Lunch Money out across the pond and then pictured his funeral.

"She just did this for the opportunity of it," I said. "Took his death and said, 'Well, we can't waste this.'"

"I wouldn't say that."

"It's exactly what you described: an opportunity to test a few theories arrived in her own house and she couldn't pass it up."

"That's too harsh, Nick. Imagine it from her per-spective: her son was suffering acute PTSD, her husband had just died, she was alone, every night she was awakened by her only child having horrific nightmares, and—"

"Having what?"

"Nightmares."

"No. I don't dream. I never have."

Her expression gave me her answer: just like the accident, my perception of myself wasn't the truth.

Once upon a time, Nick Bishop had dreamed.

"How did she do it?" I asked.

Renee exhaled as if grateful for the acceptance the phrasing suggested.

"It began the night of the accident, although it was a few years before she admitted that detail to me. It was in the early days of propranolol study. She dosed you heavily with that and did so almost immediately."

"What is propranolol?" I asked, although it sounded familiar.

"A beta-blocker. It calms the adrenal response. There's a great deal of excitement about its poten-tial for people who suffer from PTSD. The idea is that it diminishes the emotional impact of a trau-matic memory, and thus the staying power of the memory."

"I've written about it," I said, realizing now why the name had sounded familiar. "In a piece about vets from Afghanistan and Iraq."

She nodded. "That would be the focus group, sure."

"But propranolol doesn't *erase* the memory."

"No. For that, Alice—your mom, sorry—relied more on the ideas that started with Loftus's research: suggestion, implication, and reinforcement."

"What *suggestion* was made?"

"The suggestion that reality was just a nightmare. Your real nightmares were like terrible, warped flashbacks: you were always behind the wheel again. And in these recurring nightmares, you *dreamed* that you'd been at the wheel. Never mind that the dream was a mirror of reality; it was still a dream. Do you follow? Every time you slept, you descended back into a nightmare version of the memory. Your mother's contribution was to tell you that you were confusing nightmares and reality."

She paused, and her lips worked for a moment before the next words came. "And *my* contribution was to reinforce the narrative whenever you questioned it. When you brought up the wreck, I was supposed to say things like 'I can't believe any dream is that vivid. I can't believe you really feel like you were driving the car.' But I would always come back to the idea that you were remembering a dream."

"That couldn't have worked."

Her lip curled in a half smile. "Then tell me about the drive, Nick. Tell me about the wreck."

I couldn't, of course. That well was dry.

"It's not right," I said. "Ethically, it's not right. Memory is identity. Unwinding one destroys the other."

"Imagine the assault victim who became agoraphobic, or the witness to a tragedy who has become an addict, or the soldier who can't leave the war behind. Imagine those people who want—*need*— nothing more than relief from a traumatic memory."

I gave that a grudging nod. "I get that as an intellectually appealing concept, but there's a difference between seeking a therapy out and being subjected to it unwittingly."

"Agreed. How many people would pay for the chance to remove a traumatic memory, though?"

"Ah," I said. "Here I am stuck on the moral and ethical questions, and missing the capitalist one. How foolish of me."

I thought of Renee—young Renee, blond Renee, best-friend Renee—and of my mother conspiring against me, the two people I would have trusted more than anyone alive at that point, and felt not just angry but disgusted. Revolted.

"You were eager to give it a shot," I said. "Even though you were my friend."

"Absolutely," she said without hesitation, and when I looked at her, she leaned closer again and put her hand on my leg. "You were coming apart, Nick. You'd gone through this awful thing and your dad was dead, and I couldn't get you out of the tailspin. From my perspective, it was almost like you'd died in the wreck, too. You just shut off. Built walls. Wouldn't engage with anyone. It was awful. And then your mom told me about the nightmares, the way you'd wake up screaming and soaked in sweat . . . I would've done anything to help you. Your mom was a genius, too. Everyone knew that. She was an adult and she was a professional and she was your fucking *mother* and so I trusted her!"

Her voice had risen to a shout. I could feel her weight pressing down on my leg now, but I didn't look at her hand, just stared back into her face. She was, I realized, on the verge of tears.

"We fixed you," she said. "Music helped. Do you remember how much music we listened to? Of course you do; it's almost the first thing you said when you saw me the other day."

She wasn't wrong. I saw her and I remembered music.

"I remember going for runs and listening to bad rap and you talking," I said. "You were always talking. But that was just your personality."

She smiled sadly. "Actually, it wasn't. I was a painfully shy kid, Nick. Headphones on, nose in a book. When you went silent, I kept talking, because that was my role, my job. You were a shell for a while, and then you came back inside the shell, and then you just . . . were you again."

"Only without a memory of the accident."

She nodded.

"And your job was to reinforce that."

"Correct. Mostly we were just hanging out, bull-shitting about whatever I could get you to talk about. But if you mentioned the accident, I would say, 'That was one fucked-up dream.' Then move you on as quickly as possible. You wouldn't believe how many times it happened. You'd mention it, I'd say, 'Crazy dream. Let's go for a run,' or 'Check out this track,' or whatever. And you'd kind of trance out to the music and we'd eventually move on in conversation. After enough weeks like that, you started to volunteer that the dreams were just that—dreams."

"You're saying my brain was destroyed by Tupac and Jay-Z," I said. "Dan Quayle was right the whole time."

She laughed so delightedly and authentically that I had to join her. We laughed together, sitting there on the rock, and then she fell back so she was stretched out, supine in the sun, and it took me a few seconds to realize she'd started to cry.

I didn't say anything. Didn't offer any comfort. I wasn't sure she deserved it. I just knew that it had felt awfully damn good to laugh at the darkness for a moment there—and that I was very scared.

When Renee stopped crying, she didn't sit up, just lay on the rock with her face to the sky.

"You lost the bad dreams completely?" she asked. "You've never had nightmares again?"

"No," I said emphatically. "I lost *dreams*, Renee.

As far as I know—knew, rather—I never had them. But I certainly don't anymore." I paused. "Until the other night, of course. That broke the streak. With a bang, I might add."

"It was that vivid?"

"I saw a dead woman who whispered in my ear. It was vivid, yeah." I looked at my palm, the purple gash a testament to just how damn vivid the dream had been. "How was the initial *suggestion* given to me?"

"Audio cues. You lived with headphones on during that time. Your mother seized the opportunity. She gave you music. Told you it would play calming sounds, white noise, that sort of thing. Help you sleep. And it did—until you slept deeply enough. Then the real cues began. It was an idea she'd been pursuing for years but hadn't yet put into practice. Sounds beneath the music, repetitive cues. All designed to shape the dreams."

"You just described Clarity," I said. "You just described your own damn program."

"*Her* program," Renee said. "I don't think she ever intended for it to end up as the basis for what Bryce wants to do with it, but, ultimately, all things Clarity lead back to Alice Bishop. Back to you."

I looked at my palm, traced the wound with a fingertip, and thought of the dead woman's lips against my ear.

"Tell me the rest, Renee. Tell me how we ended up here together, and why I'm dreaming again."

20

By the fall, when Renee returned to Hammel's campus and I started my senior year of high school in a new school, where there was no one around who could correct my revised reality, she was less enthusiastic about the merits of memory tampering. She saw the benefits but she felt the losses. The risks. On the one hand, there were no more nightmares for Nick Bishop. He laughed easily and talked happily and generally was restored to a pre-accident version of himself. But to Renee Holland, the restoration became more eerie than exciting.

"I was just a kid, still making my way through intro classes, and now there was this world-renowned professor with whom I shared a secret," she said. "It became more than I could handle. I started looking to transfer. I didn't talk to your mom about it. I told my parents it was all about needing to get away from home, and that made sense to them, because I was one of the few kids from my class who went to Hammel. So everything was normal on the surface when I transferred to Indiana that winter."

"But in reality," I said, "you wanted to get away from the Bishop family."

She didn't deny that.

Indiana undergrad had led to grad school in Chicago, and then she'd taken a job there. She thought about my mother often but didn't reach out to her. Thought about me often, she said, but still didn't reach out. Time passed and the summer of mind games receded. Her own parents had moved, tired of the Maine winters. Only Renee's sister, Ashley, remained in Maine. I barely remembered Ashley. She'd been maybe ten years old when I'd met Renee, and I'd regarded her as a minor annoyance. She'd been a reader, I remembered that. Quiet and always with a book. Easy to overlook when you're sixteen and infatuated with her older sister.

"Home was gone," Renee said. "It's a strange thing, how your relationship with your parents changes when they move. You grew up moving around a lot, but I'd only known Hammel as a home. Then I was gone, and they were gone, and suddenly I was in a period where I . . . needed to go home. It was that simple."

I looked at her and she nodded as if I'd voiced a question.

"Bad relationship, bad choices, bad circumstances, bad lots of things," she said. "Isn't that how it goes? The first visible problem usually isn't the only one. Everything's connected. I was in a bad place, and I wanted to go home. Home was gone except for the town and Ashley. She was in college then. Those two things—Ashley and the town—they were enough. I came back. As if I didn't know what I really wanted."

What she really wanted, of course, was a taste of that unique magic she'd seen deployed on me in the summer after my father's death. Trauma not just diminished but destroyed.

"The guy I'd been with was a violent prick," she told me, "and even after I got out of the relationship, even after the charges were filed and the courtroom process was done, what do you think was left?"

"The trauma."

"There you go. This piece-of-shit asshole was gone from my life and yet still had a hold on it. Because you can remove the man but not the memories. I was sleeping with a knife next to the bed when I slept at all. To get that far, I was taking more Ambien than was healthy. I'd wake up groggy and sick and have to fight through my mornings, then come home and do it all over again. The asshole still had control over me, even though he was gone. I couldn't stand that thought. And people were advocating therapy, you know, conventional approaches, but what I wanted was for him to be *gone*. As if he'd never existed."

What she wanted, in other words, was the Nick Bishop treatment. So she came east, came home. Saw her sister, saw my mother. Made her request.

"She wouldn't do it," Renee said. "Wouldn't even consider it. By then, she was really regretting the scope of impact her work had on you, if not the result."

But never chose to mention that to me, I thought. I stayed silent, though. It was Renee's story now.

"What she *would* do," Renee continued, "was put me through the paces of the program she was working on. She gave me this set of audio prompts, ocean sounds, and breathing exercises. Not the real deal, the fix I wanted. But I tried it. One night, when I was looking at that Ambien bottle and the knife on the nightstand, I decided, *What is there to lose from trying Alice's toned-down approach?*"

"And?"

"It was like a gift from heaven. I couldn't buy into it at the start, because it was just breathing and listening and anyone could do that, right? Simple sounds, simple breaths. Generic. But somewhere in the middle, I just . . . drifted away. Up and away. Up above the pain and the fear and everything else that had infected my life. I kept the memories, though. That's the difference. The same ideas that she'd used with you, only tempered, dulled down. Targeted."

"From the atomic bomb to the cruise missile."

"One hell of a missile," she said softly. "I thought her product, when it was ready to distribute, would save lives. I still do think that, but . . . but a lot has happened now."

"When did you leave my mom to work for Clarity?"

"Never."

"Pat Ryan told me you were working for the school," I said. "Until Bryce made his offer."

"Not true," she said. "It would have seemed that way to someone like Pat, who's not really in the weeds of academia, but I wasn't employed by Hammel. I had an office there but it was all grant funded. Clarity is your mother's research, with Bryce's tech, and Marilyn's funding."

"How'd my mother cross paths with them?"

Renee pointed across the pond.

I followed her extended finger out across cove to where her family's camp had been and there on the other side of it stood the Gatsby House. The massive, postmodern house with all the glass, the monstrosity that didn't fit with the tone of Rosewater.

"The Lermonds are Gatsby. You've got to be kidding me."

She frowned. "What does that mean?"

"My dad's nickname for it. No one was ever there. You're telling me Bryce's family owned that place?"

"Sure. And you were right, no one was ever there. They bought another place out at Biddeford Pool, and oceanfront trumps pond front. This was her family's place, and I don't think her husband ever cared for it. But this is how she knew your mother."

"What did the husband do?"

"Military. West Point guy. If he was ever up at

that house, I don't remember him. She'd come by, but only rarely."

"How did I not know this?"

"Because the only person you ever saw there was Bobby Beauchamp cutting the grass, probably."

It still felt unsettling. The big empty house, looming and watchful, reminded me of the mill at the heart of town—outsized and empty and yet somehow still the nerve center.

"Marilyn Lermond bankrolled my mom's work?"

"Yes. And she sold me on joining the team by telling me that they were continuing your mother's research. Bryce was working on the coding side then. That was the first time I'd even heard of the idea of an app. Marilyn assured me it was going to be cutting-edge. Remember when you told Bryce that the idea of the app felt old, familiar? That's true." She bit her lower lip and her eyes narrowed. "But what I'd seen your mom do? *That* was definitely cutting-edge."

"Erasing memories? Indeed."

She looked up, eyes still narrowed, face intense. "It had been a decade, Nick. I knew you were alive and well. Shit, they nominated you for a Pulitzer."

"Submitted my work for one. Very different."

She waved me off. "Whatever—you were *thriving* and that fascinated me. Because it suggested your mother had been right all along. She'd taken this trauma that threatened to break you and she had removed it and the result was a thriving life."

And a dreamless one, I thought but didn't say. I wasn't sure if she would see any price to that. I never had. Not until today, anyhow.

"Then I got my taste," she continued. "I got to keep my memories. The pain from them, though?" She made a gesture like turning down a volume knob. "*That* is what excited your mother. She wanted your results without your losses."

"My losses," I echoed, thinking of the way I'd felt reading those reports of the car accident that had taken my father's life.

"It was going somewhere good," Renee said. "I don't blame you for thinking otherwise, but it really was going somewhere good. I was all in. I brought my sister in, even. She graduated and took a job with us and we were working together and it was all trending the right way. Then Marilyn died. No real surprise; she'd been fighting cancer for a long time. Then your mother had her stroke. That one was a surprise. And suddenly it was Bryce's show, and . . ."

She trailed off.

"And it's not going anywhere good now?" I asked.

For a long time, she didn't speak. Finally, I broke the silence.

"In layman's terms, what are you pursuing with Clarity?"

"The impact of auditory cues on human memory. And I swear, Nick, it was a more effective antidepressant—and a less damaging one—than any pill on the market. But it was all done in the lab back then. Controlled, monitored. When Bryce took the reins, the research began to move toward the tech sector, where he had less regulation and more room to play."

I felt a shiver of revulsion. "Just what this toy needs."

"It *can* be helpful. I understand how you would feel—"

"No," I said. "You don't. It's like having a piece of your identity removed. But if you don't like the direction Clarity is headed, then why are you still there?"

Again she didn't answer right away.

"Something changed," I said. "You wouldn't have told me all this otherwise. A guilt complex only goes so far. What skin do you have in the game, Renee?"

When I looked back at her, she was smiling, but it was anything but pleasant. It was cold and hungry, a hunter's gleam upon spotting clear tracks in the snow. Fresh tracks.

"My sister," she said.

"Have you told Ashley about the summer of fun you and my mom had yet? Or do you want me to do that and let you off the hook?"

"No," she said. "I don't need you to let me off the hook with Ashley."

"What's her role, anyhow? Bryce didn't mention her during our interview."

"No," she said. "I noticed that, too."

"So what is her role?"

"You want to know her role?" She sounded amused in an awful way, like someone who knows the joke is on her and has no choice but to go along with the crowd. *Laugh it up, gang! We're all having fun!*

"Yeah," I said. "What does she do?"

"What does she do." She echoed me again, this time without the questioning tone. "She fills an urn. That's her role, Nick. She fills an urn. Part of one, anyhow. There wasn't much of her to go into it, so I can't imagine she takes up a lot of space."

21

"What happened?" I asked finally. It was a simple question and yet I hesitated to ask it. An honest answer to a simple question can cause complex pain.

"She killed herself," Renee said.

A two-word question and a three-word response built a total silence.

Like I said, complex pain.

I was readying to speak again when Renee got to her feet.

"I told Bryce I was running for coffee. It's been an hour. I've got to get back. And I think you've got more than enough to think about until we talk again, and I hope you'll be calling from Florida. Or anywhere else. Just not Hammel. There's nothing good for you here, Nick."

Her entire demeanor had shifted, gone shadowed and cold.

"I'm sorry about your sister," I said. "I know that sounds hollow, but I am."

Renee nodded absently. She was facing the pond

but I had the sense she wasn't seeing it. She was seeing her sister, probably.

"What happened to her?" I asked.

She didn't answer. I was about to ask again when she finally broke her silence.

"Delete that damn app," she said, and turned to walk away.

"Renee . . ." I rose and followed, the granite biting into my bare feet. "You believe that app could cause true harm?"

"I think it might, yes. Can it help someone? Yes. I've seen that. Could it be dangerous? Yes. I think so."

"Bryce doesn't agree, or Bryce doesn't care?"

She stopped walking. Extended her hand and wobbled it side to side.

"'Is it dangerous to *everyone*?' would be his question," she said. "But in this case it is about *you*. You're special; thanks to your mother, you've gone deeper into Clarity than anyone else. He knows this."

"He's just curious to see what happens when he pokes at my brain? A regular Dr. Mengele. He must have been delighted when I walked in that door."

She took off the sunglasses. I could see her eyes clearly now, that bright green.

"Nick," she said, "I think you need to consider the idea that your arrival here wasn't coincidence."

"It was, actually. I took a job. It came out of the clear blue, and I had time and needed the money.

Nobody even knew I was coming to town except for . . ."

When I didn't finish, she prodded. "Yes? Except for?"

"Pat," I said. "Pat Ryan."

"Was it a lot of money for an alumni magazine story?"

"Yeah."

"Thought so. And I'll make another guess: he demanded you do the reporting in person? Said you needed to have boots on the ground for this one?"

"Yeah."

She looked away from me again—was facing the pond with her face half-hidden in shadow when she said, "If I were you, I'd be very curious about the way that came to pass."

I said, "Pat Ryan."

"I'm just telling you to ask questions," she said. "I think you need to question everyone."

"That would include you, then."

"Obviously." She spoke without a hint of concern, then spread her hands as if to say *Fire away.* My mind wasn't on her, though. My mind was on the beer-soaked night at Riptides, Pat leaning across the booth and telling me that I didn't trust enough people. This coming from one of the few that I trusted.

"You're going to think of more questions," Renee said. "I'll answer what I can. I promise you that.

You don't have to believe the answers, but I hope I have a little credibility after this."

"What's the reciprocity?" I asked.

"Excuse me?"

"You've given me a hell of a lot of information. I'd love to believe it was all the product of the most altruistic intentions, but . . ."

She smiled the hunter's smile again. "You're quite the cynic."

"I'm quite the student of human nature."

"Ah. I see."

"You don't want anything?" I said. "Not looking for an ally?"

She put her sunglasses back on. "Take care, Nick. I'll be in touch."

She walked past the camp and up the drive. There she stopped and turned back, resting one slim hand on the tailgate of my truck. A simple silver bracelet slid down her wrist and made a clinking noise when it struck metal.

"You were very curious about two things yesterday," she said. "The name of the singer and the name of the song. Still curious about those even after all I've hit you with?"

"Yes."

She gazed at me in silence for a few seconds before she said, "Me, too. I don't know the name of the songs, and I'd love to find out. The singer, though? I can tell you her name."

"Let me get my notepad," I said. "Things have a

way of slipping my mind lately if I don't write them down."

She didn't smile. Even with the sunglasses on, I felt the coldness of her stare.

"I'll do the remembering for you on this one," she said. "The singer's name was Ashley Belle Holland."

Her sister. Her *dead* sister.

This time, I didn't even try to respond. She vanished from sight behind the pines, a car door opened and closed, the engine started, and she was gone.

22

A good reporter knows how to keep his emotional distance. You form relationships with sources, different levels of closeness, but you never give them one hundred percent of your faith. You also, most crucially, do not let anyone—a source or a stranger—bait you into an emotional response. Emotion is the enemy of objectivity. It's the very reason that memory researchers had such rich material to work with on studies of eyewitness accounts of traumatic events. The more emotionally charged the moment, the less objective one feels.

It's imperative to remember that when you're reporting. Shit goes down fast, threats are real, and everyone has a different version of the events.

Sit back, breathe, watch, listen, and take good notes.

I'd been good at that. Better than most. But it's hard to keep a cool objectivity when you're the subject of the story.

After Renee Holland left, I wanted to see my mother, confront her, challenge her with Renee's version of events, and hear what she had to say.

The day for that showdown had disappeared on the Maiden Cliff trail on Mount Megunticook, though. Whatever was left of my mother's ability to explain and defend had been lost out there, and wasn't coming back.

Grackles.

An impotent exchange of my authentic sense of betrayal and her nonsensical responses wasn't going to help anything. It would just hollow me out. Instead, I took refuge with the best of friends: my reporter's notebook.

For twenty minutes, I scribbled down notes and thoughts from the conversation with Renee. I wrote down questions she'd answered and questions she'd asked. The act of reporting, treating the situation like someone else's story rather than my own, calmed and focused me the way it always had. By the time I was done, I had my first task:

Find a way to record the song, I wrote. Step one. Step two? *What happened to Ashley Holland?*

Finding out what had happened to Ashley Holland took exactly one Google search. The algorithms know what we want: tragedy. There's a reason bloody stories dominate the box office and bestseller lists. We like the voyeuristic thrill of a good death story absorbed from a safe distance. Ashley's was a good one, if you'd never known her personally.

If you had, though, it turned your stomach.

She had walked off the roof of a building. I knew

the exact spot where her life had ended—the hand-laid brick sidewalk beneath Grossman Hall, the tallest building on the Hammel College campus. No one was sure how she'd gained access to the roof of the building, but security cameras offered an undeniable account of what happened next.

Ashley Belle Holland crossed the roof of Grossman Hall in a driving rain and then stood at the edge of the roof for more than eight minutes before she finally jumped. It was a seventy-six-foot drop to the bricks below.

She fills an urn . . . Part of one, anyhow. There wasn't much of her to go into it, so I can't imagine she takes up a lot of space.

I ran another Google search, looking to see if there were more stories on Ashley Holland's life or death, and the next one I found stopped me cold.

This one was accompanied by a photograph.

I probably wouldn't have recognized her. She'd grown into a tall blond beauty. But it wasn't the progression from child to woman that froze me.

Her face looked unmistakably, undeniably similar to the woman from my nightmare. The living embodiment. Emphasis on *living*.

You're just telling yourself that. Talking yourself into it.

Maybe. Maybe not. I zoomed in on the photo and then back out and when I did that I had a crystal clear memory of red lips against dead skin as she leaned toward me, wet hair dripping, and I shut my eyes and pushed away from the computer.

"Get it together, Bishop," I muttered, running a hand over my face. "Get it together."

There was no dead woman in the room now, and there hadn't been last night. Just dreams— nightmares—and I needed to get used to them. Everybody dreams. Including, evidently, Nick Bishop.

I went back to the computer. Read another half dozen stories about the suicide. There was nothing more to learn, though. No comments from family, no reference to Clarity or to the haunting songs she'd recorded. If what Renee had said about Clarity was true—and I believed that a lot of it was—the songs mattered greatly, and yet I'd already proven twice that I was incapable of staying awake

Or conscious? Was it really sleep?

while they played. I had no desire to listen to another round after hearing her warnings, but I needed to know what the hell was in those songs, and I thought that I needed to learn that quickly. I had a feeling that Bryce Lermond wasn't going to let that app sit on my phone forever.

I took out the phone. The app was still there, and when I opened it, Sleep Song #3 awaited. I tapped "play."

Headphones required, it said.

The headphone requirement wasn't something I'd seen before. If the Clarity app was capable of discerning between Bluetooth headphones and a

Bluetooth speaker, it would be well ahead of any similar application I'd ever seen.

I grabbed the truck keys and took the phone outside with me. The Ranger had Bluetooth. I made sure it was connected to the phone and then opened the Clarity app again.

Headphones required.

"I'll be damned," I said, both impressed and baffled by the app's ability to accept one Bluetooth device and block another. The only way you could listen to the sleep songs was to bring them as close to your brain as possible. Nestle them right into your ears. Maybe there was some neuroscience-backed argument for proximity of sound and effect of sound.

Or maybe they did not want these things to be recorded.

I went back into the house, opened an encrypted phone call application I'd used when reporting overseas, and called a man named Seth Logan. He was a former NSA contractor who now did private computer security work for Fortune 500 companies. I'd gotten to know him when he was still in government work, and he'd tipped me to a source who became the centerpiece of a series of stories I wrote about government-funded hacking "research" that had gotten a little far afield of its original purview. Those stories were some of the biggest in my career. It felt a world apart from why I was calling now.

Seth answered. He always answered when the

call came from an encrypted source, and never if it didn't.

"It's Nick Bishop," I said.

"Shit."

"That's the response I like to hear."

"What kind of trouble do you want help causing this time?"

"It was never trouble. It was muckraking."

"I still don't understand that term. Why does one rake the muck? Shouldn't you just search the muck?"

"Don't overthink it, just trust it. And good news—this time, I'm not calling for newspaper publication. I was laid off, in fact."

"Aw, man. I'm sorry." There was sincerity in his voice. "I'd wondered, actually. You'd been quiet, and I see all these stories about newsroom cuts . . ."

"Yeah. It's just as fun as it sounds. The reason I'm calling now isn't to bitch and moan, though. It's a tech question that is beyond my ability but might be straightforward to you."

"That doesn't narrow the possibilities. Shoot."

"Is there any possible way to intercept or interrupt a Bluetooth connection? What I mean is, to leave the connection open but—"

"Run a BIAS."

"Pardon?"

"Bluetooth impersonation attack." He said it without interest, and I could hear that he was eating. Crunching through potato chips, it sounded like. I'd already bored him.

"That's a new term to me," I said, "so it goes without saying that I probably don't understand how to *run* one."

"How many devices are involved?"

"Two. My phone and my headphones. I want to connect them to the computer, so I guess that makes three."

"Your own computer?"

"Yes."

"Your own headphones and phone?"

"Yes."

"You don't want to hack anyone's shit?" He sounded dismayed.

"No. Just record what's playing on my headphones, and play it through the computer speakers."

"Hell, just spoof the MAC, then."

"Spoof the mack? Sounds like a rapper from the eighties."

"M-A-C, wiseass."

"Ah. The device address." I felt proud of myself, knowing that much. The MAC address was a code that identified the equipment's network interface controller, like a fingerprint.

"Right," Seth said. "Very smart. So you know how to find the MAC address for a Bluetooth device, then?"

"Um . . . I think it was on the box, but I don't have—"

He sighed like a gale-force wind and said, "Just

open your computer and do what I tell you, okay?"

"Now we're talking."

I opened the computer and followed his steps. I located the MAC address that identified the headphones, then opened my computer's settings and changed its Bluetooth signature code to match the headphones. It took about three minutes, and when it was done, I'd effectively claimed the identity of my headphones and given it to my computer.

"There's not a way to prevent this?" I said, thinking that a lot of bad things could happen with this simple technique.

"Oh, they'll put out a fix at some point, but we'll have a different script to run by then. It's the dance, man. Security to the right, hackers to the left, swing your partner, now do it again!"

"Thanks. I owe you."

"I'll add it to your tab."

"Remember that I'm unemployed."

"Just my luck. It's hard to take a guy to small-claims court for failing to pay for illegal hacking services, too. Take care, okay, Bishop?"

"You, too, Seth. And thanks again."

I already had my digital recorder out, and I was tempted to play the sleep song and test the audio. I decided not to, though. I didn't want to miss anything due to the tinny quality of the laptop's speakers, and once a sleep song had been played, it disappeared. I'd have one shot to record.

It was time to buy some speakers.

23

A lot has changed about college towns over the years, but I think there's one constant: there tends to be a good bookstore and a good stereo supply store in each one. Even in the age of online-everything, these little places seem to survive.

Hammel was no exception. There was Bev's Books, owned by a guy named Vincent who always had the right recommendation for any reader, and there was Strawn's Stereo and Music, which outlasted fresh tech until old tech became cool again. The LP collection had never moved from the shelves at Strawn's, just gathered dust for a few decades until hipsters discovered sound quality and bands discovered how their share of digital profits compared to physical album sales. Strawn's survived mostly on equipment and gear, boosted by another college-town constant: a surplus of shitty musicians who were convinced that they were just one amplifier or microphone upgrade away from playing stadium shows. Don't get me wrong, there were always great local bands, but for each one you wanted to hear there were a dozen you'd like to send out to sea. Good or bad, though, they all had to buy gear.

The guy behind the counter at Strawn's was reading a *Spider-Man* comic book when I walked in, and he didn't seem thrilled to be interrupted by a customer who wanted to spend money, but he grudgingly went along with it.

"Just give me something I can plug into the laptop that will be loud and clear, please," I told him. "I'm not worried about the sound quality so long as it is clear."

He wandered into a backroom and then emerged with a three-speaker set and a cluster of cords.

"It's used," he said. "I'd feel bad selling you new shit if you can't even hear the difference in quality."

I thanked him for pitying me, paid for the speakers, and left. The day had warmed and the breeze had died off and there was just that high blue sky, cloudless and bright. The sunlight was more than appreciated; I felt almost thirsty for it. Fall in Maine can hit you like that; there's always a back-of-mind memory that the sun is setting earlier and the nights are growing longer and that once winter settles in, it'll be for a nice, long stay.

I loaded the speakers into the back seat of the truck and then dropped the tailgate and sat on it, facing west, the sun full on my face. It felt healing, somehow. For a few minutes, thoughts of my father, my mother, Renee Holland, and her sister were gone and I was at peace.

Then the phone rang.

Pat Ryan.

I stared at the display and let it ring. I wasn't ready to answer yet. I didn't know if I should trust Renee's warning, but I also had enough questions about my article assignment to give her some credibility. When I spoke with Pat next, I wanted it to be on my terms.

He left a voicemail, telling me that he was hoping to connect and leaving his office line along with his cell. His voice was terse, none of the usual levity, and it made me wonder what he'd already heard and who had told him. Bryce Lermond had been silent since he'd seen me off with my beta version of Clarity, but I had a sense that he was watching. At the very least, I thought, he would know that I had tried the app and know which songs had played.

But what did Pat know? And why did he care?

I looked at the phone in my hand and thought of Seth Logan and how easy it had been for him to teach a novice to engineer a device takeover. What could a guy like Seth do with an app like Clarity? Track my location, for starters, but the potential data access went well beyond that. Email, browser history, phone calls, and text messages. Then there was the camera and the microphone. A guy like Seth could own your life if he wanted to.

I put the phone back in my pocket, slid out of the truck bed, and closed the tailgate. I had another stop to make before heading back to the camp.

It was time to see my mother again.

24

She was still watching the birds, but today she was outside, in a chair in the garden. A staff member led me out to her.

"Dr. Bishop, look who's here! It's Nick!"

My mother turned, looked me dead in the eyes, and smiled.

I almost left then. The swirling emotional responses were overwhelming. *How could you?* I wanted to ask, but there would be no answer, and despite all of my anger over what I'd learned that morning, there was still love and sorrow at the sight of her. I still missed her, the real her, the one who'd gone away years ago. I wanted her back, and I wanted the truth from her, and neither of those wishes could be granted.

So instead we sat and watched the birds together. When we were alone and the silence had stretched out for too long, I finally said, "So I was driving the car, huh, Mom?"

She watched a nearby suet feeder. A chickadee was working on it.

"Do you remember the accident, Mom?"

She turned and gave me the polite smile and made a gesture that was like a half wave, encouraging me to continue. It was the way you'd interact a stranger, the right amount of friendly and distanced, like two people who'd arrived at the same time in a checkout line—*No, you go, I insist.*

"The accident?" I repeated. "Do you remember that?"

"Grackles," my mother said, and smiled.

"Right," I said, and turned away. "Grackles."

"The sun is nice," she told me. I agreed that it was. We were facing into it, just as I had been on the tailgate of my truck, but the pleasant warmth was gone for me here. I wasn't sure why I'd come. Why ask anything that couldn't be answered? The conflicted emotions I had for her actions and her secrecy were mine to bear alone now. There would be no argument, no rationalizing or explaining, no hashing out of the greatest secret of my life. I could visit her, but I couldn't get answers from her.

"Do you listen to the Red Sox games?" I asked her instead.

"The sun is so nice," she said. "Just a beautiful day."

"It is."

"Grackles."

"Absolutely."

She smiled, her face upturned to the sun. She seemed younger in the bright glare, and I remembered her the way she'd been before my father died.

She'd been lighter then, more prone to laughter. Less immersed in her work. Weekends were breaks before my father's death. Afterward, they became extensions of the workweek as she turned four hours on campus on a Saturday into six and then eight and then ten. I'd understood it, of course; I was trying to lose myself in other things, too. Every meal we ate alone or each movie night we skipped had made sense because of the absence in the room. When we were together, the absence was more acute. On our own, in new places with new people, it could disappear for a time.

That was how I'd understood it, at least. Now, I looked at her and wondered if I'd always blamed grief when guilt was the real culprit.

"I'll tell them to put the Sox game on for you tonight," I said.

"They'll lose," she responded.

"Probably."

"With the sun. So nice. Just beautiful."

"It is. The camp was gorgeous this morning."

"Traps are under the porch."

"You told me. I'll get on it. That and the staining. It really does need to be stained before winter."

"Red," she said.

"Yes. I'll make sure it stays red."

"Stain, not paint."

"Yes."

"So nice with the sun."

"Gorgeous."

"Grackles."

"I'm watching for them. Haven't seen any yet."

"Just beautiful."

And so it went. I stayed for thirty minutes. We volleyed back and forth about the sun and the birds and every now and then I'd ask another question about the accident and she would return to the birds. Try something about the camp, though, and she could dial in.

"Rosewater," she said toward the end of my visit, "is a special place."

"Without question," I said. "We're lucky to have it."

She smiled at me and nodded. I patted her hand. She closed her eyes and put her face to the sun and breathed deeply.

I left her like that.

25

It didn't take me long to get the speakers set up and the recorder ready. Seth had counseled me to be sure not to use the AirPods before recording, in case it might disrupt the signal-robbing system we'd put in place, but he needn't have worried about that—even the thought of putting my AirPods back into my ears made me cringe.

The system was ready to go, but I wasn't. I opened the app, confirmed the availability of Sleep Song #3. I wanted to be able to track the progress of it through time as well as sound, but the app didn't display on the lock screen; you had to have the phone on to see it. I went into the phone's setting and removed the passcode and lock screen and changed it so the display would remain illuminated at all times. The screen glowed, the green "play" button blinking, waiting.

I moved away from it.

I told myself that I needed to work in stages, and that the next stage was some long-overdue research into Bryce Lermond and Clarity, but the truth was simpler: I was scared. The more I knew about what that song might be, the less scared I thought I would be.

Cowardly or not, the time spent on research wasn't wasted. Not in the least. Twenty minutes of investigation into the Lermond family revealed plenty of interest—and not a damn thing that emboldened me to play the next song.

The supposed paper-mill money that Pat had told me about was bullshit. So far as I could tell, they'd never been invested in any mill. Bryce Lermond's father, Kevin Lermond, was indeed a West Point man, but his wife, Marilyn, was a doctor, with degrees from the University of New England and Northeastern. She'd once held a teaching fellowship at a research hospital in Boston. Her program there had been focused in vestibular and balance studies. Among the patients serviced by the program were epileptics and seizure sufferers. When Marilyn Lermond's husband left the Army and she left her practice in Boston, they formed a joint venture and launched a company called VIST. The initials stood for Vestibular Innovations and Solutions, Tactical.

The name put a prickle down my spine. I'd done enough reporting on ex-military types who ventured into private enterprises that advertised "tactical" approaches to have a sense that many of them involved playing with the same killing toys on a private playground.

VIST kept a low profile. It was a Delaware-based corporation with a post office box address. There

was no public information on investors or contracts. The only references I could find to the
company were disturbing: articles describing the
company as a leader in research with hypersonic
weapons.

The first was a *Los Angeles Times* piece from a
few years after 9/11 that discussed the "new tech
being deployed on old battlefields." Among the
weapons referenced was a "sonic bullet" that was
in reality a narrow beam of targeted sound. The
developer proudly raved about his weapon's ability
to produce "the equivalent of an intense migraine
headache that is just totally disabling." The reporter explained that the developer had "50 different tracks, or sonic bullets, in his new weapon. For
instance, it plays backward the sound of a baby crying at 140 decibels, or 20 decibels above the threshold of pain. The noise level is similar to that of a
passenger jet taking off."

Charming stuff, right? And the potential was
not limited to the battlefield—they were also working on a version to pair with vending machines,
wherein the hapless customer standing before a
Coke machine might hear the sound of a can cracking open and pouring.

Marilyn Lermond didn't sound quite so giddy
about her pioneering work in the field.

"I'd rather not see retail applications pursued for
this technology," she told the reporter. "The average
American believes that military-grade weaponry

shouldn't be put in civilian hands. They're thinking of AK-47s and tanks and missiles, things of that nature. All very scary, yes, but I would say this: at least you can *see* the AK-47 in someone's hands."

In the same piece, she declined to comment on the specifics of VIST or their current research, only to say it was limited to Department of Defense contracts.

The next time she appeared as an expert, it was in an academic paper about the story of an American embassy in Brazil where dozens had reported suffering from dizziness, insomnia, and difficulty concentrating after sustaining inner ear damage that they attributed to a high-pitched noise within the building. The affected included diplomats and CIA officers, some of whom later demonstrated the symptoms of traumatic brain injury. The story itself seemed to have died quietly. If anyone was ever officially blamed for the sickening of more than two dozen Americans at an international embassy, it remained classified.

Marilyn Lermond's take on the idea of sonic weapons in that case was concise and chilling.

"Beyond plausible. It's already in existence. The question is the mechanism of delivery, the frequency of the tones, and whether their goals were achieved or missed. All of the reported symptoms are in keeping with the technology we already understand, but there's also the chance that those symptoms fell short of a more dangerous goal."

She was asked if that goal would be a deadly one.

"I don't think that's where the research in this area is focused—not in China, not in Russia, not here. Could you kill someone with low- or high-frequency audio weapons? Certainly. But I've seen little indication of anyone prioritizing that approach in research. It seems to be more a matter of control and manipulation. Physical, mental, what have you."

What have you. My mouth went dry when I read that gem of a quote. I noted the researcher's names and found contact information for all three of them. My newshound's blood was up, and I was getting lost in the work. Chasing the truth is a great feeling, and knocking down walls of secrecy to show the truth is a special high. One that I missed.

My next play was going to be a call to the lead author of the paper. I had just one last step in the prep work—running VIST through the Maine secretary of state's corporate records search to see whether they actually had any presence in the state or if all that investment in the mill had come courtesy of corporate-friendly Delaware.

The Maine site surprised me, though: *VIST Enterprises DBA Clarity Inc.*

Bingo. I had my on-paper connection between VIST and Clarity. I opened the articles of incorporation and saved the file, then skimmed it quickly, confirming that VIST was a Maine corporation in good standing and that the company's official address was at the Hefron Mill. Check, check, and—

I froze with my hand halfway to the keyboard. Stared at the screen. When the articles of incorporation had been filed this year, the registered agent of Clarity Inc. wasn't Bryce Lermond or Renee Holland but one Patrick W. Ryan.

I looked at the screen for a long time and then I got up and walked to the kitchen and found a cold beer. I drank it slowly and I looked at the computer from a distance and thought that the best thing I could do was leave Maine. Renee was right. There was nothing good for me here.

I didn't pick up the truck keys, though. Didn't leave the kitchen. Just stood there and finished the beer. Out across the pond the afternoon sun was descending and the light bled down in thin shafts and soon the water would glow with its namesake rose-colored sheen.

I rinsed the can out and crushed it slowly and methodically in the manner my father always had—an engineer's approach to can crushing, with a careful crease in the middle and then the left side smashed down, then the right. Everything uniform, even, precise. He taught me how to parallel park with that same obsession with angles and consistency. It had been snowing that night and the streets were empty, but we went back and forth and back and forth until he was satisfied. I would have been sixteen then, and the driver's li-

cense test loomed. Excitement. Possibility. Freedom.

I did not remember the next time I drove a car. I
tried like hell to think of it, but the well of memory
was black and endless.

"Grackles," I said, and laughed. The laugh was a
cold, mean sound, the bark of a dog with pinned-
back ears. I heard its meanness and didn't mind.

I picked up the phone then and called Pat Ryan.

"Hey, man, been trying to chase you down," he
said warmly.

"Same here," I said, in a tone I hoped was just as
warm. "Come on out to the camp, would you? I've
got a couple cold ones on ice."

"Tomorrow, maybe. Pushing my curfew with the
family today."

"We'll make it quick," I said. "Scout's honor."

"We were never scouts."

"Never had any honor, either."

He chuckled. I chuckled. A couple of old pals. My
hand was tight on the phone.

"I think we can sneak you back home before you
get grounded," I said, and then, gentle and easy,
cast out like a dry fly, "I've found out some pretty
wild shit about Lermond's mother. It's interesting.
Like, national-news interesting."

There was a hitch before his response. You might
not have noticed it if you didn't know Pat, but it was
there.

"Marilyn seemed pretty milquetoast to me."

"Prepare to be dazzled, then."

A pause. My hand ached from gripping the phone. I could see my reflection in the big picture windows. My jaw was tight, my teeth grinding. I parted my lips and took a slow breath.

"Fifteen minutes," I said. "That's all I need."

"Done," Pat answered. "See you shortly, brother."

"See you shortly, brother," I echoed.

26

He was good to his word. Less than thirty minutes after we hung up, I heard the crunch of tires on gravel and turned to see him pulling down the drive in a big black Suburban, window down, a hand waving, a Foo Fighters song blasting out of the stereo. I remembered the same one playing in our dorm room.

Good old Pat. A friend, indeed.

I was sitting on the rock, and I stood and dusted my jeans off and walked to meet him. I hoped my smile felt convincing, and, based on his reaction, it was good enough. Nothing in my body language to betray the pounding adrenaline. A reporter's response, always neutral. Just here to listen. No emotions, no opinions. One last question, though . . .

"Come on in," I said. "I grabbed a six-pack of Funky Bow on the way home."

"The good stuff."

"You know it." I grinned and held the door for him. He walked inside, ducking to get under the low-clearing doorframe without braining himself, looked around, and shook his head.

"Been a while since we were out here together!"

"You come out alone?" I asked.

"Huh?"

"You said *out here together*. I didn't know you came back here after I was gone."

"Ice fishing," he said.

"Yeah? Where do you catch 'em?"

He waved generically to the west. "Out there where it's about twenty feet deep. Good old Bobby Beauchamp pointed me the way."

"Beauchamp speaks to you? That seems odd after the sinking of the SS *Money Pit*." I was trying to lighten my approach, trying not to question every single thing that Pat said, but it was hard when all I wanted to do was jump him on the things he hadn't told me about.

"Ah, the cranky SOB actually warmed up to me in time. He likes to tell old stories about the sea and shipwrecks and he knows I'm a welcoming ear for that. Despite everything he said, I think he was partial to the *Andrea Fitzgerald*, too."

"Sure," I said, "I bet old Bob just loved that tub."

Pat was looking past me, and now he stepped around to get a better look at the open laptop with the strings of speaker cord leading to either end of the picnic table that sat in the center of the room. My phone and digital recorder flanked the laptop like a place setting, forks and knives ready and waiting. The phone was plugged in and illuminated, the green "play" button of the Clarity app blinking. Beckoning.

Pat walked over and tapped the old computer speaker.

"I see you're still rocking the same-quality stereo," he said, and laughed.

I grabbed a beer, tossed it to him.

"Had to buy that top-of-the-line gear today, actually."

"You're kidding."

"Nope."

"Why'd you buy speakers?"

I opened my beer, nodded at the table. "I've got the Clarity app on my phone."

"I still don't follow the need for speakers."

"I intend to record it," I said, and sipped the beer.

He didn't look at me. "Bryce's brainchild might not be all that enticing, I've gotta warn you. He's supposed to be a nice enough guy, but . . ." He shrugged. "If he was brilliant, we'd have heard by now, right?"

"His mother was," I said.

He turned to me. The affable grin was gone. "What?"

"Marilyn Lermond." I sipped my beer. "Serious smarts. And her husband? A West Point man. You knew that, though."

"Yeah. They endowed a scholarship at Hammel in his name."

"Generous people, the Lermonds," I said. "Cutting everybody a piece of the action."

It was quiet for a moment. Then Pat picked up his beer and drank.

"You're taking things seriously," he said. "I appreciate that, but I've got to warn you, you're unlikely to win a Pulitzer with something in my esteemed publication."

"You never know."

He gave a wan smile. "Don't push too hard."

I set my beer down on the counter. I tried to keep the low-key demeanor in place, but it was harder now.

"You don't want me to *push too hard* on a story for you? I owe you, buddy. I'll do the job right. Take it seriously."

"What I mean is—"

"Why are you lying to me, asshole?" I said.

Pat rocked his head backward. *"What?"*

"You're part of it," I said. "So why not tell me that? What's the game, Pat?"

"Part of what? Nick, you're not making—"

"You're the registered agent of Clarity, which is a subsidiary of VIST, which is the Lermonds' company, and you know all of this damned well, Pat. So why are you lying to me?"

He seemed to deflate. He took a step back, bowed his head, and ran a hand through his sandy hair.

"That'll teach me," he said. "Hire a real reporter at your own peril."

"I know I'm not here to play reporter. I'm here to play guinea pig."

He looked at me with what almost passed for real confusion.

"How much do you know about my dad's death?" I asked. "And how long have you known it?"

"What?"

"You heard the question."

Pat's mouth moved but the sound of his voice was gone and I heard the sound of water instead, a crashing, thundering wave. I looked toward the mirrored surface of the pond, then leaned on the counter, grasped it with both hands, and let out a little grunt, as if bracing after a punch.

Pat said, "Nick?"

My heart seemed to rise, buzzing in my chest like a wasp. The room tilted, spun. I closed my eyes. Held on to the counter. Heard Pat saying my name. When I opened my eyes, the room was steady and he was standing just on the opposite side of the kitchen island from me, staring with wide, concerned eyes. His expression reminded me of the sunburned man from the park, and for some reason that enraged me.

"Your *dad*?" Pat said. "Nick, what in the hell are you talking about?"

"Don't bullshit me," I said, trying not to show that something was deeply wrong inside of me, trying not to push past him for the phone. I needed the damned app again. Needed the sound of cool creek water and the feel of a deeply held breath. The pieces needed to be put back together so I could think. Clear my mind. Right now, thinking was impossible; the waves were thundering but there was no ocean in sight and the buzz in the center of my chest had turned from a single wasp into a nest of them.

He spread his hands. "I have not the faintest idea what you're talking about. As for my cut in Clarity, look, that's fair. I should've been honest about that."

I tried to focus on him but there seemed to be three of him shifting in front of me.

"There's a novel idea. Honesty."

"I didn't think it was really any of your business."

"Not my business? It's *my* brain that you pricks are screwing with!"

He frowned, his freckled face perplexed and almost believable in its sincerity. Almost.

"You're going to need to clarify that," he said. "Let me hear the damn thing for myself if we're worried about brain damage, bud. I'll admit, I'm curious about Bryce's baby."

Overlapping with his words came the sounds of the waves once more, and this time, from somewhere within the storm, a whisper.

STOP HIM NOW!

Can a whisper be a scream? I would have said no until that day, that moment, with the setting sun glaring in the front windows and Pat Ryan's face silhouetted against the rose-colored glow. The voice in my ear—against my ear and inside my ear and inside my brain, swirling and dancing, everywhere and nowhere—was both, though. A whisper and a scream.

Suddenly I was coming around the kitchen island and my hands were shoulder-high and knotted into fists and Pat was backing up with his own hands raised and one palm flat, the other occupied with the beer. The gesture was clear: he was telling me to back off, telling me that he meant no harm.

I hit him.

I swung once with my left hand, just a jab, but I had my right hand raised and my hips were ready to turn into the second punch. That one would've been a hell of a lot more than a jab. The sight of the blood, bright on his lip, pulled me up short. Barely.

He stepped backward, swearing, and bumped into the picnic table and the speakers rocked and one fell over. His beer dropped to the floor and sprayed foam as he touched his bloodied lip in shock and the sound of the waves and the wind rose and a voice trapped within them shouted *STOP HIM NOW!* and my own voice, or the closest thing I could find to it, whispered, *You need to leave, Nick. And you'd better hurry.*

Pat said, "It's not what you think, you son of a bitch, it's not what you *think!*"

I felt my left hand start to flash forward again, another lip-busting jab, but I knew that the right hand would follow this time, and if that happened, it was going to go bad fast. The sun was bright in my eyes and Pat's blood was dripping onto the old picnic table and I saw them joined together in a red haze and then I was moving for the door, pushing the old screen open. It slapped shut behind me as Pat Ryan screamed that I didn't understand.

My truck keys were in my pocket. I jerked the door of the Ranger open and fell into the driver's seat. Dropped the gearshift into reverse and hit the gas.

The explosion that followed sounded so much like a gunshot that I ducked, tucking my head below the dash. It was like Afghanistan; I just needed someone to yell *Incoming!*

Then I realized Pat's Suburban had been parked behind my truck.

I sat up as Pat came to the front door and stared at me, blood dripping down his chin. He didn't say a word. Just stared at me as if he couldn't believe what he was seeing.

I pulled the truck forward, cut the wheel hard to the right, shifted back into reverse, and hit the gas again. This time I cleared Pat's Suburban—barely, and with branches raking the truck on the other side—and bounced up the rutted drive and onto the road.

27

I drove until the paved road dead-ended in a dirt track that led steeply up into the pines. *Private Property* signs pockmarked with holes from a .22 flanked the entrance. It was an access road to an old blueberry farm and locals used it as a hiking trail.

Today, I blasted up it in the truck, the Ranger's suspension bucking and rocking. Near the crest of the hill, I gave the skid plate a workout, too, the crunching grind telling me I'd hit a good-sized rock. Then the truck growled up and over the crest and I was on a plateau of knee-high brush tinted a deep crimson, the shade that blueberry bushes take on in autumn. I slammed the truck into park, killed the engine, and sat there sweating and listening to the ticking sound the engine made as it cooled.

A bright line of red painted the knuckles of my left hand.

Pat's blood.

My friend's blood.

I shook my head as if to deny it. I could still feel the punch I hadn't thrown, felt it like a batter in the box who just barely manages to hold off on a high fastball. My whole body had wanted to uncoil, driving power from the legs up, pistoning my fist into Pat Ryan's face, all while a woman's voice whispered and then shouted at me from within the thrashing sounds of a storm I could not see.

I thought that I should go back to Florida. Job or no job. Just go back to the last place where things had been normal. From the moment I'd crossed the Piscataqua River and entered into Maine, it felt as if I'd been

Spinning on black ice.

I sat there in the blueberry field for a long time. The air cooled around me as the sun sank. I told myself to call Pat, that maybe over the phone it would be better, and the only voices would be ours. I didn't have my phone, though. It was sitting back on the table next to the laptop and the speakers and the recorder, awaiting the sleep song.

I started the truck and rattled back down the old farm road, leaving the warm glow of the blueberry fields and descending into shadow, headed back to Rosewater to find my phone and call my old friend whose dried blood flaked my knuckles.

It was nearly full dark when I pulled back into the camp, and I was surprised when my headlights pinned the Suburban in their glare. Pat hadn't left? He'd been waiting this whole time?

He's a big bastard, and he does have a temper.

Bust the man's lip up and you might want to be ready for him to respond.

I tried to imagine Pat waiting in the darkness and couldn't do it. He might take a swing at me, but he wouldn't hide to do it. I parked behind the Suburban, blocking it in, determined that we'd talk this out before he left, and then cut the engine and got out of the truck. Pat was nowhere in sight, and there were no lights on inside the camp. I stood above the broken glass from his headlight, realized that I hadn't even bothered to check the damage to my own tailgate yet, and couldn't bring myself to give a damn about that.

I called Pat's name.

No answer.

The automatic headlights on the Ranger shut off then, and I was alone in the darkness. On the rock beneath the pines it was almost black but there was still the faintest smudge of pink above the western shore. Across the cove, the green lights of the dock reflectors glittered like a jungle cat's eyes. The Lermond house. Empty as always. Still, I felt watched by it now.

There was no breeze and there was no sound. I had to stop myself from reaching for the truck keys and leaving. Running away. The place was that eerie, that unsettling, in the absolute silence.

"Pat?" I called again. "I'm sorry, man. I'm a little stressed-out today. I think you know why."

Nothing.

I walked around the front end of the Suburban, glancing to the right as I did so, as if Pat might be crouched there, waiting. There was no one, of course. Pat wasn't the ambushing sort of guy.

No? How else would you describe that little revelation about his involvement with Clarity?

What seemed more likely was that he'd sat in the camp and killed the rest of the six-pack, waiting for me to return. I pulled back the ancient screen door, almost grateful for the shriek of its rusted hinges simply because it was a sound in the silence, and then opened the main door and stepped down into the camp.

It was even darker in here, so the single light source drew my eyes immediately.

My phone was glowing on the picnic table.

I stood just inside the door, staring at the illuminated phone, and then reached out and felt along the wall until my fingers touched the light switch. The camp flooded with light, and I could see the main room, all of the kitchen, and into the bedroom.

All empty. Pat nowhere to be found.

There was a bloodstained rag on the counter next to the sink, a sliver of ice remaining from the cubes he'd apparently held to his lip while he waited for me to return. His beer can sat beside it. He'd picked mine up off the floor and even wiped up the spill.

"Pat."

Nothing. The phone still glowed. I'd forced it to stay open so that I could see the app. I crossed the room and saw that Clarity was running, but there was no sound coming from the speakers, and my computer screen was dark. The computer still had a password in place, so Pat wouldn't have been able to use it. He'd have been able to use the phone and not the computer, which meant that he wouldn't have been able to hear anything. He'd have gotten the message demanding headphones, and . . .

He'd have his own headphones. The guy lives on his phone.

The app's display featured the moon-and-stars background, dimming and brightening in a steady rhythm. Below the night-sky imagery was the track name. Sleep Song #3 had been queued up when I left.

Now it said, *Now Playing: Motivation Melody #9.*

28

I called "Pat!" again, too loud this time, a nervous shout, like the one you'd give a dog who is off the leash and headed toward traffic.

No answer. No sound.

Maybe he was gone.

Without his car?

Motivation Melody #9. What in the hell was a motivation melody?

"Pat?" By now I wasn't expecting an answer. I was still staring at the phone, watching the dimming and brightening stars, entranced by the cycle of it, knowing that Motivation Melody #9 was playing.

Playing on *what*?

I closed the app and opened the settings and clicked on Bluetooth. Four devices were logged. Three were disconnected. The fourth, currently connected, said *PatsPods*.

"Shit!"

He was listening. But that also meant he was close. He had to be. If he got too far away from the phone, he'd lose the connection. I knew from working out that you could wander a fair distance from the phone and keep a connection on the AirPods, but you couldn't go *too* far. If the thing was playing on his headphones now, he should be in sight.

I paused the app, bringing Motivation Melody #9 to a stop.

"Pat! Damn it, where are you?" I turned my back to the windows to scan the rest of the tiny cabin. There was nowhere for a six-four Irishman to hide. Outside, the wind rose and shook some pine needles down in a soft, rustling cascade, the only sound other than my own voice.

I put the phone in my pocket and walked through the bedroom, pulling open the closet and checking as if he'd curled up there to hide.

The phone buzzed in my pocket, but I ignored it as I moved through the bathroom—also empty—and checked the pantry closet—empty—and turned to face the open door. My phone buzzed again. This time I took it out, hoping it was a message from Pat.

It wasn't a message. It was a notification from Clarity.

Melody Motivation #9 Play Resumed.

Beyond that text, the starscape dimmed and brightened, dimmed and brightened.

I tapped the "pause" button but didn't even wait to see if it worked before lowering the phone and moving for the door, headed for his car. Everything on this eastern shore of the pond was blue-black with the last vestiges of dusk, and though I couldn't see him in the driver's seat, I was certain he was there. It was the only place left to check. I crunched through the broken glass of the headlight and reached the driver's door, grabbed the handle, and jerked it open. Black leather gleamed blue in the ambient lights, and the second-row seats were as empty as the first, the third row folded flat.

Son of a bitch. Where was he?

The trees rattled in the wind, a tormenting sound like soft laughter. The night woods knew what I did not.

I turned away from the car. The remaining daylight was down to a thin pink smudge above the trees on the far side of the pond. Balance Rock was barely visible, an egg-shaped silhouette in the twilit waters.

"Pat!"

Pine needles showered down on me from a gusting breeze, the soft needles grazing my neck like a dozen cool fingertips.

I took another step out onto the rock, peering into the shadows. The Bluetooth connection was an invisible leash that tethered him to the property. He had to be hiding close, a notion that chilled me. What was he doing? And, more crucially, what was he hearing?

"Pat? Turn that shit off. If you're listening to it, turn that off!"

Wind blew and the pines rattled, sprinkling me with another shower of grazing needles. I took my phone out and saw that Motivation Melody #9 had resumed playing yet again. This time I didn't even bother hitting "pause,' just turned on the phone's flashlight. The beam reached only as far as Balance Rock, making the boulder glow white against the dark water. The cove sat in silence, not so much as the ripple of a striking fish disturbing it.

Another scattering of pine needles drifted down, catching in my hair and caressing my neck. I stopped, my eyes on the cove, the cell phone light angled down across the water.

The perfectly flat, still water. The water that was not disturbed by so much as a trace of a breeze. As I stared, one of the falling pine needles drifted down to the rock, passing through the shaft of light from my phone, twirling as it descended.

What was shaking the treetops on a windless night?

I lifted the phone and tilted it skyward. The beam caught the trunk of the massive white pine beside me, a vintage north woods tree, three feet in diameter at the base and running straight and true up through green-boughed branches that drooped like the shoulders of a defeated man.

The boughs gleamed in the light as I moved it higher, past empty branch, empty branch, empty branch. The needles were falling faster now, in stark contrast to the motionless tree captured in my rising light. The tree was so tall that I had to take a step back and point my chin skyward to see the top. When I did, I almost dropped the phone.

Pat was up there.

He was on the highest branch that could support his weight. He stood tall, posture rigid, one hand grasping the trunk. His feet were balanced on the thickest part of the branch, where it met the trunk, but even there it sagged. The wood was green and lithe, able to bear a snow load while being whipped by winter winds, but green and lithe also meant unstable. The survivability of the northern white pine depends on this; it must be able to shed weight.

While I watched, Pat released the trunk, nothing holding him upright except for that tenuous perch on the branch.

"Pat," I said, "get the hell down. What are you doing?" My voice trembled.

The branch beneath him bobbed, and for an instant I was so dizzy I had to look away.

"Get down!" I shouted. "You're going to fall, Pat, get *down*!"

He didn't answer. When I looked up again, he was two feet farther out on the branch, and the boughs at the end over the pond were swaying. Beneath his feet, the branch still held. It was no thicker than my forearm. He was facing due west, straight across the pond, where once the namesake light of Rosewater had glowed, but now nothing but blackness remained.

He took another step. His footwork was nimble, a

tightrope walker's balance, his shoulders and head staying perfectly even. It was as if he'd done this a thousand times. I felt a perverse relief in seeing that he'd actually made it out that far, because now he was moving above the water rather than the rock. If he fell, he might survive this.

Might.

The old-growth pine had to be seventy feet tall, which meant Pat had to be at least fifty feet in the air, maybe sixty, the height of a five-story building.

In the faint beam from my cell phone's light, Pat's typically ruddy face looked sickly white, and so it took me a moment to see that he had white earbuds tucked into his ears.

"Damn it, Pat! You're going to fall!"

I reached toward the lowest branch of the pine, the bark rasping over my palm, with the idea that climbing toward him might help. Then I looked higher and saw the complex series of grasps and steps that it would require and feared that climbing would force the tree to sway more. I released the branch, stepped back, and called his name one more useless time.

"Pat!"

He did not look down when he took his next step. He kept his chin high and his eyes dead ahead as he lifted his left foot and reached out and brought it down squarely on the branch. The branch swayed and dipped but somehow Pat's left foot stayed planted on it while he brought his right foot into the air to follow.

He never got to bring the right one down. It was still moving through the air when the branch bobbed again with its whipcord flexibility, doing its job of shedding unexpected weight. Pat's posture was so rigid that he somehow rode the dip, following the branch's motion as he fell, downward and outward, away from the tree's trunk and toward the water.

There was no last attempt to regain balance; no final, flailing grasp at the branches as he plummeted between them, raked by the boughs; no physical adjustment whatsoever. He fell like a man who had walked off the plank and dropped into the sea, hands tied and hopeless. He faced westward the whole time, as if there were something out there that gave him a chance.

The final plunge of the branch sent him farther over the water, arcing through the air, and down directly onto Balance Rock.

I will remember the sound his back made until the day I die.

29

What I did: get him out of the water. What I didn't do: call 911.

The police asked me about that, of course. It was a fair question. I thought I had a fair answer—when you see a drowning man, you don't wait patiently for police to arrive; you get your ass in the water. Fast.

That's what I did.

The phone had been in my hand but it ended up in the rocks, its pale beam facing skyward, illuminating the towering but now-empty pine like a guard tower spotlight after a jailbreak has already occurred. I ran from the light and entered the water in the dark. I think I was shouting then. I'm not sure. In my mind it was all a scream—everything had been a prolonged scream since the sound of Pat Ryan's back breaking on that egg-shaped rock that reached out of the water in isolation, as if it had been sent out of the depths on a mission.

Balance Rock looked to be only a few paces offshore, but the pond got deep fast, and I had to swim the last few feet. Pat was already underwater. The sound his back had made—like a dry walnut in a campfire—echoed in my skull, and within the echo was a warning, a command: *Do not move him! Do not move him! Do not move him!*

You never move someone with a spinal injury, of course. You wait for the medics. This I remembered from a day outside of Bagram when a Humvee three vehicles in front of us detonated and an Army Ranger broke his back after being flung into a concrete barrier. I remembered the battle-seasoned soldiers shouting at their own comrades: *Don't move him, don't move him, nobody fuckin' touch him, medic on the way!*

I'd visited that Ranger later at Walter Reed Hospital. He'd been walking then. Not well, but walking.

What if the man with the spinal injury is underwater, though?

I couldn't wait.

I talked to Pat while I tugged him back to shallow water. Whispered reassurances, calling him *buddy* and *chief* as if we were on a backpacking trip together, everything just fine, laughing and having good times, the way we always had. In all the years of our friendship—years that included the most bullheaded, testosterone-fueled stretches—there'd never been a punch thrown, never been blood drawn.

Until tonight.

When I got him to the shore I fell to my knees and slid him, as gently as possible, up to dry ground and got him turned onto his back. We were closer to the cell phone's light then; it lanced through the darkness just to my left, looking like a portal, a beam that could carry us up and away.

It was the only light I had while I administered chest compressions. While I watched cold pond water leak from my best friend's lips, and his glassy eyes fixed first on mine and then, when his head flopped to the right, fixed on that thin beam of light leading skyward.

There were more lights soon. Bright blue and red flashers. It took me a minute to absorb what they represented.

Help was here.

A chorus of voices came at me then. It sounded like a dozen people, although the police reports indicate that only three had been on scene. I still find that hard to believe, because it felt like an invading army at the time. I was trying to explain what had happened, and I felt as if they were attacking me, accusing me, although once they had Pat secured on a backboard and moved into an ambulance, I began to recognize that my version of events sounded like gibberish. Trying to walk someone through a moment of madness rarely makes immediate sense.

By the time Pat was gone, the ambulance's wail fading into the hills as they hauled ass for Pen Bay Hospital or Eastern Maine Med, I'd gathered myself. The cop who was asking most of the questions by then was a lieutenant named Lichman, and he was more patient than the rest.

"So you got back here, and he was in the tree?" Lichman said.

"That's right."

Lichman took a flashlight off his belt, scanned the tree. "Where?"

"Right up at the top."

"You're kidding." Not a question, just stunned.

"No," I said. "He was right up there at the top."

Lichman painted the pine with the light and found the place where one of the branches had splintered, green wood exposed like the internal organ it was.

"The hell was he doing?" Lichman said.

"I don't know."

"Wearing all of his clothes, I'm going to guess he didn't intend to dive into the pond."

"No."

"Then why the hell did he climb all the way up there?"

"I don't know."

"You didn't ask?"

"I asked. He didn't answer."

Lichman clicked the light off, stared at me. "He didn't say a word? He's standing up there in the top of a tree, you're down here talking to him, and he just stays up there and doesn't move or speak?"

"Well, he moved. He was moving when he fell."

"Climbing down?"

"No. He stepped farther out. Walking along the branch like he thought it would hold him. Then he . . ." The memory of the sound of Pat's back on the rock slapped at me like a wave from the depths, and all I could do was motion toward the pond.

"Fell?" Lichman said. "Or was it a jump?"

Here I hesitated. His eyes narrowed with interest.

"I'm not sure," I said at last. "He was just stepping forward, and eventually he got out to where the tree couldn't hold his weight. Then he . . ." I remembered the straight drop, the way he'd somehow held his body rigid, his face never turning from the opposite shore.

Not until he struck the rock, at least. His face turned then. He'd been staring skyward, his body bent in an inverted V when he rolled into the water and sank.

"He dropped," I said. "He just dropped."

"But you don't think the jump was intentional?"

"No," I said, although the only thing I was sure of was that it hadn't been a jump at all. He'd walked right out of the tree and into open air. Not a dive, not a jump, not even a fall. Just a step into space.

I shivered then, but if Lichman noticed, he didn't show it. The night was cool and I was soaked, after all.

"Was he drunk?" Lichman said. "High? Both?"

I shook my head. "He'd had a beer."

"One beer?"

"All I saw him drink, at least."

"So you're in the cabin drinking together, then

you leave, alone, and then you come back thirty or so minutes later, and the man is standing up in the tree, not speaking?"

I nodded, realizing how insane it all sounded, and—belatedly—realizing that Lichman thought he smelled bullshit. He just wanted me to keep running my mouth. Because of all the things that might've happened out here, all the ways a man had ended up in the water with a broken back and a bruised face, a silent fall from the top of a towering pine tree wasn't high on the reality meter.

I looked at my hand, verifying that the pond had washed Pat's blood clean from my knuckles.

"When you left, what were you going to do?" Lichman asked. "Pick up a pizza, grab another sixer, or what?" He was trying to sound more casual now, guiding me along.

"No."

"No?" He blinked. "What's that mean?"

"No, I wasn't picking up pizza or beer."

"Sorry, that was just a hypothetical. Let me rephrase: What *were* you doing?"

I'd just punched him the face and I didn't want to do it again. You see, Lieutenant, when I hit him the first time, I felt like it was an out-of-body experience, one so damn dangerous that I needed to get away from here before I . . . did something worse. Something much worse.

"I needed to take a phone call," I said. "Reception down here is shit, so I drove up to the old blueberry farm. You go up the lane there, and it opens up, and you get a nice, clear signal."

It was a dangerous lie if they checked my phone. My phone had been here, not with me. There was no call record to support my claim. Still, I preferred it to the truth. The truth was something I needed to work through on my own.

"Who'd you call?" Lichman asked.

"Nobody, in the end," I said. "I was waiting to *get* a call."

"From?"

"A friend overseas. It never rang, so I guessed he couldn't make it, and I came back."

Why do you keep lying? Because the truth is worse. That's why.

"Overseas?"

"Bagram," I said, and his nod told me I'd picked the right lie, because he softened a bit.

"I did two years out there," he said. "MP."

"It's rough country," I said, hoping he wouldn't ask what unit I'd been with, because I had the feeling he wouldn't love hearing *The Associated Press* as an answer to that question.

"It is." He angled the flashlight up the drive and clicked it on again. Broken glass glittered in the white beam. "What's the story back here?"

"With the glass?"

"Yeah."

I tried to laugh. "I backed into his car. I'm used to having the only truck down here, and it's a straight shot backward, always clear until the road, so I just . . ." I spread my hands. "Banged right into it. That seemed like it was going to be the big problem of the night at the time. Now . . . not so much."

"Not so much," he echoed, and clicked the light off. "Then you came back . . ."

"And he's in the tree," I said, and I felt the black ice under me. Lichman was going to ask me how much time passed before I noticed Pat in the tree, and what I was doing in that time, and then he was going to ask to go inside, and he was going to see the bloody rag and the beer can on the floor and see the speakers connected to the computer and he was going to—

"He's tellin' the truth," a voice said from behind us.

Lichman and I both whirled toward the sound. The medics were gone and the only patrol officer still on the scene was pacing the shoreline, taking pictures. The speaker was standing on the driveway, behind Pat's Suburban. He stepped forward just as Lichman clicked his flashlight back on and spotlighted him.

Bob Beauchamp.

He was wearing a grungy Graffam Bros. Seafood Market baseball cap that shadowed his face, but the flashlight lit up the perfectly trimmed white beard, and he looked like an old-time sea captain. I had a bad feeling, watching him walk into the light. Beauchamp had never been a friend of mine, or my mother's, and damn sure not of Pat Ryan's. He was a gossip, and he'd also seen me—or at least the lights on in the camp—during my bloody nightmare the night before.

"Who are you, sir?" Lichman asked.

"It's Bob Beauchamp, George." His voice held none of its usual put-upon quality. He sounded rattled, in fact. I stopped being worried about what he had seen and became more curious.

"Oh, hey, Bob. What the hell are you doing out here?"

Beauchamp made a half-hearted wave. "I own the camp across the way."

Lichman's light arced left, pinned Beauchamp's log home and its log outbuildings and flower boxes.

"Didn't know you had a place here," Lichman said. It was clear he was well acquainted with Beauchamp. Most people in Hammel were.

"Only been here thirty-one years," Bob said. The words were sarcastic but he couldn't manage the tone to match. His blue eyes were milky in the light, and his usually ruddy face was white. He looked, I realized, like he was in shock.

"You saw the whole thing?" Lichman asked.

Beauchamp lifted his thick hands and held them up to the top of the pine as if framing it before a photo. His tongue slipped out and wet dry lips. He spoke while looking through his hands.

"Ayuh. I'd heard the Bishop boy come in, tearin' ass in that little truck, and I come out and was just . . . looking around. And it's no business of mine, of course, but I just took a look over and the man . . . the man was up in the tree. Just standin' there, like one of them angels you'd put atop a Christmas tree. I never seen anything like it."

"The man was Pat Ryan," I said.

"Let him talk, please," Lichman said, but Bob Beauchamp looked at me and blinked, still peering through his framed hands.

"That was Ryan?"

"Yeah. You remember him."

He looked from me to the treetop and spoke with his eyes skyward again. "He was way the hell up there, wasn't he? Yes, he sure was." His voice was a low rasp. "He was just standing there, and it was so high up, and I was afraid he would fall. I didn't want to scare him. Shit, I barely wanted to breathe."

"Did he fall?" Lichman asked. "Or did he jump? Or . . ."

"No. Or maybe. Shit, I don't know how to put it into words," Beauchamp said. "He just stepped forward. Then the tree couldn't hold him any longer."

It was as perfect an eyewitness account as could have been offered. The phrasing was so precise, so accurate: *Then the tree couldn't hold him any longer.* As if the tree had tried to. I felt, bizarrely, as if the tree *had* made an effort. Bob seemed to have shared the sensation.

"I saw the Bishop boy run into the water to help him, and that's when I called for the ambulance," he finished. He looked at me. "That was Pat Ryan?"

"Yes."

"I never seen anything like it," he said. "What in the hell was he *doing* up there? Was like he didn't know, himself."

Lichman was getting a pad and pen out, and I saw my opportunity.

"I'm going to put on dry clothes if you don't mind," I said. "I'm freezing out here."

Lichman gave a curt nod and repeated his question to Beauchamp. It gave me time to walk into the camp, grab the rag on the counter that was stained with Pat Ryan's blood, and toss it in the sink with the water running. I closed the laptop screen and disconnected the speakers and pushed them to the side of the table. Then I turned off the water, the blood washed clean from the rag—at least from detectability by the naked eye—snatched a hooded sweatshirt from the hook beside the door, and walked back outside.

"You saw no motivation for him to climb the tree in the first place?" Lichman asked Beauchamp.

"The hell kind of motivation does a man have to climb like that?"

I'm glad he didn't see me throw the punch, I thought. *I wouldn't want to have to explain that one to Jess.*

It was the first time I'd thought of Pat's wife since it all began, and it made my legs weak. I sat down on the cold rock—sat down fast. Lichman looked over.

"You okay, Mr. Bishop?"

"Just needed to sit."

"You need medical attention?"

"No, sir. Thank you." I was seeing Jess. Imagining her face when the call came.

I slid across the rock and found my phone and picked it up. The screen was cracked but the phone still worked, and when I touched it, the Clarity app was gone from the display. Evidently, its work was done for the night.

I turned the flashlight off. The enveloping blackness felt good. I could hear Lichman thanking Beauchamp and the two of them parting at the tree line.

"Should I call his wife?" I asked.

"No," Lichman said, his voice gentler than it had been. "We'll do that."

"Do you know yet?" I asked.

"Know what?"

"Did he survive?"

A pause. Lichman shook his head and then, almost immediately, realized that might communicate the wrong thing.

"I don't know yet," he said. "He was alive when they put him in the ambulance. That's all I can tell you."

I nodded. Looked down at my phone, unlocked

it, and swiped across the home screen to find the Clarity app icon. I missed it the first time, so I swiped back. Still didn't see it. Swiped right, swiped left, then right again.

The app was gone.

30

Lichman spoke with me again before he and his patrolman left, but this time there were fewer questions. Beauchamp had taken the edge off by verifying my account of the night. They took down my contact information, told me they'd be in touch the next day, and left.

I thanked them and watched them go and realized that Bob Beauchamp was still there. He stood right on the boundary of our property lines, seemingly unsure of whether to stay or go.

"Thanks for helping, Bob," I said.

"Ayuh." He wiped his mouth with the back of his hand. "I never seen anything like that."

"Me neither."

"Was Pat Ryan, you said?" Like he still couldn't believe it.

"Yes. You remember him, right?"

"Shit, yes. He liked his old boats, his old stories."

"He did," I agreed, and my throat was tight.

Beauchamp kept running his hand over his mouth. "Climbed right up there, like a man going up the rigging of a ship, you know? Quick as a spider monkey. Like he'd done it a thousand times. 'Cept he wasn't in his own mind once he got out there." He coughed and spat. "Never seen anything like that," he repeated softly.

"Thanks for getting help," I said. "Minutes are worth hours in a situation like this."

"I just made the phone call. You got him out of the water."

"The phone call was important," I said. "The phone call might give him enough time."

There was a silence, and then he said, "I'll let you be, Bishop."

"Nick," I said.

"Sure," he said, absent, distanced. "I'll let you be, either way." He started away, then turned. "What brought you back?"

"Huh?"

"Been how many years, and you ain't been back? Summer comes and goes and you stay away. It's the season to be shuttin' camp up, not opening. Then you come here and then . . . this." He motioned at the treetops. "What're you doing here, is what I'm askin'?"

Only twelve hours earlier, the question would have annoyed me. Beauchamp and all of his *It's none of my business, but some people say* . . . bullshit. Now I looked at the treetops as if they might hold an answer.

"I don't know," I said. "I thought it was a job. Now I do not know."

"It's been strange," Bob Beauchamp said.

"What's that?"

"Since you got back. I watched you bust your ass out on the dock, then saw the redheaded woman come down, then the lights on in the middle of the night, then . . . whatever the holy hell this was tonight. I ain't tryin' to fix it on you or nothing. Just saying that it has been strange here since you got back."

"I hope it quiets down," I said. "I sure hope it does, Bob. Because there's nothing I'd rather do than just sit out here and have a beer and listen to the loons and forget that anything like tonight ever happened."

"No loons," he said.

I looked at him. "What?"

"Not been a loon here in twenty years." He was speaking distantly, his eyes still flicking up to the treetops as if Pat might reappear.

"Say that again, Bob?"

He lowered his face. Squinted at me. "Huh?"

"The loons . . ."

"What about 'em?"

"They're here," I said.

"The hell they are. Haven't been loons at Rosewater since you were in diapers. The pond association puts nests out each spring, but . . ." He shrugged. "The loons don't have interest in Rosewater. Fished it out, likely."

I stared at him. He must not know the bird, must

be confused between a loon and a heron or something.

"We've got a couple," I said. "They're loud. Every night, I hear them. They make a unique, mournful—"

"I know the friggin' sound. We don't have them, though. Not at Rosewater."

I looked from him to the dark water and back. "I hear them every night. Since I came back, they've been out every single night."

Silence. When he finally spoke again, his words came carefully, as if he wasn't sure whether he should ask the question: "Have you seen them?"

I had not. They were big birds and hard to miss, with their white chests and black heads.

"No," I said. "I've only heard them."

"You haven't heard a loon," he said with finality, and he looked at me uneasily as he stepped away, heading toward his own property as if in a hurry to be behind a closed door.

"Been strange since you got back," he muttered again, and then he was gone, receding into the darkness. I saw a light go on inside of the log house when he went inside. It wasn't far from my camp to his. I'd heard the loon's plaintive calls every night. He couldn't be missing them.

I felt the cold then. I should have noticed it earlier, but there had been too much chaos for noticing much of anything. Now, though, I was alone in the dark and there were no loons crying through the night wind and I was suddenly very cold.

I went inside the cabin and turned the lights on. The computer sat on the picnic table, waiting. I opened it, remembering the grand plan of the day—recording Sleep Song #3. It was as if Clarity had sensed my intention and thwarted it.

I looked at the phone again. Went through the same back-and-forth swiping at the home screen. The app was still gone.

It had played through the sleep song, gone on to a motivation melody, then vanished. Right as the paramedics loaded Pat Ryan's body into the ambulance.

The loon's cry came from outside.

I listened to the long, undeniable sound with the soft, sad warble at the end, and then I moved to the window and stared out across the water to Bob Beauchamp's cabin. He couldn't be missing that sound. Couldn't be confusing it, either, a life-long Mainer like him, a man who'd lived on Rose-water for so many years. He'd been so certain, so positive.

The call came again, loud and sorrowful, and I felt a gooseflesh prickle along my arms, and the fine hairs there and on the back of my neck rose.

Have you seen them? he'd asked in the way that suggested the question was the end of the debate.

I went into the bedroom and found my backpack.

Put the computer in it, toiletries, and a change of clothes, and then I turned out the lights, stepped outside of the camp, closed the door behind me, and locked it. I used the key fob to start the truck from the doorstep, because I wanted the sound of the engine and the glow of the headlights before I walked farther into the blackness.

It was late, but there would be a motel somewhere with a vacancy, and I wanted to stay anywhere but Rosewater tonight.

31

I drove north up the coast. I didn't want to stay in Hammel any more than I wanted to stay at Rosewater. I wanted to go south, in fact, but I had a feeling that if I pointed the car in that direction I wouldn't stop driving until I was out of Maine entirely.

There were too many unanswered questions to take that route.

I stuck to Route 1, up past Waldoboro and South Thomaston and into Rockland, which qualified as a large town by coastal Maine standards and had a few chain hotels. Any of them would have done fine, but I continued north, Penobscot Bay spreading out on my right side in darkness, broken by the glittering lights of a cruise ship somewhere out on the North Atlantic.

In Camden, the town I'd called home before my father's death, I finally stopped. There were no chain hotels in Camden. No chain anything, actually, as mandated by town ordinance. A lonely Subway stood at the town line like a reconnaissance scout sent by big business. *They are hostile here—turn back!*

I drove down Main Street and past the harbor and found an illuminated vacancy sign at an inn called Windward Gardens. A polite but bewildered gentleman answered the bell and acknowledged that he could provide a room, although he wasn't used to doing so at such late hours. It was 9:00 p.m.

I understood his confusion once we were inside, though. It was a stately Victorian place, accented by flowers and fresh cookies and candlelight, the type of inn that catered to honeymoons and anniversaries and reservations made well in advance, not lonely travelers popping in. After getting the Wi-Fi access code—*RoséAllDay!*—and a preview of the morning's breakfast—*Belgian waffles with local blueberries and Cobb Hill Maple Syrup!*—the proprietor finally left and I was alone again in my romantic getaway inn.

I sat on the antique bed, which smelled vaguely of lavender and dust—the former no doubt applied to obscure the latter—kicked my shoes off, and lay on my back. The ceiling fan spun lazily. I was suddenly struck by a memory of Pat's face as he fell, the unblinking, obedient expression he'd had right up until the jutting boulder caught his spine. I closed my eyes with a wince, turned my head away from the fan.

And slept.

I went down abruptly, as if sedated. Slept fully dressed and stretched out on top of the bed with its arsenal of ornate throw pillows. For a few hours, it was peaceful, and my body drank in the sleep like water offered to a dehydrated man.

Then came midnight.

I woke with the same abruptness with which I'd fallen asleep, trying to jerk upward, but I was unable to lift my head. The tug of sleep was still with me, holding me down, pulling me back toward the depths like an undertow, but my conscious mind fought it with a desperation, an overwhelming sensation of urgency, a fight-or-flight need to escape sleep.

Sleep didn't want to let go, though. The riptide pulled and yanked, the sensation compounded by the smell of water. It was all around me, cool water and earthen smells—everything was damp and decaying—and as I tried to move again and failed to coax body to follow brain, I finally saw the dead woman.

She was standing at the foot of the bed in front of the old fireplace, and while I'd lit no fire, there was a glowing bed of coals in it now, soft ruby light emanating from the embers, spotlighting her pale face and pale hair and deepening her red-tinted lips.

She watched me just as she had the first time, tilting her head from right to left with the studiousness of a scientist watching a mouse in a maze. She was wearing the gray hiking pants and the black fleece top and they were both soaked. When she tilted her head, water dripped from her hair and plinked off the wide hand-hewn planks of the bedroom floor.

Her face was familiar now, a stranger no more. It was Ashley Belle Holland.

I knew a scream was pointless, and so was moving. I had to wait it out, just like the last time. Sleep through it. A nightmare, nothing more. I closed my eyes and breathed in quick, shallow gasps and waited for it to be over. It would be over soon. Just like last time, it would be over—

"You can't leave now, Nick."

Her whisper was so soft that every hair along my neck rose with the cool touch of her breath. She was right against my flesh, not speaking the words so much as breathing them into me, and I knew better than to open my eyes, I really did, but the reflex demand of terror was too much. My eyelids snapped open and there she was beside me.

She was on her knees at the bedside, her hair wet and glistening, her face bloodless except for those lips. I saw for the first time that her eyes floated in their sockets, untethered by any tissue, adrift. They rolled toward me and her red lips pursed and now I saw that the tip of her tongue was black and gray, the color of charred wood. She leaned down to me and this time I did try to scream. Tried to recoil, too.

I made neither sound nor motion, though, just lay there in frozen horror as her lips brushed my ear, damp and soft and cool, like fresh snow, and she whispered again.

"Too late to leave," she said, "but too dangerous to linger. You see the problem?"

She smiled at that, as if she'd made a joke, and that charred-wood mouth seemed to smoke from behind the red lips, like the final fumes of a cold campfire. I closed my eyes. It was the one thing I could do, but I regretted it immediately. In the trapped blackness, the sensation of her cold breath was intensified.

"You'll need to go back," she said, wisps of smoke—or was it frost?—seeping from her lips and drifting toward me, cool as ice crystals, fog over a winter sea. "Rosewater would be best. Now that you have no choice, it would be the safest place."

Safest place. That stood out, even in my horror, because she was so far worse than any horror-flick terror I'd ever imagined, and yet she spoke of safety.

"You'll need the song," she whispered. My flesh prickled in the frosted breeze that was her breath. "You know that now, don't you?"

She seemed to be waiting for a response, but I couldn't move or speak. I stared at her the way you'd watch an approaching wolf or mountain lion, some primal predator strolling your way.

"Days are growing short," she said. "Don't waste the daylight, Nick. Do not waste it. Darkness rises, fog just behind, and once you're lost there, it's the end."

Her damp hair whisked across my neck, the grazing touch of a cattail in a pond, there and gone. I kept my eyes squeezed shut, an act that felt like clinging to a cliff's edge, my whole body engaged and tensed.

"Burn the night," she breathed. "Not the daylight."

Then she was gone, and all that remained was a cool gust on my neck.

32

I woke on the floor, scrambling backward, a
trapped scream rising in my throat. I managed to stifle most of the scream, turning it into a
choked moan instead, just before I banged into the
wall.

Someone pounded on the other side of the wall
with a fist, and a man's voice called out, "People are
trying to sleep here, guys!" and right behind that,
softer, a woman said, "Let them have their fun."

I started to laugh then. It wasn't a pleasant
sound; the edge of hysteria was too clear in it. I
picked up one of the ridiculous tasseled throw pillows from the tangle of blankets I'd knocked to the
floor and pressed it to my face and laughed and
laughed and laughed like a man gone mad.

It was only when the laughter had subsided
and I lowered the pillow that I saw the glow from
my phone on the nightstand. It was lit up as if
by an incoming message. I waited for it to dim
again.

It didn't.

I rose on unsteady legs and crossed the room

and picked up the phone. The star scape screen of the Clarity app greeted me. *Sleep Song #3 has finished,* the text beneath said.

Beside my phone, my AirPods were arranged neatly—and outside of the case.

I had never put them in. Or at least I did not remember putting them in.

I clicked the side button on the iPhone. The screen went dark again. I picked up the AirPods and put them back into the case, moving methodically, the way you do when you're trying to exert control over your emotions. Calm begets calm.

My hands were beginning to shake, though.

Burn the night, Ashley Holland had told me.

No problem there. I would not be sleeping again. Not tonight.

I put the phone into my pocket and went into the bathroom and washed my face. Peeled off my sweat-soaked shirt and washed my torso with a handcloth and then put on a fresh shirt and left the room and went down the creaking steps, past a grandfather clock that glowed faintly in the moonlight, and let myself out the front door. There were old, straight-backed chairs on the front porch.

I sat there, facing east, shivering in the night air, and waited for the sun to rise.

When a thumbnail of pink finally pressed against the gunmetal sky, I took my phone out and texted Renee Holland.

WHAT IS A MOTIVATION MELODY?

It wasn't yet six in the morning, but she responded within minutes.

WHERE ARE YOU? WE NEED TO TALK, NICK.

33

She came to Camden. Told me not to leave, not to think about returning to Hammel, and then she stopped responding entirely. I stayed on the porch of the inn, watching the sea clarify under the rising sun, listening to the jingle of silverware and the hiss of a gas stove as the staff began preparing breakfast. Behind the inn, Mount Battie and Mount Megunticook rose over the coast, steep forested slopes that culminated in bold rock faces. I could see only the seaward side of Megunticook, and I was glad of that. It was on the back side that my mother had suffered her stroke. For the first time in my life, I wondered if it might've been better if the Good Samaritan on the trail hadn't seen that blinking red headlamp and climbed down the rocks to find her. If she'd died out there in the cold and the snow, avoiding her years in the twilight chamber that held her now, in the world but not of it. Died and taken her secrets with her.

Horrible thoughts, to wonder if her death might have helped us all. And yet they were my only companions that morning until Renee Holland arrived.

She wore no makeup, her red hair was up and tied in a loose tangle, and her green eyes gazed at me from behind glasses. She'd rolled out in a hurry, and yet somehow was more immediately attractive for it. There was none of her contrived distance, the cool façade she'd carried herself with for most of our encounters since my return to Maine. She wore a hooded sweatshirt and black leggings, and when I looked at her face, I saw the resemblance to her sister and shivered.

Darkness rises, fog just behind, and once you're lost there, it's the end.

"I heard about Pat on the drive up here," she said. "What happened?"

"Your app happened."

"What?"

"He played it. I was gone. He put his headphones in and he played it and then he climbed sixty feet in the air and walked to his death without so much as a glance down, let alone a scream. Walked like he had no idea what he was doing."

"He's not dead. At least, not as of this morning. The news said he was in intensive care."

I heard the sound of his back on the rock again, and I said, "Let me guess—he's nonresponsive."

She nodded.

I leaned forward and braced my arms on my knees and clasped my hands.

"You said it was about me. That was a lie. It's a threat to *anyone* who listens to it. I feel like you knew that."

As if on cue, the front door opened, and the older man who'd checked me in poked his head out, smiled, and said, "Breakfast will be served shortly. Waffles with blueberries and Cobb Hill Maple—" He saw Renee then, blinked, and said, "Oh—are we two? I can correct that."

"We're none," I said. "No breakfast. Thanks, though."

"I'll have breakfast," Renee said.

For a moment it was silent, the innkeeper looking awkwardly from Renee to me.

"We can bring it to you on the porch," he said, sensing the obvious tension, and then ducked back inside.

I turned back to Renee. "You're going to have a *waffle*? Pat Ryan might be dead! If he's not, he'll be paralyzed, and you're going to chat over breakfast?"

"I don't like being bullied, so, yeah, I'll have breakfast. You're standing here looking at me as if it's my fault—"

"I saw him hit the rock. I heard the sound his back made. His spine snapped like dry firewood split with a maul."

She winced. Put one hand on the railing and looked away.

I raised my voice. "His face never changed until his back broke. He stepped out and away and didn't even seem to sense that it was dangerous. That's what your little app can do. But you already know that, don't you?"

She inhaled through her nose, her chest rising and falling, her lips remaining in a tight line.

"Yes, you do," I said. "Because it's the way your sister died. Or pretty damn close, right?"

"Be very careful with the way you talk about Ashley."

"I don't think you have the right to tell me that anymore! Because you're not the one she's talking to in the night. She doesn't whisper in your ear. She comes for me, and so I'll be the judge of how someone can speak about your dead sister."

My voice was rising, on the edge of a shout. Renee leaned back against the railing, tightening her grip on it, as if the porch were in motion and she needed to brace herself.

"What are you saying? 'Talking in the night'— what does that mean?"

"She comes for me," I said. "The first time I wasn't sure it was her. Last night, though, after seeing her picture in the newspaper articles, I couldn't be more certain. And she's dead, she is very, very dead, but she's there." The rising shout had dropped to a near whisper, and I could hear the tremor in my own voice. "She's right *there*, Renee. And it is the most frightening thing I have ever experienced."

She was watching me with horror but also without disbelief.

"What did you do?" I asked, and the anger I felt didn't keep the plaintive tone from my voice. "Tell me what you people have made—and how *I* make it stop."

"What does she say?" Renee asked.

"That's not an answer. I need to—"

"Tell me what she says!" she shouted. Her hands were balled into fists, her body rigid.

"She's got a few messages," I said. "She tells me that I can't leave but it's dangerous to linger. She tells me to stay out of Fog Town. Tells me my days are numbered. Sweet little messages like that. She likes to whisper them into my ear. It's beyond terrifying."

"It's a dream," Renee said, but her voice was uncertain.

"Tell that to her," I said.

Renee looked down at her hand, considered it, then released the railing and stepped away. It was as if she had to convince herself to let go, like a rock climber making her way across the face of a sheer cliff, afraid that a free hand would invite a fall.

"She speaks to you?" she asked, voice low.

"Yes. She doesn't always speak, though. Sometimes she just stands there and watches me. Other times, she comes close." My voice trembled, and not with anger this time. "She comes very close, and she feels very real. I want *you* to tell me a few things, starting with what in the hell you and Bryce Lermond put out into the world that made my friend jump from—"

"You kept it *in* the world! I told you to delete it! You

knew it was dangerous. I took risks that you can't possibly begin to imagine to prevent *you* from making a deadly mistake, and now you're blaming *me*?"

The innkeeper emerged at that moment, two coffee cups in his left hand, a steaming carafe in his right.

"Ah . . . I'll come back."

"I'll take coffee, please," Renee said. She smiled at him, and it looked as if she'd never tried the expression before and didn't know how to execute it. "Smells lovely."

He looked like he'd rather cross hot coals. He approached Renee warily, poured her coffee, then handed mine to me and vanished inside again. I put the coffee down beside me, but Renee leaned against the railing and sipped hers. She'd gone from bridling anger to the appearance of complete calm, as if she could change circuits at will. The juxtaposition of scene and circumstance made my head ache.

"You did tell me to delete it," I said, "and I appreciate that, but I'm no longer in control of it. It's not optional."

"What does that mean?"

"Just what I said. Last night I woke up from a nightmare that starred your dead sister and I was playing the app. I not only hadn't intended to play it; the thing was gone from my phone. But it came back, and I played it without making the conscious choice to do so."

She stared at me with horror and wonder and didn't speak.

"Renee, what in the hell did Pat listen to that made him do . . . that? And why doesn't the same thing happen to me? Or will it in the end?"

"I don't know," she said, and then held up a hand before I could object. "I honestly do not know. I can distill it, though: Pat listened to a weapon. That's what it is. A cutting-edge weapon with an ancient twist."

"Excuse me?"

"It is the worst of all worlds," she said. "A weapon that combines the most futuristic ideas of neuroscience with a ballad that's older than this country."

34

A week ago—hell, two days ago—I might've laughed at the claim. A lot had happened in those recent days, though.

"How does it work?" I asked.

Renee swung her weight off the railing and crossed to the chair beside me and sat. We faced the sea together, watched a lobster boat cross in front of the islands, carving a white wake, and it struck me that, to any passerby, we would look like a happy vacationing couple. Certainly not two people discussing madness and death and exchanging accusations.

"I don't know," Renee said, her voice soft. "It's why I'm still there, though. I intend to find out. Somewhere along the line, Bryce altered the effect. It went from soothing the sick and calming the anxious to . . . to . . ."

"Killing them."

She nodded.

"Ashley went up on the roof of Grossman Hall," I said. "I read about it. But what in the hell happened before?"

"She listened to the song," Renee said. "The new one. Or the old one presented in a new way. I'm not sure. Regardless, it was the first time she'd heard it, I know that."

"You're a terrible liar."

"It's not a lie!"

"Then what you told me yesterday was. You said I was hearing her voice."

"That's right."

I spread my hands, palms turned skyward, imploring. "If she sang the song, Renee, then she'd *heard* the song before."

"Actually, she hadn't." Her voice was a neutral tone that unsettled me, a conscious emptying of emotion. "She never heard her own voice. And before you tell me that's impossible, let me explain. She recorded the song in a soundproof booth while wearing sound-canceling headphones. Every single time. You've seen the mill, you've seen the level of security investment that's been made, so just imagine if they wanted to bring that same approach to preserving silence."

I thought of the voice I'd heard, the melodic beauty, and I felt a core-deep chill.

"Ashley seems real to you," Renee said, watching my face. "Like a ghost, not a nightmare."

"I wouldn't undersell her—she definitely feels like a nightmare—but, yes, it's a ghost. It's every ghost story you've ever heard or imagined. The difference is . . ."

"What?" she prodded when I fell silent.

"I don't know what she wants," I said. "To hurt

me or to help me. Usually, that's clear in a ghost story, right? But I think that might not be her choice to make."

I hadn't articulated this before, but once the words were out there, I found myself nodding as if someone else had posited the idea.

"She could go either way," I said. "I'm pretty sure of that."

Renee looked sick, drained.

"Who came up with the song?" I asked.

"I don't know. Bryce hired Ashley to sing it. At first, he wouldn't tell her anything at all about it. When she kept pressing, he finally said it was a folk song that dated back to sometime before the Revolution."

"No titles, no names, nothing else?"

"No. Bryce put the rules of the game into play. He didn't tell me anything about it. He told Ashley. He was entranced by Ashley. Maybe in love with her. I don't know. Regardless, he picked her to sing his song. A good choice: she was a wonderful vocalist. But he demanded she not tell anyone."

"Surely he knew you two would talk."

"Considering all of the NDA's he made her sign, he probably thinks he scared her into cooperating. She was excited about all of it. She thought it was grand intrigue and adventure."

"But she did tell you."

"Eventually. She thought the secrecy was over-the-top. That came up the day he ordered the cell phone–sensing system, ironically. The one that triggered when you stepped off the elevator, remember? That hadn't been installed yet. I had to order it, and Ashley and I were talking about that when she mentioned recording the song, how he made her wear earplugs beneath noise-blocking headphones, then played white noise through the headphones while she sang. She thought it was all crazy, because carrying a tune when you can't hear your own voice is pretty damn hard. She told me that Bryce seemed deeply excited and deeply afraid at the same time."

"What did you do when you heard all that?"

She closed her eyes. "I asked her to record it for me," she whispered. "I told her that I had some concerns about Bryce, about his goals for Clarity. I told her that what he was doing with the recording sessions sounded like madness, so I wanted to hear it for myself. There was only one way to do that: have her record the song."

"Did you ever hear it?"

"No. I asked Ashley—*told* her—not to play it until we were together. We were going to meet at my house at eight. That didn't happen. She was dead by eight."

Now it was my turn to be silent. At length I said, "Is it just the song that matters? Or does the rest work, too? Because the breathing and the meditations seemed powerful."

"They are," she said. "Those were your mother's work, Marilyn's work, the passion project of all these years of research. But the sleep songs and the motivation melodies? All Bryce."

"No idea where the songs come from?"

"Song, singular. He's broken it up for you. And I do not know where it came from. Answering that question is my job. My whole reason for being. I will get that answer." Her eyes found mine, the hunter's glimmer back in them. "I will not let you hinder that process, either."

It was a threat, but there was so much sorrow in her voice that it made me more afraid for her than for myself.

"Will you let me help you get those answers?" I asked. "Because you want them, but I think that I *need* them."

"You should go, Nick, leave Maine, go home, go anywhere else. Let me do what I need to do—alone."

"I think it's a little late for that. I'm pretty sure your sister won't let me leave."

Her lip trembled, and she bit down on it. "You're sure it's her."

"Yes."

"Have you asked her?"

"When she appears, I feel paralyzed and mute and utterly fucking terrified. I'm not in a position to ask her anything. I can only listen."

"What does she say?"

"That it's too late for me to leave, among other things," I said, and my voice thickened. I cleared my throat, tried again. "That the fog is bad. That I could get trapped in it."

"The fog?"

"Yes. That's where they wait."

"Where *who* waits?"

"Trust me, I'm curious myself."

She stared out at the bay, but her eyes didn't track any of the boats cutting wakes across its sapphire surface. Finally, she said, "It's not her. She is dead and gone. The songs may conjure nightmares, but they don't conjure a ghost."

"I'm the wrong audience for that argument, after the past few nights."

She kept her back to me when she said, "I would like you to watch my sister's video."

"Her video of what?" I said, picturing Ashley Holland in a recording booth. "I don't want to hear that song again, whether she says I need to or not."

"You won't," Renee said. "There's no audio, in fact. Just Ashley."

I raised an eyebrow, waiting for more.

"It is a security camera video," she said softly. "Of her death. I want you to watch it. Please."

I felt sick. "What is the point of that?"

"If there was a video of Pat, I'd watch that so you don't have to watch this. There isn't, though. And you'll be able to tell me." Her voice was low, earnest, almost pleading.

"Tell you *what*?"

"If they were in the same . . . state or condition." She turned to me. "Please."

I thought of Pat's face, expressionless as he fell.

"All right," I said, and my mouth had gone dry. "All right, let's see it."

35

Renee picked up her shoulder bag, and I extended my hand, thinking she was going to pass me a computer or tablet with the video. She pulled back and looked at me as if I'd gone mad.

"Not out here. Don't you have a room?"

I had a room. A room where her dead sister had breathed into my ear.

Renee saw the hesitation in my face and said, "What's the problem?"

"No problem," I said, and I almost believed that was the truth. It was daylight, after all. No visions had appeared for me in daylight. Not yet, at least. It wasn't the most promising reassurance, but it was better than nothing.

We went up to the room. I left the door cracked when I stepped inside. The room was empty and the fire was out, but I'd seen it like that before, and this time I wanted to be able to leave in a hurry if it changed again.

Renee walked to the little desk beneath the window that faced Mount Battie, with its circular stone tower overlooking Penobscot Bay. She set her bag down and withdrew a MacBook.

"I've watched it a dozen times," she said, opening the laptop. "That sounds terrible, I know, but I keep searching for something, *anything*, that will tell me what she's experiencing. It's as if there's someone just outside of the frame, calling her forward. I've watched it over and over and still I want to scream at her, as if I can shake her out of it, bring her back, call her off."

Someone just outside of the frame, calling her forward sounded very similar to what I'd seen with Pat.

I moved behind Renee so I could see the monitor over her shoulder. Renee opened a video player. The display was black with a white play button in the center, waiting. She looked back at me, her eyes searching mine. I saw the pain, the desperate need for answers. I was certain that I wouldn't be able to provide them—I was the one with the questions, not the answers—but I nodded.

"Go ahead."

She pressed "play" and then took a half step back, which brought her up against me, her back grazing my chest. I was just tall enough to still see the screen, although the bottom corner was now obscured by a wave of dark red hair. I could hear her breathing, slow and controlled. Consciously controlled, I thought. The way you breathed before some physical challenge.

The screen stayed black, but a clock appeared

in the upper right-hand corner. It was in military time, 17:57:03. Nearly six in the evening.

The screen filled with a color display of a tar-covered rooftop that was pockmarked by utility vents and one large block of electrical switchgear. A light rain was falling, and the drops left a few filmy bubbles over the camera, clouding the display. On the left side of the frame was a concrete-walled utility room with a steel door. Out beyond, brilliantly colored trees were visible, their crimson or orange leaves bright against a pewter sky. A white smoke-stack rose in the corner of the frame. The Hefron Mill. Home to Clarity.

The temperature in the room seemed to dip, a pocket of cold air riding through. I reached out and put a hand on the back of the chair for balance. It pulled me closer to Renee, and I was grateful for the human warmth of her. If she was aware of anything happening in our room, she didn't show it. The monitor was her entire world right then.

On-screen, the steel door of the utility room swung open. For an instant, only darkness was visible on the other side. Then a woman stepped out and walked forward with the measured strides of a marcher, heading straight across the roof. She was blond and wore a black fleece and gray hiking pants. Ashley, in the same wardrobe she wore in my nightmares. Just not soaked. Yet.

She crossed the roof with that brisk stride and pulled up short just at the edge. She was absolutely motionless now, indifferent—or unaware—of the wind that whipped her hair and drove rain into her face.

I leaned closer, pressing against Renee, and peered at the screen, then pointed. There were pinpoints of white on the sides of her head, but she was too far out of the frame for me to identify them.

"Are those—"

"Earbuds," Renee confirmed. "Yes. She never takes them out."

Ashley had walked up to the last inch of roof. Even from this vantage point, the dizzying height could make your stomach clench, but from where she was, it should have been terrifying. The surface beneath her was slick with winter rain and the wind was blowing hard off the ocean and there wasn't a handhold to grab for if she slipped. There was nothing but the brick sidewalk waiting far below. Yet she never looked down; she simply stared into the pewter sky as if something out there captivated her. Watching her, I felt very dizzy, the solid oaken floors seeming to turn into the pitching deck of a ship, but I gripped the back of the chair in front of me and kept my eyes on the screen. I felt as if something very bad would happen if I turned away. My heart raced and staggered, raced and staggered, and I wanted to take my phone out and see if the beautiful undulating Clarity icon was there—wanted nothing more than a few minutes of deep breathing and soft water sounds, the restoration it promised.

"Nick," Renee began. "Are you okay? Should I stop it?"

"I'm fine." I squeezed the chair tighter. "Just let me watch."

So we watched.

For eight minutes, we watched Ashley Holland stand motionless on the edge of the roof, facing the leaden sky, the wind drilling the rain into her face and lifting her hair back with each fresh gust. Her hiking pants rippled along her legs at first but then went still as the rain saturated them and plastered them to her flesh. Her hair clung to her neck in soaked strands. The wind rose and fell, sending autumn leaves pinwheeling across the roof. Even in the worst gusts, she never moved. Never reacted. She was static, absolutely inert.

Until she walked off the roof.

Ashley Belle Holland stepped off the roof and into the void without ever looking down or to the side. She stepped into eternity with her face fixed dead ahead, staring at something unseen by the camera but all-consuming to her.

Then the roof was empty, and it was just the rain hammering the puddles across the tarred surface, and Ashley belonged to the bricks down below.

36

I became aware of Renee's soft sobbing as if it came from far away. When she turned away from the computer, she turned into my chest, and I held her while she cried. She leaned into me as if grateful for the contact, but holding on to her was the only way I remained standing. My knees were shaking and the room was filled with gray light that shimmered at the edges.

We stood like that for a while. Renee pressed her face into my chest and I held her even though she'd gone very still. There was nothing romantic to the moment, and yet there was something deeply intimate to it. A simple but profound need for shared warmth. We stood motionless, and yet I had the sensation of sliding, whirling, skidding.

We are on the black ice now, I thought, still staring at the screen, though I had no memory of the black ice I'd crossed on the day my father died. Maybe the event was gone but the physical sensation remained.

Some circuits stay lit.

Maybe I'd get lucky. Maybe I wouldn't remember

this day, either. For the first time since Renee had told me the truth, I thought that I could argue in defense of my mother's point of view on the ethics of erasing memories. I had absolutely no desire to remember the way Ashley Holland had stood on the edge of a roof, staring into the rain before stepping off to her death.

"Was he like that?" Renee said finally. "Was Pat Ryan anything like—"

"Yes. Exactly like that."

She pulled away from me, stepped back, and paced the room. She had her hands in the pocket of the hooded sweatshirt, tucking in against herself, her back and shoulders rounded, as if she were bracing herself. I knew she had to be imagining the way it felt to fall like that, and the last instant before impact.

"It's as if she's listening to something, isn't it?" she said. "And she has the earbuds in the whole time, but she acts like she is listening to a speaker, someone not just heard but seen, someone who commands all of her attention. Do you know what I mean?"

"Absolutely. You had it right when you said it was as if there were someone just outside of the frame."

"She never looks down. The only view from outside of that frame would be the sky and trees and hills beyond. You couldn't see the ocean, not from there." She paused, and her voice darkened. "You can see the mill, though. She's staring straight at it."

I could tell from the way she said this that she thought it might matter, but I shook my head.

"Pat was doing the same thing, and he couldn't have seen the mill. He was looking west across Rosewater, into the hills, and the sun was going down, so there wouldn't have been much to see at all."

"Ashley is totally focused," Renee said. "Never a glance away, not even when the wind blows that leaf into her face. She doesn't flinch. She's focused until—"

"What direction is it?" I asked.

She blinked. "Huh?"

"What direction is she facing?"

"I don't know. Grossman Hall is south of the mill, right on the edge of town. You can see the smokestack from the mill."

She was convinced the mill mattered. I wasn't.

"Pull it up again," I said. "Please. Start it anywhere. We don't have to watch the end."

She started the video clip over. I oriented myself the way she had, using the mill's smokestack as a reference point. The smokestack appeared in the far right corner of the frame. On the far left corner, I could make out the bell tower.

"She's looking west," I said. "She's facing due west. She even walks at an angle to get there. The easiest path across that roof would be north. But she went due west."

"Why does that matter?"

"Because it's what Pat did," I said. Pat had been facing the sunset the entire time.

Burn the night, Ashley Holland's ghost had whispered to me, breathed to me, in that cold-fire wind that had caressed my neck like dry ice, *not the daylight.*

I looked at the security camera time stamp at the bottom of the frame. It was paused at 18:14. Ashley was still on the edge of the roof, gazing through the wind and rain.

"What day was it?" I said.

"September 30."

I took out my phone and pulled up Safari and entered "sunset, September 30, Hammel, Maine."

A site called TimeandDate.com was the first response: sunset on September 30 in Hammel had been 6:18 p.m.

Ashley Holland had been out of the frame by 6:19.

"They waited on the sun," I said. "Both of them did. When it disappeared, they stepped toward it."

I was positive that I was right—but being right about this didn't provide many answers.

"It's a starting point," I said, speaking as much for myself as for Renee. "The first thing we understand, right? That sunset is important."

"Second thing we understand," Renee said. "We also know the result of listening to whatever they each heard."

I acknowledged that with a nod and then closed the screen on her laptop. It was frozen where I'd paused the image, with Ashley still on the edge of the roof, her last step all that remained. I didn't want to see it any longer.

"There are three things," I said. "We know that sunset matters, we know the result, and we know that Bryce understands a hell of a lot more about it than we do. He knew it was dangerous. He tried to prevent her from hearing it."

That was the wrong thing to say, because it had been Renee who talked her sister into breaking that rule. I saw the pain on her face and spoke quickly.

"But he didn't prevent me. He *gave* it to me. Why? Because I didn't respect his company? Because I didn't take him seriously?"

"No," she said. "That's not enough."

"Maybe it is. I showed up and challenged his genius and he thought 'Okay, smartass, why don't *you* beta test this shit?'"

She shook her head. "He wanted you here, Nick. He has for a while. He asked me if I knew you well enough to invite you up, and that was before Ashley died."

I stared at her. "When did that happen?"

"Months ago. He brushed it off as being interested to talk to you about your mother. Considering what I'd seen"—she checked herself—"considering what I'd been *involved* with where you and your mother were concerned, that idea wasn't appealing to me. I told him the truth, which was that I'd had no contact with you for years, and he let it go." Her eyes found mine. "This is why I asked you about

Pat. How it all came to pass that Pat enticed you to come back."

"I took it at face value. I called him looking for work, and the Clarity profile was what he had. That simple."

"You called him."

"Yes. I'd been laid off and . . ." I stopped. Thought about it.

"What?" she said, watching me.

"He knew I'd been laid off," I said, "but I didn't ask him for a job. The idea of finding work in Hammel wouldn't have crossed my mind. I just shared the scenario with him. It was two friends talking, nothing more. After that, he called a little more often, checking in, you know? We'd had a few of those calls before he offered me the gig. By then it felt like I'd asked him for help, but you're right—he made the offer."

Someone passed in the hall, and a bedroom door opened and closed, which pushed the door to our room open another inch. I didn't move to close it. I liked having it cracked.

"He didn't know what in the hell it was, though," I said softly. "Pat might be an investor, might be Bryce's friend, might be a lot of things that he wasn't honest about, but I don't believe there's any chance he knew what really happened to your sister."

"How can you be so sure?"

I looked back at her. "If he had known, do you think he'd have put in his earbuds and listened to the thing for himself?"

"Unlikely."

We stood there in silence for a few seconds and then I said, "I'll need to see Bryce again."

"Don't ruin what I've been working on," Renee warned. "If you tell him what I've said, it gives him a chance to protect himself. So, to borrow your phrase from yesterday, let's remember that we each have some skin in the game."

"You think Bryce doesn't know that? You think he buys your enthusiasm for the company?"

"I think he buys my curiosity for it," she said. "And I'm quite sure he believes that once I'm shown the full power of Clarity, I'll hang around."

"For money?"

"For simple proximity to something extraordinary," she said. "His mother would have told him that. And yours."

"You've been working with him for almost a year. What *is* that work?"

"What does the mighty COO of Clarity Inc. do? Not much. The research your mother started has stopped. Where she partnered with hospitals, he partners with coding experts in other states and speaks with them privately. He talks about how close we are to launching the product—he's always saying that—but I don't think he means it in the way that you'd expect: he's not thinking of an IPO or a billion-dollar sale."

"What is he thinking of?"

"Power," she said. "Pure power."

I waved a hand at her laptop. "You don't talk about Ashley? You haven't asked him what she was doing, what she might have heard?"

"No," she said simply, "because he would lie."

"I thought you said he was enchanted with her—infatuated."

"Yes. We pretend that love of Ashley bonds us. Grief. We pretend we're moving on in her honor. But we each know better. I'm watching him, he's watching me. Yoked together. Keep your enemies closer and all that. I knew in time I'd find an opening. Someone or something would come along."

I smiled grimly. "And here I am."

She didn't argue.

37

We left Camden and drove south separately. Renee was returning to the Hefron Mill, to Bryce Lermond's right hand, and I had to trust her. It was harder than I'd have liked. Pat Ryan would've said this proved his point: I didn't trust many people.

Hometowns, he had said, *are complicated places.*

What had he known that night? What was Pat actually expecting out of my return to Hammel? There would be no answers coming. Would there? I assumed Pat wouldn't be able to talk, but I also hadn't confirmed his condition. People survived terrible things, recovered from horrific injuries, emerged from comas. It wasn't impossible. I could call and see.

I was on Route 1 in Bath, driving down toward the shipyard, when Jessica Ryan answered her phone with a question.

"What the fuck happened, Nick?"

I'd hardly been expecting pleasantries and small talk, and yet the question jarred me. I drove down to the bridge in silence, the seconds ticking by.

"How is he?" I asked at last.

"That's what you called to ask? Twelve hours go

by and you decide it's time to check in on his progress? You didn't think to call and explain?"

"I don't know how to explain," I said. "I can't tell
you anything that will make it clearer. All I can tell
you is that . . . he wasn't himself when it happened."

"What does that even mean, he wasn't himself?
So he was drunk, high, what? What was he *doing*?
You showed back up and decided to pretend it was
college again: Let's get drunk and climb trees like
little boys? Is that it?"

"I wasn't there when he went up," I said, which
only amplified the sense of childishness, but it was
all I had to offer. How else to explain the madness?
*He was listening to some kind of song, Jess. I don't
know what the song is, but I do know that it makes
you climb high and chase the sunset.*

"What shape is he in?" I asked.

"He's on life support, Nick. A machine is breathing for him right now. He can't speak and can't walk
and can't even breathe and . . ."

She ran out of words and into tears then. I
listened to her cry while I drove across the bridge
and up the hill and the sea fell behind me.

"Where are you?" I asked when she began to
regain control.

"Eastern Maine Med."

"I'm going to head your way."

"Fine," she said in a faraway voice. "He won't be
going anywhere."

38

Jess was waiting outside of Pat's room when I got there an hour later. She was wearing yoga pants and a frayed Celtics sweatshirt and I knew without asking that she'd been in the hospital all night and all day.

She rose when she saw me and stepped forward swiftly. I was bracing for a slap, when she hugged me instead. She didn't say a word, just held on to me. I could feel her heartbeat against my chest. Over her shoulder, Pat lay in the hospital bed. He looked impossibly frail under the thin sheet with the intubation tubes running from his nose and the wires of a heart monitor snaking away from his chest.

"Where's April?" I asked. Their daughter.

"My house. My mother is with her. She wants to see him, but I'm not ready yet." Jess stepped back, pushed her dark hair away from her face, and held both hands to the bridge of her nose as she tried to gather strength and focus. "Nick . . . *what . . . happened?*"

I told it the way I had to the police, trying to

sound like a sane eyewitness. It was far easier than telling her the truth.

"He fell," I said, and that much was true, of course. In the end, he fell.

"Out of a tree," she said, and then she laughed in an awful way. "That is what I will have to say for the rest of my life. Why is he in a wheelchair? He fell out of a tree! Why was he in the tree? Well, I haven't the faintest idea, but his best friend was back in town, and you know, boys will be boys."

"Jess . . ."

"No." She shook her head furiously, hair whipping, and stepped back. "No, you don't get to say anything to me. He's in there in a medically induced coma and looking at medical bills that will bankrupt him unless Bryce Lermond decides to ride to the rescue and—"

"Unless Bryce Lermond rides to the rescue?"

"Of course," she said with a bitter little smile. "That's what he has to count on now, right? When the benefits disappear and you break your back, charity is the only thing that can save you."

"The college benefits disappeared?"

"When the job goes, the benefits go, Nick. That's how it works."

"Jess, what are you talking about?"

"The school turned the alumni magazine into contract-only work last spring. Everyone in a salaried position got laid off."

"He hired me to write about Lermond's company for the alumni magazine. Just days ago."

"He can't hire anyone. He doesn't even work there." She stared at me. "You really don't know this?"

"I really don't know this," I said. "Why didn't he tell me?"

"He was embarrassed. And he's never liked to share his own troubles."

She was right about that. For a gregarious guy, Pat was always tight-lipped about his own life. But the performance he'd put on with me was more than tight-lipped. He'd been pretending everything was normal. Why?

"What does he do for Bryce now?" I said. "For Clarity."

"For *what*?"

"Clarity. He's the registered agent of the company."

She leaned forward, head tilted, looking at me as if I was insane.

"If he has a job that isn't 1099 work for the school, I should know about it. I don't think he does, though. The past few months have been fruitless interviews or distractions, like the book."

"What book?"

She gave an exhausted wave. "Legends and folklore, some anthology of all the stories he's always been collecting. Nobody wants to buy it, though. All he needed was Bryce's magic money wand."

She looked back at Pat and tears began to well. "No healthcare, in this country? You'd better find a magic wand."

"What happened to *your* job?"

She gave me that *Are you insane?* look again. "I'm still working, but that doesn't really help him. Not now."

"You didn't put him on your . . ." I stopped talking. Looked at her left hand. The ring finger was bare. I looked up again, met her eyes.

"He didn't tell you," she said, less a question than a shocked statement.

"No. When?"

"Nine months ago. He was . . . I don't need to get into all of it, Nick. I don't have the energy. Suffice to say we tried and tried again and eventually I couldn't try anymore. We separated last year. The divorce was final in February."

"I'm sorry," I said. "I can't believe he didn't tell me."

"I can't, either. Except to say that everything was different with him. He was so distracted. Just knowing that he was out on that damn boat during winter, that was bad enough. Now . . ." She nodded at Pat in the hospital bed.

"He was living on his boat?"

"Yep. Cooking on the little galley stove, reading his old books, and supposedly writing a new one. I never saw him generate much in the way of pages, though. He sent out query letters, I know that.

Then he found Bryce and became convinced that was going to lead to the next great thing."

"Why?"

"Because he was a broke man with dreams and Bryce was a rich man with patience," she said simply. "That's how it works with benefactors, right? The problem was, Pat stopped looking for other options. I don't know if he even interviewed for a job these past six months."

"I need to talk to Bryce," I said. "We'll get him to deliver."

"I'm sure you're just the guy to convince him to help."

Her voice was thick with sarcasm and tears, but I nodded. I thought she was right.

I *was* just the guy to convince him.

39

The fog was building again near the harbor, thin sheets of it drifting past the mill with its whitewashed brick and smokestack. I stood in the mist and buzzed the intercom and heard Renee's voice a moment later.

"It's Nick Bishop, hoping to see Mr. Lermond," I said, sticking to formal, to the façade that I was just here on business.

"Come on in, Nick."

The locks ratcheted back and I tugged the heavy glass door open. The elevator door was opening by the time I reached it, and Renee stood inside, looking at me with barely concealed annoyance.

"Usually we'd prefer to schedule an appointment," she said, and her bearing reminded me there were cameras in the elevator. Probably cameras everywhere.

"I'll explain to Lermond. His app disappeared. Hard to write about something I can't see."

I joined her on the elevator. We both stood facing the doors as they closed. It was awkward, and the feeling of being watched was palpable. We went up to the third floor, and as the doors opened again, I offered Renee my cell phone.

"I remember the rules. Put this in your little velvet coffin until I leave, right?"

She took the phone. Our hands touched, and for an instant she was looking me full in the eyes, and it was the Renee I'd seen that morning, but then she stepped away. The security box for the phone was on a table beside the elevator. She dropped it inside, and before we'd turned away, Bryce Lermond spoke from behind us.

"Nick Bishop. Pleasant surprise."

He was dressed in jeans and a Patagonia vest over a gray button-down and the same shining leather boots. He smiled at me over a steaming cup of tea as he lifted and lowered the tea bag.

"The app's gone," I said.

"Pardon?"

"It vanished from my phone. Beta versions are buggy, I realize, but . . ." I shrugged. "I'd like it back. I was growing interested in it."

He gazed at me through the steam. "Were you."

"Absolutely. It was working. I was sleeping. Hell, I could barely make it through the songs without falling asleep. Impressive."

He nodded, studying me with a little half smile. I matched it.

"I'm glad you were enjoying it," he said. "Mind if I ask how the dreams have been?"

"You can ask, but I can't tell you. I don't remember any."

His half smile faded. He looked down at the tea. "I heard there were some bizarre events with our mutual friend Pat last night. How's he holding up?"

"Not well," I said. "I just came from the hospital, in fact. He's in a medically induced coma."

"Terrible."

"Yes."

Silence drew out. I was fine with that. Silence is one of a reporter's best tools. The typical person either likes to fill silence or feels a need to do so. You learn a lot when someone talks more than they'd intended.

"Mind my asking what in the world happened?" Bryce Lermond asked.

You know what happened, you son of a bitch.

"Bad result of a very old game," I said. "We're not kids anymore. He made the mistake of thinking we were. A few beers probably helped it along."

I could feel Renee's stare, but I didn't turn my attention from Bryce.

"A game?" he asked.

I nodded. "When we were in college, we'd go out to Rosewater, fool around, hang out, and inevitably end up jumping from the trees into the pond. Back then, I think we had better balance and reflexes."

"That's what he was doing?" Bryce said. "Fooling around, having fun, and took a spill?"

"Yeah."

More silence. He lifted and lowered the tea bag. Looked at Renee, then at me.

"About the app . . . ," I said.

"Would you like to see my apartment, Nick?" he asked.

"Pardon?"

"It's right upstairs. Stunning harbor view. Let's go up there and have a drink, shall we?"

"I really came for the app. Didn't want to intrude on your time."

"No intrusion."

"Or have you intrude on mine."

He smiled. "You're unemployed except for this story, correct?"

"Exactly. I should finish it up and get back to Tampa. Back to the job search."

"Let's go upstairs. I insist." He glanced at Renee. "Hold down the fort."

An unsubtle way of telling her that our conversation would be private. She nodded. She wasn't looking at me. Bryce punched the elevator button and the doors parted again. He waved me ahead. We got on together and rode up in silence and then the doors opened and revealed an expansive apartment with slate floors, exposed brick, and ductwork painted a gleaming black. Urban-industrial chic. The kitchen was outfitted with soapstone countertops and stainless steel and the living room was fronted by wide windows facing the harbor.

"Keep your chin up, Bryce. When Clarity starts

making money, you'll be able to afford someplace decent."

Bryce Lermond chuckled. "You're a throwback, Nick. That you are."

"Meaning?"

He didn't answer. He crossed the living room and went to a wet bar where he set the mug of tea down and took out two crystal tumblers.

"Are you a whiskey man?"

He was standing before a row of bottles. There was an unopened twenty-three-year-old bottle of Pappy Van Winkle in the mix. I tapped it.

He'd probably paid ten grand for the bottle at some auction, but he just smiled again and opened it without a word. Poured two fingers into one of the tumblers and handed it to me, then poured another into his own and lifted it.

"A toast," he said. "Here's to honesty."

I didn't lift my glass.

"Don't like that idea?" he asked.

"Just waiting to see where you're going here."

"Ah. Time's wasting. I forgot. The unemployed man with the hectic schedule."

I drank some of the bourbon. Waited. Bryce Lermond stared out at the harbor where the gathering fog was obscuring the boats at anchor.

"Your mother," he said, "was ahead of her time."

I didn't answer.

"But you realize that now. Surely you do." He took a sip of the bourbon, still facing the harbor, and then sighed and turned to me. "We're going to need to get into the thick of it now, aren't we?"

"The thick of what, Bryce?"

"Your friend is in the hospital. He might be paralyzed. Might die, who knows? Too early to tell."

He said this casually, indifferently, and my hand tightened on the tumbler.

"You'll have some medical bills to cover," I said. "One way or the other."

"I will?"

I nodded. "It would be a good idea. For his family, and for your privacy. You do value your privacy."

"That sounded almost like a threat, Nick."

I stayed silent. He smiled.

"Tell me," he said, "what could you do to me?"

"Write the story. You know that."

He crossed to a Herman Miller lounge chair in front of the windows and sat. Swirled the bourbon. Watched me.

"What's the story? Give me the gist."

I smiled and shook my head.

"Let's assume a few things, just to expedite this," he said. "Let's assume your story features an accusation that Mr. Ryan listened to the contents of the Clarity app in the minutes before his unfortunate tumble, and that Ashley Holland had, too."

He waited for a reaction. When I didn't give him one, he sighed.

"Let's not waste each other's time. Of course I know why Renee is still here. She *thinks* she knows, too. But she's too curious of a woman—and too philosophical—to play the avenger. Renee will continue to be an asset to the company."

We'll see, I thought. He might be right. He might be very wrong.

"So when you threaten to reveal things," he continued, "you'd be counting on people to take all of this seriously. I'm not sure how that will play. A phone app that has some sort of deadly mind control capacity? Nobody's buying that one."

"Maybe it's not the app," I said. "Maybe it's the song."

He sipped the bourbon. "A song that guides people to their deaths? Feels a little Satanic Panic, doesn't it? Interview Ozzy Osbourne about the old days. More people will read it then."

"It may take some time," I said, "but the story will be there. Trust me. And when it appears, you won't be happy."

"Probably not. But I agree that the story will take some time, and that adds to your dilemma as an extortionist. I'm not sure you *have* the time, Nick."

I tried to keep my eyes steady and my breathing normal. Tried not to show any hint of fear. I looked out to the harbor and the incoming fog and for the first time I realized that his apartment occupied the front of the mill, which meant that its only windows faced east. The sunset would never be visible from in here.

"Why'd you give it to me?" I asked.

"The app?"

"Yeah. I'm a special object of your affections. I'd appreciate understanding why."

He leaned forward, braced his elbows on his knees, and gazed at the caramel-colored bourbon.

"You need to consider your leverage here. You're not in an ideal position to make threats. It's your natural reaction—expose the evildoers, all that— and a reasonable default. But from a standpoint of leverage? You should consider different terms. Perhaps not a threat. Perhaps an offer."

"An offer."

"You know, cooperation." He looked up at me. "Ask not what you can do to hurt me but what you can do to help me. I assure you, it's a better way to make money."

"Sorry. Old journalist's instincts. We're used to avoiding cooperation with sources, and we're damn sure not used to making money."

The corner of his mouth twitched. "You really hate me, don't you?"

"I don't know enough about you to hate you, Bryce. You can fix that. Tell me how it works and why it's worth the cost, the lives."

He laughed. "Just like that, right? I'll just . . . tell you. Sure."

I waited.

"As I think I mentioned, I'm concerned about your personal timeline at the moment," he said. "*Concerned*, mind you, not certain. You're a

question mark. Regardless, it's probably imprudent
to waste time, so let's get to it. You'd like to see that
your friend and his family are cared for."

"Yes."

"You might like some money yourself?"

"No thanks."

"Come off it. You're jobless and broke. If I give
you, oh, a half million, you'll appreciate it."

"Keep it. You're going to spend more than that
on Pat."

"Fine. You just need to earn it for him. I don't
want to insert myself into a friendship, but I could
make an argument that you owe him. When I found
out that it was Pat playing through that many songs
and not you, it was disappointing, but also not my
fault. *You* violated our agreement, not me."

The anger was building in me now, the avalanche
beginning, scattered pebbles sweeping downhill,
driving rocks of rage ahead of them. I drank the
bourbon just to have something to do. My hand
trembled a little, so I loosened my grip on the glass.
Bryce Lermond watched it all intently.

"I think it's a fair offer," he said. "A guarantee
of your friend's care, removal of financial burden
from his family, and some cash in your pocket. All
for work that could be done in thirty minutes."

"What work, Bryce?"

"Listen to Clarity," he said. "All of it. Sleep songs
and motivation melodies."

"I was offering to do that for free."

"Bullshit. You've got ideas now. Recording, am I right?"

I shrugged.

"Give up on that," he said, "and agree to simply listen. To let it play out the way it was always intended."

"I never intended on any of this."

He leaned back in the chair, swiveled to look out the window, casting a reflective gaze over the village and the sea beyond.

"I need to see how good your mother really was," he said.

"Clarify."

"To the best of my knowledge," he said, "there are ten people across generations who have heard that song completely, in verse and with melody. Of those ten, nine are dead. Suicides. Every . . . single . . . one."

He turned back from the window and met my eyes. "Except for Nick Bishop."

40

I'd been determined not to let him knock me off stride, convinced that I'd heard enough madness now to be hardened to it.

I was wrong.

"Bullshit," I said, but I knew that it wasn't, of course. By then, even the strangest of claims had credibility. Ashley Holland's ghost saw to that.

Bryce Lermond gave me an appraising stare.

"Impossible for you to believe, Nick? You know what happened to Ashley. You *watched* what happened to Pat Ryan. He's not even on the scoreboard yet, by the way. He may make it ten dead out of eleven."

I stepped back and leaned against the bar. The solid support felt necessary.

"Give me the other names so I can judge for myself," I said.

His laughter, rich and genuine, echoed in the open space with its hard surfaces, all that stone and steel.

"Admirable effort," he said. "But come on, buddy."

"If you want me to believe you, then you'll need to prove—"

"I won't need to prove a damn thing. Remember our little lesson about leverage? You don't have any. You want the app back, right? You need the song."

I didn't like the way he said I'd *need* the song. It was the word Ashley's ghost had used, and I very much wanted to believe they were both wrong.

"You also want Pat's financial difficulties addressed, and maybe a bit of cash in your own pocket. And someday—a day to which we agree, of course—you'll even have the story. I don't care who tells it. You do. Am I wrong?"

He wasn't wrong. Horror story or not, I wanted to be the one who told it.

"All of this awaits," Bryce said. "You just need to play your role. To think about cooperation rather than confrontation."

I put my free hand down on the bar, felt the soapstone surface, and tried to draw some strength out of it and spread it into my core, to rob its cold, hard sturdiness.

"Nine of ten, eh?" I said.

"Nine of ten," he said. "Not Nick Bishop, though. He's still here. Fascinating, don't you think?"

I felt like the mouse in a maze, loaded up with some new cocktail of mind-altering drugs, pursuing a path I didn't understand beneath the watchful eye of a man who didn't care whether I lived or died.

"How did I make it?"

He spread his hands, the bourbon sloshing in the glass. "That, my friend, is the question. That's why you're here. To see how far it can go."

"How far it can go," I echoed. "Whether I continue to survive, you mean?"

"Correct." He sipped the bourbon, unfazed.

"How did you know I could take it when others couldn't?"

"I didn't know; I was curious."

"Fine, asshole: Why were you *curious* to see whether I'd walk off a roof?"

"Because you don't remember trauma," he said calmly. "And you do not dream. Clarity involves trauma and dreams. Intimately. While I'd love to take credit for your unique condition, the credit belongs with your mother. She bulletproofed you."

"I don't remember my dad's accident," I said. "But I don't think that extends beyond—"

"False," Bryce Lermond said with a terrible, giddy delight. "You do not remember *trauma*, Nick. Pain, violence, agony—none of it sticks."

"You're wrong. Crazy, but also fundamentally wrong. I've been all over the world recording traumatic events. War zones, hurricanes, homicides. I can send you the story I wrote about the family they found on the border, sealed into a shipping container and left in the desert heat. Tell you how that looked and smelled and sounded. My whole career has been—"

"Reporting on other people's trauma," he said. "Yes. I am well aware of that. It's most intriguing, because it suggests you were either drawn toward their traumas or toward the act of recording it, but it's an irrelevant topic for our current discussion. Tell me something about your *own* trauma."

I set the bourbon down. I wanted both hands on the cold surface of the bar now.

"Seeing those things, recording those things, is trauma. I assure you that it is—"

"Is not your story," he said, shaking his head. "Not your pain. Tell me about a time when *you* felt pain. Go ahead. Tell me."

I stood there, palms down on the bar, the stone cool against my skin, and searched for a memory of pain. It would be easy. It *had* to be easy.

Bryce Lermond leaned back in his leather chair and crossed his right leg over his left.

"I'm waiting," he said. "A man of your pedigree, with all that travel to dangerous parts of the world, surely, *surely*, has suffered pain."

"Damn right I have."

"Excellent. So tell me about it. One memory. It doesn't need to be dramatic, by the way. Maybe a broken finger, a bloody nose? You've got some scars on your face. Tell me about them. How they happened, how it felt."

Scars. I felt the soapstone cool against my palm and a wild relief rose out of the touch. I lifted my right hand and held it out to him.

"Right here," I said. "From broken glass, after my first night with your psychotic little mental infection."

"You remember that experience?"

"Yes, I remember it! I woke up . . ."

He saw me hesitate, and a smile spread across his face.

I wanted to kill him right then. The only restraint was my own horrified realization that he was right. I didn't remember the cut. I remembered the aftermath. I remembered waking up with my hand painted in blood. I remembered going to the doctor. I remembered—

"Oh, shit," I whispered, and Bryce's smile widened. I wasn't paying much attention to him anymore, though; my mind was back in that doctor's office. The one the nurse had told me I'd visited years earlier after shredding the ligaments in my ankle. I didn't remember that visit. Didn't remember the injury. I remembered the game, remembered the open lane to the basket, and then . . .

Nothing.

"How?" I whispered.

"You're with me now, aren't you?" Bryce said. "Excellent! However, I warn you that all of this will probably be distracting. I suspect you'll spend a lot of time searching for memories now. Don't. I realize that's easy for me to say, but I assure you that you're not missing as much as you might fear. You're missing pain, and only pain." He paused. "And dreams, of course."

Those are back, I thought, but I wasn't going to tell him that. I felt as if there were nothing I could hide from him; he knew more than me about my life. The dreams, I could keep to myself.

The ghosts.

"How?" I repeated.

He got to his feet, crossed to the bar, and poured himself another bourbon. He offered the bottle to me, and when I didn't respond, he shrugged and set it down and then took the glass back to his chair. He sat and looked out at the harbor, which was filling in with more fog by the minute.

"Your mother was a brilliant woman. So far ahead of the rest of her field. She set out to block a single traumatic memory. There are dozens of elite researchers working on the same thing. No one has come close. The only problem was that she over-achieved. She didn't just erase a single bad memory or remove a single recurring nightmare. She blocked them altogether." He turned back to me. "If it holds up . . . well, I can hardly imagine the value."

"You're a sick man," I said. "And you're wrong about my lack of leverage. I've got contacts at the highest levels in—"

"The Department of Defense? FBI? Pentagon? CIA? By all means, give them a call. I suspect there are a few people in each of those agencies who have familiarity with the work I call Clarity, and a hell of a lot more interest in protecting it than exposing it."

I couldn't tell you how many times I've read the phrase *his eyes twinkled* and—embarrassingly—how many times I've written it when too lazy to find an original phrase. I'd never seen it happen, though. In real life, it doesn't happen, right? Well, when Bryce Lermond taunted me with the result of my potential calls to the Pentagon, the son of a bitch's eyes *twinkled*. They really did. He was that damned delighted with himself. He looked like a puppy crouched over a new toy, daring you to take it from him.

"You're a smart man," he said. "Smart enough to understand the enormous value of a weapon so simple—and cheap, I might add—as an auditory signal that can end a life. That tool on its own would revolutionize the very idea of power, wouldn't it? But it's still a weapon, still an arm's race, and what risk do you see to that?"

My mouth was dry, the vestiges of the bourbon harsh in my throat when I breathed.

"If someone else got ahold of it, the power tips."

He pointed at me. "Exactly! Then we'd have real trouble. Imagine—nations rushing out earplugs and noise-canceling machines. The tinfoil hat approach to national defense. It would be something to see, wouldn't it?"

He sounded almost wistful about the idea.

"So we have a source of unprecedented power," he said. "Affordable, portable, incredible. Almost omnipotent power. You can't unleash it, though. Unless . . ." He smiled at me again. "You see how this ends, right?"

"Unless you can deploy a defense for it."

"Precisely. A vaccine, so to speak. If I could say, 'Here is the weapon, and here is the shield' . . . well, then. Well. We would really have something."

It was silent for a moment, and then he clasped his hands together, leaned forward, and smiled up at me.

"Nine out of ten, Nick. Nine out of ten. One soldier still standing."

"I haven't heard it all, though." I didn't mean to whisper, but that was how it came out.

"I know." He nodded grimly. "We will have to see how you do with the whole thing, won't we?"

I saw Ashley Holland standing on the edge of the roof in the rain, saw Pat standing in the upper reaches of that white pine, and I shook my head.

"I'm not doing it. Fuck you."

"Confrontation in your blood, eh?"

"I won't listen to it."

"You're missing the point, Nick. You'll *have* to listen. One way or another, it's going to happen. Do you think you can just walk away now? Be real, man."

I remembered the night before, in Camden, when I'd found myself listening to the song without any conscious memory of beginning it.

"I'm not the monster you want me to be," Bryce Lermond said.

I laughed.

"Really," he said, "I'm not. If I were, I'd have you handcuffed to a chair right now, locked in a sound-proof room while I blasted the song at you. But I won't do that. I think there's too much risk."

"Microdosing," I said, remembering his odd choice of terminology in our first conversation. "That's what you want me to do."

"I think it's best," he said, nodding, as if he were a trusted doctor agreeing on a treatment plan. "That's why I broke it up for you. Verse by verse, bit by bit."

"What's the song? Where in the hell did this thing come from?"

He smiled and shook his head. "I'm going to let you walk out of here. I'm going to let you go at your own pace. It's more than most in my position would do, I assure you. Originally, I didn't much care what happened to you. I'll confess that. But now? Why, now, Nick, I'm almost rooting for you."

He got to his feet and nodded at the windows, where the banks of gray fog were thickening.

"Let's go downstairs and retrieve your phone, shall we? The Clarity app will be restored to it, as you wished. This has been a fine talk, but we need to send you on your way. The sun will be down soon. I think you should be someplace comfortable when that happens."

41

The last man standing.

It's a phrase that usually signifies victory, a triumph against the odds. The way Bryce Lermond had explained it to me, though, I felt anything but triumphant as I walked out of the mill with my phone in my hand, the Clarity icon restored to the home screen.

Of those ten, nine are dead, he had said. *Suicides.*

It was the wrong word. He knew it and I knew it. They weren't suicides; they were murders.

I faced down toward the harbor, where the incoming fog was now thick enough to hide the buildings just a block away, and I almost hesitated, as if afraid of the fog. I wanted to look back to see if Renee was at the door. She'd walked me out of the mill in absolute silence. We'd talk soon enough, I knew. It was the idea of another watcher—not Renee but Bryce Lermond, up there in front of his wide windows with his bourbon in hand—that made me push past the fear and into the fog. I didn't want to show him so much as a hesitation. I should throw my phone into the storm sewer while he watched. The app held the means to my execution, and I'd walked in and asked for it. Let him watch while I destroyed it. Not a victory, maybe, but at least I'd have the satisfaction of knowing that he'd be disappointed.

I didn't throw the phone, though. I held tight to it.

You'll need the song.

Ashley had said that. She'd also told me to return to Rosewater.

I sat in my truck for a long time, running the defroster, waiting for the windshield to clear. It wasn't much help, though. The fog was outside of the truck, and there was no choice now but to drive through it.

By the time I reached Rosewater, the sky had cleared and the sun was visible in the west. This was the way of the place. The fog massed on the coast and was pinned in the eastern valleys by the mountains.

I'd been awake for fifteen hours already, coming off three hours of sleep. I was exhausted. Sleep would come easily if I let it. I put a pot of coffee on to brew and then went back outside and walked down the rock to where the stone was still bathed in sunlight. The sun was descending in the west and the cloud cover was thickening. It wouldn't take long for full dark to fall tonight.

Out on the water, a loon called, its echoing cry piercing the stillness.

I looked over at Bob Beauchamp's cabin and saw that he was working in the garage, the door up and the light on. He was sitting on a stool in front of his workbench. I left the rock and pushed through the pines, crossing the soft, permafrost-like soil that would be a bog in spring.

"Bob? Bob!"

Beauchamp turned. He was holding a tube of wood glue in his right hand.

"Whaddaya need?" he said with all the enthusiasm of a man answering a telemarketer's call.

"Come out for just a minute. Please?"

He gave one of his customary Yankee grunts that could have meant *That's fine* or could have meant *Screw you,* but he got down from the stool and walked out of the garage, the wood glue still in his hand.

"Well?"

I held up one finger. "Shhh. Hang on, please. I want you to hear it."

He waited. I waited. Not a sound came. Beauchamp shifted impatiently, but I lifted my finger again, pleading for a little more time. Surely, the sound would come again. Surely.

Then it did. Clear as a church bell, undeniably the song of a loon, the high, echoing cry, the haunting sorrow.

"There! Right there. You heard that."

Bob Beauchamp stared at me, and I didn't like the look on his face. There was neither recognition nor confusion—just pity. Pity and maybe a touch of revulsion.

"You're gonna tell me there's a loon on the pond," he said, a statement not a question.

"You *had* to hear that one, damn it!"

He reached out and slowly and purposefully tightened the cap on the wood glue. He kept his eyes down when he spoke again.

"It ain't like it was before, Bishop. Nobody's greasing my palm to tell you what did happen or what didn't, all right? Never felt good about it then, and I sure as hell don't feel good about it now."

When the loon cried again, I didn't even bother to point it out.

"What did you say?" I asked.

"Your mother's gone. Good as gone, anyhow. Not comin' back to put the screws to me." He looked sideways, as if she might be standing there, and added, "Or the dollars, sure. I always took her money, didn't I?"

"What are you talking about, Bob?"

He tugged on his beard, stubby fingers moving though the white hair as if he was trying to tamp down rage.

"It wasn't any business of mine."

"It never is," I told him, and his eyes flashed at that, but then I said, "Just tell me what the hell you're talking about."

"There were never any friggin' loons!" he shouted, waving his overmuscled forearms toward the lake as if shooing something away from him. "But we had to pretend, ayuh, oh, ayuh, we all had to pretend. Dollars in our pockets then."

"Bob . . ."

"I don't know what she did to your head," he said. "I truly don't. Some people say she just wiped your memory clean. I have trouble believing such a thing as that. But—"

"What people say that?"

"But I've lived too long in this world to dismiss anything out of hand. All I know is I'm done going along with your imagination. Because it's . . . disturbing, is what it is. You hearing shit that's not there and comin' down here to ask do I hear it, too, just like when you were a kid, jeezum, just like that summer all over again."

I felt as if I were in the harbor park again, facing Renee as she told me that I'd been driving the car, and that memory made my legs unsteady. I shifted, tried to concentrate on Bob Beauchamp's grizzled face.

"You were paid to lie to me about the birds?" I asked.

"About everything!" Beauchamp said, and it was a good thing he'd closed the cap of the glue, because he was squeezing it tight now, the muscles on the back of his hand standing out. "If you said it happened, I was supposed to agree. Workin' through trauma, you were. That's what she told everyone, at least. Nick was working through trauma. Your old man had died and everyone felt bad enough, but it still wasn't right. It still wasn't—"

"Everyone?"

"Sure."

"Who else knew, Bob?"

"Whole friggin' pond knew, I expect. Well, down here to the cove, anyhow. The Luces, Cayas, Hollands, Wickendens, Lermonds—anyone who might see you on a regular basis knew. We were just supposed to go along with what you said, and we weren't supposed to ask any questions. If you said your old man had been lost at sea, we were to nod our heads. Abducted by aliens? Sure thing, kiddo! It was bullshit, and it was dangerous. I knew it then and I know it now. It might've helped the nightmares, but that doesn't make it *right*, son, you know? But she was your mother, and you were just a kid, so what the hell was I supposed to say? I kept my mouth shut. You and I didn't run into each other much anyhow."

I felt as if gravity had tripled in strength, no longer tethering me to the earth but threatening to pull me down into it.

"Marilyn Lermond knew?"

"Ayuh."

"I don't even remember her. Or any of them."

He shrugged. "They don't use the place much. Never have. For all the money it costs them to build and rebuild, they're hardly ever there. Too much money to know what to do with it, I guess."

"But they were there when I was a kid," I said slowly. "The summer when you were all asked to lie to me—*paid* to lie to me—they were there?"

"She was. The husband and the kid, they were down to Boston or someplace. She was alone. Except for your mother. They took to each other. A glass of wine in the evening out on that lawn, things like that. Talking. Just a lot of talking."

It went quiet. The loon broke the stillness. I watched Bob Beauchamp's face. His expression never changed. He hadn't heard a damn thing.

"I'm sorry, Bob," I said. "And thank you. Truly. Thank you for telling me what you just did. It's important."

"It's in the past," he said.

I shook my head. "I wish it was, but it's not."

"You feelin' all right, son?"

"I'm fine."

"Looking peaked."

"I'm fine." I took a breath and stepped back. "Thanks again. And I'm sorry. For all of it."

He looked nonplussed now. "Nothing for you to apologize for. Wasn't your idea, not any of it. Rosewater is not a good place for you. Wasn't then, isn't now."

"Excuse me?"

He frowned with what seemed real concern. "If you're hearing shit that's not real, son? I'm no scientist, no one like your mother—and some people say she was a genius, the real deal, a no-doubt genius—but what she was doing felt risky to me. When a boy—or a man—gets to hearing things that aren't real . . ." He shook his head. "The last thing you should tell him is that you hear it, too. That ain't good."

"No," I agreed. "It's not good. Thank you, Bob. For telling me the truth."

He whirled as if relieved to be dismissed and hustled back to the garage. I turned and walked back up to the camp, moving slowly, taking in all the porches and windows that faced me.

They all knew.

The green reflectors of the Gatsby House—the Lermond house—glimmered in the afternoon sun.

When I reached the rock on which our camp was built, the loon called again, and its usually soothing sound made my heart begin to hammer. The wind rose and pine needles showered down and I looked up at the towering tree where last night Pat Ryan had walked to meet the end of his life, or at least the life he'd known.

Nine of ten. Then there's Nick Bishop.

"Immune," I whispered. "Thanks, Mom."

I wanted to believe it. It was one thing to say and another to trust, though.

The loon called again, and this time there was an answering cry. Her mate? His mate? A rival? I had no idea. Maybe an expert could tell me, if the expert could hear them. They were louder here, though. There was no question about that. Even if they were imagined, they were louder up here by the camp.

Another cry came, and this time I walked toward the sound.

The camp's floor rested up on concrete blocks on top of the rock, a cheap approach that was common with seasonal places in Maine. You drained the pipes in the fall and buttoned the place up and let the winter do its worst. I knelt and studied the foundation and when the loon called again, the sound was even louder, piercing. I could have sworn the bird was right there, shrieking as if I'd threatened its nest. I reacted instinctively and looked for the source of the sound. There was no bird in sight, of course.

There was, however, a pinprick of red light glowing beneath the camp.

I moved toward the shadows under the building, sidestepping in a crouch like a catcher shifting to take an outside pitch. Smells of dust and moss and old, cold stone waited in the darkness. The light grew brighter, a single point of crimson against the black.

Traps, I thought. *Some kind of electronic trap for the chipmunks. Mom remembered those, of all things.*

I ducked all the way under the building, pushing my face through a sticky spiral of cobwebs that I wiped clear with trembling fingers. As I shuffled forward, I saw that the red light was coming from the center of a black plastic box about the size of a paperback book. A power indicator, I thought. But to what?

The loon cried again. It was deafening down here, so loud that I tried to jump away from the sound, moving backward and rising up simultaneously and braining myself on one of the joists, a jarring, painful blow. I reached up to grab my aching skull and my fingers met something thin and slick and cool. No spiderweb this time.

It was a wire. Fine-gauged, snaking from that black plastic power supply box, running along the length of the joist, held in place by wood staples.

I traced the wire back toward the daylight, and there, at the edge of the structure where the joist met the wall, I found a speaker.

It was hung with what appeared to be double-sided tape or maybe Velcro. It had a metal protective grid but felt surprisingly light. I peeled it off the wood and tugged it outside so I could see it clearly. The loon cry came again, and again it was so painfully loud that I reacted instinctively. When my palm covered the speaker, the loon's cry was undeniably muffled.

"Traps," I whispered, remembering my mother's gibberish about traps for the chipmunks.

Had she said they were for the chipmunks, though? No. She had not. I'd assumed that was what she was talking about. All she'd said was that there were traps under the house.

And Renee had told me that years ago my dreamless, trauma-free sleep had been the product of two careful approaches: reinforcement and audio cues.

I withdrew my clip knife from my pocket, flicked the blade open, and severed the speaker wire. The red light signifying the active connection to the power supply went dark.

42

It easily could have been a birdsong. All I know was that it was a repetitive cue, played at a frequency that was supposed to be inaudible. Your mother researched birdsongs, though, particularly how much a baby will know instinctively, even if its parents are gone and it is isolated."

Renee said this while turning the little speaker over in her hand as we stood in the kitchen together. She'd come straight from the mill, and though she said Bryce hadn't showed any interest in her destination, I suspected he knew exactly where she was.

"The sound was played at a frequency that was inaudible?"

"Yes."

"It's *loud* to me," I said. "An undeniable sound. So you think she put that speaker down there?"

"Yes. If it's a bird's song, yes. That's what she was working with at the time. Later, she moved on to words and tones. A language study from Germany was particularly fascinating to her. They had a group of students who were learning Dutch. The researchers played Dutch words while the students slept, and retention improved. Their memories were clearly enhanced from merely hearing the words while they slept. Then the researchers put a twist on it—they played the same words and added a single, one-pitch tone immediately after. A beep, basically."

"And?"

"The tone blocked the formation of memories. It was astonishing: the students in that control group didn't simply fail to improve; they regressed. Their memories *weakened*."

I had that black-ice sensation again. It was becoming more common and thus less disorienting. If you spend enough time on black ice, does an illusion of control return? I was about to find out.

"Marilyn Lermond and her husband worked on sonic weapons," I said, staring at the little speaker I'd removed from under the camp. Renee had set it down on the counter, and it looked menacing to me, its metal grille suddenly reminiscent of Bryce Lermond's smile.

"Sounds very James Bond."

"It is. Read the recent complaints from our embassies in Cuba and China: strange sounds, memory loss, dizziness, headaches. Children waking up with nosebleeds." I stopped there, remembering the sudden nosebleed I'd had after walking out of the Hefron Mill on my first visit.

"They called it Havana syndrome," I said slowly. "One of the diplomats described the same sound every night—like a marble dropped on the floor, he said. A single, sharp crack. Then he'd show up at work and not be able to remember the names of simple objects. The sound came at night, and in the day his mind wasn't right. Wasn't his own. That's pretty close to what you were talking about with the language study, isn't it? A repetitive tone that disrupted the formation of memories."

"Yes. You wrote about this?"

"Tried to. Mostly I just read about it. The State Department stayed silent. The people who would talk all said the same thing—it was likely some sort of sonic or microwave weapon that affected the inner ear."

I looked down at the speaker with its cut wire, the copper showing like an exposed vein.

"Nine out of ten are dead," Renee said softly, and I knew her curiosity in the speaker was gone. I'd caught her up on my fun chat with Bryce Lermond—most of it, anyhow—and the list of the dead that I'd avoided joining thus far.

"That's what he said, yes."

She walked out of the kitchen and stood with her arms folded beneath her breasts, staring out across the pond. There was a smudge of dull ruby light over the western hills.

"You're not actually going to listen to it again, are you?" she asked.

"I don't know. He thinks I'll need to. Your sister—"

"It's not really my sister!" She almost shouted it. "It's a dream," she said, voice lower. "The song brings her into your dreams somehow."

"Fine. The nightmare version of your sister says the same thing."

But the word *nightmare* for Ashley wasn't any more accurate than the word *suicide* was for the cause of her death. She was a ghost. I was sure of it.

Renee turned her back to the window and sat on top of the picnic table, facing me, her feet propped on the bench seat. She reminded me of her younger self then, something in the posture calling up the blond girl I'd bonded with in the months after my father's death, oblivious to her partnership with my mother. Hell, oblivious to a lot of things.

"What are you going to do, Nick?" she said.

"Try to burn Bryce's life down," I said simply. "Pat's in a coma and Ashley is dead. He doesn't believe I can touch him. He made that clear. I intend to prove otherwise."

"Will you listen again?"

"I think I'll have to." I put my hand in my pocket and touched my phone almost unconsciously, as if to reassure me that it was there. "I'm not sure when, but I've got a feeling it will be clear."

She was silent, watching me. I looked over her shoulder, to the place where the red light had died. The hills were blue and gray now. Sunset.

"And I won't sleep tonight," I said. "The next time I sleep, I want the sun to be up."

"You think the sun matters that much?"

I thought of her dead sister's red lips framing the ice-fogged blackness where her mouth belonged. *Burn the night.*

"Yes," I said. "I think it does."

I brewed another pot of coffee. The fatigue that had been building throughout the day was settling into my brain as well as my body. That last wisp of sunlight had seemed important. Now that it was gone, I was more afraid.

As I watched the coffee drip through the filter and fill the carafe like sand in an hourglass, I said, "Maybe I'll tie myself to the truck, make sure I can't do any midnight climbing even if I wanted to."

It was supposed to be a joke, but after watching Pat the night before, it didn't seem funny, at all, and from the way Renee grimaced, I knew it hit her the same way.

"I'll stay with you," she said.

"You don't need to."

"You kidding me? I'm going to drive home and, what, cross my fingers, hope that when I wake up I don't hear news about you walking off a roof somewhere?"

It was my turn to wince.

"Sorry," she said.

"It's true," I said. "It is absolutely insane, and yet it's true. I don't know if I'll make it through the night." I shook my head, trying to process the madness of all of it. "How did he *get* the song here? How do you think he managed that?"

"By get it here you mean . . ."

"Across generations, to borrow his own phrase." I pulled the coffeepot out, found two mugs, and filled them. "It would seem impossible to preserve that song if what Bryce says about it is true. If the people who hear it die, then how do you keep it alive? See my point?"

"Maybe there are more people like you."

"My mother created a zombie army that we're unaware of?"

"No. Maybe the thing that she created within you is natural to some people. The lack of dreams, the selective loss of memory."

I brought the coffee over to her. She took it without a word and held it between cupped hands as if she wanted to absorb its heat.

"I wish she could talk," I said. "Really talk, I mean. I feel like she has the answers, you know? Some of them, at least."

"I've shared that exact wish so many times since my sister died."

I was standing in front of her, facing the window, and the darkness beyond made me uneasy, so I turned around and sat beside her on the picnic table. I could feel my phone pressing against my leg. The AirPods were in the other pocket. All within my control—until it wasn't, like the previous night, when I'd awoken to discover I'd been listening to the sleep song without ever intending to play it.

I sipped the coffee, tried to imagine the caffeine spreading through me like hot blood. *Stay awake. Just stay awake until morning.*

"Your mom saved you from this," Renee said.

"Maybe. And at what cost? My memory is gone."

She reached up with her left hand and touched my temple. "Your memory of *pain* is gone. And what I'm talking about"—she caressed the side of my head in a slow, circular motion—"is truly lifesaving. When others heard that awful song, they died. You listened and lived. That's your mother's work."

"It's the silence that I hate," I said. "She could have told me at any point. Should have."

When Renee stopped massaging my temple, I wished I hadn't spoken. It had felt good, soothing. Probably would have put me to sleep, though. Less good.

"I understand that," she said. "I could have told you, too."

"Eventually you did."

"A little late, though."

"Maybe not."

We were still sitting side by side, almost touching. I looked at her in silence and she cocked a quizzical eyebrow.

"What?"

"Why'd you change your hair color?"

"Why does *that* matter?" Her face darkened.

"Sorry," I said. "It doesn't. I just—"

"My sister and I looked more similar the older she got," she said, and reached up to touch her hair as if it contained a memory. "By the time she was in college, everyone commented on it. The resemblance. I liked it, back then. When she died, I couldn't stand it anymore. I'd look in the mirror and see her. I didn't want to look anything like her. Not after watching that surveillance video. The way she just . . . stepped out of this life . . ."

I put my hand on her leg, and she caught my arm and leaned into it, wrapping her own arms around my biceps, hugging me tight. She leaned her head into my shoulder and for a long time neither of us said a word.

"I'm sorry that I never told you the truth," she whispered.

"You did eventually. Better than most."

"Still, I'm sorry."

"Thank you."

She lifted her head and looked up at me. Our faces were very close.

"I did care," she said. "I hope you believe that. You were never some sort of game or experiment, Nick. You were a friend who was going through hell and I wanted to help. Your mother was desperate to help. That's what we were doing."

"I know. I believe that. Really."

She smiled weakly and then squeezed my arm and leaned up to give me a peck on the cheek. I turned toward her at the same time, though, and for a moment she froze, her face an inch away from mine. I started to turn away when she tugged on my arm, pulled my face lower, down to meet hers, and we kissed.

It was a long, slow kiss, the kind that can make the rest of the world fade away, at least for a moment. I twisted on the table and brushed her hair away from her face and let my hand rest lightly on the back of her neck. I could feel the heat of her along the cut in my palm, a throb that seemed to transfer from within her to within me. We were overeager, hungry, and hunting, like two teenagers who've waited too long. I guess that's what it was, in a way.

When we finally broke apart, we were both breathing hard. I pulled back and looked into her green eyes and said, "Bad idea, right?"

"Maybe?"

"Which implies maybe not?"

"You think?"

"Felt nice for a bad idea."

"Didn't it, though?"

Another pause, and this time I thought the moment had passed. Then she smiled and said, "I did promise to keep you up all night, didn't I? Wasn't that the deal?"

My throat tightened and my heart raced. This time, it was a very good sensation.

"Yeah," I managed. "You did promise that."

She bent close to me again. As we kissed, she shifted on the table and swung one leg around me so that her weight was resting on my thighs. I put my arms around her and leaned back, pulling us down onto the table—and directly into the coffee cups.

They tipped over spilled, coffee dripping between the gaps in the old picnic table in fat, mud-colored drops. We both laughed, and I straightened up.

"Very smooth of me, I know. Hang on, I'll get a towel."

But she rose with me and took me by the hand and pulled me toward the open door of the bedroom.

"The coffee can wait, Nick. I'd rather not."

I was happy to oblige.

She guided me into the room and I was so lost to her touch that I didn't even think to find a light as I swept the door shut with my heel, leaving us in blackness save for a thin band of light bleeding through from the kitchen.

We fumbled in the dark, bumping against the old furniture in the too-small room, hands colliding as we reached for each other's clothes, laughing at the awkwardness of it all. Then the clothes were off and we were on the bed and Renee was beneath me, warm and soft and sensual, and all the horrors of the day were fading.

I kissed her neck and down her past her collarbone and lowered my mouth to her breast and she made a soft sigh and ran her fingers through my hair and down my back, an electric crescendo riding along her touch. Then she slipped her hand away, found me, and guided me into her. I closed my eyes, sealing out that final band of light, and lost myself to the steady rhythms of her rising hips.

"No rush," she whispered. "We've got all night."

She pulled away then and swung out from under me, the old bed creaking as I rolled onto my back and she slid on top of me and over me without ever taking her hands from their tight clasp around the back of my neck. She arched her back and her breasts rose in the shadows and I grasped her hips and pulled her tighter, pushed deeper, closed my eyes again, lost to the perfect, exquisite heat of her. She rocked slowly at first, excruciatingly slowly, then faster, moaning as she lowered her face and her hair spilled across my chest. I reached up and ran my fingers through it, felt the dampness of the spilled coffee but barely registered it, all of my brain and body devoted to the one place where we were joined.

Her hair wasn't just damp, though. It was wet. Soaked, dripping. Cold water running through my fingers. I opened my eyes.

That was when I saw her hair was blond, too. In the faint filtered light Renee's hair was the color of straw, darkened only by dampness. I was staring at it, frozen, as she leaned forward, her tongue tracing a line between my pectorals and up to my neck, and then lifted her face to mine.

It was Ashley Holland, dead-fleshed and dead-eyed but ruby-lipped. Her lips brushed mine as she whispered, and cold air flooded into my mouth like a gust of winter wind. Then her lips were on my ear, and she was whispering.

"You have to listen now, Nick. You must. It's the only way. Otherwise, you'll have to stay. You must listen very carefully now. Hear only the right things."

Her mouth left my ear and her cold, wet hair trailed across my cheek and we were face-to-face again, her lifeless eyes fixed on mine.

I screamed. Pulled back and away, scrambling, falling from the bed, the darkness rising as Ashley followed me down, lowering her lips to mine.

43

Waves rose and broke, rose and broke. Massive, undulating swells of charcoal-colored water foamed with white spray. Behind the sound of the waves was the relentless drilling and dripping of rain and a high moan of wind. Wood grated, creaked, and cried out. Somewhere a flag flapped and snapped as if determined to escape its tether.

All I could see was the endless storm-tossed water—and the fog.

All around me, the fog. It floated with calm stillness, in perfect contrast to the angry waves. It drifted placidly above the churn. I watched it and dizziness slapped at me like one of the great furious waves and I was sure that I would fall into the water to be hammered into the ink-dark depths.

I looked down. My feet were bare and bloodied and too white, the fine bones visible like gray threads beneath skin so pale it was nearly blue. I was standing on a jagged wet rock, a few feet above the tide line. Moss-colored rockweed blanketed the surface closer to the water, and it looked impossibly soft, soothing as fleece. I wanted to step down onto it and ease my aching, bleeding feet, but it seemed too close to the water, too dangerous. I needed to get higher and could not risk descending. The big waves were on the way, I knew, promised by the thundering bass of the sea out beyond the blackness.

The fog kept coming. Thicker now, and faster, though still patient. A steady creep, like a spider that races ahead only when you take your eyes off it.

"Help," I said. The sound of my voice was lost instantly to the rain and wind and waves. Somewhere behind the fog and blackness was the relentless *snap, snap, snap* of that flag or sail whipped by the wind.

"Follow the song," Ashley Holland said from behind me, and I whirled but couldn't find her. I was alone on the rock and I realized now that the rock was disappearing quickly. The tide was coming in fast. Already the rockweed was underwater, tendrils of it moving like fingers waving farewell.

I stepped higher, lacerating my feet. Hot blood sluiced across that pale—too pale, far too pale—skin.

"Where are you?" I shouted. My voice loud enough to hear now, amplified by fear.

No sound answered but the storm and the sea.

I walked higher still. My feet throbbed and jets of blood darkened the rock ahead of me. I wanted to stop and sit but the tide was coming in fast, the water chasing on my heels, spray dousing my back even as I climbed, and I knew that if I sat down here, I would never rise again.

I was going to run out of rock, though. Soon it would all be under.

"I will have to swim," I said, and this time Ashley answered me.

"Don't swim," she said. "Follow the song. Do not go into the water. You have to follow the song."

"I can't hear the song!" I screamed, and now I saw her moving in the mist, a figure floating through the fog, only a few steps ahead. I scrambled toward her, the pain in my feet excruciating, the blood splashing knee-high in glittering red arcs.

There she was. Just ahead now. Almost there.

I slipped in my own blood and a wave broke frigid and fierce across my back and now I was down on the rock, pulling myself ahead with my hands. A fingernail split and peeled back, blackened, already dead. The water covered my feet, salt scouring the open wounds. I scrabbled across the rock, grasping a handful of needlelike rock each time, fighting higher, higher, until finally I caught up to Ashley.

Except it wasn't Ashley. It was a shirtless man in tattered trousers. His torso was laced with ribbons of flayed flesh and his hair fell to his shoulders in matted tangles. Sores crusted his lips. They split when he smiled, and blood filled them. He had no teeth, just a mouth of decaying flesh and blackened tongue.

"You'll stay now!" he cried, gleeful, as the blood ran down his chin. "Right here with us, down here below. You'll wait with us down here below!"

I spun away. Scrambled to my right as the cold spray whipped into my face. The rock ended in a cliff, and just beyond the sea waited impatiently, tossing with the lumbering fury of a beast too large for speed but too powerful to need it.

The steady cracking of the flag lashed, louder now, and I looked toward the sound. Something large and pale swooped out of the fog and I ducked and raised my arms to protect myself. A shadow flickered by and then circled back, but nothing attacked. I finally looked up and saw what was above: a ripped sail flapping on a frayed rope. That was the source of the snapping sound I'd associated with a flag. The sail was rotting and blackened along the edges, snapping, snapping, snapping. Barely hanging on.

I stepped closer, trying in vain to see what the sail was attached to, and then a clatter of wood drew my eyes back to the ground.

An oaken plank rode the waves in against the rocks, bashed against them only to be tugged back out and thrown forward again. It had to have been twelve feet long, jagged and splintered at the ends. It was colored dark green by either paint or rot, but something was written across it in a glistening red ink that I knew was blood.

I knelt, leaned forward, strained to read.

PURGATORIUM

The word was clear one moment and gone the next as water broke over the plank and the tide swept it back again. Then the fog came in and wiped the sea away and then there was nothing but the rock and the mist and my bleeding hands.

"I don't hear the song!" I screamed, and Ashley Holland answered in a voice that was as calm as the sea was angry.

"Listen," she said. "Just listen."

I stopped moving. Clung to the rock as the waves pounded and the fog thickened and swirled. I heard the storm and the sea and the *snap, snap, snap* of the flag. The creaking and rasping of wood.

And then the song.

A woman's voice, faint but pure and steady as a mountain stream:

Do not fear, oh, do not fear
For no man among us must die
No man among us must die

"It's there," I whispered. "I hear it now."

"Shhhhh," Ashley answered, and a bracing breeze passed over me, as if her voice were trapped within the wind. "Listen. *Liisssten.*"

I peered into the fog and strained to hear.

No man among us must die
No man among us must die

If you want to see home
I ask you to rise
Tell you now to rise
Now, now you must rise
For no man among us must die

"Offer your hand, Nick," Ashley Holland told me.

I reached into the fog, saw now that my hand looked as my feet had before, emptied of blood except for a red-black sore where my fingernail had been. A wave hammered my legs, waist-high, staggeringly powerful. It dragged me across the rock face, granite shredding my skin, and I cried out just as a cool palm found my own and a strong hand closed on mine and tugged me upward, out of the cold, dark sea.

"Nick," Renee said. "Nick, are you there? Are you there?"

44

She was staring at me, her eyes horrified, and until I heard my own voice say "Yes," I wasn't sure that I could answer.

She let out a long exhalation and sagged to the ground beside me. She was wearing nothing but my sweatshirt, her long slim legs bare beneath it. We were on the rock outside of the camp, and I realized that I was fully dressed—jeans, a button-down shirt, socks, boots, belt, even my watch. I was trembling and felt at once cold to the core and hot to the touch, as if racked by fever.

"What happened?" I said, and then I tried to sit up and the world swam and spun and I slumped forward again, felt the rock cool and rough against my cheek.

Renee's hand was on my back, rubbing it gently, calming, and I could hear my own breath rattling in my lungs. I closed my eyes and concentrated on the cool steadiness of the rock, as I had with the soapstone counter in Bryce Lermond's apartment, high above the harbor, high above the fog. The memory of the fog brought on the memory of the shirtless man with the bloodied torso and the lips crusted with sores, and I began to shiver while Renee Holland rubbed my back and whispered my name.

The fear passed in time. I'm not sure how long it took. I know only that it passed and that she did not leave me until it did.

It was only after the shaking stopped that I became aware of an ache in my right ear. I reached for it instinctively, a response to the pain, but my fingers found hard plastic instead of flesh.

I removed an AirPod from my ear, stared at it there in my cupped palm, and then looked up at Renee. In her face I saw that whatever horrors I'd just experienced, she'd matched. A different movie, maybe, but with the same goal: terror.

"Tell me what happened," I said. "For you, I mean."

"I will. Can you stand?"

I nearly said no but decided to try. I rose on shaking legs, with Renee bearing most of my weight. Beneath the sweatshirt, her own legs were goose-pimpled from the cold night air. The only light came from inside the camp.

Holding tightly to each other, we walked toward it.

PART THREE

PURGATORIUM

45

I'd been on the move for twenty minutes prior to waking, a busy man without being conscious of any of it.

We'd made love, Renee told me, and then I'd slept. She'd considered waking me—that had been my request, of course, to make it through the night without sleeping—but I'd drifted off peacefully and slept deeply and she saw no cause for alarm so long as she remained awake and alert. All we needed, she thought, was a sentry. A single guard would be enough.

"You looked so relaxed. I kept my hand on your chest for a while because I wanted to feel your heartbeat, feel you breathing. You were fine. You were just fine."

At midnight I rose.

"You didn't say a word at first, but you moved like yourself," she said. "At ease, perfectly normal. I said your name, that was all—just *Nick?* like a question—and you smiled and put your finger to my lips. Like, *I'm fine, don't worry.* I thought you were going to the bathroom. It all felt fine. Then you got dressed. It was dark and I couldn't see much, but when I heard you putting on your boots, I asked why you needed your boots on in the bathroom. Still joking, then. Still believing you were . . . yourself."

I hadn't answered her, though. I'd said nothing at all as I walked out of the bedroom. Then a beam of light broke the darkness in the bedroom. It was coming from the floor. From my phone.

She got down from the bed and picked up the phone and saw that Clarity was playing. Motivation Melody #4.

"I called your name then and got no answer. But the air felt cooler suddenly, fresher, and I knew then."

She knew that I was on the move, and outdoors. She pulled on my sweatshirt and ran in pursuit. The front door was standing open, a cool breeze coming through it, and when she burst through, she found me standing in the darkness, eyeing the treetops.

"You seemed curious, nothing more. As if there was something up there that didn't fit. But you didn't look frightened, and you didn't look as if you . . . intended to do anything."

"Climb, you mean."

She acknowledged that with a nod.

"Still, it was terrifying. Because you were there but you were not yourself. All of your expressions were perfectly normal, the way you carried yourself was right, but it was as if I didn't exist at all.

Then you started to shake. You shook like . . . I don't even know how to describe it. As if you were in a blizzard. Only that's not even right, because it was almost boneless, just this awful shudder . . ."

She had to stop and gather herself.

"I saw that you had them in," she said, lifting the case of the AirPods. "And I ran to you and tried to take them, but . . ."

A single tear dripped from her left eye, ran down her cheek, traced her jawline, but didn't fall.

"But then you spoke in my sister's voice," she said, barely audible.

"What?"

"You opened your mouth and spoke but it was my sister's voice," she said, louder now, firm and undeniable. "You said *'He'll need to hear it now. Don't try to stop him. It's too late for that.'*"

"Don't try to stop him," I echoed.

"Yes. As if she was speaking for you." She stopped, shook her head, took a breath. "It was the most terrifying thing I'd ever experienced. And yet I listened and did what I was told." She choked out a laugh. "How about that? I felt like screaming at the top of my lungs and running until I couldn't run another step, but instead, I did what I was told. I let you listen. And the shaking stopped. You sat down. I sat with you. I sat with you and held you and waited for something to happen. For a long time, it was like you were comatose. There in body but not in mind. Then you were *all* there again. I can't

tell you exactly how I knew you were back. Something shifted—not physically, more like an energy
change. A warmth. I don't know how to explain it;
I just knew you were there. I said your name." She
swallowed. "When you spoke, it was in your own
voice again."

I put my hand on her leg and she covered it with
her own, but it was a hesitant move, as if she wasn't
sure she trusted my touch.

"What was it like to you?" she whispered. "Or do
you not remember a thing?"

"I don't remember getting dressed or walking
outside or anything that you just described. What
I remember is very different from that."

I told her all of it—the way her hair had gone
damp in my hand and her face had become her
sister's and then I was alone on the rock island in
the storm-tossed sea. I told her about the shirtless,
bloodied man who waited in the fog and told me
that I would be staying there now. Of the torn, flapping sail and the way her sister's voice guided me
back toward the song.

"These are not nightmares," I said. "It's real."

"*What* is real?"

"The place."

"The rock island?"

"Yes."

"You're serious."

"Yes," I repeated. "I'm not saying I can sail off
and find it, Renee, I'm just saying that it's more real

than a dream. It's something in between, maybe. But I could stay there. Your sister is keeping me from doing it, I think, but I could stay there."

"Which means she is there," Renee said softly.

I didn't answer that.

"It's a dream," she said at last. "A vivid and wickedly powerful dream, evil, yes, but still a human product. At the end of the day, your experience is a human creation. Engineered."

There was a desperate insistence to her tone. I understood. There are some things it's healthier *not* to believe in, maybe. Until the time comes when your experience forces your mind to expand, at least. Then belief takes care of itself, and doubt detonates.

"There was a plank in the water," I told her. "Banging against the rocks. It looked like the stern of an ancient ship, with a name scripted in blood."

"Do you remember the name?"

"*Purgatorium*. Not subtle, right? But I doubt anyone named a ship after . . . Renee? What's wrong?"

She'd gone stiff and pale, her mouth pressed into a thin line.

"Purgatorium," she said.

"Yes."

"That's a Bryce joke."

"Pardon?"

"It was his nickname for Clarity," she said. "Back in the early days, we were debating names for it.

Everything felt either too familiar or too desperately hip. He started calling it Purgatorium then. Made jokes about the ads, how we'd promise to take all of human stress and anxiety and put it on hold, a reprieve. It stood out because it's an odd phrase, you know? *Purgatory*, fine. *Purgatorium* is Latin, though—it's not the kind of word that just comes to the tip of the tongue."

"Does it mean the same thing? Being trapped between worlds, awaiting a fate?"

"Yes," she said.

If the lonely rock island in the fog was as real as I felt it was, then the idea of being trapped there was utterly terrifying. Scrambling on and on through the darkness, endlessly searching for some safe dry stone that was always just ahead of me in the mist.

The feeling was so acute and so horrifying that I had to suppress a shudder. I rose and walked to the bedroom.

"Nick?" Renee sounded alarmed, and with good reason—last time I'd set off alone, the madness was just beginning.

"I'm just getting my notebook."

"Why?"

"Because even though I said I'll never forget it, I don't want to take that chance. I want to write the song down while I can still hear it."

"You remember the words?"

"Yes."

I brought the notebook and pen out and flipped to

the page that was scrawled with my attempt to capture the pitch and cadence of the song. I looked at those lines and now saw them in an entirely different fashion—as a whole rather that individual beats.

"They're waves," I said.

"What?"

I traced the rising and falling lines with my index finger. "Big swells, out deep."

"That's what it sounded like?"

"Yes." But I was almost more interested in what it looked like. Giant rolling breakers, the kind that sounded peaceful and pleasant from a distance but would pummel and pull you down. Drown you. I stared at the image for a few seconds and then turned the page and began to write. The melody returned to mind easily, and the words rode in on it.

Do not fear, oh, do not fear
For no man among us must die
No man among us must die
If you want to see home
I ask you to rise
Tell you to rise
Now, now you must rise
For no man among us must die

Renee was reading over my shoulder. "Sexist," she said. "'No *man* among us must die'? I guess the women and children were screwed."

We both laughed then. The laughter felt good.

Better than good: it felt necessary, like a lifeline tossed from the shores of sanity.

You'll stay now! the shirtless man had cried as blood ran down his chin. *Right here with us, down here below. You'll wait with us down here below!*

I took a breath and wrote *purgatorium* below the lyrics.

"It won't be a real ship—it can't be with a name like that—but it means something."

"The HMS *Terror* was a real ship," she said. "I wouldn't rule out any disastrous name ideas. The HMS *Fatal Voyage*."

She was pushing too hard for humor now, but I understood it, of course. She'd been terrified. She still was. The world had gone mad around her. You either laugh or you cry, right? Renee wasn't the crying kind.

I smiled. "Fair point. I'm sure Pat would have . . ."

"Would have what?"

My smile faded and I stared at the notebook and thought about that night at Riptides when Pat and I drank beer and talked about old times. We'd joked about shipwrecks that night. Then, in the hospital where he lay comatose, his ex-wife told me that Pat had been casting about from one dream to the next after he'd been laid off. Including writing the book about shipwrecks.

"He would have known any story about the ship," I said. "And I think it might be real."

"The ship might have been real? Should be easy

enough to find that out." She took out her phone and began to enter in a search. I watched in silence. I'd meant the ship, yes, but it wasn't the ship that lingered in my mind.

My mind was on the rock island where the bloodied man had told me I was going to stay with him in the fog.

46

There was no ship named the *Purgatorium* that had sailed off the coast of Maine—or anywhere else, so far as Renee and I could tell. We spent the remaining hours of darkness together, sitting on opposite sides of the old picnic table, searching for phrases from the lyrics, the ship name, anything that might replace nightmares with realities. We didn't find anything, but I was happy to have the task. It passed the hours, at least.

It burned the night.

Dawn was rising when we stopped. There was no discussion of this; we simply stopped when the sky went from black to gray to pale pink. Renee set her phone aside, folded her arms on the table, and rested her forehead on them. I realized how exhausted she must be.

"Thank you," I said.

"Didn't find anything," she said, her voice muffled.

"For staying awake. For staying with me."

"Oh. Of course." She didn't look up, and I was glad for that, because I wouldn't have wanted her to see my expression. When thanking her for staying awake with me, I'd finally paused to consider the alternative. What if I'd been alone?

I was thinking about that while I got up and made yet another pot of coffee. Watching it brew, I found myself hearing Ashley Holland's voice.

Now, now you must rise

The lyrics had been looping through my brain for hours now, but as day brightened around the camp, the idea of *rising* lingered. There had been two commands, I thought: the instruction of the song and the instruction of Ashley's voice. They had seemed in sync at the time, but were they? What would have happened if I had listened only to the song?

Now, now you must rise

Ashley had told me to offer my hand. I'd done so, and then I was back in my own life, back at the camp, saved from that hellscape of rock ledge in the angry sea. If it had been only the song, though . . .

Renee's shoulders rose and fell slowly. She was asleep facedown on the table. I moved quietly to the door and stepped outside and stood watching the pond in the dawn light while the coffee steamed. I didn't like the steam. It reminded me too much of fog. The morning was silent except for the wind in the trees and the soft lapping of water in the cove. No loons. They were never there to begin with, of course. Bob Beauchamp had been right.

I turned and looked at his cabin reflexively. A

thin wisp of smoke rose from the chimney. Bob was an early riser.

Now, now you must rise

No surprise from a retired harbor master, though. You had to be up early. That was when there was the most boat traffic. I frankly hadn't the faintest idea what a harbor master did other than take violation complaints and make calls to boat owners when there was a problem. Like, for example, when their boat sank.

A ghost of a smile came over my face, remembering that night in the old apartment in Hammel when a drunken Pat learned that the SS *Money Pit* had found its way to a watery grave without having even left the harbor. He'd then purchased and christened the *Andrea Fitzgerald*. He'd never met a salvage project he didn't like.

I was one of them, maybe. According to what Jess had told me in the hospital, rescuing me had been high on Pat's priority list even while he foundered in his own career. One wild dream after another, she'd said, and Jess didn't even know about Clarity. She'd known about the book about shipwrecks.

When I was reporting in combat zones, I'd trained myself to remember a single phrase by echoing it, usually unspoken but always moving my lips, the physical sensation designed to anchor it in the brain. I was doing it now, I realized. *The book about shipwrecks.* Four words, mouthed silently. Anchored.

I looked back at the Beauchamp cabin. Watched the smoke rise.

The night at Riptides, when Pat told me about Marilyn Lermond, he'd said she was a fan of old Maine legends. *She was full of stories, man. You wanted to hear the old legends, from shipwrecks to windigos, you just needed to buy Marilyn a chardonnay. She could go toe to toe with Bob Beauchamp any day—and did.*

Bob Beauchamp, the man who'd stood in the dark trees for a long time before emerging, white-faced and shaken, to talk to the police after Pat had fallen.

I looked back in at Renee. She was still sitting at the picnic table with her head nestled in her arms, her back rising and falling slowly.

Bob Beauchamp, though, was awake.

I walked through the pines to pay him a visit.

He answered my knock right away but didn't open the door fully. He was wearing baggy trousers and suspenders over a flannel shirt, and his milky-blue eyes were narrow and set back in deep hollows above his broad nose.

"You were up late to be up so early," he said.

"Those lights bother you again, did they?"

"I notice 'em, sure."

"Should've hung the curtains like I recommended." He grunted. "You need something?"

"Wanted to talk to you about Pat Ryan."

"I told the police what I saw. Can't tell you anything different."

"Not about the night he fell," I said. "Just in general. Curious if you talked much with him over the past few years."

"Can't say that I did."

"What about Marilyn Lermond?"

"Marilyn's dead," he said, but he was wary.

"I know. Did you talk to her much before that?"

"Don't see how it's any of your business if I did or if I didn't."

"Some people say," I told him, jabbing him with his own phrase, "that you would go toe to toe with Marilyn, telling old stories, shipwrecks and ghosts, campfire shit like that."

He looked at me without speaking.

"Did you ever hear of a ship called the *Purgatorium*?" I asked.

He blinked, pulled back from the door. "Ryan told you that one, eh?"

I shook my head. "No, sir. He never did. I was hoping you might."

He regarded me uneasily.

"Bob?" I said. "It's important."

"It's just an old tale," he murmured, but he didn't look so confident in that. "Can't be important."

"I think it may be."

He seemed to debate for a moment, but then he stepped back from the door.

"Come on inside. That one don't tell quickly. I'd like to be sitting down for it."

47

Bob Beauchamp's cabin was sparsely furnished, with a battered gray leather sofa and a burgundy upholstered recliner both angled to face a forest-green Jøtul woodstove. None of it matched in color, fabric, or era, and yet it all seemed a natural fit. There were clocks, barometers, and thermometers on the walls. None of the instruments were in agreement, not even the ones that aspired to measure the same thing. The only calendar in sight was four years old, but the photograph of Marshall Point Light in winter with its holiday wreath was festive if nothing else.

Beauchamp knelt by the stove and used tongs to rotate a chunk of burning birch until the coals baked red and fresh flames curled up. Satisfied with the fire, he closed the stove door and hung up the tongs and then sat in the recliner, which wheezed beneath him. I took the couch. If there was a spring left beneath the cushion, it wasn't evident. I sank so far into it that my knees seemed higher than my head.

"An old tale," Beauchamp said again, speaking

to me but looking into the stove. "Why'd he tell you that one?"

"I already said he didn't."

"Then who did?"

"A dead woman."

His eyes left the fire and found mine. I waited for a challenge that never came.

"*Purgatorium*," he said, drawing the word out. "Ayuh, that's not one you hear of much anymore. Don't know that anyone ever heard much about it, of course. But these days?" He shook his head. "Nah. Your buddy was the only one who gave a damn. But I was never comfortable talkin' with him, to be honest with you."

"Why not?"

"Always huntin'. Like he was hungry for something and wouldn't say what."

"He was writing a book," I said. "Maybe that's why."

"Maybe," Beauchamp allowed, but I could tell he didn't believe it.

"It was a ship, though? The *Purgatorium*?"

His milky eyes reminded me of a snake's. They seemed to suggest his age and bulk were deceptive and that he'd be pure speed whenever he wished to be.

"The ship's name was the *Arabella*. Till it wasn't."

I'd spent enough time around Bob Beauchamp to know he wasn't one to be rushed through a story, so I waited.

"You know Boon Island, surely?" he asked.

"No."

"You don't know Boon Island?" He said it with such incredulity you'd have thought we were talking about the Statue of Liberty. "Down off York Beach, near Kittery?"

I shook my head. I knew York and Kittery—you passed by them as soon as you crossed the New Hampshire border into southern Maine—but I'd never heard of a place called Boon Island.

"Hell," Beauchamp said with disgust, "if there's one thing every kid in Maine once knew, it's Boon Island. How you got outta school not knowin' that, I can't even begin to guess."

"Let's make up for it now."

He grunted. "Ain't much of an island, of course, just a rock ledge."

I felt a cold wave pass through me and was grateful to be sitting in the sagging couch instead of being on my feet.

"Rock ledge?" I echoed hoarsely.

"Ayuh. Lighthouse there now," Beauchamp continued, oblivious to my discomfort. "Used to be wrecks out there all the time, but only one famous one, and that was in 1710. A ship from England called the *Nottingham Galley* sank there, six miles off the coast from York."

"I thought you said the ship was the *Arabella*."

He shot me a rebuking stare. "I'll make my way there."

I lifted my hands. "Sorry."

"Fourteen sailors from the *Nottingham Galley* made it out of the sea and onto that rock. It was December 11. You know what December in Maine is like. They all fought their way out of the ocean and onto that rock island in a storm, soaked and with no provisions. They never managed to build a fire. But most of them survived until rescue. Ten, anyhow."

"In December," I echoed, thinking of the way the wind howled across the tossing pewter waves off the coast of Maine in winter, of how you didn't want to spend much time on the beach even if you were dry and dressed for the elements.

"That's right. It became a famous story. All the right sensational aspects—the shipwreck, the survival." He paused. "The cannibalism."

"Nice touch."

"True touch. They ate the carpenter after he died. The rescuers found raw human flesh wrapped in seaweed, bound up like one of them sushi rolls."

If he'd wanted to turn my stomach, he succeeded.

"More than two centuries later, a Pulitzer Prize–winning writer from Maine, Kenneth Roberts, wrote a novel about it," he said. "For a while there were boat tours by the island. Maybe there still are. The point is the story lingered—because of the horror."

"That's usually the way. Horror stories outlast hero stories, I think. Unless they're paired together, of course."

"I don't know if there was any hero to the Boon Island story," Bob Beauchamp said. "They were rescued by a corpse."

"Say that again?"

"Two men tried to make it the six miles to the mainland. They knew rescue was there, because on a clear day they could see the village, watch folks walking to church on a Sunday. No one was searching for them, because no one knew they were missing. They'd set sail from England months earlier. Their families didn't expect to know the result of the voyage, good or bad, for a year or more. They were just out there, part of the ocean. So two of them left in this pitiful excuse for a raft. It foundered almost immediately. They drowned. One of the frozen corpses washed up on the shore. The locals discovered that and took to the sea to search. They found the ten remaining survivors. Without having found the frozen man first, though, they'd never have gone looking. So, saved by a corpse."

He looked pleased with himself. A natural storyteller. The problem was most natural storytellers are bullshitters. What I needed was the truth.

"When they were finally found, they were brought ashore in what is now Portsmouth," Beauchamp said. "Local families took them in, nursed them back to health. A few died but most survived. Extraordinary, considering the circumstances."

"How many days had they been out there without a fire?"

"Twenty-four."

I stared at him. "Twenty-four days in December and January without a fire. Off the coast of Maine."

Beauchamp nodded grimly.

"That's almost unbelievable."

"Look it up, you don't believe me."

"I believe you," I said, but I also fully intended to look it up. "What's it got to do with the *Purgatorium*, though?"

His grin showed his yellowed teeth. "That makeshift raft the dead man rode in on? One that was found washed up with his frozen carcass still aboard? The folks who came across it never talked much about the way the corpse looked. Too shaken up by it all, I suppose. But a young boy was with them. Little kid. But old enough to remember what he saw. Years down the line, he told folks that there was a name painted on one of the planks of the raft. The name, he said, was *Purgatorium*."

He watched me, wanting to be sure he had me captivated.

"Only problem with that little tale," he said, once he was convinced that his audience was in the palm of his hand, "was that there wasn't any paint to be had on Boon Island."

He grinned that cold grin once more.

"Blood," I said. The word loud and toneless in the quiet cabin.

"You tumbled to that pretty quick. Got a dark mind, Bishop."

I didn't need to tell him that it was anything but a guess.

"So that was the story of Boon Island," he went on. "The wreck happened in 1710, and the boy became a man, and the man became a soldier, way it always went in this country back in those times. Always fightin' a war. He got himself into a good one, French and Indian. He moved up north, found himself in a French settlement. My people. Acadians. You know anything about the Acadians?"

"They were deported. Taken from Maine and Novia Scotia and New Brunswick and relocated to Louisiana. The Cajuns in Louisiana are descendants of the Acadians in Maine."

"That's maybe twenty percent of the story, but I'll grant you still know more than most folks. The British *deported* them, as you called it. Others would call it genocide. There were more than twelve thousand people rounded up and loaded onto ships. Children were separated from parents, farms were burned, churches destroyed. Some were shipped to Louisiana, yes, but also to Pennsylvania, Maryland, Virginia, and Massachusetts. Was the governor of Massachusetts, William Shirley, who helped devise that grand plan."

Beauchamp stared into the fire, gathering his thoughts.

"Shirley was your original 'Masshole.' After luring the Acadian men into churches with talks of peace, they were captured and held hostage until their families would come to join them so it would be a nice, easy thing to load them all up like cattle into the holds of ships. Some of them got sick along the way. Go figure. That wasn't real popular news in the colonies where they were supposed to be deposited. Of course, neither was the fact that they were French and Catholic. Or mixed race with Mi'kmaq people, in some cases. All that was a real risk for good Puritan folks of Massachusetts, you know. So Shirley, he came up with a nice, humanitarian plan—he had the ships overwinter at sea. Four months, they waited. Four months off the coast of Maine in winter."

He paused, letting me consider that.

"More than half of 'em died. Nobody knows the exact number. Lost to time now, the details, but it was terrible. All the ships out there on the winter sea at anchor, people dying every day, and everyone just waiting, waiting, waiting. Many so sick they could hardly speak. One of the Acadians—he was said to be part French, part Mi'kmaq, though who knows—requested to go from ship to ship in a dory. He'd row over and back. Eventually, the Brits agreed, because of what he was doing."

"Which was?"

"Singing songs for the dying," Bob Beauchamp said, and I felt an electric prickle at the base of my skull. "The British let him move between the ships because he was effective. Picture it like a hospice of sorts. Peaceful. And by then, after wintering so long, waiting for a place—anyplace—to put their captives ashore, the Brits were more than ready to have them die peaceful. It had to beat the howling and crying in the night."

I leaned forward and clasped my hands together. To Beauchamp, it probably looked as if I was simply listening intently. In reality, I was steadying myself against the memory of the shirtless, gaunt, blood-spattered man on the rock island.

"The singer never took ill, which was amazing in its own right," Beauchamp said. "He'd go down in the hold with the stink of sickness and death and sing his song. Bring some peace to things. The end would come, and the bodies would go into the sea."

"Do you know the song?" I asked.

"This went on for several weeks," Beauchamp said, as if I had not spoken, "and then came the gale. One hell of a blizzard, blowing down across the Bay of Fundy. The sickest of ships was the *Arabella*. It was also the least seaworthy. That brig was so loaded with death and despair that the British simply abandoned it. A winter storm rising, they didn't think the ship would survive it anyhow, and they were terrified of the plague. All those French Catholics and Mi'kmaqs down in the hold, talking in their foreign tongues, sick with fever and starvin' . . . why, it had to be a frightening sight, don't you think?"

His cloudy eyes brightened with anger as he spoke of his ancestors.

"The British moved their officers and crew off the ship and onto another, and the *Arabella* was left to ride out the gale with its dead and dying. On came the storm, wind and ice and rage, and in the morning the *Arabella* was gone."

"Sank."

"No. She'd sailed it out. The least seaworthy vessel—and one without a crew. Come the sunrise, there she was, under full sail. The last any man alive saw of the *Arabella*, she was sailing north by northeast, right back to Acadia."

"Did they make it?"

He spread his hands. "You tell me, and we'll finally have an end to the tale. The ship was never seen again. The dory was, though. Washed up on a rock island miles away, not too far from what is Cutler, Maine, today. The rock had no name then, but today it's Evangeline Ledge. You got any idea why that might be?"

"The poem," I said, and I knew it because Pat had told me his new boat was named *Evangeline* after the poem.

"Ayuh, good for you. *Evangeline* was Longfellow's poem about the genocide of the Acadians. That one was popular when it came out, about a century after the crime was done. Evangeline Ledge is nothin' but rock and weed and water."

I was squeezing my hands together tightly, crescent-shaped white lines appearing and fading as I moved my fingernails from one grip to the next.

"You've told me two stories," I said.

"No, son, I've told you one."

"Then where does Boon Island meet up with Evangeline Ledge?"

He smiled humorlessly. "When the dory from the *Arabella* was found," he said, "there was a name painted on the stern. You tell me what it was."

"Purgatorium."

"That's right," Bob Beauchamp said, and his storyteller's voice faded into a near whisper. *"Purgatorium."* He breathed it like a prayer.

For a time it was silent save for the fire popping and the old stovepipe ticking as the heat spread.

"You don't know the song?" I asked.

He shook his head, eyes intent on me. "You're the second man ever to ask me that question."

"Was Pat Ryan the other?"

He nodded. "And I'll tell you what I told him— it might just be an old tale. I know that. But everything beneath it? The foundation it's built on? That's gospel, Bishop. Boon Island and the Acadian exodus and William Shirley's sick ships left at sea. You can look all that up. Look hard enough, like your buddy did, and you'll find one thing I never knew, too."

"What's that?"

"The first mate of the HMS *Arabella*," Bob Beauchamp said, "was named Lermond."

"Bryce's family."

"Most likely. The Lermonds have been here so

long, they make the Daughters of the American Revolution look like they just passed through customs."

I looked from him back to the fire. Stared at it and thought. Said, "In your story, the song was peaceful. Helpful, even."

"Why's that bother you?"

I didn't know how to answer that, so I didn't.

"Well," he said at length, "somethin' to consider about my story—the song was peaceful, as you say, and helpful. But we don't know what it became out on the *Arabella*, when the sun went down and the storm blew in."

I turned back to him. His eyes were bright.

"What more do you know, Bob?" I asked.

"I just told you."

"Not the old story. I'm talking about today. The Lermond family and Pat Ryan and . . ."

"You," he finished for me.

"Yes."

He gazed out the window, across the pond. "I know that some people say you got your head turned around out here when you were child. All messed up. Truth became fiction. Fiction became truth."

"Some people say that, eh?"

He nodded, unbothered. "And I know that was the summer your mother and Marilyn Lermond took to each other."

I thought of the speaker I'd found under the deck.

"Did they work together on me, Bob? Marilyn's tech and my mother's research?"

"I think many things became parts of a whole out here at Rosewater."

"Stop being so damn vague. Say what you mean."

"I *am* sayin' it. What addled your friend Ryan's head the other night, or what addled yours all those years ago, I don't know. I truly don't. But I wouldn't be holding everything separate in my mind if I were you."

His eyes returned to mine. "I suspect it's all one story," he said.

That was when Renee screamed.

48

I ran to her, but Bob Beauchamp didn't follow beyond his door, just stood there and watched as I bolted through the pines. Renee was standing on the rock and staring out across the pond in the now-bright light of the new day. She was just beneath the towering pine and I was certain, absolutely certain, that she would do what Pat had done, what her sister had done, that in my absence she'd played the terrible song and the rest of the story had been written for her.

Then she screamed again, and I realized she was shouting my name. I called back. When she saw me, she ran to me and grabbed me, her fingers digging into my arms.

"What the hell were you doing?" she shouted.

"Nothing. Just—"

"I fell asleep, woke up, and you were gone!"

"I'm fine. I was fine. I just—"

"You don't *just* walk out! Not after last night! You have no idea! You weren't there to see . . ." She stopped then, her voice torn between a shout and a sob, and pushed back from me and put her hands to her head. "You can't do that," she said, softer now.

"I'm sorry," I said. "I'm sorry."

We stood there for a moment. The scare was done, we were together again, the sun bright and the night gone. It should have been fine. What struck me, though, thinking of her terror at waking and finding me gone, was a chilling sense of finality.

"You can't always be there and awake," I said. "Last night you were, and even then . . ."

"Yes," she said, because she understood what I meant.

At some point, the song would summon me again. Alone, I wasn't sure how it would go. I wasn't sure how long her sister could help me out there in the fog and the storm. At some point, I thought that I'd have to listen to the rest of the song.

I looked back at Bob Beauchamp's cabin. He was standing in the doorway, watching us.

"I learned some things—" I began, but Renee cut me off.

"Pat's ex-wife called," she said.

"What?"

"It's what woke me. Your phone was ringing. I saw her name and I answered. I was disoriented and looking for you but she said she didn't need to hear your voice." She looked away from me. "She told me she just wanted you to know that they'll be removing the ventilator today or tomorrow."

There were only two reasons to end assistance

for Pat's breathing—because he was doing it on his own now, or because the doctors knew that he never would again. Renee's face told me which one it was.

"Who made the decision?" I asked, my voice brittle, the sound of dried leaves in the wind.

"His father. He's flying in from Montana now. I hung up on Jess in the middle of her explanation, though. I realized you were gone, and I thought . . . I was afraid that—"

"I know," I said. I knew exactly what she thought I'd been doing.

"How does it end?" Renee said softly.

"How does what end?"

She waved her hand around us, exhausted. "All of it. I can do another night like this. Another night, two nights, a week of them, but . . . how does it *end*, Nick?"

"I'm not sure," I said, although I thought that I was. I'd seen the island.

I looked up at the shafts of sunlight filtering through the pines and let them shine full on my face. It would not last long. It was autumn in Maine, and the days were growing short. What mattered—what I could control—was what I did with the hours.

"Go home and get some sleep," I told Renee.

"No way."

"Yes. Seriously, you need it and I need it."

"*You're* going to sleep?"

"At some point, yes." I pointed at the sky, at the sun. "I'm fine during the day."

Already, the sun seemed too high, though. The newborn day was aging fast.

"Sure," she said, but there wasn't much conviction in it.

"I'm steady during the day," I reassured her. "When the sun's bright and the sky's clear, I'm fine. Only time I've struggled in daylight hours is when the fog comes in."

"The fog."

I nodded. "Yesterday afternoon was tough, I'll admit that. But the fog cleared as I drove out here, and it's as if my mind clears with it. Once I got away from the harbor, I had my feet under me again. As bright as it is today, I'm feeling good."

Renee was looking at me strangely. "You came to the mill yesterday afternoon."

"Right."

"It was clear, Nick. It was bright and clear. All day."

"Not down in the harbor," I said. "While I was talking to Bryce, the fog was . . ."

Her face told me all that I needed to know.

I looked away, out across the pond, and then over to Bob Beauchamp's cabin. He was gone, and the door was closed.

"How has the weather been since I got back to Maine?" I asked. It was hard to find my voice. "There have been so many times when the fog has seemed thick to me. You know the kind that comes rolling in and all of the sudden the islands are gone and then the whole bay—hell, the mountains?"

"I know the kind," she said. She looked pale. "And it hasn't happened. Not once since you've been here."

I took a deep breath and nodded. "Okay," I said. "Okay, that's good to know."

DO YOU WANT TO LEAVE FOG TOWN BE-HIND? the Clarity app had asked me cheerfully on that first test run, while I sat on the Adirondack chair at the end of the dock, a smirk on my face. That wasn't how it worked, evidently. You went into the fog, not out of it.

And after last night, I knew what waited there.

"I'll stay here with you," Renee said.

"I'm not ready to shut it down and sleep just yet. I can't waste the day."

"I'm not leaving," she said, and I saw the set of her jaw and the spark in those emerald eyes and knew damn well that I wasn't talking her out of anything.

"Okay," I said. "We're going to need to make the daylight count, I think."

"Where are we going?"

I opened the door to the camp, stepped inside, and picked up the strange speaker I'd cut loose from under the house the day before.

"One stop to inquire about this," I said. "And then one at the harbor."

"The harbor?"

"Yes. We're going to find a boat called the *Evangeline*."

47

The kid at Strawn's Stereo and Music was watching a movie this afternoon instead of reading a comic. The movie was *Hot Fuzz*. I respected that choice, at least.

"No refunds on used equipment," he said when he saw me come in. "We'll take returns, but"—he saw Renee walking in behind me—"oh, hey. Last time, it was just this guy."

Renee gave me a quizzical look.

"Last time I was buying speakers."

"Crappy speakers," the kid offered helpfully.

"Indeed. This isn't one of those." I set the small speaker I'd removed from beneath the camp on the counter. "I'd like to know what it is."

He was sitting with his feet up on the counter, back to the door, eyes on the TV, where Simon Pegg was hurdling hedgerows. He lowered his feet and swiveled the chair around. He was wearing a Marvin the Martian T-shirt. I looked at Renee, who gave me one raised eyebrow. I tried to make my smile reassuring.

"He knows equipment," I said.

The kid picked up the device and studied it.

"No brand logo." He turned it over, traced the rough metal. "It's taken some weathering. Where was it?"

"Outdoors."

"No shit. I mean, like, was it for a patio or a deck or something? It's got a pretty serious protective casing."

"I only found it," I said. "I didn't install it."

"Yeah, it's definitely not cheap stuff like what you got last time," he said. He reached into a drawer beneath the counter and withdrew a set of small screwdrivers. Selected the right size on the first try. Unscrewed the back panel of the speaker.

"Was it wired into a receiver?" he asked.

"Just a power supply. I think."

"You think?" He looked from me to Renee meaningfully, as if telling her that she could do better, and then returned his attention to the speaker. He removed four screws, set them carefully to the side, and then separated the metal panels.

"That's what it looked like to me," I said. "'Hardwired to a junction box of some sort that had a red light to indicate the connection was active."

He stared at the components inside. Then he said, "Weird."

"What is?"

He pointed with the screwdriver. "There should be membranes in here for a woofer or tweeter, right? That's how a speaker works. Instead, there are these disks."

He was indicating thin disks, shaped like wafers, that were aligned but not touching.

"Would it produce anything like a beam?" I asked.

"A beam?"

"Yeah. Not light, but sound."

"Oh! You mean like directional. Huh." He tilted the speaker right and left and then said, "Shit, I think it could. Where did you get this?"

"I think it belonged to someone who did research on hypersonic sound."

"Hypersonic?"

"High-frequency. I don't know much about it."

"This could definitely be directional," he mused. "But when you say *high-frequency*, do you mean like out of the human ear range? Ultrasound?"

"I think so. Maybe."

"These are interesting," he said, tapping a pair of small chips that were staggered below the wafer-shaped disks. "Semiconductors. But I haven't seen anything quite like them before." He traced the wires with the screwdriver tip and then picked up the exterior wire that I'd severed and studied that. "This went to the power supply?"

"Yeah."

"Why'd you cut it?"

Because I wanted the loons to stop.

"Lazy, I guess," I said.

"Dumb, anyhow," he offered.

"Customer service isn't really your strong suit, is it?"

He shrugged, didn't look up. "What do you want me to do with this thing, dude?"

"Find out what it does, how it works, any damn thing you can."

"Bro, it's a store, not a research lab."

Renee stepped past me then, leaned on the counter. The kid looked up and his eyes fixed on her cleavage, at which point they went as wide as Marvin the Martian's on his shirt.

"What's your name?" Renee asked.

"Uh . . ." He seemed to have forgotten his name. "Alex," he finally managed. "I'm Alex."

"Okay, Alex." She reached into her purse, came out with a checkbook and a pen. "I'm going to let you write whatever number you think is fair onto this check, and then I'll sign it if you just find a way to do what you can by the end of the day. Think you can do that?"

"I've got to work the register all day," he said.

We were the only customers in the store.

Renee smiled sympathetically. "All work and no play, right? But maybe—*if* there's any free time— you could at least try? And I'm not kidding about the check. You pick any price you think is fair, write it in, and cash it. I won't complain."

"I could try," he said. "Sure. Give me an hour with it? Whatever I don't understand after an hour, I'm not going to figure out just because I have more time."

She scribbled her signature at the bottom of the

check. I saw then that the check wasn't from her own bank account—it was Clarity's. I had to suppress a smile. Bryce Lermond was paying for my research. I liked that.

"I appreciate it, Alex," I said.

He ignored me. Smiled shyly at Renee. Said, "I'm on it."

Renee and I walked out, and I was laughing by the time we hit the parking lot.

"Company checking. Nice touch."

"It's the least Bryce can do."

"Agreed."

"You think that goof in there can actually learn anything useful?"

"He's definitely going to stand a better chance with it than I did," I said, fishing the truck keys from my pocket. "I'm not betting on . . ."

I stopped talking and walking. Renee kept going for a few strides before she noticed. Then she stopped and turned back.

"What's wrong?"

I was looking down the hill, toward town. Fog was gathering in thin sheets. The street and the buildings were still visible but from behind a haze. A day ago, I wouldn't have thought anything of it. Now . . .

"Do you see anything down there?" I asked, pointing.

Renee looked. "See anything, meaning?"

"Fog."

She looked back at me too quickly. I knew the answer then.

"You're seeing fog? Across the street?"

"Yeah. Down the hill. It's coming in fast."

She didn't even bother to look back, as if she might have missed it. She knew that she hadn't missed anything, and I did, too. Overhead, the sun was clear, and warm for a fall day. That was all she could see.

"Let's get down to the harbor," I said, trying to keep my voice steady. "I don't have any idea where Pat kept his boat, and I don't want to waste time."

50

The harbor was shrouded in fog when we arrived, but I didn't mention that.

I parked at the public landing and looked out across the bay. There were a few dozen sailboats tied up alongside the docks, nestled into slips, and a few dozen more tied off to moor buoys in the open water.

"Start with the docks," I said. "We can skip any motorboats. It will be a sailboat."

"You know what it looks like?"

"No, but I know the name. *Evangeline.*"

We separated and began to walk the docks. The bay was perfectly calm, glassy, and yet I could hear waves like distant breakers. I could hear, in other words, the opening background noise of the Clarity app, those deep-sea tones I'd once taken for harmless, familiar white noise. It felt anything but harmless now.

I didn't tell Renee about the sound of the waves. I also made certain she wasn't looking when I slipped my AirPods out of their case and kept them in my curled left hand, like a gunfighter unsnapping his holster.

I didn't want to play any more of the song, but if it came to that, I wanted to be ready.

No man among us must die.

"Nick? I think this is it."

Renee was standing at a slip beside a sailboat that was desperately in need of new paint and had ropes strung through stanchions where stainless steel cables belonged. It looked like a boat Pat would've purchased, and there was a moment when that brought a smile to my face. Then I remembered him stretched out in the hospital bed, nonresponsive, with his family flying in to say goodbye, and the smile was gone fast.

I walked down and joined her. The sound of the waves seemed to soften while we looked at the boat together. The only fresh paint on the craft was on the stern, where the boat's name had been lovingly applied in gold script with a black shadow line. *Evangeline.*

I climbed aboard. Renee looked up and down the dock, making sure no one was watching us, and then followed. The hatch cover that led below deck was secured by a padlock. I had a small Leatherman multi-tool as a key chain. I took it out and set to work unscrewing the hasp from the weathered teak.

"You're sure it's his boat?" Renee asked.

"We'll find out fast if I'm wrong."

When I'd loosened the screws, I was able to pry the hasp free from the wood. The lock dangled impotently. I lifted the hatch cover and stepped down into the dimly lit cabin below. Or at least it was dim to me—the fog blocked sunlight from filtering through the galley windows.

The stairs were steep, to allow maximum space inside, but still it felt cramped. I looked at the tiny galley kitchen and the bathroom stall with the accordion door and the berth with a bunk the size of a twin bed and thought about how long Pat had been living down here. Nine months, Jess had said? No romance of the open ocean, either; he'd been tied up at the dock. It was a depressing idea.

He'd stayed busy, though, based on the clutter of paperwork spread across the dining table and the U-shaped settee that surrounded it. Legal pads, photos, old books, ledgers, binders, folders.

"Mind my asking what, exactly, we're looking for?" Renee said, stepping down to join me.

"Anything about the song."

"Pat knew about the song?"

"Yes. I don't know exactly how to begin searching, but anything about the exile of the Acadian people might be worthwhile."

Renee picked up one of the books on top of the clutter. It was a history of the Acadian exile.

"Easy enough."

I laughed. "If all of this stuff is about that, though, I don't know how to narrow it down except to look for anything about the song or a ship called the *Arabella*."

I slid down the settee, reached for one of the legal pads. When I picked it up, I set my earbuds down on the table, then saw Renee staring at them.

"You just holding on to those?" she asked.

"Yes."

She looked at me hard.

"I'm okay," I told her. "Just seeing the fog."

And hearing the waves, of course. I could hear the waves and the wind as if we were out on open water ahead of a rising storm. I didn't tell her that, however. I picked up the notepad and started searching.

We'd been combing through Pat's notes for about twenty minutes when Renee opened a manila folder and withdrew a stack of photocopies. The images were from a very old book, what looked almost like parchment but might have been merely paper so old, it was beginning to age to dust.

"You said the *Arabella*, right?"

"Yes."

She slid one of the pages across the table to me. The writing was elaborate, antiquated penmanship, but it was legible. The document was titled *Journal of John Trenchard*.

"Who's John Trenchard?" Renee asked.

"No idea."

Her index finger traced a line in the middle of the page: *I have been moved from the* Winslow *to the* Arabella *under the command of Ephraim Knowlton, Her Majesty's Navy.*

"Right ship, though," Renee said.

"Yeah," I said, and I heard Bob Beauchamp's low voice telling his grisly tale and felt a shudder.

Renee slid in close and we began to read together.

51

Journal of John Trenchard

We sailed from Grand Pré on the first day of September, Year of Our Lord 1755, with 230 of the Acadian men aboard. We were told as many as two thousand were spread between the ships. On departure, Winslow's men set fire to the villages. We took to open water with flames and smoke at our backs. Everything was burned. Houses and fields and even their church. That troubled me then and it troubles me now.

We were told we'd be two months at sea, but illness had ravaged some of the first ships to arrive in Massachusetts Bay and the townspeople feared more captives might spread pestilence. So we waited, day upon day, week upon week, in the coldest winter I have ever known. Meanwhile, the illness did spread. We lost track of the dying, but I know at least three score were sent into the sea from the Arabella alone.

It was in late December when the death song began. I was among the first to observe it. The singer had no known name. If his people called him anything, we never learned it. He was a small but strong man with dark features and kind eyes. He almost never spoke, not to our crew nor his companions, yet inevitably each night he would find his way to the sickest, the suffering.

Then he would sing to them.

He had a beautiful tenor voice that would inspire a writer of hymns. He would sing his song while holding the hand of the dying, of the anguished. This would occur always late in the night, exquisitely timed so that the song ended unerringly at the first light of day.

By the time dawn was fully upon us, the afflicted would be dead.

Upon first encounter, I was shaken by the entire event. It called to mind old tales of Druids, or boyhood stories whispered about the church graveyard in the village of Mohune where I was raised. It felt less real than imagined, a story that would have been at home within The Arabian Nights or Chaucer. And yet I was watching it before my own eyes.

Time passed, though, days fell to night, the singer moved on, and the anguished ended their lives in peace as the sun broke in the east. I watched these men with interest. The song soothed them, assuredly, altering even their breathing and their muscular response. Men who had been shaking violently became still, and those struggling for breath seemed to fill their lungs deeply and restfully as the song went on. It was, I remarked to Captain Knowlton, both a troubling sight and a beautiful one.

I believe the Captain agreed with me. The true misfortune began when word of the death song reached the first mate, William Lermond.

At first, I believed Lermond's interest in the strange exercise was no different than my own. It was a remarkable sight, after all. As the days passed, though, it became clear that he wanted to understand the song, to learn it for himself, and it was evident that he viewed the solemn ritual as a kind of dominance. He saw none of the grace of it, none of the compassion, only the power. In his mind, such qualities could be extracted one from the other. When power is wielded without grace and compassion, we behold a dark world, indeed. I told him as much even though he was my superior, and he mocked me and asserted his rank. What might I have done then, I am not sure, but the question has never left me and I know it never will.

"What might I have done?" is, I suspect, the final earthly thought of many men.

I know it will be mine.

Lermond's first attempts to learn the song came through questioning of the singer. He asked what might occur if such a song was offered to the healthy, and not the dying. Would they gain strength? Would they feel nothing at all? He then asked what might occur if the song was offered to the dead.

These questions clearly troubled the singer. Though the man spoke little, he warned Lermond that a gift could become a weapon swiftly if used with the wrong spirit. It was one of the few times I ever heard him speak.

It was also the first time Lermond had him whipped.

As the long winter drew on, and the Acadians grew sicker, Lermond's obsession deepened. He reversed tack and attempted to cajole the singer, to bribe him with brandy and promises of privilege. The singer would have none of it. Lermond then tried to break his spirit. He withheld first food, then water. He administered more lashings. Throughout this abuse, the singer never said a word.

It was only when I brought the situation to Captain Knowlton's attention that the abuse ceased. Lermond wanted to quarrel with the Captain, and for a moment it seemed he might actually bring a mutineer's violence to the day, but he cooled his temper. The next night, however, he sent our cabin boy with instructions to sit as close as he might to the singer and to listen carefully to the words of the song. To memorize them so that he might record them later and share them with Lermond.

The singer was a keen observer and noticed the boy fairly quickly. How much of the song the boy heard, I cannot say, but his notations for the first mate were minimal. Lermond was unsatisfied, and sent the boy back again, and again.

It was on the fourth day that the boy climbed the rigging.

It was just before sundown on one of the few clear days we'd had in weeks. The sails were stowed, and there was no reason for him to make his way up the mast, but he did. He climbed all the way to the yardarm and walked out to its end. He never so much as reached for a jackstay or a line but proceeded as indifferently as if he were on a footpath. A few of the crew laughed, thinking he was having a bit of fun, nothing more. A boy's game.

I was unsettled watching him, because he'd never played such a game before and because it was a dangerous one, with the ice covering the yardarm. Moreover, he walked in such a fashion that it seemed he was not in his own mind. Some of the men believed this was for sport, part of the game, but I did not then and do not now. He walked that icy yardarm into the wind as if called by his own mother. He stood there, surefooted as a cat, and faced the sun. It was vanishing behind that unforgiving rocky coast and he watched it all the way down. At last light, he stepped off the yardarm.

Others blamed the ice, blamed the wind, blamed him for a fool's fall. But I tell you, he did not fall! He stepped forward at last light. I know this to be true.

He went into the water and a line was thrown but he did not surface for it. Two men went in after him at great peril to themselves, but he was not to be found. We were all deeply shaken by the events. The boy was no more than fourteen and a good lad, quick with a smile. He shared my name, John. He had been no trouble and much help, maintaining good spirits despite our circumstances in that grim winter. He was far from home and from his mother.

I will readily admit that I did not even consider the song at that point.

It was three nights later when Lermond ordered another man to carry on the work that the cabin boy had begun, documenting the death song. The new man, Dennison, was a good sailor but a cruel man who had recently been lashed for theft, and I believe he was happy to perform any task that would keep him from further lashings. I don't know how much he added to Lermond's record, but I do know that he was only two nights at the task.

He was in the rigging by sundown on the third day.

By then, of course, no one believed it was a joke. Men tried to shout him down, but he did not so much as cast a glance below. He simply faced the sun. It was an overcast day and the light wasn't more than a smear of tin color in the darkness but still it was all *he looked for. He did not speak. Captain Knowlton sent a man after him.*

He had just reached the yardarm when Dennison stepped off it.

This time, being in a terrible way prepared for the event, we were quick into the water. I was the first one in, and the sea off that forsaken shore was as brutal a cold as I've ever endured, but I was able to reach him. With the help of two others, we got him out of the sea and back aboard the Arabella and all of us who had been in the water huddled close to the stove in blankets.

Dennison came around slowly. As the night went on, though, he began to tell strange, horrid tales. He spoke of an icy ledge of rock in a gale-thrashed sea. He said he had been on this rock and that he was not alone there. He claimed there were men from another ship on the rock, and that he'd sighted our own cabin boy, John. It chilled my heart to hear him speak of the boy. My fear grew to outright terror when he clutched me and pulled my face close to his own and insisted that the other men on the rock had come from a ship called the Nottingham Galley.

Whether Dennison had heard of the fate of the Nottingham Galley, *I'll never know, but most of us had heard the grisly tale of the crew shipwrecked and left without a fire in a brutal winter. Of the unspeakable acts that occurred.*

Dennison fell silent when the sun rose, and I was grateful to be away from him. When I next saw him, he spoke of the fog and wind as if it were present. The sea was becalmed and the sun was bright and yet he appeared convinced a gale was near.

For several days his condition worsened. He had not slept and soon he refused to eat and the shock of his exposure to the cold sea began to claim his body. He was ravaged by fever and seized by muscle spasms and spoke only of the rock island in the storm, of howling winds and furious seas and of our boy, John, and the men who'd been there before him. They were waiting on him, he said. He was bound for the island, and this terrified him. I endeavored to reason with him, an approach I hadn't seen any of the others take, to indulge the terrible talk in effort to show him the madness and folly of his imagination.

Dennison, however, could not be reasoned with. He clutched my arm with a thin but strong hand and pulled me close to his ghastly face, which was gaunt and riddled with open sores.

"They get stronger," he told me. "You can feel it in the fog. Thicker it gets, stronger they are. Sundown is the worst of times. They're terribly strong at sundown, and I'm getting weaker. There's a price to be paid for listening to the death song, and a greater one is due for any man who shares it. It was a solemn thing, any fool could see that, and yet we tampered with it."

I told him that this was nonsense, that there were no men waiting for him in the fog. I told him that he was returning to good health and needed to maintain his faith. He would have none of it. He listened patiently—more respectfully than Dennison ever had in all our months at sea, in fact—but ultimately dismissed me.

"They want me badly," he said, and told me of grasping hands that reached for him in the fog, determined to pull him down and away. "When I arrive, one of them will be released," he said.

"One man comes aboard and one departs. That's the special hell of it, Trenchard. I'll be among them so long, waiting while others come and go. I see that clear. My wait on the island will be long."

I put forth that it was his fever speaking and that when it broke he would feel not only of renewed strength but of logical mind.

He smiled at me the way a mother smiles at a child.

"They require a full crew on the PURGATORIUM," he said. "No more and no less. Each man aboard releases another, but until then it is an endless stay. They all want me, don't you see? They wait for me because when I arrive one of them can go into the sea and be quit of it. Just one, though. They wait for me, Trenchard, and they are not kind."

I told him I'd not heard of any vessel named PURGATORIUM. I argued that if any from the Nottingham Galley were on the rock, he was confusing not only his ships but his nightmares and his reality. He listened in silence, his face wrought by the most awful, knowing smile. At length, I could bear the smile no more and I ceased my efforts.

What might I do for Dennison? I had attempted all that I understood, and so at last I turned to that which I did not understand, and suggested we summon the singer. Lermond wouldn't hear of it.

Then came the days when Lermond spoke with Dennison alone. Their conversations appeared intense, and the other men stayed away, fearful of Lermond for his brutality and authority, and fearful of Dennison for things they dared not speak of.

It was on the afternoon ahead of the gale that Lermond

sought out the singer once more. This time, he demanded the truth of the song with such a ferocity that even I was astonished by the monster within him. When the singer refused to speak, Lermond had him bound to the mast and commenced a lashing so ghastly that to recall it roils my stomach even to this day. I've lived a life among hard men and much brutality, and yet I've never seen any occasion more terrible, more inhuman, than the beating Lermond administered to the singer that day.

And what did I do? You are well entitled to ask the question. I wish only that I had a better answer. I did not intercede directly but chose instead to seek out Captain Knowlton. I might write that it was not my place to intercede with Lermond, that it would have been insubordination of a kind I would never have tolerated aboard any ship. These words would be true.

Truer, however, are these: I was afraid.

Captain Knowlton had been sleeping and Lermond had the watch. By the time I roused the Captain and we returned together, the destruction done to the body of the singer was such as I had never seen before or since. He had been lashed almost to pieces, bones laid bare, flesh flayed in a red mist over the deck.

Lermond was still at it, too.

Captain Knowlton brought it to a stop and commanded me to put Lermond in shackles. The first mate resisted but others came to my aid and together we wrestled him down on the deck that was slick with blood and ice. He was raving by then, starved with desire for the singer's knowledge, driven mad with an ugly lust for power.

Lermond was taken to the brig and the singer was transported belowdecks for such minimal aid as could be administered. Two of the men who carried him were made sick by the task. Such was his physical condition.

On the day after the lashing, Dennison died and was buried at sea. It was blowing fifteen knots at least and snow was falling and in the wind on the icy deck the men slipped so that his body tumbled from the bag and struck the side of the ship before going over. He floated there for what was surely mere seconds but felt every bit of eternity, his face upturned, one dead hand stretched out, as if reaching back for us.

The next day was a terrible one. The wind blew unceasing and the snow and ice came and the captives continued to fall sick in ever-larger numbers. Because of Lermond's awful actions, the possibility of even spiritual comfort was denied to the dying. The singer was now too devastated in mind and body to offer solace. How he'd clung to life even that long, I shall never know.

That evening, when the ship began to take on water from a fracture in the hull directly amidships, it was difficult not to believe that the vessel was cursed by the horror that had taken place on her decks. I know I was not alone in that belief. Lermond had doomed us all, it seemed.

I preferred not to venture belowdecks any longer. The winter wind off that coast was crueler than any I'd known before, and yet I preferred it to the scene below. Lermond, you see, had begun to sing his own song. How much of it he'd learned from the cabin boy and from Dennison, I cannot say. How much was his own. How much was the Devil's. They were all a piece of it by then, I believe. Lermond lay in shackles and sang his own song.

The day after we began to take on water, a meeting was

held between Captain Knowlton and Captain Whittaker, of the Anne, as well as an ambassador from Governor Shirley. It was agreed that the Arabella was in an untenable situation, with a storm approaching, hull damage worsening, and the Acadians frightfully ill and no doubt contagious. Word was passed that we would disembark ahead of the storm and transfer to Whittaker's ship, the Anne, and wait out the worst weather. It was my understanding at this point that surely our human cargo would be transferred as well, and not left to a helpless, hopeless death. Only once we were aboard the Anne did the truth of Governor Shirley's decision strike us. The sickest of the Acadians had been left alone on the Arabella. Only the healthy were transferred to the Anne.

Captain Knowlton took an action that I understood in spirit but distrusted in effect. He removed Lermond's shackles and ordered him to remain aboard the Arabella. He was in command of the vessel for the duration of the storm, Knowlton said, and while we all knew that to be a death sentence, Lermond seemed authentically pleased with the commission. He also seemed to understand the death sentence, however, as he tasked one of the men with taking his personal belongings from the ship and seeing that they were returned to his wife should anything dire befall him.

We were about to disembark when, against all better judgment, I decided that I must see the singer one last time and say a prayer over him.

He was wrapped in blankets that had become crusted to his body with his own blood and juices, as vile a sight as you can imagine, yet his eyes were open and he watched me with a raptor's gaze, one which unsettled me so deeply that I nearly left. I steeled myself and approached and whispered an apology. The words couldn't have meant anything to him, and my voice was unsteady until I began a favorite Psalm of David, which I recited with closed eyes. When I opened my eyes, the singer was smiling at me so kindly that I might have wept, because I had stood idle while inhuman harm was done to him and he knew this as well as I did. Yet, still, he was kind to me.

When he spoke, I was so startled I nearly cried out. The words were in French and I spoke almost no French then, but I'll forever remember the words.

"Il navigue avec moi maintenant."

The translation records as: "He sails with me now."

Upon uttering this, the singer nodded at me but once, and yet it was enough that I understood clearly that he'd appreciated my efforts, clumsy though they might have been, and that he wished me to depart.

And so I did.

I have never been so eager to be gone from a place as I was from the Arabella.

The gale that night was the fiercest I have been in. Only one other in all these years since comes close. Even aboard the far stouter Anne, there was fear of sinking. No one spoke of the Arabella because there was no doubt as to her fate. She simply could not survive. We all knew that. We all knew how many sick men had been left aboard as well. And Lermond.

The storm ceased a few hours after dawn, and as the skies cleared we beheld a ship headed toward us out of the fog.

For a long while I refused to believe my own eyes, but with

so many shipmates aboard, there was no denying the truth of it. The Arabella was not simply afloat but moving under full sail, swift and sure and with an able crew. They passed near enough to us that we could see the men, and while they looked healthy, I did not like the way they moved, let alone the set of their faces. They were cold men, empty men. Not men at all beyond their form. The singer was nowhere in sight, but First Mate Lermond was clearly visible—lashed to the mast.

I knew then that the singer had indulged Lermond's evil wish: he had demonstrated what might happen if the song was offered in a spirit other than solace, with darker ambitions. I cannot suggest the details because I wasn't aboard, but I do know that dead men seemed to fill the rigging and all among them looked sound of body, if empty of spirit.

Then the ship was past and gone, sailing east, the sunlit water red as blood before her. We watched until she was out of sight. It is my understanding that as of the occasion of this writing no trace of the Arabella has ever been found.

I believe that might be a good thing. There was evil aboard. It had not always been there, perhaps, but in that long winter of death and sickness, in that winter when we abandoned our burdens to care for the least among us, there was certainly evil aboard the Arabella.

For many years, I hesitated to blame the song itself. I had heard it when it carried grace, peace, beauty. Could anything of beauty that existed in the world created by our own Lord be turned cruel, turned evil? Could beauty and grace be forged into a cold dark stake that was then driven into the minds and hearts of the innocent?

No, I thought, no, it cannot be.

But then I ask myself to remember the day we departed from the Acadian land. I ask myself to remember the men taken from their families, forced from the part of the earth where they'd endeavored to build a home and live with the most modest of luxuries in exchange for the unmatchable gift of freedom. They were taken at the point of a musket or sword, loaded aboard a vessel with no destination known to them, free men turned captive, and while we sailed away, they looked back to see the fires consuming their fields, their barns, their homes, their churches.

I consider all of those sights and realize that, surely, a gift of beauty and grace can be turned to a weapon, a destroying force. Surely, this can happen, because have I not seen it happen? Have I not, in fact, participated in such destruction in the name of the Crown?

It is, I believe, the very nature of man. As surely as Christ turned water into wine, so can men turn power into poison. This they shall continue to do until He has seen enough, I'm afraid. Some days, I hope that He has already seen enough. Then I pray for forgiveness for such dark thoughts.

I will wonder of the fate of the Arabella until the end of my earthly days. When the sun is full on my face, I feel content that the men aboard found peace, or at least not further suffering. I believe that the island Dennison described is no more than the fevered nightmare of a dying man. But night has fallen now, and I write this by candlelight, and I wonder if *the island is not real and if it does not wait for me, an earned fate, for I stood idle when I might have helped the innocent.*

"Il navigue avec moi maintenant."

He sails with me now.

It is when I hear those words again in full darkness that I know to the marrow of my bones that the island is real, a place of trapped evil. Sleep then denies its comfort to me, so I sit by candle or lantern light and wait out the dark hours. My hope is that in the days that have passed since my voyage on the Arabella, *I have earned the sunrise.*

One never knows, though. The only assurance is that we exit into a mystery.

52

We read in silence, and I have no idea who finished first, because neither of us seemed inclined to break the silence. I know that I went back and read segments again, and I suspect that Renee did, too. At last there was no pretending that we weren't done with the story.

"I wish Trenchard had learned his name," I said softly.

Renee looked at me, dark red hair swinging under her chin. "The singer's?"

"Yes."

"You believe the story, then. That it's real."

"Yes. You don't?"

She touched the photocopy gingerly. "I'd like to believe it's Pat's work, some attempt at fiction, but I can't. I don't know where he found it, but I believe it's real."

I nodded. "The history is accurate. The dates, the ships, the overwintering off the coast."

"And the dreams are the same," she said. "Dennison's fever dreams. They're so similar to yours."

I nodded. I had not read them as fever dreams,

though. I had read them with a very real and fore-boding sense that Dennison was reaching out to me across the centuries through the pen of John Trenchard, by way of Pat Ryan, and communicating with me directly.

The *Purgatorium*, he said, would require a full crew.

They wait for me, Trenchard, and they are not kind.

I had a feeling, awful but certain, that I had seen Dennison on the island. And he had not looked kind at all.

"Let's go," I said, gathering the documents.

"You're going to take them?"

"Pat has no need for them now. I might."

I stood and felt the boat rock beneath me and for an instant I heard the wind rise and towering waves curl and thunder down on sagging timbers. It was so sudden and visceral and so undeniably *real* that I was convinced I was on a foundering ship somewhere over deep water. I reached out and gripped the table to steady myself and Renee put her hand on my arm.

"Nick . . ."

"I'm fine. I'm fine." The sound of the wind died off and the waves softened into quiet breakers, distant again. I stood holding the table for a long time. Finally, I released it and we climbed together out of the boat's cabin and up to the main deck. The harbor was thick with fog; the parking lot hidden from view. I didn't bother asking Renee what she saw.

I slid the hatch cover back into place and then used the Leatherman to screw the hasp back in and leave it locked, as Pat had intended. Then I turned back to Renee, who was standing in the stern.

"Do me a favor, please," I said. I meant to speak in a strong voice but it was scarcely above a whisper.

"What's that?"

"If you have to play the song for me, try to hold off as long as possible. Make it as close to sunrise as you can."

She didn't say a word. Her jaw worked and her lips parted once but then she flattened them into a hard line and settled for a single nod.

"Thank you," I said, and then we left the *Evangeline* and returned to my truck.

53

"Where to now?" Renee said once we were in the truck. She asked it in a detached, disoriented way. I knew her mind was still on what she'd read in the journal of John Trenchard and what her sister might be experiencing. If the horror story described in those pages was real, then her sister was ensnared in a uniquely awful hellscape.

"I need to speak with Bryce," I said, "but the kid with the speaker asked us to give him an hour. It's been more than an hour. I don't want to leave that thing behind."

"What do you want from Bryce?"

"His time," I said, staring at the inbound fog.

"What does that mean, Nick?"

"Yesterday he was candid with most of the questions I asked him. I have fresh ones today."

"He's not going to help you. Every answer he gives you could hurt him."

I watched the fog and shook my head. "I don't think so. I don't have time to hurt him. He knows that."

"Nick . . ."

But she didn't finish. Whatever argument she was going to make about my future died before it left her lips. I started the engine and put the truck into gear and we drove up the hill. The town and the tall buildings of the campus beyond were hidden from me, most of Hammel cloaked by the white-gray fog, but out in the western hills where Rosewater waited, it looked to be clearer.

I saw the fog now as sand in an hourglass. As it filled in, my time ran out. There would be another attack soon, a seizure, whatever you wanted to call it. The men of *Purgatorium* would reach out for me. Maybe I'd avoid their grasp again, but maybe not.

They get stronger. You can feel it in the fog. Thicker it gets, stronger they are. Sundown is the worst of times. They're terribly strong at sundown, and I'm getting weaker.

The kid at the stereo store, Alex, was ready for our return.

"You were pretty close," he said, looking at me.

"How so?"

"It's high-frequency and directional, just like you said. Here." He motioned us over and lifted the speaker back onto the counter. The back panel was still removed.

"These guys?" He tapped the semiconductors. "They're actually emitters. And these"—he tapped on the thin crystal wafers—"think of them as a projection beam." He glanced up at me, intrigued beneath his hooded eyes. "Just like you thought."

"Explain the emitters, please. I'm not following that."

"Yeah, I figured it out," he said, enormously satisfied with himself. "This piece"—he tapped something that looked like the socket of a very tiny lightbulb—"is a transducer. Don't think of it as a speaker, okay? That's where you were wrong. It's a self-contained unit, not part of a system that requires a receiver or anything. It has everything it needs right in here."

"Including the source sound?"

"Including the source sound." He put the screwdriver down, picked up a pair of long tweezers, and slid a chip out from beneath one of the semiconductor arrays. "Right here."

"Looks like a microSD card," I said, thinking of my old digital cameras, the ones that sat unused as the camera technology in phones became better and better.

"Exactly. It's an audio file. Really simple stuff; it's just that I'd never seen anything quite like it before."

"Any way to find out what's on the file?" Renee asked.

He smiled at her. It was his full-on, impress-the-ladies smile. It was a damn shame he had granola stuck in his teeth.

"Asked and answered," he said.

"Pardon?"

"Asked and answered. It's what lawyers say."

"Only in response to a bad question," Renee said.

He flushed and frowned and the granola vanished.

"I mean, like, I've already figured it out. I put the card into a reader and pulled up the file . . ." He swiveled away, tapped on his computer keyboard. "And got the file. It was just sitting right there. No password or anything. I was sort of surprised by that, because the rest of the device seems so sophisticated, right? But the file was just right there. Until I played it. Then it does this."

He angled the monitor so we could see the screen. An audio player window was open, and the progress bar tracked from left to right as the seconds passed.

A loon's cry came from the speakers, plain and clear. I pointed at the computer and started to speak but then realized that neither Renee nor Alex had reacted to it at all. Before I could say anything, he spoke again.

"It seems like it's muted, right? But there *is* a file. Now, I probably wouldn't have figured the next part out if you hadn't mentioned the high-frequency idea." He frowned at me, as if unhappy to give me that much credit, and added, "But I took a look . . ."

He toggled between windows and now we were viewing a player that displayed the file in megahertz.

"And it's playing at twenty-five *thousand*," he said, sounded awed. "I recorded the file and altered it. The sound is distorted but at least audible."

He changed windows again, then pressed "play" on his new version, and a garbled but undeniable loon cry came from the speakers.

This time, Renee looked at me.

"Hear that?" she said.

I heard the first one, I thought, but our pal Alex didn't need to know that.

"Yes," I said. "Weird, right?" I was eager now to simply push the conversation along and get out before he asked many questions or took any interest.

"I don't think it's so weird," he said confidently. "Someone wanted to lure them in, right?"

"Excuse me?" I was uneasy, thinking that he knew Bryce Lermond, that Strawn's Stereo and Music was a trap I'd wandered into.

"The loons. Birds hear in a totally different way than we do, man. Not just frequencies and distances; they hear everything but with a totally different *purpose*. It's how they mate, migrate, everything. If you were trying to attract a loon up by your cabin or dock or whatever—or scare one off maybe—you'd want to communicate with it. But that would probably piss off the neighbors, right? Or even if you didn't have any neighbors, you'd be liable to drive yourself crazy, listening to that over and over."

He stopped the player and the distorted loon song died.

"So that's my guess. Whoever put this up is, like, *seriously* into birds. Studying them or whatever."

He tugged at his ear and peered at the screen. "Kind of smart, if the loons can actually pick it up at that frequency. I wonder if it worked."

"I think it did," I said, but whether the birds had ever heard it, I had no idea. I knew that it was my cue, though. The sound my mother had chosen when she set out to stop my nightmares and erased my knowledge of reality instead. It wasn't so different from the story John Trenchard had recorded in that ancient journal of the *Arabella*. Something conceived with the best intentions could go bad in a hurry when you played with power you didn't fully understand.

"Thanks for the help," I began, but he cut me off again.

"There's one more, and it's a wretched friggin' noise." He toggled between windows, pressed "play," and winced at the sound that emanated from the speakers. It was a high, harsh squawk, nothing like the loon. It reminded me of failing brakes on an old car, or the protesting screech of an ancient screen door.

"What is that one?" Renee said, grimacing.

"An undesirable," he said, turning it off. "Which makes me think maybe the point of the system is to scare birds away. People like to have loons around, but not grackles."

I stared at him, feeling an ice-water sensation slide down my spine.

"Grackles," I echoed.

"Yeah, you know, those annoying little bullshit birds. Here." He opened another window, hammered the keyboard, and then the screen was filled with the image of small but fierce-looking bird with a black body, shimmering bluish head, and bright golden eye. It looked like a small raven.

"Grackles," Alex said, and smiled at me.

54

My mother was in a session with an occupational therapist, but they allowed me to interrupt it when I told them it was an emergency. They didn't ask after the nature of the emergency, which was a relief. I couldn't begin to explain it.

I came alone. Renee wanted to join me, but I'd asked her to wait. I saw the disappointment in her face, although she didn't object.

"You said she can't answer questions," Renee said.

"I didn't think she could. Now, I'm not so sure."

I left her sitting in the truck and went into Harbor House by myself. The staffer who led me into the room explained to the OT that I needed a few minutes alone with my mother. I could tell that they were both puzzled, and I didn't care. Just as they were stepping out of the room, I turned back.

"You told me she likes to be in the garden," I said.

"That's right." This from the staffer who'd led me in, a woman I'd met on my first visit.

"Does she like the birds in particular?"

"Loves them."

"Any specific kind?"

She looked at me as if I were mad. "Not really. Just . . . birds."

"Okay. Thank you."

"Sure."

The door closed, and I was alone with my mother. She smiled at me.

"We had lunch," she said.

"That's great, Mom. That's great."

"Sometimes I'm not hungry."

"I know the feeling." I pulled a chair up close to her. Looked into her eyes. Tried to find a vestige of the woman who'd raised me. "Mom, I need your help. Can you help me?"

She patted my hand. Smiled. Her eyes didn't change.

"Thanks," I said. My mouth was very dry, and it seemed hard to find words. "I found the traps under the porch, Mom. Out at camp. At Rose-water."

Those blue eyes didn't seem to shift in the slightest, but her posture might have stiffened a little. Might have.

"Good," she said. "They're hidden."

"Yes, they were." I felt like we were making progress, edging toward reality, when she added, "My brother will fix them."

I bowed my head. Closed my eyes. Breathed. Then I looked up and tried again.

"Are the loons good or bad for me, Mom?"

"We had lunch early today," she told me. "Sometimes I'm not hungry."

My hands were clasped tightly together. She reached out and patted them again. Kept smiling.

"Are the loons good or bad for Nick?" I asked.

This time I thought there was a perceptible change in her expression. Not quite a frown, but close.

"Are the loons good or bad for Nick?" I repeated.

"Both," she said, and I could have screamed. Renee was right: there was no point to this. I wouldn't be able to get an answer. The day for dialogue with my mother was long gone.

"Okay," I said. "I'll let him know."

We stared at each other. She wasn't smiling now, and while she was looking right at me, she didn't seem to see me. Certainly, she didn't seem to recognize me.

"Grackles," she said.

The ice water found my spine again.

"Tell me about them," I said. "Tell me about the grackles."

"At Rosewater," she said.

"Yes. The ones at Rosewater."

She shifted in her chair. I had the sense that she was trying to coax something forward, that she was putting a physical effort into a mental task, just trying to roll the boulder of communication up the hill. It was an awful feeling.

I reached out and took her hand. Felt her cool, papery skin against my palm.

"It's fine," I said. "It's fine, Mom."

But still she looked pained.

"Are the grackles good or bad for Nick?" I asked.

"Both," she said. The word left her thin lips force-fully, enunciated sharply. This time I didn't feel the surge of helplessness. I'd dismissed her answer the first time. Now I just studied her face.

"Both," I echoed. "Does that mean I— Does that mean that *Nick* needs to hear them? Or should he stop listening? Which is better?"

Again she shifted in the chair. She pressed her lips tight. Took a breath. Said, "One day we all went to see them."

"See who?"

"The Red Sox. That was a good day."

We'd all gone to Fenway together exactly one time. Sat in great seats along the third-base line on a perfect July day, ate hot dogs and popcorn. It was the first and last time I ever saw my mother eat a hot dog. My father and I had laughed about that. We'd all laughed about it, actually. It had been a warm, pleasant day of laughter. When the game was over, we'd gotten back into the car and driven up I-95 northbound to Maine, headed home. We'd driven right past the place where my father would die on black ice just a year later.

"I remember the game," I whispered. "Wakefield pitched. He drove you nuts. You never trusted the knuckleball."

"Well, it moves," she said.

"It sure does," I said, and my eyes were hot and stinging. "It's all over the place. He kept them down that day, though. Beat Cleveland."

"Up and down." She lifted her hand, made a wavering motion, like the flight of a knuckleball.

"It was a good day," I said.

She smiled again. I felt relieved to see it. As badly as I wanted more answers, I didn't want to put her through the agony of trying to come up with them. I thought that we'd gotten as close as we could to real connection.

"Thank you," I said. And then, because I wasn't sure what she saw versus what she heard, I added, "Nick thanks you. He wanted me to tell you . . ." I swallowed. "He wanted me to tell you that he understands."

She squeezed my hand.

We sat there in silence for a few moments. When I glanced out the window, the fog was coming in thick.

"I need to go, Mom. But I'll see you soon."

"Up and down," she said. "Like Wakefield."

"Right. Hell of a knuckleball."

She hunched, seemed to fold in on herself, and pressed her lips tight again. Then she said, "Grackles." Pause. Breath. "Up."

I watched her. She was looking right through me, but the force of effort from those two words was obvious.

"Grackles go up," I said.

Her body seemed to loosen, unwind.

"Up," she said. "Yes."

"The loons . . ." I drifted off, thought about it, and then said, "Well, the loons descend. The loons dive down, don't they?"

"Down," she said. "Up and down."

I studied her. Thought about the random, disassociated speech—what I had *perceived* as random and disassociated, at least. Wakefield and the Red Sox and the good day. Birds and sun. Traps under the porch. Grackles. The fluttering rise and fall of a knuckleball crossing the plate.

I thought of the song.

"I need both," I said. "Nick needs both sounds, doesn't he? One to dive, one to rise."

"Nick has both."

She looked so grateful then that I wanted to cry.

The only problem was that the fog was seeping in through the closed window and clouding the room. I squeezed her hand.

"I love you, Mom. Nick loves you, too. We all do. Dad does, too."

She smiled. Her body seemed to loosen again, like an unclenching fist. I watched her thin chest fill with a deep breath. She settled back into her chair. Outside, a bird was singing.

"Thank you," I told her, and then I kissed her cheek and left.

55

"There were two cues," Renee said. "One to take you down, and one to bring you back."

"Sound right?"

"Yes," she said. "It sounds absolutely right."

We were sitting in the truck in the parking lot. She looked away from me, gazed at the building.

"She can communicate that well?"

"I think so. I just didn't know how to hear it. I wasn't working hard enough."

"You think the sounds are a help to you, then?"

"I don't know. She called them traps, too. That doesn't sound good."

"Did she know where you were staying?"

I nodded. "I talked about Rosewater. She talked about the traps. At the time it was just gibberish to me. Hell, it might still be."

"You don't believe that, though."

"No," I said. "I don't believe that."

I started the truck and drove down the hill and back into town. The speaker—or emitter, the proper term now—rested on Renee's lap. When we passed the mill, I slowed, and both of us looked up, searching Bryce's windows on the high, east-facing floor. We could see only tinted glass. And the fog. Well, *I* could see the fog.

"I need to bring Bryce to Rosewater," I said.

"What?"

"But I need to make that work again, first." I pointed at the emitter. Reattached to the power supply, it should work again.

"You want it to work?"

"Yes."

I was the only one who could hear the birds at the frequency the emitter used. I had feared this initially, but now it occurred to me that I'd never seen the fog at Rosewater, either. The terrible dreams followed me from place to place, voices and visions and the rising wind of an angry storm out at sea, but at Rosewater the fog had cleared. Until I listened to the sleep song.

Ten people had heard the song, Bryce Lermond had told me, and nine were dead. Then there was Nick Bishop.

"Things felt stronger to me at Rosewater," I said, "but I think I was safer there."

"It sure as hell didn't feel that way last night," Renee shot back.

No, it hadn't.

"I'd cut the speaker wire before last night," I said. I was thinking about where I'd found the emitter and picturing the building above it. The speaker had been mounted beneath the room where I'd slept as a kid, sixteen years old, my dad just lost to a car accident where I'd had the wheel. From within that room, I'd emerged with no memory of the accident. Of pain.

Renee hefted the emitter. "This doesn't matter anymore. Maybe once it did, but not now. What matters now is what you heard on that app."

I shook my head. "You're wrong. Some circuits stay lit, sure, but even they might need help. That sound—or the memory attached to it—was a help. You're the one who told me that all of my mother's approaches to removing my nightmares were rooted in audio cues."

She didn't argue but she looked uncertain. I could spare only a glance at her, though; the fog was blanketing the pines and birches and reaching out across the road with experimental fingers, as if the banks on either side of the road would soon join hands and block my path entirely. It was as if the clouds were massing in a hurry to prevent me from returning to Rosewater. I willed my foot off the brake and kept driving, telling myself that this latest fear was not high on the priority of terror I'd endured, let alone high on the scale of what was to come. I'd seen the island and I'd felt Ashley Holland's dead lips against my ear.

"You really believe you need to see Bryce," Renee said. She sounded reluctant.

"Yeah. He's proud of his little song. I'd like to

listen to it with him. On my turf." My own voice sounded foreign to me, but not unhappy.

"Listen to it with him?"

"Yes. He says I'm the lone survivor of it. Let's test the theory."

"You'd kill him?" Renee said. She sounded curious, not shocked.

"He'll kill himself," I said. "Isn't that the idea? Isn't that what he's done? What his family has done across all these years? They wanted to watch from a safe distance. To play with pawns. I'm on the board and I want Bryce to be, too. If I'm bound for that island, Renee, I damn well want to see him there with me."

Ahead, the fog and the birches shared the same shade of winter white. The road was becoming hard to see. A car swerved around the truck and crossed the double yellow to pass us, honking as it blew by. I knew the speed limit on the road from Hammel to Rosewater was thirty-five and I was doing only twenty, crawling along, but it was the best speed I could manage in the fog.

I remembered sailing with Pat in Penobscot Bay when we were both still in school, his freckled face confident as he sat at the tiller. Then the fog had closed in around us and all that I'd been able to think of was the number of rock islands that we'd passed on the way out. I'd wanted to stop then, too, but it's always easier to press ahead when you're traveling with a friend, even if you're scared. Especially then.

"I want Bryce to hear it," I said. "He and I can sit together and listen to your sister sing. What happens then, I don't know. But he's going to be part of it."

"He won't just sit there and listen, Nick."

"Correct. It will take encouragement."

I could feel her stare on me, but I didn't look her way.

"You think you're running out of time," she said. This wasn't a question.

"I know I am."

Another horn blared, and this time it was coming toward to me, not from behind me, and Renee grabbed the wheel and jerked it to the right. Branches lashed the passenger side of the truck as I hammered the brake and brought us to a stop.

Renee and I sat in silence. I thought I could hear her heartbeat, but I wasn't sure. It might have been my own. She released the steering wheel, exhaled, and moved the gearshift to park.

"Maybe I should drive."

"Maybe." My mouth was dry again.

"Is it the fog?"

"You're seeing it, too?"

"No."

I nodded. Worked my tongue around my mouth, tried to call up some saliva. "Yeah," I said. "It's the fog. Thicker now. Darker."

"Let's trade, then," Renee said, and opened her door. I opened mine and stepped out onto the shoulder of the road. The fog behind was so thick that I could see only shadows where the closest trees stood. One of the shadows moved toward me. Renee. I started in her direction. Then she spoke from behind me.

"Nick?"

I looked in the direction of her voice, then turned back to the approaching shadow I'd thought was her.

The man from the island stepped out of the fog and smiled at me. The sores on his dehydrated lips burst open and blood leaked from them, running hot and red, twins of the lash marks that laced his torso. I smelled blood and salt water, the scents so overpowering that I brought a hand to my nose.

"Close now," he said, and as he stepped forward, I stepped backward.

Right into Renee's arms.

As soon as I made contact with her the man from the island was gone, as if we'd interrupted the circuit that brought him here.

"Nick, are you okay? Are you with me now?"

"Yeah. Yeah, I'm okay."

The fog was thinning. Not vanishing but thinning. My head pounded and I could hear the sound of distant breakers and the *snap, snap, snap* of the torn sail but the man from the island was gone and the fog was thinning.

I closed my eyes and breathed and felt Renee's body warm against my own. I heard a car pass by, close to us, and then opened my eyes again and saw the road more clearly, glimmers of daylight returning.

"You need to hurry now, Nick," Ashley Holland's voice said.

"Yes," I said.

"Yes, *what*?" Renee asked.

I ignored her at first and searched the road for a sign of her dead sister. Ashley didn't appear, but I knew whose voice I'd heard. I knew it without a doubt.

"Nothing," I told Renee. I squeezed her arm and stepped away. "Let's go. Let's get back to Rosewater." I took my phone out. "You drive. I'll call him."

"Okay."

As she put the truck into gear, I found Bryce Lermond's number and dialed. He answered immediately, bright-voiced and chipper. My hand curled into a fist at the sound of it.

"There you are, Bishop! I confess, I was beginning to worry."

"We need to talk," I said.

"Oh? Bad day? Or was it the night that troubled you?"

"Come see me, Bryce. I'm running out of time, and you know that. I'm asking for a few more answers before I go. Don't deny me that."

"I hate to hear you sound so fatalistic."

"Just come see me, you son of a bitch."

"Of course. Happy to."

"I'll be at the camp at—"

"Rosewater, yes, yes, I know. I'll see you soon, buddy. Take good care until then, all right? Regardless of what you think, I really *do* want to see you one more time."

I ended the call. Lowered the phone and looked ahead. The fog was still there, but thinner. The emitter rested on the floorboards between my feet.

"We'll get it set up the way it was," I said, talking to myself as much as to Renee. "It did help. It will again. I know that."

"Okay. Is he coming?" Renee turned onto the camp road, glimpses of the pond showing through the mist and the trees.

"He said he would. He said he'd like to see me one more time."

Silence while she digested that.

"I'll splice the speaker wire under the porch and we'll bring it back to the way it was before," I said, picking up the emitter. "It will help me, but I don't think it will do a damn thing for him. Regardless, you'll need to be gone."

"Like hell."

"You'll need to be gone," I repeated. "When I play that thing on the speakers, Renee, you can't be anywhere near it."

She turned into the drive and angled down the steep descent. A black BMW was parked at the base of the hill. Beyond it, Bryce Lermond was standing on the rock, gazing out across the pond.

"He was already here when I called him," I said. "He was just waiting."

"What do you want me to do?" Renee asked, foot on the brake, the Ranger stopped halfway down the hill. I looked down at the emitter, its cut copper wire bright against the black rubber backing, and I felt just as Bryce intended—helpless.

"Put it in park," I said. "We'll see how it goes."

It wasn't until I stepped out of the truck that I saw Bob Beauchamp standing in the pines between our houses, gun in hand.

56

Nick!" Bryce called brightly, as if greeting an old friend. He was wearing his trademark jeans-and-fleece combo and three-hundred-dollar Danner work boots that didn't show so much as a crease in the leather. He stood with complete confidence, and why not? The man with the gun was there on his behalf, not mine.

I got out of the truck, holding the emitter in my left hand, and looked from Bryce to Bob Beauchamp. His face was drawn and waxen. He was holding a semiautomatic handgun, maybe a Taurus, something a tier below Glock but plenty deadly. Bob saw the question in my eyes, and he shifted his weight from left to right and muttered, "This is on you now, not me."

Bryce Lermond spoke before I could respond.

"Bob's going to join us for our talk," Bryce said. "I hope that's okay. Come on in, come on in."

I'd locked the camp door when we left, but now Bryce opened it and beckoned me toward my own home. I turned back to Beauchamp, the only man who had a key.

"You're a hell of a caretaker, Bob."

He didn't respond. I felt the weight of the emitter in my hand and understood for the first time how involved Bob Beauchamp had probably been in my mother's project. I lifted the emitter, making sure he saw it.

"Could've told me about this old thing a few days back, couldn't you? I'm pretty sure my mother didn't crawl around under the camp installing it herself. Let me guess: You did that work?"

He narrowed his gaze. "Doesn't matter," he said shortly.

"I think it matters greatly. I think you knew about it, too."

"That old thing hasn't been active in a decade, Bishop. It doesn't matter. Not now."

But I knew better, because I'd heard the sounds.

"Let's go inside," Bryce repeated, and this time his voice had some bite to it. Beauchamp stepped forward and waved the barrel of the gun toward the door. I looked at Renee. She was staring at the gun with a sick look of understanding—and no trace of shock.

Bryce was watching her, too. He said, "Cheer up, Holland. By the end of the day, you'll thank me. Trust me on that. We just need to stay the course. Please go inside."

I walked across the drive and entered the camp. Bryce leaned against the kitchen island and nodded at the picnic table.

"Sit."

I sat. Renee stood just inside the door, at a distance from me. Beauchamp stood a few feet to her side.

"I think our time for indulging this game is over," Bryce said. "I was happy to give it a shot. Pretty curious to see how you'd do, actually, but all of this intrepid-reporter bullshit is not helpful. The things you think matter actually don't matter at all . . ." He pointed at the emitter, which I was holding in both hands as if it were a weapon or a shield. "Exhibit A. But you're going to cause trouble at some point. Which is a shame, because Bob here gave you more than enough background. There was no need to break into Pat's boat."

"Trust but verify," I said, and Bryce laughed.

"Very good, very good. I suppose I should have anticipated that. And I'll admit I was a little hot when I realized I hadn't already taken steps to ensure Pat Ryan didn't leave anything around, so I appreciate the nudge. Where are those copies, by the way? The ones you took from his boat."

It was as if he'd watched our movements all day. I'd paid attention to the mirrors, though. I'd been alert for followers, and hadn't seen any. So how did he know so much? I looked at Renee.

"Don't blame her," Bryce said, reading my thoughts. "My guess is that all she knew was that I could track your location with the app enabled. She had no idea the app activates the microphone as well."

Renee stared at him. He smiled.

"Invasive, I know. But necessary. I don't love the alliance you two seem to be developing. Last night, for example. Quite the alliance last night."

Renee said, "Go to hell, Bryce."

Bob Beauchamp shifted position, and I saw the gun move from his right hand to his left. He reached back with his right and slid the dead bolt home, then leaned against the door, moving the gun back to his right hand. I watched him and then returned my attention to Bryce Lermond.

"It's a family legacy, isn't it?" I asked Bryce. "Your ancestor recorded it. With help—sorry, with sacrifice—from the cabin boy on the *Arabella* and then from Dennison. Two dead men. Your ancestor saw that the record was sent back to his wife when he died, and it has been passed along all these years. You're still trying to figure it out, aren't you?"

"Every family has a legacy."

The emitter was cold in my hands. I rotated it, feeling the weathering and corrosion on the metal frame, and found myself distracted even from the gun by what Beauchamp had said about it being years since the thing was connected to a power supply. I'd heard the loons, though. I had heard them.

"Curious about that toy?" Bryce said. "You understand it for the most part, I think. It was one of your mother's tools. Your family's research, my family's tech. A beautiful little blend of talent that conspired together right here at Rosewater. Someday, this place may be a museum." He pursed his lips as if pondering that and then said, "Or not. We'll probably cut this chapter from the history, actually."

He crossed the room and came close to me, reached out.

"May I?"

If I swung the emitter into his face, he'd never get a hand up. Beauchamp would end my fun pretty quickly, but I'd at least get the satisfaction of seeing the son of a bitch bleed.

"Nick," Bryce Lermond said, watching my eyes, hand still extended, "we don't need to behave like children. The situation is what it is. Accept that, ask your questions, and I'll give you the answers."

"And then?"

He didn't blink. "You're going to die. How long that will take if you're left to your own devices, I'm not sure. Probably not long. You're seeing the fog pretty consistently now, aren't you?"

I thought of him listening to every word I'd said in the past hours—days—and felt foolish, exposed. I would hurt him, I decided then. It was a small satisfaction, but the only one I could extract. Maybe, if I got very lucky and moved very fast, I could even kill him.

A cold breath touched my ear, a chill spread down my neck and between my shoulder blades, and Ashley Holland's familiar voice whispered, "Let it ride."

Bryce leaned closer. Put his hand on the emitter. I loosened my grasp and let him take it from me. He smiled, and I saw that he thought he'd taken more than the device from me. He thought that I was beaten. Maybe I was. I was damn tired, I knew that.

Let it ride, the dead woman had told me.

Okay.

"Yes," I said, my voice sounding loud in the room as Bryce took the emitter away and set it down on the island, "I am seeing the fog consistently now."

I turned and looked out the window at the pond. There was fog gathering over its surface, a crystalline cloud. The sunlight could still penetrate it, but I thought that wouldn't be true for long.

"Who's been in my shoes before?" I asked.

"What's that?"

"Someone has. You seem to understand the process, and you didn't get all that from Pat Ryan's old journals."

"Oh, definitely not. Yes, I must confess that I misled you a tiny bit yesterday, although in my defense it wasn't by much. I told you nine of the ten people to hear the song are dead. That's only half-true."

"Half?"

"Sixty percent? I don't know, Nick, you tell me—how *alive* is your mother?"

I pivoted back from the window. Stared at him.

He smiled. Rapped his knuckles off the metal cover of the emitter. "She gave it a hell of a try. And this part of the story I actually *do* want you to know, because it's fucking *noble*, man. All I ever wanted was you. You were going to be the test. I mean, you were the one who couldn't dream and didn't remember trauma, right? But she put you off-limits. Even promised to play the role herself, if that's what it took, and considering how much she knew about the risks by then . . ." He made a little inclination with his head and seemed almost sincerely moved. "Very brave. She was a very brave woman."

"You made her go through this?"

"She volunteered."

I thought of her stroke. She'd been hiking when it happened. At least, that was what I'd been told, the only thing that made sense. They'd found her down in the rocks below Maiden Cliff. She'd taken a long fall.

"She fell at sunset," I said aloud.

"What's that?" Bryce asked.

"Yes," Renee said, and everyone looked at her. She didn't take her eyes off mine. "She walked off the cliff edge just like Ashley from the roof, like Pat from that tree, like Dennison from the ship's mast. It was at sunset and she was facing west. The only difference is someone found her while her heart was still beating. Like Pat and Dennison. Not like Ashley."

Her eyes were bright and shimmering.

"You knew that?" I asked.

"No. But I understand it now."

"Is she there, Bryce?" I asked.

"Who? Where?" Bryce said in a bored tone that made me wish I'd swung the emitter into his teeth after all.

"Is my mother on that island? Is she trapped out there, in her own mind, her own perception?"

"I don't know," he said. "But you're going to finish her work now."

"What's that?"

"The song soothes. It *heals*. We know that. We are very well aware of that. I could show you screenshots of an MRI, Nick . . . It's remarkable. The song calms the brain almost instantly." He made a finger-snapping gesture that moved too slowly to produce any sound. "A beautiful thing. But then, if you let it play on? The brain illuminates, lobes that shouldn't be active are suddenly bright, the whole brain seems to be *on fire . . .*"

His voice drifted off and then he refocused his gaze on me and smiled.

"It's something special," he said. "Power like that scares people. There's a reason that the song has been silent for so long. My family has hidden that thing across so many years, across multiple continents and generations, all out of fear. They were afraid to embrace what their ancestor discovered. Even my parents were. My father had more curiosity, but my mother undermined that. Frightened him. A shame. Because there's no *need* for fear when you have *control*."

"You don't have control over it," I said.

"Not yet," he agreed. "But closer every day, Nick. Closer every day."

There was a long silence that felt like a held breath. Bryce's dark eyes were locked on mine.

"There is a power here that you don't even fathom yet," he said in a voice just above a whisper. "A power that could change . . . well, everything. Everything we understand about our own world. And we're going to give it a try now. Yes, we are."

"We've already got plenty of ways to kill people, Bryce. You're not changing the world by inventing another."

His eyes gleamed. "I wouldn't be, would I?"

I waited for more, but he didn't say anything. He looked at me for a few more seconds, as if we were locked in a private communion of some kind, and then straightened abruptly.

"Okay, kids, field trip coming." He took a few steps toward Renee, and though his tone was light, his face had hardened. He stepped past Renee, motioned Beauchamp aside, and unlocked the door. "Walk behind us, Bob, and please don't be shy about pulling the trigger if you need to. Just shoot low, man. Legs, not brains. Nick's important to me."

He pulled the door open and Ashley Holland stood on the other side, framed against the fog.

All that had once terrified me about her was now familiar: the eerie blue-white pallor, the bloodred lips, the salt water that dripped from her tangled blond hair, the smell of the sea. She looked tired, though, and I was beginning to understand that. It was a long trip from the island to me, and however she made it, I suspected that it wasn't easy.

It came with a cost.

"Almost there," she told me, and extended her hand and beckoned me forward.

Bryce Lermond seemed surprised when I rose without a word and walked for the door.

"Easy, tiger. I'll lead the way."

I let him walk in front. Let him believe he was leading. There was much he didn't understand, I realized now. Just as much as I didn't, or maybe more. The who, what, where, and why of the living did not matter so much. Not when squared off against the will of the dead.

I'd expected to be instructed to get into a car, but Bryce led us through the pines instead, following a narrow path that the deer used when they came down to drink from the pond at dusk. We moved up and away from the camp and curled through the trees and I understood that we were walking toward the house his family had owned all these years, the monstrosity looming over the water with its always-empty dock marked by the bright green reflectors.

The Gatsby House.

It was right in front of us, but I couldn't see it. I could scarcely make out anything beyond Bryce because the fog was so thick. I caught my foot on a root once and stumbled and I heard Bob Beauchamp shift behind us, but I didn't look up to see if he'd lifted the gun. Let them worry about me all they wanted; I didn't intend to run.

Up ahead, visible here and there through the fog, Ashley Holland led the way.

We were deep in the trees when I heard the loon cry. It brought me up short, and Renee nearly walked into me.

"No one hears that," I said. Not a question, but a reassurance.

"Hears what?" Beauchamp said. "Move along, asshole."

I started walking again, and the loon wailed once more. The sound my mother had chosen to calm me long ago was alive again, and the sound was deceptive. What the uninformed believed to be a peaceful birdsong was in fact a guardian's war cry. The emitter that she'd used to play it sat on the table inside the camp, its power cord severed.

So how was I hearing it? And I had never heard the grackles, not once. She said I needed both. Up and down, one to descend, one to rise.

No. That wasn't entirely right. She'd said "Nick has both." *Has.* As if it had been hardwired, a permanent change, and all I needed to do was listen and understand.

For the first time, I thought I *did* understand. The emitter had mattered once, had mattered greatly. But maybe its job was already done.

Some circuits stay lit.

"How's the fog, Nick?" Bryce asked.

"I don't see it now," I told him, although he was no more than three feet in front of me and all I could make out was his silhouette. Ashley was farther ahead yet clearer to me.

"It will be back," Bryce said. "I'm quite sure of that."

"We'll see."

We walked on through the fog. I could hear the waves again and the whistling wind. The *snap, snap, snap* of the sail. Figures moved in the mist around us and once I saw Dennison, laughing with blood on his lips, and then another man reached for me, a cold claw of a hand grasping at mine. Ashley Holland didn't break stride, though, so neither did I. Somewhere out there, the loon cried again. Fainter but present. Loons are expert divers, capable of pushing fast and deep when necessary. When they dive, they are not prey; they're predators.

I liked that idea.

We came off the trail onto a path of crushed stone that led to one of flagstone and then on up to the house. The glass doors gleamed black against the mist. Ashley had vanished from sight, leaving a swirl of mist, a vortex like steam drawn upward by a fan.

Bryce walked beneath the deck to the lower level of the house, which had as much glass as the upper level. He went to the center door and slid it back and motioned me inside.

"Come on in. We're about to revisit that conversation about the power of the song, Nick."

I stepped out of the fog and into the Lermond house and found myself facing a casket.

57

I stopped just inside the doorway, five feet from the casket. It was a sleek polished mahogany or walnut, wood so dark it looked almost black in the dim light. The lid was down and the silver handles gleamed.

Renee slipped in to stand beside me, silent. When I looked at her, her face was so pale that I thought she might faint. She looked at me with a question in her eyes but neither of us spoke. Behind us, Bob Beauchamp muttered something about a merciful father.

"Don't need your commentary, Bob," Bryce said in a low voice. "Just need you to keep the peace. You want to stand outside, go ahead."

Beauchamp took him up on the offer. He left the glass door open but backed out of the house in a hurry, stumbling over the threshold.

"What's the joke, Bryce?" I whispered. "You want me to climb in?"

"No joke. You're about to do something very special. Change the world, in fact. I believe you can do that." He walked to the head of the coffin and let his fingertips trace its smooth surface. "The song, I've solved. I can capture it, conceal it, replicate it, alter it, aim it. I can do most anything with the song. The problem is the singer. I haven't solved that one just yet. I think there's a more significant process there. Human touch seems to matter."

I got it then. A horrible sense of clarity crept over me, and I remembered the journal of John Trenchard, his description of how the *Arabella* had been abandoned with no one left aboard save for the dead and dying. I remembered this and then I heard the words of the song:

If you want to see home
I ask you to rise
Tell you to rise
Now, now, you must rise
For no man among us must die

"No, Bryce," I said. Whispered.

He looked at me and smiled. "Ah—you understand, don't you, Nick?"

"It won't work."

"Perhaps not. But I think it might. Worth a shot, isn't it?" His eyes had that fevered gleam again. And why not? He intended to raise the dead.

"No," I said again.

Bryce Lermond grasped one of the silver handles and lifted the lid of the casket. The top third of the lid rose, but I couldn't see inside of it yet, and I moved backward to ensure that remained the case. As I moved backward, though, Renee moved forward, passing me in a rush, closing to within a stride of the casket before she screamed.

Her body went rigid and she screamed from her core, from within the deepest part of herself, and she was still screaming when Bryce slapped her.

I moved forward then, but so did Bob Beauchamp. I felt a wrenching pain in my shoulder and the press of cool metal to my skull as Beauchamp grabbed my arm and put the gun to my head. It didn't matter, though. I was already on my knees, beaten—and not by Beauchamp or the gun. By then, I could see the contents of the casket.

Ashley Holland's corpse had been as artfully reconstructed as could be done with the remains of a woman who'd fallen to her death on a brick sidewalk. Which is to say that her body was the ghastliest carnage I'd ever seen outside of a battlefield, and far worse in its own way than any I'd seen *on* one. It was worse because someone had spent time on her. They'd drained her of blood and fluids and tried to mend shattered bones and stitch torn flesh and then they'd covered their horrible creation with a black velvet blanket. Even the blanket couldn't hide the reality, though; it draped in unnatural dips and valleys while other areas rose like a volcanic mountain range.

I knew as I looked down at her that she had struck the bricks feet-first. The damage—devastation—

had worked up the chain. Legs to spine to shoulders and neck. Her face had been left largely intact. Extra care had been given to preserving this illusion.

Renee had stopped screaming and slumped to the floor. She looked up at Bryce with horror.

"What have you done?" she asked, voice trembling. "What . . . what is this?"

"You may well thank me," he said. "If Nick does his part, I think you'll be most grateful for *what I've done*."

Renee just stared at him, sickened and shocked. Then she looked at me.

"I thought she was cremated," I whispered.

"Yes," she said, and there were tears in her eyes now. "So did I."

"And what a waste that might have been," Bryce said. "Hate me now, Renee. That's fine. Reasonable. But soon? Soon you'll thank me. It's up to Nick."

Renee didn't answer. Her eyes were fixed on mine.

"He thinks I can bring her back," I said. My voice was as toneless and empty as her scream had been anguished.

"Yes," Bryce said. "I think he can."

"No," Renee whispered—moaned, really—and the word wasn't argument; it was a plea. "No, no, please, do not—"

"Bob," Bryce said warningly, and Beauchamp stepped forward and grabbed Renee around the shoulders and dragged her backward. He seemed to want to be as far away as possible. Renee didn't even fight him. She was staring at the casket with wide, terrified eyes—until she looked at me again.

"Bring her back?" she whispered.

"Yes," I said. "The song has been sung to the living. He wants to know what happens when it's offered to the dead. Am I right, Bryce? You've got the same big idea your ancestor had on the *Arabella* all those centuries ago."

Bryce looked to Renee.

"I loved her," he said. "I love her still. And you? You have the arrogance to look at me with blame. To see her now"—he waved at the casket—"and say this is *my* fault. When *you* were the one who coerced her into removing every protection, every caution, every protocol. Together, she and I were going to change the world. Together, we were going to . . ."

His voice trailed off. He wiped his mouth. Shook his head.

"You hid the truth from her," Renee said. "She didn't know a fraction of what you knew."

"There would have been a time for that! My time, according to my plan!"

"To your control. That's the only word that matters to you, Bryce. Don't you *dare* speak of love when you mean control."

He stared at her, nearly trembling with rage. Then he whirled from her and returned to me. Squatted beside me. Spoke softly.

"I'm going to need you to sing it for her," Bryce said. "As they did on the *Arabella*. You understand this, don't you."

I nodded.

Now, now you must rise

Yes, I understood it. He thought he could raise the dead, with my help. He'd read the same story I had, and he knew that the doomed crew of the *Arabella* had emerged from within the storm and sailed on. He probably knew much more than that, if William Lermond's private letters home had contained details that John Trenchard's journal did not. He knew exactly what his ancestor had sought from the song: defiance of death. No, triumph over it.

"You know a lot about the song, but not enough," Bryce said. "Contact seems to matter. The song's power can extend only so far on its own. The full effect requires human touch."

"There's nothing human about this," I said.

"I ask you to try," Bryce said, and I heard the phrasing and almost sang aloud: *I ask you to rise.*

"I won't," I said simply.

"Understand that when I say I am *asking* this of you, that's a generous phrase."

Tell you to rise

Now, now you must rise

"I'm going to die, anyhow," I said. "So why would I try? For *you*? Your madness? No."

"For proof," he whispered, and his dark eyes looked like oil on asphalt. "You want to see it home,

Nick. I know that you do. You're a storyteller above all else. Not a man who skips the ending. No matter the cost."

I wanted to tell him that he knew nothing about me—tell him that of course I would never reach into that casket and lay my warm, living hand on Ashley Holland's cold, crushed dead one. I couldn't speak, though. I just looked into his eyes and heard the song in my mind—*Now, now you must rise*—and I thought of the journals of John Trenchard and of the story of the *Arabella* and the question, the simple but oh-so-troubling question.

Was it possible?

I thought of the Acadian singer, enduring the lashes of Lermond's whip on the deck of the *Arabella*, bearing that agony and never saying a word. Then I thought of Ashley, pacing the rock island in the unrelenting wind and rain, pacing through the fog in the howling endless storm.

"Renee," I whispered. "Do you want me to try?"

Bob Beauchamp murmured something that sounded vaguely like a prayer, but for a long time Renee stayed silent. Then she whispered, "If you can help her, please do it. Please."

If you can help her.

I wanted to hear Ashley's voice then. Hers was the only desire that mattered—not mine, not Renee's, certainly not Bryce Lermond's.

I looked down at the dead woman's face and said, "Ashley?"

"Yes," Bryce breathed, as if he thought I was coming closer to what he wanted so badly. "It's worth a try, isn't it? For her. For *her*, Nick, just try."

I was about to tell him that if he wanted to see such horror so badly, he could try it himself, but then I stopped myself. Why *couldn't* he try? He knew the words; as he'd said, he had the song. Why had he needed me at all?

And then, finally, I understood.

If the simple act of listening could do damage to the living, then the act of singing it to the dead? That was damnation.

It was written plainly in the journal of John Trenchard, quoted from the dying Dennison. There was a price to listening to the death song, and a higher cost still for those who shared it. Once it had been a gift, a peaceful passage, but out there on the winter sea where Lermond's whip had gone slick and red with blood and flesh, flaying innocence in pursuit of power, it had become something else.

"Yes," Ashley Holland's ghost whispered into my ear, that soft icy gust that had once repelled me and now felt like a comfort. "You know what to do. Sing the right song, in the right way. Please."

I couldn't see her ghost in the room this time. It was not at all like the visions. This time, the only version of her I could see was the atrocity that lay before me in the open casket. But I could hear her.

I could listen.

I faced Bryce once more. "All right," I said. "I'll try."

Beauchamp muttered, pacing with gun in hand, and on the floor behind me Renee was whispering to herself, and suddenly their voices were exhausting to me, infuriating.

"Shut them up," I said from between clenched teeth, and Bryce Lermond looked at me and smiled, as if we'd made an agreement, come to a private understanding.

"Bob," he snapped. "You heard the man. Shut up."

Beauchamp fell silent and Renee did, too. Bryce rose and moved briskly past the casket, not even sparing Ashley's ruined body a downward glance. He opened a wall-mounted cabinet and withdrew sets of headphones. For an instant, I thought he intended to play the song through them. Then he returned and handed one to Renee and one to Beauchamp, keeping the last for himself. I realized that they weren't headphones at all but ear protection, the kind you'd wear at a gun range where large-caliber weapons are being fired. It wasn't a poor comparison.

Bryce put his on, eyes aglow, his excitement a palpable thing, and I could see his ancestors in him, that feverish thirst for unnatural power that had led William Lermond onto the deck of the *Arabella* with a blood-soaked whip in hand.

I turned back to Renee. She sat on the floor with her back against the glass door. Like Bryce, her ears were covered and her eyes were bright. The only difference was the tears.

"Try," Bryce Lermond said. "Try, Nick."

I lowered myself to my knees beside the casket. Leaned closer. Looked at Ashley Belle Holland's poor, ruined face. Took her hand.

Began to sing.

58

On the island the storm was raging, and so were the crew of the *Arabella*. I saw them all now, their faces clear despite the fog. They all looked like Dennison, with ragged, bleeding lips, hollow eyes, and gaunt cheeks. Ravaged by the storm, the wind, the thirst.

They begged for me, their hands scrabbling across mine, fingers like parchment-covered bones. They begged and they laughed and they wept, a furious, frenetic swirl of human madness and anguish.

I kept my eyes on Ashley Holland.

She was standing on the jagged outcropping of rock where the high waves broke and the shattered board bearing the word *Purgatorium* smacked against the rocks. The word was written in blood, and where it had originated, I did not know. The first sighting off the coast of Maine might have come at Boon Island in 1710, but I thought that the ship had been sailing the night seas long before that, and would sail them again. Wherever desperate men gathered, the ship might find them.

The torn sail snapped overhead, and the wind lashed, and the sea crashed down. Ashley faced the storm calmly, resolutely.

She was different from the others. They seemed to understand that. They kept their distance. She'd boarded the wrong ship in the darkness but that was not her fault and there was no reason she couldn't be rescued. The others, I thought, had cast their lot knowingly. I wanted to ask for their names, wanted to understand their histories, but I couldn't bring myself to look into their faces. Their fingers clawed at mine, raked my back, tore at my hair. Papery flesh peeled from their bones like zested rinds, leaving shallow furrows behind. Always, always, there were their sounds—screams and laugh and sobs.

They could touch me, but they couldn't seem to get ahold of me. The touches were terrible, but they didn't slow me down, didn't knock me off stride. I stayed in pursuit of Ashley, crossing the rock in the fog.

Ashley finally turned from the storm. Looked back at me. A question in her eyes.

"Leave!" I shouted. "Leave now!"

She stared at me for a long time as the wind and rain pummeled her. I was missing something, I thought. I was missing a key rule. It was the rule Dennison had shared with Trenchard: the waiting could be brought to an end, but not without sacrifice.

"You'll be replaced," I called. "I promise. I'll see to it."

Ashley's expression changed to one of exquisite sadness. Not the sorrow of disappointment or anger but of heartbreak. She gazed at me like that for a long time before she turned and stepped down from the rock and into the sea.

The water was deep and the water was dark. Blissfully, wonderfully deep and dark. I lost sight of her swiftly.

The storm rose in fury then, the wind shrieking as if the loss had wounded it, the waves a torrent, salt spray all around, cold needles against my flesh, drying my lips, stinging my eyes. A terrible thirst overtook me then, but when I wet my lips the tissue peeled from them in dry flakes and all I could taste was salt and blood. I could no longer see clearly, my dry eyes tormented by that cutting spray, and so I squeezed them shut and huddled on the rock, trying to get low, out of the storm, already aware that wouldn't be possible. The storm would go on endlessly for me now.

I had made a terrible choice.

Then came a sound just a pitch below the howl of the storm. Soft but clear and decidedly out of place on this forsaken rock.

It was a bird's song. Not a beautiful one, not the mournful cry of a loon nor the harsh cawing of a seagull, but something higher, shrill, rising, rising, rising.

I kept my eyes closed and let my mind chase the sound.

I came back to consciousness on my knees beside the casket. I was gripping the sides of it with both hands, using it to hold myself upright. My body was soaked with sweat, and my muscles trembled and twitched. I lifted my head and looked at Bryce Lermond.

He was staring down at me with great disappointment.

"Nothing," he said. "Nothing."

I turned to Renee. She looked at me with a question in her eyes. I nodded.

"Try again!" Bryce shouted. "You were close—I know you were close! Try again!"

I rose unsteadily and looked down into the casket. Ashley Holland's body lay in ruined rest just as it had before the song.

That was good. It meant that I had picked the right words and sang it the right way. I was learning the art now. In the end, it was all a matter of craft. Of intent.

Bryce Lermond looked like a dejected mad scientist. A child who'd discovered his lightsaber was nothing more than a toy. I tapped the side of my head, indicating that I wanted him to remove the headphones. He did, lowering them to dangle loosely in his right hand.

I watched them carefully. Breathed deeply and waited for the trembling in my muscles to cease.

"I'm closer than you think," I said. "It's just a matter of a few words."

"Exactly!" He sounded relieved. He took two steps closer to the casket, his eyes on Ashley's corpse. "It might not be easy, but it can be done. I'm sure of that. I've read so much more than you, Nick; my family has tracked it across eras and continents and learned every story. It *can* be done."

"Yes," I agreed. "It can be. All I need are the right words. I'm very close."

I hummed in cadence, the rising and falling melody, the sound of a peaceful sea. I made myself look at Ashley so that it would appear my full attention was on her. Bryce's protective headset was clear in my peripheral vision, though, held loosely in his fingers, and he was distracted. He, too, was focused on the contents of the casket. If my humming bothered him, he betrayed no indication of it.

"A few words off," I said, and then, cautiously, softly, I sang, *"Far, far down we go, Fearless though we are prey . . ."*

Early words, the first I'd heard of the song, but I remembered them well. Once you'd heard the song, you had no choice but to remember it.

Bryce didn't interrupt me. He stepped closer, his protective headset forgotten now, and rested one hand on the edge of the casket, peering down at Ashley. Waiting for a glimpse at power no man should have.

"Nothing ahead that we know," I sang, *"but all behind we must flee . . ."*

Bob Beauchamp spoke from behind us in a high, frightened voice.

"Stop that! Stop it!"

He understood what I was trying to do before the others did. Renee's hearing was still protected by the headset, but Beauchamp had removed his to follow Bryce Lermond's lead. Two of them could hear, and only one of them feared that.

I could control them with the song, I thought, if I had time to get through enough of it. Given enough time, I could probably get them to take a long climb and a last step, and nobody's gun would stop me from that.

"Shut him up!" Beauchamp shouted, and this time Bryce looked at him, and when he did, I lunged for the headset, his beloved protection. I got ahold of it and knocked it free, sent it skittering across the floor, beneath the casket. He pursued the headset rather than attempting to stop me. It was the wrong choice.

I sang louder now.

"So run, run on with me, Dive, dive in with me, Swim, swim deep with—"

There was a scrabble of motion behind me, and I turned, still singing, to see Bob Beauchamp stepping forward, wild-eyed, lifting the pistol. I stammered, losing the words and cadence, and our eyes locked as he leveled the pistol and moved his finger to the trigger.

Renee stepped in front of me with one hand outstretched, reaching for the gun.

She made contact as he fired, and the bullet blew through the center of her palm and then bored through her chest just below her collarbone and whatever was left of the round tunneled into Ashley Holland's casket.

Renee dropped, and Beauchamp stepped backward, stumbling for the open door behind him and pawing at his face, which was now wet with Renee's blood. The pistol fell from his hand and his heels hit the lip of the threshold and upended him. He fell to the stone patio on the other side of the door, and he was still down when I reached the gun. He made it halfway to his feet before I shot him. It was a good shot. Center mass. That's a good use of a bullet, as any instructor will tell you. Not many instructors have shot a man.

I heard a howl of fury from behind me, a sound that might have come from the island itself, from out there in the waves and wind, and I whirled as Bryce Lermond ran toward me, and then I fired twice more.

Center mass.

They were both down then, the two of them joining Renee, all down in their own hot blood, and I
got back to my feet, so that the casket and I loomed
above them.

Beauchamp was already dead. Bryce was moving his heels and opening and closing one hand,
trying impotently to crawl. Renee lay curled on the
floor beside her sister's casket. The only hand that
she had left was held to her breast and soaked with
blood.

She was dying but not dead. Very close, though.
Her gorgeous green eyes told me that. She knew she
was close, and she wanted help. Wanted peace.

I dropped the pistol and went to Renee. Touched
her face as gently as possible. Cleared my head and
my heart, and began to sing.

"Far, far down we go . . ."

60

She died in the night, but I sat with her until dawn.

I didn't want to leave her there alone after sunset. Not in that place, where such terrible things had been conceived and had occurred. Not beneath her sister's coffin.

I sat with her in my arms until there was no warmth left in her body, and only then did I lower her tenderly to the floor. I went upstairs and found a blanket and covered her with it and placed a pillow under her head. In the darkness, I could convince myself that she looked almost restful.

I thought of the island, of Ashley's walk into the water, and the knowledge that she had to be replaced to be released. Bob Beauchamp was the first to die, but my song had been for Bryce Lermond.

I believed that mattered. Hoped that it did.

I left Renee and stepped outside. The fog was gone and the stars were clear and bright. Ashley Holland's ghost did not whisper to me in the night. No one spoke at all. The wind was still and the water was calm while I walked back to my own camp.

Three times, I heard the loons.

The fact that they were not real no longer bothered me. They were there, a gift from my mother, a passage to deeper sleep, peaceful sleep, no nightmares, no pain.

A cost to that? Yes. Of course. A dear one. But still I was grateful.

I'd heard the grackles now, too. An unpleasant sound but a demanding one, insistent. They had chased me from the island just as I'd prepared to surrender myself to it.

I cleaned the camp shower with bleach and took my time scrubbing it down. Gathered my clothes in a plastic bag and tossed in the rubber gloves I'd worn for the cleaning before I changed into canvas work gloves and knotted the bag. I took the bag with me while I walked to Bob Beauchamp's cabin and found the gas cans in his garage. It took me three trips to move it all to the Lermond house. I sat beside Renee again then, though I kept my distance now.

The blackness of night lightened in that remarkable way of pre-dawn hours, something at first imperceptible that grows to undeniable. Inevitable.

When the first pink hue touched the blue-gray sky, I sang what I hoped was the right song, in the right way. I didn't know if it mattered, so long after Renee's last breath, her last heartbeat. I was certain it could not hurt.

When I was done, the sky was ruby-colored and

the trees were taking clear shape across the water and I knew I couldn't wait any longer. I poured out the gasoline, applying it most liberally beneath the exposed trusses that held up the second floor of the house, and then splashed a healthy dose in the furnace room, just below the electric panel.

Before I left, I lowered the lid on Ashley Holland's coffin. I didn't look down at her. What was inside of that box was not Ashley. Then I knelt beside Renee one last time and closed my eyes and touched my lips to her forehead.

The house was engulfed in flame when I left, Rosewater reflecting crimson and orange light in my rearview mirror. I heard the first sirens when I was halfway to town. The trucks began to pass me then, but I did not slow, and neither did they.

It had been a long day and a longer night and I knew that I would need rest before the next visit. Pat Ryan's parents were due in town, and I knew that soon the ventilator would be removed. I wanted to be with Pat when that happened. I thought that I should hold his hand and sing him a song. I would face to the east, where the sun rose. I would hope for the best.

61

I am a dreamer now, as I think any singer must be. The two are interwoven, inseparable. I've come to understand that the song is already there and that it is my burden—and blessing—to find it and share it, but I am well aware that I did not write it.

I know that all too well.

The singer, I believe, must be gifted with vivid dreams and visceral memories. With clear eyes ahead and the breath of the past against the ear. You don't choose these gifts; they choose you.

All we control is what we do with them.

The camp at Rosewater sold swiftly and at a good price. I was surprised by that, considering the new notoriety of the pond, but the real estate agent told me not to be. It was, after all, waterfront property close to town. Besides, the fire damage hadn't spread to the pines, she said, and by next summer, when the grading was done and the seeded grass sprouted, there probably would be little evidence of the devastation, scarcely a hint that the Lermond house had ever existed.

The special value in our camp, she told me, was the way it was sited, looking across the cove and over the pond to the western mountains. A perfect sunset view. People love a sunset view, she assured me. People will pay for that.

The house I bought with the profits from the camp is a small but tidy cottage in Port Hope that faces east across the bay toward Little Spruce Island. The sun goes down early out there, but the sunrises are spectacular.

I haven't missed one yet. Each morning I sit on the covered porch or out on the patio, watch the sun come up, and listen to the birds. They are loud gulls mostly, but I've added feeders and houses and begun to keep a count of the species. So far, I'm at thirty-three—or thirty-four if you count the pair of grackles in the cage inside.

My mother loves those birds. She watches them for hours, and their harsh, shrill sounds make her smile.

Grackles are disliked by many people, often viewed as a nuisance, and yet they are extraordinary creatures, gifted, capable of uncanny navigation. I learned all of this while reading through my mother's research archives. The grackle is one of a very few North American birds that can navigate through an extraordinary sense of the earth's geomagnetic field. Some research suggests that humans might carry the same ability on a subconscious level. Others dispute this.

I don't understand all of the research, but I know my opinion.

I also learned something new about the loons of Maine that first winter after I left Rosewater. When the lakes and ponds freeze and force them from their freshwater homes, they don't migrate far. They head for the coast, for open stretches of salt water, and overwinter at sea. In the spring, they return inland and prepare for the eternal battles—birth, life, death. Finding a home. Feeding a family. Protecting those sacred, hard-won things.

My mother seems happy here. She eats well and moves without evidence of pain and smiles often. If she's troubled by her condition, she betrays no indication of it. I feel as if she's well aware of who I am. That thought may be naïve, but it is hopeful, and I see nothing wrong with that. Some circuits, as my father used to say, stay lit.

Each day I work with her on the memory exercises that her doctors and therapists recommend. They caution me not to expect much. For a long time, I thought about recorded cues and guidance offered up to the unconscious mind during sleep. The research is undeniably promising. I had my reservations, of course, but the thought of being able to reach someone who is lost and guide them back toward you—to restore them to how they once were and how you wish them to be again—is a powerful one.

It is far easier to seek power than to forsake it.

One morning, while we were watching the sun crest in the east and listening to the grackles bicker, my mother turned to me, her placid smile in place, and said, "Sometimes, even the best ideas."

That was as far as she got with it, but I told her that I understood.

I think that I did.

I took my job at the hospice three months to the day after Renee Holland's funeral. Public relations work. We have a monthly newsletter and multiple social media channels. I write the stories that reassure the grieving. I make the promises that this place is the right one to spend the last days of a life.

It could feel like grim work if you didn't aspire to make it count. Being around the building is what I need, though. In time, the staff became acquainted with my odd hours and laughed them off as I'd hoped they might. I'm a night owl, that's all. They seem genuinely appreciative of the time I spend roaming the halls, taking interest in the facility, the work, the lives of the residents.

The deaths.

The residents seem to appreciate the song.

My days are my own. I treasure the sunlit hours. I write, I wander, I watch. It is a beautiful and fascinating world. My mother and I sit in the garden on a good day, or inside the covered porch beside a heater on a foul one. We watch the birds, listen to their unique calls, their songs. I watch her smile and I wonder what she hears and knows. We face the east, of course. There will come a time when I must sing the song for her, and all I know about that is that we will watch the sun rise together when I do.

There remains much I don't understand about the song or my role as its singer, but I know that what was once good became evil and that there will likely come a time when those interested in attaining power at any cost will find their way to me, much as a man named Lermond found his way to a singer on the deck of the *Arabella* two and a half centuries ago. They will come in search of the song, come with weapons in their hands and hate in their hearts.

I will be ready for that moment, I think. This much I am sure of—the song will endure long after I'm gone, and thus my role is to share it with pure intentions for as long as the stage is mine. It is a temporary role.

What then?

Well.

At night I dream of the island. The fog reaches for me with its wispy fingers and then draws me in tight and I can hear the cascading waves on the rock, the sounds of creaking timbers, the snap of a torn sail tugging in the wind. I can see the ones who wait, moving within the mist. I can hear their laughs, their screams, their wailing howls.

Then I wake. A dreaming man now, I have developed a fresh gratitude for dawn. At dawn, the memory of the island recedes, and as the daylight rises, I'm convinced that when my time comes, the ones on the island will let me pass. I've spoken for them, after all, have told their story, sang their song. I owe them no more. They will let me pass. I am sure of it.

Then comes the night, and the fog reaches out with the wind blowing hard behind it, and I am no longer so sure. This is the rhythm of my life. The island comes and goes, night becomes day, dreams and memories change hands. Familiar faces become foreign, dire moments become distant, and the only thing I can be sure of is that I'm sure of nothing at all, which leaves a great capacity for hope.

I hope that maybe the worst of this world is imagined, and the best of it assured. It is so easy to become fearful when you are alone in the dark. When the sun emerges in the east and the last of the blackness recedes, it is possible to believe that too much weight was granted to fear, and too little allocated to hope.

This is, of course, the gift of dreams.

ACKNOWLEDGMENTS

Emily Bestler is responsible not just for this book but for Scott Carson's very existence. She is an editor without peer, and her grace, enthusiasm, wit, and unflagging support make the books better and the process a pleasure. A million thanks, Emily.

Richard Pine steers the ship—and sometimes powers it. Troubled waters and unanticipated fog banks don't faze him. He can even quiet the ghosts. Wouldn't want to make the trip with anyone else. His team at InkWell Management is the best.

Lara Jones keeps us all in line and brings the most fun to the party.

Thanks to the incredible team at Atria: Libby McGuire, Dana Trocker, Karlyn Hixon, David Brown, Milena Brown, Paige Lytle, Jessie McNiel, Al Madocs, Jimmy Iacobelli, and so many more. Writing and publishing during a pandemic made for an admittedly strange experience, but the Atria team provided a great sense of stability and support and enthusiasm, and somehow sold the books! You guys are the best.

Erin Mitchell promotes, publicizes, supports,

counsels, and edits. And those are just the things I'm aware of!

Angela Cheng Caplan and her team are always invaluable, and early readers/supporters such as Bob Hammel, Michael Hefron, Kaleb Ryan, Gideon Pine, Tom Bernardo, and Pete Yonkman are more crucial than they know.

Scott Carson came into existence as the world shut down, and yet people kept finding the book. For that, I need to thank every bookseller and librarian and reader, and also some people who went out of their way to spread the word—Stephen King, Michael Connelly, Dean Koontz, Richard Chizmar, Brian Freeman, Stewart O'Nan, Christopher Golden, Alma Katsu, Bev Vincent, and many more. Such generosity means the world.

So do family and friends, last year more than ever. Jenn and Ben Strawn in Indiana and Adam and Annie Thomas in Maine kept me going in ways they probably don't understand. The secret societies of the Puzzle Guild and the Pizza Posse kept me sane in 2020. And Christine—you did it all. Inspired, encouraged, tolerated, even edited.

Ryan Easton hiked the Cutler Coast with me last year, and my father gave me the book Moonfleet many years ago, and those two experiences coalesced into something unexpected and appreciated in these pages.

Read on for an excerpt from
Scott Carson's next novel,

LOST MAN'S LANE

AUTHOR'S NOTE

A conversation about earthquakes made me decide it is time I tell the truth.

Let me explain the lying first. That started in 1999, when I was sixteen years old, and became the coconspirator of a murdered man. I turned forty last summer, staring down the barrel at middle age, and much that once seemed as distant on the horizon as a mirage now feels welcome. Professionally welcome, anyhow. Nobody's referring to me as the "next" anything these days, no more wunderkind talk—though it's already been a long while since I heard that one. Maybe I'll miss those predictions someday, but I'm not sure, because the predictions were born of the truth that I refused to tell.

I had my reasons to avoid the truth. Ego was one of them. It was nice to be viewed as a natural talent. When it comes to motivators, though, I don't think anything trumps fear.

"Vain and afraid" doesn't have the same flair as "talented and hardworking," does it? But you could make your peace with it.

What about lying, though? Could you make your peace with that?

Probably not.

Is refusing to tell the truth different from lying? Most would tell you it is.

I'm not so sure.

All I know is that when it comes to telling ghost stories, people tend to regard the storyteller as a liar or a fool. Except, of course, for the hard-core believers. In nearly two decades of book tours, I've determined that there's a disconcerting correlation between ghost stories, close talkers, and halitosis. Keep the skepticism close and the Listerine closer before you tell someone a ghost story, I recommended on one television appearance. It's always easier to make a joke of the experience.

Now I'm going to find out what it's like on the other side. I'm going to find out what it's like to be the wild-eyed man with the hushed voice and the hand on your arm to prevent you from turning away, imploring you to listen, please, *really listen*, because this is how it happened. *This is the truth!* You believe me, don't you?

With a ghost story, it's always easier to turn away than it is to believe.

I've done all right telling the made-up ones. I've published a dozen books, made a living, even had a couple movies made. The people who liked the books hate those movies, but most of the people who watched the movies never read the books, so I guess it's a wash. The books that sell the best aren't the novels about ghosts. The bestsellers are the true crime stories. They please the critics, who sometimes use words like "prescient" and "perceptive" to describe my reporting. They never use those words with the ghost stories, which amuses me on my better nights, and keeps me awake on the bad ones.

I've made it this far with my secrets. I could keep going. But here at the proverbial crossroads of midlife—supposing that my body holds off illness and my truck's tires hold on to the pavement—I'm at that point where you're supposed to look back. You charge forward in your twenties, you strategize in your thirties, but somewhere in your forties, you're supposed to look back. To develop a taste for nostalgia that you didn't have before, as you realize that you're going to have plenty of occasions to stare into the past whether you want to or not. Time has a way of forcing that. Sometimes the looking back is sweet and sometimes it's bitter, but in my experience, it is almost always involuntary.

The past calls you, not the other way around.

I can hear it knocking now. Can feel it beside me on the porch on this unseasonably warm spring evening, with that glorious humidity that clings even into darkness, like summer is sealing winter out and taping the seams. We're bound now for the sun and the heat, the swelter of dog days, and then the first crisp night when a cool wind rustles brittle leaves and reminds you that it was all a circle, dummy, and there's only one way off this ride, so stop wishing that time would pass faster.

1

Driver's Education
February, 1999

"I said, 'What you wanna be?' She said, 'Alive.'"
—Outkast

"Da Art of Storytellin', Part I"

I got my driver's license on February 11, 1999. This would be easy to remember even if I didn't have the speeding ticket with the date on it.

But I do.

My mother drove me to the BMV that afternoon, which was a Thursday, and she talked about the weather the entire way there. It wasn't idle small talk; she was a meteorologist, and that day was closing in on a February heat record in Bloomington, Indiana. We'd had snow only a few days earlier, but we drove to the BMV with the windows down, welcoming the 70-degree air like a gift, which is the way those days feel in a Midwestern winter, a jump start for your draining battery.

My personal battery was running high already—this day had been a long time in coming. If you didn't take the formal driver's education course, you needed to wait six additional months after your sixteenth birthday to apply for a driver's license. This was the state's way of bribing teenagers to take driver's ed—and my mother's way of buying time before releasing me to the world in a "two-thousand-pound killing machine."

Finally, the wait was over.

I wasn't worried about the written portion of the test, and while I expressed high confidence about the driving portion, let's all admit that our heart-rates picked up at the phrase "parallel parking" when we were sixteen. I took the driving portion first and passed without trouble. Even nailed the parallel parking—no small feat in the Oldsmobile Ninety-Eight my mother had given me, which was the length of a hearse. On to the written test—twenty-five questions, multiple choice, fill-in-the answer bubble on a separate Scantron sheet with a No. 2 pencil. I cruised through twenty-three before a male voice boomed out, "It's Miller Time!"

I heard my mother's laugh in response. Melodic, practiced, unsurprised. When you're Monica Miller the meteorologist, you can't go long before some dimwit producer decides to affix a famous beer slogan to your segments. People often recognized her, and they loved to indicate it by shouting out "It's Miller Time!" When you're sixteen and this is the way the community responds to your mother's presence, it's not a great deal of fun.

Particularly when your mother is beautiful, and it's mostly men shouting at her.

I didn't bother to turn around at the exchange, so I never saw the cheerful citizen who recognized my mother, only heard him, and then my mother's on-cue laugh, but the distraction was enough that when I filled in my test circle, I missed the twenty-fourth line entirely, and filled in the twenty-fifth blank on the accompanying Scantron sheet. I then dutifully answered the next question in the twenty-sixth line, stood, and handed my exam to the bored clerk.

"You are allowed two mistakes out of the twenty-five questions," she intoned in a voice that said she could—and maybe did—recite this in her sleep. "You may return no sooner than tomorrow to re-take the examination."

"Great—gives me extra time to figure out a way to cheat," I said, a remark designed to make her smile. It did not make her smile. She lined her answer key up beside my test and peered through the top halves of her bifocals as she scanned the results. Her red pen made little taps of contact with each correct answer—a nice, steady rhythm.

Slow ride, I hummed softly, *take it easy* . . .

The clerk's red pen paused. Hovered above the test.

I leaned forward, frowning, and immediately

saw the mistake. There was no answer to question twenty-four.

The clerk's mouth twitched with a barely concealed evil smile.

"Mr. Miller," she said, in a voice exponentially louder than she'd used previously, "you have missed question twenty-four by failing to answer it."

"I did answer it. I just got out of order."

"You have also missed question twenty-five," she continued. "And it is my duty to—"

"What happened was, I filled in the wrong—"

"*It is my duty,*" she snapped, glaring at me over her glasses with a look that effectively severed my vocal cords, "to inform you of the correct answer. Question twenty-four reads: If you encounter a law enforcement officer whose command differs with the signal at an intersection, what do you do?"

The easiest question on the whole damn test. A question that half the kindergartners in the county would answer correctly.

The clerk smiled at me.

"The correct answer," she said, still loud enough for the room, "is option C: 'Obey the command of the law enforcement officer. You selected option B: Honk and proceed with caution.'"

Laughter erupted. One man repeated my answer for his wife. Another woman snorted and clapped. I didn't dare turn around to look at my mother. I stood there imagining the responses from my friends when I informed them that even after a six-month wait, I still didn't have a driver's license. I was so lost to my horror that it took me a second to realize that the clerk was still speaking.

"You have missed only two questions, which means you have passed the test. Please follow me over to the back of the room so we can get a photograph for your driver's license, Marshall Miller."

I'd passed.

I also spent four years carrying a driver's license photo in which my face was so red, it looked freshly sunburned.

When I finally looked at my mother, she was smiling that 100-watt, television-approved smile of hers.

"Honk and proceed with caution," she said, and handed me the keys.

We laughed about it then, and we laughed even harder in the car on the drive home. If we'd had any idea how much of our lives would soon be lost to my interactions with law enforcement, we wouldn't have cracked a smile.

I dropped my mother off at home, knowing that I wouldn't see her again until breakfast the next morning. She'd been offered the prime-time broadcasts on numerous occasions when I was younger, declining them each time, but when I turned sixteen, she agreed to move from days to nights, guaranteeing a better paycheck and larger audience—and requiring a hell of a lot of trust in her teenage son. I was determined not to screw it up. I was the only child of a single mother, and if you can make it to sixteen without disaster in that dynamic, you're carrying at least a little bit of extra maturity. Extra concern, anyhow. I did not want to disappoint my mother.

I also genuinely did not believe that I would.

There's no confidence like a sixteen-year-old's confidence in the future.

I dropped her off in the driveway of our simple two-story Colonial on its tidy lawn. We lived on Raintree Lane on the north side of town, west of what was then State Road 37 and is now Interstate 69. It was a neighborhood of modest but well-kept homes and mature trees, and I appreciate it more now than I did then, but I suppose that's true of a lot of things.

I made about a thousand assurances that I would be careful, gave my mother a one-armed hug without relinquishing control of the steering wheel, and then pulled out of the driveway, headed for the Cascades Golf Course, intending to hit a few buckets of balls at the driving range on this strangely warm day, but mostly ready to experience my freshly minted freedom. I put the windows down, and that unseasonable warm air flooded in. The ancient Oldsmobile didn't have a CD player, so I had a Sony Discman resting on the bench seat beside me, connected to the stereo through an auxiliary cord that ran to the tape deck. Badass. With my mother out of the car, I turned the volume up on Tupac's "2 of Amerikaz Most Wanted." Badder-ass.

Beside the Discman rested not one, not two, but three massive binders of CDs, divided into three categories: rap mixes, rock mixes, and make-out mixes. The former two, unfortunately, saw more airplay than the last. I let the Oldsmobile's speakers blast all the bass they could handle and bobbed my head in rhythm, and had Pac still been alive, he'd have no doubt laughed his ass off at me, but in that moment, alone behind the wheel, I didn't care about the old car or the shitty stereo. I was a free man, no chaperone required.

Life was good.

I made it four miles before the colored lights came on behind me.

It was more frightening than it should have been, maybe. I'd never been pulled over; hell, I'd never been alone in a car. Police were the ultimate authority figures, like principals with guns.

In the adrenaline rush of the moment, I forgot a key rule from the BMV study guide: When one is pulled over by police, one is to pull off the road on the right-hand side. I opted instead for what struck me as the clearest area: the wide expanse of grass that ran between the road and the fairway of the thirteenth hole of the golf course. This required crossing a lane of oncoming traffic, a maneuver that I executed without so much as a turn signal.

The siren went on. A single, bleated chirp that chilled my blood.

On a normal day in February, the course would have been empty and even the driving range closed. Because we were chasing that heat record, it was busy, packed with cabin-fever sufferers taunted by new sets of Christmas clubs. Wonderful. I had an audience.

Four miles as a free man. A good run while it lasted.

I parked the car and waited while a muscled-up officer with a crew cut approached. The window was already down, and he leaned in and studied me, seeming torn between anger and exasperation. His stiff uniform shirt strained around his chiseled chest and arms as if determined to escape it. His name tag identified him as CPL. MADDOX.

"Son, what in the hell were you doing, crossing over here?"

"It seemed safer for both of us," I said. This was up there with honk and proceed with caution in terms of poor answers.

"Safer? On the wrong side of the road?"

"There was lots of room to park."

"Are you trying to tell me that I'm wrong, son?"

"Not at all, sir, I'm just . . . the thing is, it's a big car."

"Does it steer itself?"

"Pardon?"

"Does it steer itself?" His eyes were the same dark blue as his uniform shirt, which was pressed against pectoral muscles that looked like they belonged to a creature from Jurassic Park.

"No, sir."

"So let's stop blaming the car for your decisions."

"Yes, sir."

"It is not a 500 Benz," he said without a hint of emotion.

"No, sir. It's an Oldsmobile."

"Do you think the district attorney is really a ho?"

My lips parted, but I didn't offer any words. I was stunned and confused—and then, oh-so-belatedly, I realized my music was still playing. Tupac's "Picture Me Rollin'." Pac was describing his Mercedes and expounding on his theories about the personal lives of the law enforcement members who'd put him in custody.

I am going to jail, I thought as I punched the stereo power off just as Tupac offered a few words to the "punk police." I wondered how handcuffs felt.

"It's a song," I said. "I mean, not a . . . you know, the lyrics aren't mine. They do not represent my views."

"Oh. I was confused. The voice sounded exactly like yours."

When I looked at him this time, I thought I saw the barest hint of a smile. Then it vanished as he said "License and registration, please."

Shit.

"I, uh . . . I only have this." I showed him my temporary license. The real one would be mailed. And now, no doubt, dropped directly into the garbage disposal by my mother.

Maddox eyed the temp. "You got this today."

"Yes, sir."

"Off to a heck of a start."

"Yes, sir. I mean, no, sir."

He lowered the temp license and fixed the steel blue eyes on me again. "Registration?"

I found the registration, wondering how long it would take for my mother's insurance rates to soar. Teenage males were more expensive to insure even without points on their licenses.

"Please wait in the vehicle," Corporal Maddox said, and then he returned to his cruiser.

I wanted to punch something—mostly myself. I hated the tight-throated sensation and the rapid heartbeat and the echoing words of my ridiculous exchange with the state trooper. All of it so stupid. All of it something a kid would do. I did not feel like a kid, either.

At least, I hadn't until those colored lights had come on.

I looked in the sideview mirror, trying to make out what Maddox was doing. I deserved a ticket. But he'd smiled—almost—when he made that remark about confusing my voice for Tupac's. Was he smiling like a jerk, or like someone who'd give a kid a break?

The driver's door of the cruiser swung open, and

Maddox stepped out. It was only then that I realized someone else was in the car. Not another cop, a partner riding with him, but someone in the back, behind the steel grate. A blond-haired girl, wearing a teal polo shirt with a white logo and script over the left breast. Her hair was tied up loosely in a bandana that matched the teal-and-white shirt. The combination was immediately familiar to me, the uniform of the Chocolate Goose, a local ice-cream shop that had been in business for generations and was a townie staple in summer. The logo on the polo shirt would show a version of the Mother Goose character, complete with reading glasses and a babushka and a chocolate ice-cream cone held jauntily in one wing. It was strange to see the outfit in February. The Chocolate Goose was strictly seasonal, opening on Memorial Day weekend and closing on Labor Day. The girl, who looked about my age but wasn't familiar, seemed to stare directly at me, as if searching my face in the mirror. She looked the way I felt: frustrated and foolish and a little frightened. Maybe more than a little.

Then Maddox swung the door shut, and my attention returned to him, the girl's face relegated to a faint outline seen through dark glass.

Maddox approached, holding my license in his right hand and a ticket in his left.

"Mr. Miller," Maddox said, passing me the license and registration, "this is not an ideal day for you to receive a traffic ticket, is it?"

"No, sir."

"Points on your license before you even get started. Not good."

He gazed down at the golf course, seeming to follow the descending slopes down to the dark wooded valley that traced Griffy Creek into the heart of downtown Bloomington. His big chest swelled. I wondered how much he could bench press with those arms and that chest. I wondered if he was as intimidating to that girl in the back of his cruiser as he was to me.

"What's your father going to say when you show him this?" he asked.

I didn't answer. He shot me a hard look.

"What's he going to say, Mr. Miller?"

"He's dead," I said.

I was afraid that he would ask how it had happened. It was hard to explain that I didn't know. Harder to explain that he might not be dead at all. He was to me, though. That's the way it feels with a father who bailed before you were born. Closer to dead than alive, but more hurtful than a dead man could ever be.

"I see," Maddox said. He seemed to mull over something, and then he separated the two halves of the ticket—one original, one carbon copy on pale pink paper. He handed me the copy.

"I clocked you at 39 in a 30," he said. "That's the first violation on the ticket. The second is for improper lane movement. These are lessons you shouldn't have to learn the hard way."

I couldn't come up with anything to say and didn't see the point in trying. The consequences were already in hand, and that question about what my absent father would say sizzled in my brain, temporarily as troubling as the ticket itself.

"That copy is yours. This one is mine, property of Corpo*real* Maddox, until it is filed with the court."

He'd drawn his rank out in an odd Southern drawl, as if enjoying the flavor of it. I kept staring at the ticket. His thumb had left a grimy print on the bottom corner, probably from the carbon paper. It looked like ash, though. Appropriate, for the document that would burn my freedom down.

"Sometimes," Maddox said, "I forget to file them."

It was as if the ticket in my hand had gone from traffic citation to lottery winner. He was granting me mercy.

"*Thank you,*" I said, looking up from the carbon-stained ticket.

"For what?"

His broad face was empty, the eyes still cool, but I was sure he knew exactly what I meant. He was giving me a break.

"For the second chance. I won't screw it up."

"Did I say you have a second chance? I said sometimes I forget to file paperwork with the court. I made no fucking promise of it. Where the fuck did you hear the words '*second chance*'?"

I was so shocked I couldn't even begin to answer. I'd heard adults swear, but I'd never had an adult swear at me. Not like that.

"You make assumptions," he said. "That's a dangerous way to live, Mr. Miller. It is a better way to die."

A better way to die?

I glanced at the golf course, this time hoping that I had an audience. Everyone had their backs to me, heads bowed over their balls or tilted to watch them in flight. I suddenly felt alone and afraid.

"Do you know what I hear when you say *second chance*?" Maddox snarled. For the first time, I was aware of the gun and baton on his belt.

"No, sir." I managed to murmur this.

"I hear a little prick who thinks the world owes him kindness."

A police officer had just called me a prick. No one was listening to us and there was no one I could call for help. I didn't have a cell phone. I had only a few friends who did, and they weren't with me. I was alone. The only person who was still paying attention to us was the girl in the back of the police car—and she was also alone, and worse off than me.

For now.

Maddox let the silence spread out like his massive shadow. He hadn't asked a question, and I didn't know what to say, so I didn't speak.

"Driving a car down a road filled with strangers who are just trying to get home safe," he said at last, "is responsibility, Mr. Miller. Not a joke, not fun, not a privilege. It should feel damn serious to you. Nobody is promised a second chance at getting home safe. You will learn that."

The ticket was trembling in my hand now.

"Go on your way," Maddox said. "Now."

He turned and walked away. I sagged in the driver's seat, the carbon copy in my hand. Right then, I didn't care if he filed it or not. I felt as if I'd glimpsed the chasm between the kinds of consequences that existed in the world. There were tickets and there was violence.

He wouldn't have hurt you, I told myself.

Right? No way a police officer would have hurt me. There were people not far away and . . .

What if there hadn't been?

I looked in the mirror in time to see him settle back behind the wheel. In the half second before the driver's door swung shut, I saw the girl in the backseat again.

She'd started to cry.

I would have remembered her face even if I never saw it on a MISSING poster.